"It was the first (...) **hands under wat**(...) **like small balloons. Rich red would bubble up to the surface and float thick like feathers on a lake. The more I scrubbed, the dirtier my hands got."**

In the food we eat—milk, ice cream, baby food, cooking oil—is death. And no one is safe from the superbly intelligent killer who is systematically tampering with innocent items found in grocery stores all over the country. Only one man has a chance of finding a pattern to this random, spreading horror—David McAdam, an antisocial computer genius, the FBI's only hope in this baffling case. McAdam's search takes him into the labyrinth of giant food companies who will lie to an unsuspecting public to satisify their insatiable hunger for profits . . . into the heart of a government that may be sabotaging his most brilliant efforts . . . into a nightmare world where a twisted killer is always one maddening click of a computer key ahead of him. And finally, in a battle of mind versus menace, McAdam comes to a shocking conclusion no one wants to believe and to a deadly confrontation he may not survive. A brilliant mix of high-tech suspense and old-fashioned gut-churning action, this dazzling thriller will keep you riveted until its final provocative twist.

RED DAYS

RED DAYS

Stephen Kimball

A SIGNET BOOK

SIGNET
Published by the Penguin Group
Penguin Books USA Inc., 375 Hudson Street, New York, New York 10014, U.S.A.
Penguin Books Ltd, 27 Wrights Lane, London W8 5TZ, England
Penguin Books Australia Ltd, Ringwood, Victoria, Australia
Penguin Books Canada Ltd, 10 Alcorn Avenue, Toronto, Ontario, Canada M4V 3B2
Penguin Books (N.Z.) Ltd, 182–190 Wairau Road, Auckland 10, New Zealand

Penguin Books Ltd, Registered Offices:
Harmondsworth, Middlesex, England

First published by Signet, an imprint of New American Library,
a division of Penguin Books USA Inc.

First Printing, September, 1993
10 9 8 7 6 5 4 3 2 1

 REGISTERED TRADEMARK—MARCA REGISTRADA

Printed in the United States of America

PUBLISHER'S NOTE
This is a work of fiction. Names, characters, places, and incidents either are the
product of the author's imagination or are used fictitiously, and any resemblance to
actual persons, living or dead, events, or locales is entirely coincidental.

To Peter Patrick

Because you never know

And everywhere
The ceremony of innocence is drowned;
The best lack all conviction while the worst
Are full of passionate intensity.
>   —William Butler Yeats,
>   "The Second Coming"

I'm only scared of people.
>   —Sam Shepard,
>   *A Lie of the Mind*

Chapter 1

They want you to believe you can prevent cancer. They want you to believe you can control it the way you would a machine or a child.

But I knew better.

The particular horror of cancer is that it lurks quietly benign in each cell, an evil embryo waiting for seed. You can't see or feel it. One moment a cell is normal and healthy, the next it explodes into a predator that terrorizes the entire body. What happens in the meantime to trigger this reaction? How could such uncontrollable violence simply occur without warning?

The answer is in the blood. In the rush of countless cells through the bloodstream, each with its own purpose, comes a rogue cell, an outlier. Its hereditary predisposition to cancer is shoved forward by a stimulus or a trauma that flips the switch, turning order into chaos.

But, after extensive research, I have discovered a vaccine for it. I have learned as so many others before me that the solution to the problem lies in the problem itself.

The solution is death.

It was the first of the red days.

Morning: the sky was blue in its usual way and the sun was in the sky in its usual place. But later the day grew high and dark, and rain fell in its usual way—down.

Wind blew the mindless rain through windows not yet closed to the red day. I could not get the lower half of my body to move, so I had to drag myself over the floor to close the window.

The pane of glass, clean outside but dirty and streaked on the inside, was alternately a window looking out or a mirror bearing my own reflection. Through the window the rain looked like lines of static on a television screen.

Spring was pushed forward by the rainfall. Buds flared from the ends of tree branches. Life was ignited out of the comfortable dimness of winter. As the sun rose earlier and set later, one was forced to endure more of the day.

The wolf of the red day was relentless.

And I could not get my hands clean. I could feel microscopic organisms leaching into them, searching for the slightest opening in my skin. Having found one, the cancer cells burrowed in deep, invaded arteries, and held on like debris in flood waters, until they coalesced in tumors.

I would hold my hands under water until they swelled like small balloons. Rich red would bubble up to the surface and float thick like feathers on a lake. The more I scrubbed, the dirtier my hands got. My fingers would stick together. Best to tuck them tight under my arms.

I tried to watch the limits. But the first red day expanded like a hall of mirrors. So I sat on the floor of the room with my hands under my arms and wished hard that the room would not grow.

Red day number two. Clearer. No rain.

Being a somewhat cautious person, I took my time deciding how to get out of bed in the morning. There were so many ways of hurting oneself in the simple act of rising from bed.

For example, by raising one's shoulder and turning toward the edge of the bed from a supine position in an improper motion, one could damage muscles in the neck and upper and lower back. Bones could also be affected, nerve endings.

The real damage lay in stepping out of bed and onto the floor. The soft linen slope at the edge of the mattress ended with a dark line, beyond which was the hard floor littered with glass, nails, or slippery substances. On certain red days the floor was so foul and distant that one wouldn't even try to muster one's energies to leave the bed.

Today, driven by a newly realized purpose, I stepped forward. I negotiated the ambiguity of my home with precision—four steps to the closet for my robe; eight steps to the bathroom; six steps back to the bedroom; nine to the kitchen; and four to the front door. The entire process lasting forty-seven minutes, a respectable time.

Leaving home, I gave up considerable control. Oh, I might have known the number of steps from the front door to the corner (eleven), from the corner to the subway station (one hundred twenty-nine, give or take five), from the station to my office (eighty-four).

But once out in the undefined openness, one was at constant risk. Terror hung in the spaces of the vacant lots and in the city's telescopic streets. Dark eyes and unseen hands waited patiently around corners.

No amount of planning could prepare one for the potential danger. Every choice brought new threats. Each decision created its own peril.

The openness gave one the freedom to choose one's poison—to take the subway or a taxi to the airport.

I chose a taxi.

"What airline should I drop you at?"

"The red one."

Once there, I walked along the wall and found that by putting one foot in front of the other and keeping my eyes straight ahead, I could get to where I had to go.

But the wall grew with each step I took. The ceiling grew higher and all points in the room became destinations impossible to reach.

One of my hands gripped a bag, the other left a slight liquid film on the surface of the wall.

People moved past, shadows. Voices from the ceiling wrapped around my head like steel wire. Someone somewhere turned a switch that started a machine that caused the room to pitch and yaw like an amusement park ride.

It would have been easy enough for me to escape. I knew precisely how far I was from home and what was involved in getting there. And I had counted how many steps I had taken from the curb to this very point.

But the room held just long enough for me to get to the ticket counter.

"Any baggage to check?"

"Yes, this one. Mark it 'fragile.' It contains very delicate articles."

"Very good. Your seat to Rochester has been confirmed. The flight departs in twenty minutes from gate six."

In the waiting room a chair kept me off the floor. Here in the open space the clouds massed and darkened. The darkness drew strength from the openness, the disconnection of things. The air grew moist and thick.

A drop of water sizzled on my upper lip.

The flight was called. There was a general commotion toward the gate.

The rain began, a light drizzle. We entered a tube.

So many biological processes transpire through tubes. Fallopian tubes. Eustachian tubes. Esophagi. Intestines.

Rubbery matter reductio ad absurdum.

The storm followed me inside the airplane. Water ran down my brow and into my eyes. I groped my way into my seat and drove home the lock on the seat belt.

I recognized this plane as a DC-10. I had researched the safety records of all aircraft for the last three years. DC-10—a flying mausoleum.

The cabin had 32 rows, six seats to a row—a total of 192 seats, 192 seat belts, 192 fold-down trays. I always sat toward the front, believing the pilot's instincts for survival would preserve him and the passengers nearest him in the event of a crash.

Who was our pilot? Was he sober, sane, capable of balanced judgment? And the mechanics, did they show up for work today? Were the proper checks and balances in place—checklists, tests, inspections? What if they forgot to fill the tires with air?

The design of the cabin's interior was abstract floral. I counted twenty-four stylized daisies on the back of the seat in front of me.

In the seat pocket were the safety instructions. *In the event of a water landing. . .*

I couldn't bring myself to read them. I gripped the armrests and closed my eyes. The skies opened and floodwaters seeped through the walls.

I held my breath as water surged at my lips, gushed through my teeth and into my mouth, finally bursting out my nose. The outside became my inside.

Wave after wave pounded over me. I felt my skin puckering from the constant drenching. It was all I could do just to hold on, squeezing my eyes closed as virulent water rose above my neck. I tried to collect myself.

Soon it would be time to choose my poison.

Chapter 2

Closing the door of her apartment, Carla Moon finally shut out the world, at least for the night. It was a relief to be home, safe among familiar things.

What a day. More than tired, Carla felt disintegrated. But home was a sanctuary where she had control over her life. She snapped home the three dead bolts on the door and chained it.

Carla's apartment was in a high-security building with a twenty-four-hour guard, TV monitors in the stairwells and hallways, the works. She would have preferred a funkier place, maybe a loft. But her father insisted on the Attica look if she was to live in downtown Rochester. And he took care of the rent.

Carla didn't bother to hang up her coat or put away her purse and camera bag. She left them in a heap by the door. She cleared away clothes and magazines from the couch and eased down. It felt good to be sitting, to be alone.

She closed her eyes and tried to clear her mind of the day's images that clicked by in black and white, like an old newsreel.

One image was the translucence of the early spring fog as she drove to her 8:00 A.M. film class at Rochester College. Another was her own hands, in white cheesecloth gloves, handling 36mm tape as she tried unsuccessfully to sync the sound track to a scene from her thesis film.

With the backs of her hands Carla tried to rub from her eyes the faces of people at the Rochester Hilton, where she had just finished a shoot. They swirled out of the blackness and around her head—gray, flaccid faces with cracked ceramic smiles. And then the worst one of all flew into her consciousness.

The face belonged to Mitchell Bryer, and it was hovering in the darkness of the Hilton bar when she arrived for her shoot. Mitch looked like the aging college professor he was, in his usual jeans, tweed jacket, and sixties hair tied back with a rubber band.

Carla had wanted to break away completely from him, to wash herself clean and start over. She hated herself for getting sucked into a melodrama: boy meets girl. Boy abuses girl. Girl acquiesces to boy's prestige. Girl finally loses boy, but boy won't get lost.

Earlier that day she had left a note in Mitch's film-department mailbox in which she asked him for the four keys to her apartment. She hoped he would just send her the keys. But he tracked her down on campus and insisted on talking. She agreed to see him before her shoot at the Hilton and hated herself for not telling him to go fuck himself.

Carla slid into the booth, keeping to the far end of the seat. Mitch was drinking a Cape Codder and, not bothering to order her anything, immediately went to work on her.

"How could you even think to do this to me after all I've done for you?" he said in his "hurt" voice. "Tired of the old guy now? Found some young stud you can lead around by the nose? Get what you can and get out. That's the story, isn't it?"

Carla kept silent as Mitch explained how grateful she should be to him for improving her, for teaching her good taste. He even brought up how he had "helped" her in his graduate seminar.

He aimed a finger at her face. "Face it, Carla, you wouldn't make it in the film program without me. Remember, I chair the graduate fellowship committee. You walk away from me, you can kiss your free ride goodbye."

Carla was stung but wouldn't let him see it. "I don't want your help," she said, steady. "And I don't want to see you again."

"What is it, Carla?" he shouted, almost hysterical. She noticed people were looking at them. "Need to be humped more often? Fine, I can handle that. I can even start on Vitamin E, if that will make you happy."

He lowered his voice. "But you ought to think about your future, Carla, and about the people who are in a position to help you. You don't want to do something you'll regret."

"The only thing I regret in my life, Mitch," she said quietly, "is getting involved with you."

"Cunt," he hissed, and threw his drink in her face.

Carla blinked back the vodka burning in her eyes. She grabbed for a napkin and stood up, but Mitch pulled her back. She felt her blouse rip down the front. Finally able to see, she tore his hand loose and walked out, never looking back.

Carla had to rush home to change and return to the Hilton for her photography assignment. On the way she was stopped by a black and white police car.

"What's that stain on your blouse?" the policeman asked before giving her a breathalyzer test.

Carla was late for her assignment, a shoot of a reception for Kodak sales managers, another group of drunken businessmen and their even drunker wives. But Kodak was an important client for Carla's studio, and she had to get her shots right.

As a private act of rebellion, she used Fuji film stock.

The lighting in the Hilton ballroom was strong and directly overhead, casting deathly shadows under the eyes of her subjects and bright reflections on balding foreheads. Carla remembered to pick out the vice president for sales and get plenty of flattering shots of his wife. As difficult as it was to flatter a woman in a wig and forty pounds overweight, Carla managed to keep the woman's double chin in the shadows and soften her harsh look.

Normally, Carla tried to have fun on the job by talking with subjects and bringing out their personalities in their faces. But tonight she just wasn't into it. In her first hour on the job, she had to deflect come-ons from three men (one in the presence of his wife). For the rest of the night she stayed off to the sides of the ballroom, perfunctorily snapping group shots and candids. The evening became a blur of loose gray faces.

One face caught her eye, that of a young man in a dark suit with a fine nose and high cheekbones. Apparently alone, he stayed seated in the back of the room. Carla watched him from a corner as he made small talk with the people at his table. He appeared to be somewhat ill at ease in the forced social situation. She found him in her viewfinder and focused.

Just then Mitch walked into the frame of her viewfinder. The bastard!

Carla stayed behind the camera like an ostrich, hoping

he wouldn't see her. She slowly crouched down as Mitch surveyed the room, sipping another drink. Then he spotted her and, smiling, he reached in his pocket, pulled out something, and held it up. Her keys.

Even though Carla wanted to stay as far from Mitch as possible, she knew she had to go to him to get the keys. She took in a deep breath and went toward him, keeping her eyes away from his and focusing on the keys. He said nothing as she took them and walked away.

She took a few more shots of the crowd and packed it in. Back home, she fished her keys out of her bag and tried the lock. But it wouldn't turn. She tried another and it didn't work either.

Mitch had given her the wrong set of keys.

The fucking bastard. She berated herself for even trusting him to give her the right keys. Then she told herself it wasn't her fault. She would just have all the locks changed tomorrow.

Once inside the apartment, she felt better, more secure. She pushed her bookshelf in front of the door, in case Mitch tried to get in that night.

Carla rubbed her eyes and opened them. Without wanting to, she looked around the apartment at all the projects she had started but never finished. In a corner were the frames and mats for portraits of her sisters she had taken and wanted to frame. On the kitchen table, almost buried by the empty boxes of Chinese food, were invitations she had designed for a party that she was to have had last weekend but never did.

Spread out on the floors of the living room and bedroom were months of unopened newspapers and film and photography magazines. Carla had taken to sleeping on the living room couch because her bedroom had become nearly impenetrable, what with all the clothes, darkroom equipment, and stacks of books, not to mention a bicycle.

Cobwebs sprouted in corners of the ceiling. Propelled by warm air blowing from ducts in the wall, a dust ball shaped like a feathery skull tumbled by her across the floor. The silence was delicious, the lighting soft.

Before going to bed she liked to have a cup of tea and milk while watching *David Letterman*. That always helped her to unwind. She slid out of her coat, left it in the chair, and walked toward the kitchen. Carla noticed the light on her answering machine. She ignored it.

Suddenly she felt a wave of dizziness overcome her, and she had to steady herself against the counter.

"God, it's been over ten hours since I last ate something," she said to herself as she waited for her head to stop spinning. She had eaten some yogurt around lunchtime but nothing else after that. She rummaged through the cupboards and found the tin of Earl Grey— empty.

"Great," she said out loud, "the perfect end to the perfect day."

Her last hope was the refrigerator, where a pint of milk she had bought yesterday stood as the solitary item on the top shelf. It would have to do. She opened up the carton, poured out the milk into a pan, and heated it on the stove.

A cup of warm milk before bed. At least her mother would approve.

Carla felt a little stronger and managed to pick her way through her bedroom and change out of her black dress and into a robe. When she returned to the kitchen the milk was beginning to simmer.

Just then a portrait on the side of the milk carton

caught her attention, that of a young boy missing from home for over a year. The photograph was grainy and amateurish, blown up from a small negative but, despite its technical shortcomings, very powerful, contrasting the child's innocent smiling face with the horrors one could imagine he was experiencing.

Carla could not stand to look at it any longer and threw the carton into the overflowing trash basket.

She poured the hot milk into a mug and found a comfortable place on the couch. The sheets, pillow, and blanket were still where she had left them the night before. Carla was too tired to watch television. She would just sit and relax and hit the sheets a little early tonight. Tomorrow morning she and her younger sister, Carol, were going shopping, and Carol didn't like to be kept waiting.

The milk was still too hot to drink, so she blew on it. She tucked her lower lip under the rim of the mug and began to sip. The clay mug felt stubbly and pleasantly warm against her lip. She blew again into the mug and took a mouthful of milk. The liquid slid down her throat and hit her stomach in a warm rush. She took another sip, a little longer this time.

An instant later she felt the tightness of invisible hands around her throat. She desperately tried to cough but could not collect enough air in her lungs.

Then she felt an awful jolt, as if she had been kicked in the midsection. Another jolt shook her, this time driving her to her knees. She let go of the mug and it shattered on the hardwood floor.

Carla flailed her hands and tried to support herself against the couch, but the tremors continued, each worse than the last. An awful terror of being smothered overcame her, and she tried to scream but could only manage to whimper.

She lost all control of her muscles. She began twitching uncontrollably and clawed the floor with her fingernails. Nausea welled up in her stomach and throat, causing a thin stream of vomit that oozed down her cheeks.

Her eyes filled with tears, splintering the light. Images crowded her mind, of the child on the milk carton, her mother's face, the young man in the dark suit at the reception. The images floated through her mind as if they were on a carousel. Her breaths grew shorter, more difficult.

Carla's field of vision narrowed to the point where the light was no more than a pinprick on a black background. The images grew fainter. She gulped hard for air.

Then she had no more breath and no more images.

Chapter 3

California Key was the kind of place where a story usually ended.

It was barely an island, more a spit of earth, a geological afterthought, separated from neighboring Kettle Key at high tide and connected at ebb tide by a mushy, sinkholed stretch of oolite. The key looked like it had simply gotten fed up with the earth around it and split off.

California Key somehow escaped designation on maps of Florida. Even the U.S. Geological Survey map of the area missed it.

It was about three-quarters of the way down the Keys—that necklace of coral islands stretching gracefully some one hundred fifty miles from mainland Florida to the southernmost and only tropical point in the continental United States, as the guide books said. Most of the islands around California Key were uninhabited, and many no one had bothered to name.

Bordering California Key to the north was the Gulf of Mexico—rimmed by the sclerotic retirement towns of West Florida and the consumer wasteland of the Texas coast. To the south was the Atlantic Ocean—traversed by cruise ships packed with tourists holding fistfuls of Yankee dollars and hell-bent for a good time in the fun-ravaged Caribbean.

Even for Florida, the Keys were different. Folks on the mainland would tell you that people there were strange, different, as if by some arcane decree all American nomads, gypsies, and bohemian types had to spend a requisite amount of time there before moving on to that ashram in Boulder or commune in southern Vermont. The Keys were California in miniature, Shangri-La with reggae and piña coladas.

But the people weren't the only thing different about the Keys. Animals, like the Big Pine miniature deer, that grew no larger than a small dog and wouldn't think of being seen anywhere else in the world, found a home in the spooky glades of the larger deserted keys. The sun-sucked soil coaxed out plants with names like gumbo limbo and poisonwood that escaped most documented phyla.

The air itself seemed to carry subversive ions that imbued the place with a self-conscious breeziness and stylized decadence. Entering the Keys, a traveler could conclude that he had entered some kind of zone—a kind of Bermuda Triangle of decorum.

Quiet as a graveyard, California Key was actually a riot of information storage and retrieval. Here, nature functioned with the precision and elegance of a very large-scale integrated circuit. Flora and fauna interacted through layers of binary signaling—something–nothing, something–nothing—translated into a single message: survival.

Life on California Key was the closest human approximation to being encased in silicon. It was something like a sensory-deprivation experiment where you spend weeks or months in a controlled environment, a dimly lit tank of body-temperature water with muzak pumped in.

After a while you have trouble distinguishing between night and day, your circadian rhythms gone awry.

Toward the Gulf side of the island stood a house—a rambling three-story Victorian with carved bentwood railings, doors in improbable places, corner turrets festooned with weathervanes, and a wide, inviting open-air porch that wrapped around the ground floor.

It was the kind of place where a story ended, where the hero would go to lick his metaphysical wounds after doing battle with the forces of evil. A fortress of solitude, the end of the rainbow.

From the gloom of the house, David McAdam slowly stepped out onto the back porch. He shaded his bloodshot eyes from the sun, but that did nothing to shield him from the glare shooting off the ocean. It had been another long night and his head felt like it had sat front row center at a heavy metal concert.

He sniffed the air. What was that strange smell?

He sat down heavily on the top step of the porch and wondered why he had never thought to bring sunglasses when he came to Florida almost a year ago. The house was no more than fifty feet from the ocean, and every time he came outside he would recoil from the glare like some cave-dwelling bat.

He pictured the kind of sunglasses he would get: those French kind, not the wrap-arounds, but the ones in the shape of a cat's eyes. He made a note to himself to go by Toshi's sometime soon and order a pair.

David tried to remember the last time he had seen Toshi over at the Bar and Marina on Kettle Key. Was it a month ago? Three months?

For David, time was the hardest thing to keep straight. Whenever he bothered to think about it, he observed that he usually fell asleep sometime after midnight and woke up in the early afternoon of what he assumed was the next day. But it could have been two days later, or a week.

And those didn't include the days he just stayed in bed and stared at the water-pocked ceiling of his bedroom and compared the patterns there to those of integrated circuits he had designed early in his career.

Of one thing at least he could be certain: he hadn't seen anyone since Toshi.

David sat still on the porch and took inventory of the components of the white noise on California Key—the lapping of the waves, the rattling of the wind in the pines, the dull roar of a jet tearing toward the naval air station down on Boca Chica Key.

But no pelicans.

A colony of them roosted over on the east side of the island, a chattering, gregarious flock. David wondered what made them so quiet today—maybe a snake or some other predator was stalking California Key. If something was on the island, it would've had to have been there for almost four hours or so since the tide went out.

He pushed it out of his mind and let the sun bake his face and shoulders. He dreamily remembered the first time he had felt that sun, newly arrived from his previous home, an estate outside a village in the Austrian Alps.

David had lived there in hiding for almost two years until the paparazzi from a German magazine tracked him down. After a wild trip through Europe, and a detour to North Africa just to get the damn photographer off his trail, David showed up on California Key early one morning. The sun was shining and the house looked invitingly desolate.

He had all his worldly possessions stuffed into a nylon

duffel bag—four passports, three printed-circuit boards, a toothbrush, a few clothes, a Swiss army knife, back issues of *Computer World*, and a number for his secret Danish bank account. (The Danes, he had found out, were as discreet as the Swiss in their banking practices and gave better interest rates.)

After a few months on the island, David sensed that the big white house needed a certain something, a final touch, to make it the home of his dreams. By then he had picked up a nice stereo and cleaned out the Key West record stores of every rock 'n' roll tape or CD he recognized. He installed a computer system to meet his needs and stocked the twenty or so freezers around the house with enough food to last him through to the next century.

Taking his time, David covered the house with alternating strips of brown, olive, and mustard yellow paint—camouflage—that hid it from view and added a nice punk look to the place.

He had bought the island and house from the estate of a writer who had built it in the 1950s. When he had first seen the pictures of the property in a real estate catalogue, David had been taken by its forsaken look. He could understand why the writer had selected this as the site of his home.

To find California Key, you'd have to be intensely interested or intensely lost. Or crazy.

The tiny spit of earth was several times removed from those infectious anthills up north called cities. As in "civilization." What a joke.

David felt reasonably safe here. California Key was far enough away from humanity to suit him. The air separating the key from the rest of the world was still and clear. The tropical sun cauterized the marrow. The ocean waters scrubbed the city filth from the skin.

David began to feel the hangover tighten around his skull like a hat two sizes too small. To take the edge off, he went inside, navigating around the computer system in the middle of the floor, the Fudgesicle sticks he used to trace circuits, and a year's worth of garbage waiting to be taken away. He made his morning drink—vodka and mango juice—and went back outside.

Not thinking, he let the screen door bang shut. The noise sounded like a lunatic banging trash can lids inside his head.

Taking his seat, he began to wonder about the pelicans again. Where were they today? Had they all flown farther south, the seasons changing without his knowing it? And what was that smell?

Moving his eyes from the horizon toward the shore, David realized that something was wrong. The gulf waters, usually clear, were a strange shade of pink. And the smell—heavy, pungent . . . what *was* it?

About twenty yards out he noticed a silvery glint of light on the water's surface. Then another, and another. Dead fish, hundreds of them, bobbing under the waves.

David was witnessing a red tide, the first he had ever seen in his eleven months on the island. He had heard about the phenomenon—blooms of plankton caused the algae in the sea to multiply in great numbers and discolor the water. These algae, called dinoflagellates, were highly poisonous and probably the cause of death for the hundreds of fish that began to pile up on the shore, flipping and twitching as the poison worked through them.

David picked up handfuls of fish and hurled them back into the murky gulf. Their scales felt rubbery and disgusting. He worked quickly, purposefully, throwing back the red tide's harvest. If he could save a few, just one or two. . .

But it was useless. Fish of all sizes and description accumulated on the beach. Many more rolled in with each wave. The smell grew stronger, overpowering.

David grew short of breath. He gave up and went back inside, looking for a drink.

Chapter 4

Hugh Lawson, special agent in the Investigations Division of the Federal Bureau of Investigation, tried not to appear too obvious as he listened in on the conversation going on in the associate deputy director's office. Sitting in the waiting area directly outside, Hugh found it was hard not to.

Hugh fidgeted in the chair. His muscles were a little tight from moving furniture all weekend and painting his new house in Arlington. He had just gotten bumped to a GS-12 and made the decision with Pat, his wife, to move in closer to the city. She was a ward nurse at Fairfax Hospital and had wanted to be closer to the job than they had been way out in Herndon.

Hugh shifted his legs, thick and heavy from his days playing collegiate football, second-team All Atlantic Coast Conference at North Carolina. He strained his neck toward the door. He couldn't make out much of what was being said, only an occasional rise from Edmund Brady, the old man, as he read the riot act to Dean Stiles.

Hugh wondered what Stiles had done to deserve this kind of flak. He was a top agent in Investigations, and had one of the Bureau's highest collar and conviction rates.

But he was also known for playing fast and loose with FBI procedures. Hugh had worked under Stiles on two cases and had been horrified how Stiles routinely ignored standard Bureau practice. Apparently, his irregular methods were starting to catch up with him.

A bellow from Ed Brady shook the door on its hinges. The door opened and out came Dean Stiles, his face hard and red. His blue eyes glowed like nuggets of uranium. Hugh tried to think of something to say but thought better of it.

"He wants you," was all Dean Stiles said before he stalked away down the corridor. Hugh swallowed hard and entered the office, prepared for the worst.

Hugh had been in Ed Brady's office only twice before and then in the company of Stiles. Brady was at his desk, removing something from the bottom drawer. He made a vague motion for Hugh to sit down.

Ed Brady was somewhat of a legend at the Bureau. Story had it that he had been hand-picked by J. Edgar Hoover as one of the newly minted young agents assigned to ferret out fifth columnists before World War II. As the associate deputy director for Investigations, the Bureau's number-two man, Brady had overseen nearly every one of the FBI's most sensitive cases over the years.

He had the memory of Methuselah, a reputation as a methodical, meticulous investigator, and an unshakable faith in the law of the land. Hugh had always looked up to Ed Brady. To him, Brady embodied law and order.

Brady's head and hands were massive, like a statue's, and he wore old-time rimless glasses that reflected the milky light of the office and hid his eyes from view. He held out something toward Hugh.

"Have one," Brady said offhandedly. Hugh looked down. Brady was holding a bag of caramel candy.

Hugh took one and watched as Brady popped two of them into his mouth. Brady folded his hands in front of his mouth and looked up at the ceiling, meditating and chewing. Hugh squirmed a little in the chair. Don't rush him, he warned himself, although curiosity was tearing at him like a hungry rodent.

"Style," Hugh thought he heard Brady say as he chewed the candy. Here it comes, the old man wants to rag on Stiles.

"I just saw him leave," said Hugh, "he looked pretty—"

Brady shook his head. "I said 'style.' Every agent has one. This . . . diversity makes the Bureau as effective as it is, in my opinion. Take Mr. Stiles. He leans very heavily on his imagination—hunches, if you will. Judging by his record, one may assume that his style has its place here.

"But there are limits to that approach. So it needs an offset, a balance of some kind. . . ." His voice trailed off and he remained quiet for several long seconds.

Hugh waited patiently, trying to see into Brady and anticipate what would come next. But he could see only his own reflection in his superior's glasses.

"I was at the briefing yesterday when you challenged Mr. Stiles on the tampering investigation."

"Sir, I wouldn't presume to challenge a senior officer, especially in public. I was questioning his theories."

Brady held up a huge hand. He popped another caramel in his mouth. "Very well," he began, his speech slightly slurred by the candy. "For about three months now, Mr. Stiles has led the investigation on the product tamperings. There are forty-eight such tamperings the

Bureau is investigating. It is absolutely our highest priority at the moment."

"Forty-eight?" Hugh said, thinking out loud. "Yesterday there were—"

"There has been another. But more on it later. Stiles believes that some of these incidents may be . . . connected in some way. But you don't find the evidence persuasive?"

Hugh wasn't sure what Brady was up to, but he knew he had better say something and that it had better be the right something. "Well, as usual, Dean makes some interesting points. But I just don't see any connections in these incidents worth pursuing at this time.

"For instance, Dean puts a great deal of emphasis on the use of cyanide in three of the incidents. We know that different kinds of cyanide were used, even though that information has not been released to the public. It's unlikely that one killer, even a smart one, used different *kinds* of cyanide.

"Another problem is with the products that have been tampered with—mostly different. The first product was milk, followed by cough medicine, cooking oil, ice cream, and a string of others. Granted, there have been some repeats in products—cough medicine was hit three times, milk twice. But certainly no trends."

Hugh was on a roll and, judging from the attention Brady was giving him, he was making an impression. "And next we look at the poison–product relationship," he said. "The first was milk–hydrogen cyanide, then cough medicine–arsenic, cooking oil–strychnine, and ice cream–potassium cyanide. It goes on. No connections there."

Brady was quiet for a moment. Hugh could almost hear the gears clicking in the man's head. "Tell me, Lawson, how would you respond to Stiles's conjecture that a connection might exist among the dairy tamperings?"

Hugh gripped his hands, trying to force his brain to work faster. "It's just too far-fetched, sir. The locations are so diverse. The milk tamperings occurred in New Jersey and Maryland, the ice cream in Minnesota.

"What's more, five people were killed in the Maryland incident, eleven in New Jersey, and nine in Minneapolis. And these poisons are easily available, Stiles said so himself. Any kid on the street could get his hands on them. There's even that obnoxious book—*The Poor Man's James Bond*—that gives you directions for making cyanide at home."

Brady smiled slightly. "Now let's put your skepticism to the test. This morning at approximately nine thirty the body of a twenty-three-year-old woman from Rochester, New York, was found in her apartment. She had been dead for about eight hours.

"The police were puzzled because no cause of death was apparent. They checked for evidence of suicide, homicide, heart failure due to a reaction to a drug she might have been taking—the usual. But nothing looked promising.

"They were ready to pack it up when a detective on the scene noticed a sticky substance on the floor around the body that had come from a broken coffee mug. He had the wit to bring in for testing a container of milk he found in the kitchen garbage."

He fished another caramel out of the bag. "Cyanide, extremely large quantities, were present in the milk. An autopsy showed the same thing—the woman's body was riddled with it. More tests are being conducted on the milk, the container, and the body, of course. And Rochester police are tracking down the store where the milk was purchased. Do you still believe there are no connections?"

Hugh said nothing for several seconds. He was so close to getting his first investigation that he could almost taste it. And his instincts told him that the reason he was in the running was due to his skepticism.

"Copycats," he said finally. "We've seen it before. One sick mind following another."

"So you would investigate the Rochester case as an isolated incident?"

"Yes, sir."

Brady stood up and Hugh followed his lead. "Sit down, Lawson," he said, slightly annoyed by Hugh's eagerness. Hugh sat.

Brady paced behind his desk, hands in pockets. Hugh squirmed in the chair. "How long have you been with the Bureau, Lawson?"

"Six years, sir. And it's been a very—"

"You've probably guessed that we're putting you in charge of this investigation. Dean Stiles has taken it as far as he can, I'm afraid. Normally, something of this magnitude would be given to someone more . . . senior. But I think you're the man for the job."

Hugh tried to think of something to say, but nothing came to mind. It didn't seem to matter, anyway.

Brady peered out the window and spoke softly, almost to himself. "I met with the director this morning after he spoke with the attorney general. They agree that these tampering incidents are getting out of control. The White House is under pressure from captains of industry to take drastic measures. But the Administration has taken a, er, soft stand on the tamperings. But that may change."

Brady turned back toward Hugh. "Think about it, Lawson. Any sociopath in the country now knows he can plant poison in the milk at the corner grocery store and get away with it. The public is panicking. Pockets of hysteria are spreading."

From somewhere deep in his mouth Hugh felt the onset of a vague paralysis. It coated his throat like thick mud and slowly slid down his spinal column and legs, settling in his feet. He felt embalmed and watched passively as Brady pulled a manila folder marked "TOP SECRET—EYES ONLY" from a drawer in his desk and placed it in front of him.

"That's the file on the tampering investigation. You'll be going up to Rochester today. I'm told there's a flight out of National at three. Be on it."

Those last words stirred Hugh from his inertia.

"The Department of Agriculture is in on the investigation and wants to take it over in the worst way. They have some jurisdiction over dairy-product inspection and have staked out a place for themselves in the investigation. Suffice to say there is some maneuvering at the Cabinet level over this. The Secretary of Agriculture, as you know, is a close friend of the president.

"Now I have the Food and Drug Administration clamoring for a piece of the action. Goddamn politics. But we have to deal with them, as well as with the local authorities and the Bureau's field office in Buffalo.

"So the director has struck a deal with all parties concerned. With their knowledge of the dairy industry, the USDA people are keeping computerized records on the tamperings, primarily those concerning milk products. They may also attend any briefings and press conferences related to the case, and have assigned a computer technician to the FBI agent-in-charge. That's you.

"We agreed that, after thirty days, if we see no tamperings of dairy products, then the FDA takes over these roles. Should that happen, we'll revisit the whole arrangement and get this monkey off our backs."

"That's some fancy footwork, sir," Hugh said, admiring the director's savvy.

Brady harumphed. "Goddamn politics." He leaned his back on the mahogany bookcase built into the wall and folded his arms.

"And then there is the matter of the press. I have considered sending an information officer up with you but decided against it. Public affairs in Washington will be on top of the situation, so don't you worry about it."

"Has anyone released a statement?" Hugh asked.

"Yes. Special bulletins have been broadcast to alert the public about the milk. No doubt the national press will pick it up before long. You can expect leaks on this one. The best thing you can do is spread information around, not trust any outsiders, especially the USDA, with substantial information."

"But they'll be in on everything. . . ."

"Then you will have to do your best," Brady said sharply. "In a nutshell, Lawson, your job is to get this investigation back on track. I will hear no more of any conspiracy theories unless there is significant, and I mean significant, evidence to back them up. All we need now is public hysteria."

Brady started pacing. "Most important, you are to keep me apprised of everything. Call me anytime, anywhere. Any questions so far?"

"No, sir," Hugh answered, a little too quickly, he thought. He looked at Brady, who was thumbing through a row of books in the bookcase. Plaques and citations cluttered the shelves. Hugh noticed a photograph of Brady shaking hands with J. Edgar Hoover in front of a Brinks armored truck.

"You read poetry, Lawson?" Brady asked, his back to Hugh.

"Sir?"

"Poetry. Do you read it?"

"Well, in college . . . some."

"Ever heard of Yeats, William Butler Yeats? Irish poet. Are you Irish, Lawson?"

Hugh thought fast. His family was as WASP as they came. "Uh, on my mother's side," he answered.

Brady wasn't listening. "I have a collection of Yeats's works somewhere here on my bookshelf. Mr. Hoover used to read him very closely, liked him a lot."

"I believe that I have heard of him," Hugh said.

"You should read him," Brady said. "Yeats had a theory that every thousand years or so there is a cataclysmic event, like the birth of Christ and the decline of the Roman empire, which was followed ten centuries later by the rise of feudalism and the medieval church. Another millennium later the world as it was known began to topple, the great European monarchies overthrown or emasculated, the world's religions fading in importance."

Brady's huge head was tilted sideways, gazing out the window with a look of . . . was it ecstasy? Hugh noticed a glob of caramel wedged between two of Brady's teeth, lateral incisors.

"Yeats described this as a widening gyre, an unraveling of civilization as we know it. He uses the metaphor of a falcon, a wild bird, no longer able to hear its keeper. From the chaos emerges a beast so strong, so terrible, that it is able to establish a new world order."

Hugh sat transfixed, unable to move, as Brady continued. "Not many people know this, but Mr. Hoover believed that communism was the embodiment of that beast. He was absolutely convinced that Marxism was the portent of a great movement that would lead to world anarchy. An incarnation of evil. I'm of the opinion that his relentless pursuit of suspected communists was based on that belief. You *are* familiar with the so-called witch hunts of the fifties, Lawson?"

"Yes, sir."

"We all know better now, of course. Communism has faded like every other ideology."

Despite himself, Hugh spoke up. "But not democracy, sir. That's an ideology that's still very much alive."

Brady shook his head. "That's a matter of opinion. We are fast approaching the end of this millennium, Lawson. I believe the rhythms Yeats described are rapidly accelerating. We now see major shifts in the world order every hundred years or less.

"What we have here with these tamperings is a shadow of that beast, a first spasm. Think of these incidents as previews of coming attractions, if you will. Most assuredly we will be seeing much more."

Hugh tried to move his tongue, but the paralysis was back, holding him fast. Ed Brady moved in toward him, close.

"The widening gyre, Lawson, is the disintegration of man's soul. That soul is being replaced with something else, something terrible. A manifestation of chaos coming from within."

"The beast?" Hugh managed to say.

"Most assuredly."

Hugh rushed out to call Pat. He tried to shake off the clamminess he had got from his seance with Brady. What the hell was *that* all about? he wondered. No time to think about it. It was already 1:47 and he still had to read the file and attend a briefing before he could leave for the airport.

Hugh waited almost ten rings before Pat picked up the phone. When he had left the house that morning, she had been busy scraping wallpaper in the foyer before the kids got up. She might be still working on that project.

Her voice was tense and shrill. He heard Lynn, their youngest, crying in the background.

Hugh tried to give Pat a sense of the excitement of the case, how it was his shot at a major investigation. He would have to leave as soon as he got home and needed her to pack a suitcase for him.

"How long this time?" she finally asked. There was something strange in her voice, emotionless and empty.

"Couple weeks, maybe longer. I'll call home every day."

"Don't bother, Hugh."

"What?"

"I'm taking the kids, we'll be in Richmond." Her mother lived in Richmond.

Hugh was running late. "Fine," he said. "Gotta run." He hung up as Pat was about to say something.

At his desk, Hugh flipped through the tampering file. Not much there, but he had a few questions for his briefing with Dean Stiles and a USDA liaison.

During the briefing, Hugh tried to read Stiles to see if he harbored any resentment toward him for getting the investigation. But the senior special agent gave away nothing, delivering his report in his unusual inscrutable manner.

Hugh had to race home to get his bags for the three o'clock flight. As he pulled into the driveway, he noticed that Pat's car was gone and the curtains were drawn on all the windows that had them. He tried the bell, but no one was home.

Hugh unlocked the door and, entering the foyer, stumbled over something heavy in the darkness. He found the light and snapped it on, a bare bulb on the ceiling. The garish red wallpaper left by the previous owners had been scraped away, leaving tear-shaped spots on the walls. In the middle of the room stood two pieces of luggage nestled among white drop cloths.

Chapter 5

"The cyanide killed her before she even digested the milk," the doctor from the Monroe County Medical Examiner's office whispered into Hugh Lawson's ear. "It's quick, faster than even the potassium chloride we use in lethal injections for executions."

Hugh nodded and looked out the gritty window of the 7-Eleven store. Nature itself seemed to be thrown off balance. On this bitter day in May, the Rochester snow was falling up.

Small, hard flakes were blown straight up into the sky by gusting winds. The wind whipped the snow around the army of reporters and TV crews camped in front of the store since morning. It stung their faces and upended spotlights and microphone booms. Hats, pages of script, and styrofoam cups were caught in the fast whirlpool of cold air and swept away.

Inside the store, two aisles wide, the confusion was even worse. Investigators of every stripe—FBI, USDA, FDA, city detectives, among others—were bumping into one another, sweeping the place, trying to get a piece of the action.

The Rochester P.D. was supposed to be in charge, but you would hardly know it. And they were following a vague lead, that the victim, Carla Moon, had bought the milk from this store. All they knew was that this was the store closest to her home that sold Beverly Farms milk in pint containers. She could have bought it anywhere.

Hugh had just arrived from Washington and was sorting through his options. He could hang back, let the Rochester P.D. finish its sweep, and then jump into the investigation. Or he could assume control, clear the place of non-essential personnel, and get this going by the numbers.

Whatever he did, he knew his opening moves would be watched, his credibility evaluated. Nobody up here knew this was his first investigation, and he wanted to keep it that way.

A question for the doctor occurred to Hugh. "How did you know it was cyanide?"

The doctor, bleary-eyed from filling out forms for hours, perked up. "That's an interesting question. When they brought her in, we had no idea on the cause of death. Best we could come up with at the time was a coronary, but she was pretty young for that. We found a lot of acid in her blood and we thought she might have gone into diabetic shock.

"While the lab downtown was running tests on the milk in the container, one of our toxicologists was examining a sample of the decedent's tissue. He noticed that the sample gave off an odor of almonds, which can indicate a presence of cyanide. Only a few people with certain genetic traits are capable of smelling it like that.

"We first do a screening test, which takes two or three hours. We draw a blood sample and free up the cyanide, which will turn a strip of green indicator paper blue. If we get a positive, we do a much longer test in which cyanide gas is produced by adding acid to another blood sample. The gas is captured and shot into a yellow acid-based solution that will turn a bright purple if any cyanide is present.

"Now, if you really want to split hairs about the *type* of cyanide, then you need to do a refractory kind of analysis.

"Our results came in just before we heard from downtown. We both got the same thing—potassium cyanide. Somebody meant business, Mr. Lawson. That's an extremely powerful toxin."

Two people Hugh had met earlier drifted over. One was Ellen Sherwood, from the New York State Office of Toxicology, and the other, Harry Rentschler, an aide to the mayor.

"You said acid was found in her blood," Hugh said to the M.E. "Where did that come from?"

The doctor took a step closer. "Cyanide is a very insidious form of poison. It binds to the iron in the mitochondria, the part of the blood cell that produces all the cell's energy, and deprives the cell of oxygen. This caused dysfunction in the cell and produces lots of acid."

Hugh stepped aside as a USDA inspector carried out a case of test tubes marked against the milk containers in the dairy case. As he left the store, the inspector was momentarily blinded by the flash bulbs and spotlights aimed by the hungry reporters. A vial of milk fell from the case, splattering on the ground.

"No use crying," said Rentschler. Hugh looked at him, taking in his tortoise-shell European-style glasses, cashmere scarf, and Burberry coat. Another smart-ass political type.

Hugh turned to Sherwood, the toxicologist. "How would someone around here get hold of cyanide?"

"*Potassium cyanide,*" she said, asserting her territory. "The distinction is important. There are the mercurics, sodiums, and calciums, but it was potassium cyanide, the most lethal, that got the Moon woman."

"But how would you *get* it?"

"It's not much harder to get than drugs on the street corner," she said, grinning. "PC's used in a lot of industries around here—agriculture, mining, pharmaceuticals—to name a few. And you don't need much."

"Isn't it a controlled substance?" Hugh asked, indignant.

"Nope, no federal law controlling it. Some states regulate its distribution, though."

"That's hard to swallow," said Rentschler, giggling. "Hey, did anybody hear about that tampering in California last month?" he said, still laughing. "What a hoot. One of the victims had donated his organs for transplants, and after most of his guts had been distributed, they found out he was poisoned to death. Can you imagine how the *donees* felt, their new kidneys filled with cyanide?"

Hugh started to say something to him, but Sherwood said, "I understand you've been seeing a variety of cyanides in these tamperings."

Hugh stopped in his tracks. How did *she* know that? "That information's classified," he said, and left it at that.

"I also heard," Sherwood went on, "that the last milk tampering killed an entire family in New Jersey as they were eating breakfast. Cheerios I think it was."

"Cheerios?" gasped Harry Rentschler, grinning stupidly. "I guess that means we've got a cereal killer on our hands."

Hugh was about to have him thrown out when a blast of wind and snow swept through the 7-Eleven, followed by an elfin-looking man in trenchcoat and tweed hat. He surveyed the chaos in the store, obviously amused by what he saw, and came straight toward Hugh.

"You Lawson?" he said.

"That's right. How did you know?"

He held out a hand for Hugh to shake. "Nelson Oliva. Special agent-in-charge of the Buffalo field office." He nodded to the others.

He turned to Hugh. "Listen, can we go somewhere and talk?"

Hugh looked around the small store, nearly every inch of which was occupied by cops. "Let's step over here," he said, leading Oliva to a corner next to a video game that bleeped "Take Me Out to the Ballgame."

Nelson Oliva stamped his feet and made a broad motion toward the reporters outside and the scene breaking up in the dairy section. "What a circus, huh?"

"Tell me about it," Hugh said.

Oliva unbuttoned his coat. "Yeah. Listen, I just came from the Hilton, place where Carla Moon was working last night photographing a reception. We might have a suspect."

"What . . .?"

"A waitress at the Hilton lounge says she saw Moon there last night. With a man. She also says they had an argument, the guy manhandled Moon."

"When was this?"

"Around eight, just before the reception Moon was working. Hey, have I ever worked with you before?"

Hugh was thinking, trying to keep down the excitement building inside him. "Do we have a description of the man?"

Oliva's eyes dropped to the floor. "The lounge was dark, the waitress said. Never saw the guy's face. She did remember he had a ponytail and didn't leave a tip.

"We checked, he paid in cash. Otherwise we'd have had his name on a credit card."

Hugh felt a surge of anger. "That's it, just a ponytail and a cheap tipper?"

Oliva stamped his feet again, not so much from the cold as from nerves. "We're checking on other customers who were at the bar at the same time. And we're still talking with Moon's family and friends, anybody who might know who the guy is.

"One interesting thing, Lawson. When the police arrived at Moon's apartment this morning after a call from her sister, the door was barricaded from the inside with a bookcase. They had to call the fire department and two locksmiths to get in. She definitely wanted to keep someone out."

"What about a doorman, anyone see a guy there last night?"

Oliva's eyes went back to the floor. "We got the night doorman out of bed this morning. Says Moon came home alone, no visitors before or after. But he does remember a guy visiting her over the past few weeks."

"Ponytail?" Hugh said, hopeful.

"No description."

"Shit," Hugh muttered. "They pay those guys to keep an eye on things. Don't they at least look at people?

"We're fighting time. The tamperer is probably somewhere in Canada by now."

Oliva was looking at him now and Hugh was suddenly aware of himself and lack of experience.

"The borders are sealed," Oliva said. "And all of my men from Buffalo are here assisting the city detectives. For the moment, the best we can do is interview the woman's family and acquaintances, collect names, run down leads.

"We're checking on employees of the milk company, looking for anybody with a record, as well as disgruntled employees, recent fires."

"All right," Hugh said, composed. "I've got to call Washington and then set up at the field office. I doubt if we'll get anything, but can you finish up here? And let's keep the details on the suspect out of the papers."

On the other side of the store, Harry Rentschler was bantering with the police commissioner and munching potato chips he had taken from a rack in the store. Hugh excused himself and stalked over to him.

With a handkerchief he always carried, Hugh snatched the bag of chips from a surprised Rentschler.

"This is evidence," Hugh said, his teeth clenched. "I'll make sure to mention your tampering with it in my report."

Rentschler stomped out of the store, grumbling under his breath.

Oliva came up to Hugh. "Easy, Lawson. We all know he's an asshole, but we're going to need help from the mayor's office on this case."

Hugh handed the bag to one of the five or six forensics specialists working over the store.

"What else have you got?" he said to Oliva.

"The USDA guys are waiting for you at a field site we set up in the D.A.'s office," he said. "And speaking of the press, they want a statement. They already have one from the city police, but want one from us, from the agent-in-charge."

Pressure rose in the back of Hugh's neck. Coping with the authorities was enough, but he wanted no part of the media. "Let me check on it," he said.

Oliva shrugged and drifted off. "Where's the phone?"

Hugh asked a forensics specialist dusting the video game for prints.

"Behind the counter," she said. "It's already been dusted and printed for latents."

He called Brady and filled him in on the suspect and, sure that he would be refused, Hugh asked permission to make a statement to the press. To his surprise, Brady agreed immediately.

"Another thing, Lawson," Brady said. "Our Behavioral Sciences people at Quantico have come up with a profile of the tamperer—quiet, middle-aged Caucasian male, extremely intelligent but very reserved."

"Probably just some kid," Hugh said under his breath.

"What?" Brady bellowed.

"Nothing sir, it's confusing in here. Lots of people pushing and shoving."

"Well, get it organized. I'm sending some people to back you up. Let me know if you need more help."

Hugh hung up and peered outside at the crews of reporters pushing through the police line, mobbing anyone leaving the store. He knew he would have to make a statement to them now. Like any federal bureaucrat worth his weight in paper, Hugh feared and hated the press for the vultures they were. Under the layers of clothing he felt drops of perspiration running down his ribs.

Get it over with, he said to himself. Stick to the facts. Take no questions.

A little while later, on his way to the field office, Hugh realized that he hadn't minded delivering the statement to the press. In fact, it was the most exciting thing he had done in a long time.

Chapter 6

Gardening is one of life's few pleasures. It had a singularly calming effect on me, forcing me to shut out the world, if only for a while. On some red days my gardening helped contain me, gave me focus, and I could just ride out the worst of it.

Because I traveled so much I didn't give the garden the attention it deserved. A few hours after getting back from Rochester, the first thing on my list was to check on my flowers.

To my relief, they looked fine. The rains had been good for them. Some of the perennials were in bloom while the annuals would come later. I hummed as I weeded and enjoyed the fine order of the garden.

Now, there are gardeners who concern themselves with color. Others experiment with textures, heights, blooming sequences. These gardeners have their place, I suppose.

I was a methodical gardener. I did not mix species, preferring instead to keep tulips with tulips, anemones with anemones, phlox with phlox. My garden had definition, a steadiness you often don't find in gardens these days. It was a structured micro-world that I controlled.

My garden had purpose.

Since my Rochester trip, I felt calm, placid. How frequently we underestimate the restorative powers of work. The trip succeeded beyond my greatest fantasies, even though the accomplishments were somewhat modest.

Only one subject had been immunized. I did not know what happened to the other cartons of milk I had injected. Perhaps they were discarded or were never consumed. I consoled myself with the thought that someone, somewhere, had been immunized by these other cartons, but that the true reason for their deaths was never discovered.

What was truly exciting was the reaction—on television, radio, the newspapers. All over the country—and the world, I found out—attention was focused on me without anyone knowing who or what I was. Armies of police and federal investigators were mobilized. And it was all my doing.

I would have liked to have been there as the subject drank the milk. I would have liked to have seen her face as the reaction hit. I would have liked to have heard her last sounds as the vaccine went through its final stages. Perhaps there was some way of overcoming this distance I suffered from my subjects.

As I weeded I recalled, savored, the experience of immunizing the milk in Rochester. I remembered the trembling excitement of preparing the two syringes in my hotel room and securing them in my bag.

On my way to the place where the act was to be performed, I felt such power as I had never known. The air around me bent from the force of my magnetic field. The terrible openness was neutralized by this power, reduced to nothing more than a thin gauze that I cut through like a knife.

When I reached the place I approached the lines of

milk steadily, sure of purpose. My eyes took in everything around me, perceiving light waves normally invisible to the human eye.

But I was more than human. I was a god who had to stoop low to get to the milk cartons. No one was near. If there had been, he surely would have been dissolved by my magnetic field.

I drew out the first syringe. In a great rush, I felt ancient, heavy in armor, a Greek warrior hidden in the belly of the wooden horse left before the walls of Troy. With sword in hand I waited silently as the gates of the city swung open and the trap was sprung, a force released from the inside.

I held a carton of milk tenderly and brought the syringe near it. I spoke softly to the milk.

"You won't feel a thing," I whispered.

The syringe exploded into the milk with the force of an atomic reaction, its aftershocks propelled into history.

Months before I went to Rochester I planned my strategy. It is always important to understand one's instruments thoroughly before undertaking an operation. Doubly important when human subjects are involved.

Poisons are subtle, delicate instruments. They must be approached with due respect. I read up on them, devouring the literature. I visited zoos and aquaria to observe the poisonous exhibits, making a special point to see the black mambas, the deadly death puffer, and the king cobra. A few botanical gardens and academic nurseries I called on grew lethal species such as the monkshood, deadly nightshade, belladonna, and death camas.

Most fascinating of all were the lowly snails—the members of the *Conus* family. So beautiful but deadly. These, like the *Conus textile*—the cloth-of-gold—had gorgeous shells of bright colors and vivid designs and a remarkably sophisticated method of poisoning their prey. By harpooning their victims with a hollow, disposable tooth, the *Conus* injected a deadly venom that ravages the cells of the neuromuscular system. Swift, sure paralysis and death.

Poison, I learned, was basic to nature, merely one of many methods of survival. Some animals had claws and speed to defend themselves and prey on game. There were insects with camouflage or rapid breeding patterns that ensured their survival.

Only the poisonous ones interested me, especially the organisms that used their poison to regulate populations. An important role not unlike my own.

Almost anything can be poisonous if one takes enough of it. And no two people are affected by any one poison in quite the same way. For example, as little as ten milligrams of atropine, the toxic agent in belladonna, have been shown to be fatal to humans. But there are cases of people surviving doses of up to five hundred milligrams.

Poisons have a long and illustrious history. Witness Socrates, Cleopatra, and others who used poisons as an agent of their own deaths. Men of knowledge—sorcerers and medicine men—used poison to heal and kill. Neuroscientists and others used toxins to develop medicines.

In poison there is physic.

I had a difficult time choosing my poison, there were so many to select from. More than ten million chemical compounds are capable of producing some toxic reaction in humans. And every year more than a million and a half people are exposed to a poison in some way.

Again, the burden of choice, of too much freedom.

But I focused on the lethal toxins. They were the strongest vaccines.

I knew the reaction I wanted: swift, certain death with a minimum dosage. I looked into the alkalies, lye and potash, that often were fatal when swallowed but required large doses, sometimes as much as thirty grams.

The chlorinated insecticides in solution looked promising. Compounds such as DDT, dieldrin, and DMC go straight for the central nervous system and usually cause death. But most of them were very hard to get, having been banned in most areas. That also made them relatively easy to trace.

Strychnine was another possibility. One advantage was that it caused severe muscular contractions in the victim, sometimes leaving *risus sardonicus*—the smile of death. A fine irony.

My poison would have to stay active in milk, so that ruled out the vaporous poisons. Nor could I have used extreme corrosives—they'd eat right through a carton.

I wanted something colorless, odorless, undetectable to even a suspicious consumer.

I first experimented with hydrogen cyanide, HCN, an extremely powerful toxin and popular rodenticide. It could do the job, inducing tachypnea, dyspnea, paralysis, and respiratory arrest in fairly short order. But HCN is available only in gas or liquid form. I needed maximum flexibility, something also in a solid form.

I found my answer in the *Handbook of Poisoning,* the pocket-sized edition. A wonderful read. There it was, the perfect choice, with an incredible class six rating—super toxic—right up there with the most poisonous substances known to man.

Surprisingly, it was a natural product, contained in such mundane sources as apricot and peach pits and cassava roots. It was widely used in industry and therefore easy to obtain and hard to trace. Another advantage: its lethal dosage is extremely low, weighing in at less than LD five milligrams—a mere taste for a one-hundred-fifty-pound man.

Another advantage: it is one of a family of poisons, all extremely toxic. If I used all of them, one for each immunization, then no one would ever know how to find me. I could work safely from the shadows.

The best thing about it is the effect. Most poisons affect a single organ like the kidneys or the heart. This one attacks every cell in the body. It is utterly and ruthlessly efficient, boring down to the level of the cell and inhibiting all oxygen utilization and electron transport.

The result: each cell in the blood is strangled, deprived of oxygen. Certain death, almost instantaneous.

The chemical symbol for this wonder drug is KCN. Ah, potassium cyanide, the perfect vaccine.

Chapter 7

Duffy Stambaugh, computer specialist 1 in the Division of Fertilizers and Biodegradable Compounds at the U.S. Department of Agriculture, stood at parade rest before Hugh Lawson. They were in the cafeteria of the Rochester Hall of Justice, where Hugh was taking a break, eating a sandwich and reading a book, after six straight hours of computer work on the investigation.

Stambaugh screwed his eyes, trying to make out the title of Lawson's book, *The Poems of William Butler Yeats*.

"Is it good?" he asked, not really interested.

Hugh looked up at Stambaugh, six feet four inches and 229 pounds of hayseed. Stambaugh was the USDA's liaison to the tampering investigation, a computer jock pulled from his farm detail to follow Hugh around like a puppy and meddle in everything. When Stambaugh was close by, Hugh could smell the fertilizer in his hair and the oil under his fingernails.

"It's very edifying," Hugh answered dryly.

Stambaugh nodded, not getting the sarcasm. "Oliva sent me down to tell you that those lists you wanted are here. We got them on floppies, so they're already on the computer."

Hugh tucked a coffee stirrer into the book to mark his

place. "On my way," he said, and followed Stambaugh up to the sixth floor, which was shared by the FBI, the Secret Service, and other federal agencies. They took their now familiar places at the USDA computer terminal set up in a back office, more of a glorified closet, in the FBI field office.

"So, what do you want to do?" Stambaugh said, crunching down on pork rinds he had picked up in the cafeteria while looking for Lawson. The pork rinds, Stambaugh's lunch, were individually sealed in tamper-resistant plastic that was stamped with a batch code that ran across the perforation. The idea was that you would notice if someone opened the plastic after it had been sealed.

The individual pork rinds were then sealed again in rows of heavy-duty blister packs. Finally, the blister packs were enclosed in a thick plastic box. And this was just the minimum—four protection features—set by the government on food items.

To get to a pork rind, Stambaugh had to labor to pull back the seal along the perforations and then peel away the plastic. Sometimes a pork rind broke up as he tried to open it with his big, meaty hands.

Hugh shook his head at the question. "What do you *think* I want to do, Stambaugh? Run one of the lists against the file." Jerk.

"Which one?"

Hugh exploded. "I don't give a shit which one. We'll do both of them anyway. Do the milk company employees. See if your computer can handle that."

"Oh, it can handle it, all right."

"Wonderful."

Hugh, at the tail end of his patience, took a deep breath. He was not good at suffering fools, he knew that.

But dealing with hicks like Stambaugh, having to rely on them for his investigation, was a different matter.

Ed Brady had given him strict orders to cooperate with the USDA, but he couldn't have known what a liability they'd be. Stambaugh knew nothing about conducting a criminal investigation. Each time Hugh needed anything from the computer, he had to go through this so-called computer specialist, having to explain everything in minute detail before Stambaugh could go to work.

And the damn database the USDA had set up was breaking Hugh's butt. Slow and cumbersome, it could have been designed by a seventh-grader as a science-fair project. Hugh wasn't surprised to find out that Duffy Stambaugh was one of its designers.

Hugh had one promising lead—the man in the Hilton bar—but it was fading fast. Experience had taught him that for every hour that went by in a murder investigation, the killer got a hundred miles away. Now, three days after the crime, the killer could be halfway to the moon.

But the worst thing was the press leaks. Hugh had no idea where they were coming from. First, classified details from the forensics report on the Rochester murder were plastered all over the papers. Next to appear was the description of the man in the bar. No informer in his right mind would come forward now for fear of exposure. And the man in the bar with the ponytail, whoever he was, probably had a crew cut by now.

FBI agents in Rochester were running over each other tracing down hopeless leads. Friends and family of Carla Moon knew of no boyfriends she had, claiming she was too busy with her studies and her job. There was no evidence she was into drugs, weird sex, or anything else that would put her with a homicidal psychopath.

It sure was tempting to simply write it off as a suicide. But the question troubling Hugh and the Rochester police was: why did Carla Moon barricade her door that night?

Hugh was now finding out about life in the hot seat. The Washington types he was dealing with played tough. In the middle of the night he was getting urgent phone calls from Congressmen, anxiously demanding information on the case for their constituents. Hugh could hear the desperation in their voices. To calm fears and build some cachet for himself, he appeared on Sunday morning talk shows and held regular press conferences. His friends at the Bureau wanted to know the name of his agent.

The investigation wasn't the only thing troubling Hugh. For the first couple of days he'd been in Rochester, he called Richmond nearly every hour. And each time he called, Pat's mother answered, telling him Pat was either on her shift at Fairfax Hospital, where she worked as a nurse, or taking the kids somewhere, or busy with something else. He was being stonewalled.

There wasn't much he could do about it now. Dumbly he and Stambaugh watched as the computer whined and clicked through the cross-walk of the former employees of Beverly Farms Dairy—the company whose milk was poisoned—for any convictions. On the FBI's computers it would have taken thirty seconds or less.

Hugh kept an eye on his digital watch as the USDA computer clunked along through its analysis and then slowly squeezed out a printout like a hard bowel movement. It took exactly three minutes and twenty-eight seconds for the whole process.

Stambaugh grabbed the printout and read it over. "Four arrests total, with convictions," he announced. "Two for possession of grass, one for aggravated assault—he beat his wife—and another for shoplifting. Otherwise, zippo."

Hugh swore to himself. "O.K., we'll let Oliva's people check them out. Let's do the other one."

"You got it," Stambaugh said merrily and crunched on a pork rind. He typed in a command to check another list, this one of the tenants in Carla Moon's apartment building. After doing so, he sat hunched over, watching the screen, showing no sign of fatigue or frustration. The perfect machine.

"Stambaugh," Hugh said, "did your bosses at the USDA ever mention that you people would have to turn over the data collection on this case to the FDA if a month went by without any dairy tamperings?"

Stambaugh's eyes screwed up at the question. "You know, I did hear something like that. But it doesn't look like it'll ever happen, does it?"

Hugh studied his watch. Minutes went by, three, four, and then five. No printout.

"It's taking longer this time," he said. "What's the problem?"

Stambaugh shrugged and cracked his knuckles one by one, squeezing first the large joint of each finger and then the small one. Abruptly he stopped.

"What the fuck?" he gasped.

Hugh spun around toward the computer. On the screen, strip after strip of data, each representing a major file on the investigation, disappeared as they watched.

"What's happening?" Hugh said, seized with panic. "Talk to me, Stambaugh."

Stambaugh, stupefied, said, "I don't know, we're in a

crash situation. It went straight out of database and into DOS, and I didn't get to save a damn thing."

"Well, do something," Hugh shouted.

Stambaugh nodded and furiously typed in a command. He slammed his big thumb on the return key. The lines on the screen, now into the second page of the five-page menu, continued to melt away.

This isn't happening, Hugh prayed.

"Stambaugh," he said, "is this the only copy of the database?"

"Let me try something else."

"Do it, for christsake."

Stambaugh bore down, his fingers moving in a blur as he keyed in a series of commands to stabilize the program. He looked up. Over four-fifths of the database was now gone.

"I'm bailing out," Stambaugh screamed. Agents and secretaries from the field office had heard the commotion and were gathering at the door. Hugh felt his shirt sticking to his skin.

Stambaugh shut the computer down just as the last of the information, collected over three months of intensive investigation, slipped away from them.

"Maybe I can boot up again and get back into DOS," Duffy Stambaugh said, avoiding Hugh's eyes.

"You do that," Hugh muttered.

Chapter 8

Hugh had to wait five days for the report from the USDA on what had happened to the database. He had insisted on a report, something official and on the record to use to get the USDA out of his life. When the report finally came, it stated the obvious: someone had planted a self-replicating virus in the USDA computers and eradicated just about everything in them.

An army of specialists from Agriculture went through the database backward and forward but had no idea who had done it, other than it was not the job of a professional hacker. And they were able to trace the source of the virus only to a computer "somewhere east of the Mississippi River."

Normally, Hugh would have been panic-stricken at the thought of losing all computerized information on a major case. But the virus gave him his chance to start over and set up a decent system. Back in Washington, he stopped by to see Denise Katchadorian, section chief for Systems Development in the Bureau's Technical Services Division.

Hugh had seen Katch in action on several cases back in the days when he worked in counterespionage. She was one of the best in the FBI, and knew just about

everybody who was anybody in the mercurial world of
the state-of-the-art.

Tucked away behind its innocuous title, the FBI's
Technical Services Division housed such crucial offices
as the National Crime Information Center, Planning and
Analysis, and Katch's shop—Systems Development.
More like a laboratory, the office buzzed with activity,
and there, in the center of it all and right where Hugh
thought he'd find her, was Katch, chain-smoking while
glued to a computer screen.

Denise, her dark hair now streaked with gray, hugged
him when he came up to her. Hugh had to bend low to
return the hug and caught a snootful of cigarette smoke
still in her hair.

"It's great to see you, Hugh," she said, "even though
my antennae tell me I shouldn't even be talking to you."

Hugh let the reference to his computer problems pass.
"Just one question, Katch."

"Let's go in my office."

Hugh's eyes needed a moment to adjust to the darkness in Katch's office. She kept the blinds down and the
curtains drawn so that she could give her full concentration to the five computer screens that circled her desk.
Hugh could make out the inscription on one of the many
commedations and diplomas framed on the walls, a
Ph.D. in computer science from Carnegie Mellon University.

"Why don't you just contract a big company, like IBM
or PanTech, to do the job for you?" she suggested after
Hugh had explained the situation to her.

He frowned. "Brady would never buy it," he said.
"That would mean letting a company in on the total operation."

"Split up the contract, then. Bring in two, maybe

three, companies. And put controls on the data. You know, series of passwords, key codes. We do that here."

"Denise, I need somebody—one person—to take over for Agriculture, to set up a system for them. They're lost and I'm stuck with them. Who's the best out there?"

Katchadorian looked at him, her head encircled by a cloud of smoke. "You want the *very best,* or the *most feasible* best?"

"The very best, unqualified."

"Then your man is David McAdam. He's the best."

Hugh had to think a moment. "McAdam? You mean the PanTech David McAdam?"

Katchadorian lit up another cigarette. She hadn't finished the other one. "Exactly. He assisted the Bureau on a project some fifteen years ago when he was very young and before PanTech was what it is today."

"What project was that?" Hugh asked, encouraged.

"The Recidivist Interface Matrix—RIM. Simply stated, it's a multi-processing system that interfaces a number of variables to predict when and how known criminals will commit their next crimes. It was brilliant. We still use it."

"Did you work with McAdam?"

"For the part of the project involving encryption, yes. I was supposed to be the specialist and he the generalist. But he knew twice, maybe three times what I knew about my specialty."

The story about David McAdam was coming back to Hugh. He remembered reading about charges of embezzlement, fraud, and other felonies when McAdam had been bounced out of PanTech. Bringing him into the investigation, Hugh realized, could present some problems with Brady.

"Weren't there some pretty strong allegations of impropriety surrounding McAdam at the time of his departure from PanTech?"

Denise smiled and shook her head as she stamped out her cigarette butt in the already full ashtray. "Hugh, you sound like a perfect bureaucrat. A man like David McAdam is too creative to be confined to the corporate structure for very long. He will always be challenging old thinking, threatening the status quo. That was his 'impropriety.'"

Hugh didn't particularly care for a sermon just then. It sounded like McAdam might be his man despite his checkered past. But he wasn't convinced. "What's McAdam like?"

An alarm went off on one of the computer terminals, and Katch leaned over and poked something on its keyboard. "Damn thing," she said, "too finely tuned for its own good."

She sat back and smoked her cigarette, the tip glowing in the darkness of her small office. "David McAdam," she said, her eyes drifting off. "Exceedingly bright, strong in everything—chip design, software, general electronics, you name it.

"And extremely imaginative. When I worked with him I noticed ideas came to him in bursts, out of nowhere, apparently. You know he virtually built from scratch, in his parents' garage, one of the first versions of the personal computer. I think he still holds a dozen or so basic patents."

"That's all fine, but what's he *like*?"

Denise looked at him. "You mean, what's the dirt on him? Plenty, if you read the supermarket press. I found McAdam to be a very gentle, generous man with a good sense of humor. Something you don't often find in a computer scientist. A bit quirky, perhaps, but no more so than most state-of-the-art types.

"When he left PanTech, he reportedly pursued several unsuccessful ventures. You may have read about his short-lived career as a rock-concert promoter. His name surfaces from time to time in some of the more gossipy computer journals I subscribe to.

"My contacts in the industry tell me that he was embittered when his partner in PanTech forced him out of the company, trumping up the charges on him."

Hugh nodded. "That's Sandy Slade, isn't it?"

"Yes, the slick one. McAdam was the creator, Slade was the marketer. Now, Slade is president of PanTech."

Hugh had one more question. "Earlier you called McAdam the 'very' best, but not the 'most feasible' best. What did you mean?"

Katchadorian laughed and then coughed deep in her throat, a terrible smoker's hack. "Your problem is finding McAdam," she said as she seized a cup of water. "No one's seen or heard from him for, my gosh, five years now."

Chapter 9

After nearly a year on California Key, David McAdam had perfected the art of puttering. Take today, for instance. Here he was, on the floor of his living room with a Fudgesicle stick, trying to find a burned-out circuit in the motherboard of one of his computers.

David rarely did anything without background music. Jimmy Buffet, wasted away yet again in Margaritaville, shook the drywall of the house at three-quarters full volume on the stereo.

The circuit had burned out late last night while he was working on a project, a computer game he was tentatively calling "Toxic Dumping." It called for two players; one to take the role of a midnight waste dumper for a nuclear reactor in New Jersey (designated on the computer screen as a small truck illuminated with radiation). The other role was that of a lone investigator for the Environmental Protection Agency, designated as a black sedan.

But David was getting bored trying to debug the problems in the program. He was sure there was a bad circuit in there somewhere. He cleared away a pile of semiconductors on a crate he used as an end table and set down his fourth vodka and mango juice that morning. The motherboard was spread out on the floor like a patient undergoing multiple-organ transplants.

Using the Fudgesicle stick, he traced the circuits in search of the bad one. This would be the last time he looked. No more chances for this mother.

And then it hit him. Here he was, David McAdam, creator of some of the most complex computer systems ever conceived, reduced to building stupid children's games. This was what he had come to. In disgust he tossed the Fudgesicle stick into a corner.

David was restless again, pissed off with himself and the world. Sometimes working on computers wasn't even enough. He needed something else to do and dimly remembered that he needed to see Toshi about something. With his memory frayed by Wild Turkey and vodka, David had to rack his brains before he could manage to recall what it was.

Sunglasses.

O.K., he would do it, he was going to Toshi's. Having made the big decision to go, David had to overcome one obstacle before he could leave: he had to get dressed. It took him at least an hour to find a pair of pants. And then he noticed that the sweatshirt he was wearing had a blood stain up and down the sleeve. Where had that come from?

Rather than take another hour or two to find another shirt, he turned the one he had on inside out. That seemed to work. You could hardly see the stain.

Going to Toshi's was an event that David attempted every few months or so, but since he didn't keep track of time he never knew how long it had been since his last visit. Usually he would just stop by to pick up a computer component he'd ordered, have a few drinks, or get Toshi to wire him some cash out of his Danish account.

David really had everything he needed right here in his house—food, music, and a reasonably good computer system. And, of course, booze.

On his way over, David remembered why he made this trip so infrequently. The thorny underbrush on California Key, grown dense in the months since he had last hiked through the island, snagged his clothes and scraped his shins. Fragrance of tamarind and oleander invaded his sinuses like a drug.

At the edge of the island the tide was out long enough for him to slog through the oolite that connected or separated him from the United States, depending on how you looked at it. The soft white mud covering the oolite was slippery and pocked with sinkholes, causing him to jerk and slide across like a second runner-up in a slam dance contest.

The hike through sun-dappled Kettle Key was always a relief, but it stopped abruptly at the shoulder of U.S. 1, where tractor trailers and mini-vans roared past in both directions. David felt the shakes coming on, followed closely by a titanic headache. This was the worst part of the walk, getting across the highway. If only he'd had a couple more vodka and mango juices before he left.

His head swiveled back and forth in robotic spasms as he searched for a break in the traffic. He figured he needed about five minutes to cross the highway, given his present condition. Finally the traffic stopped and U.S. 1 was peaceful, at least for a highway. He made it across intact.

Toshi's Bar and Marina stood shy but proud at the end of a dirt road curving off the highway toward the Atlantic. The place was in only slightly better condition than David's house, although it lacked his bohemian flair.

Behind the nondescript building that included the bar and Toshi's apartment, at the end of a trail of smelly diesel fuel, was the marina and the odd assortment of fishing and pleasure boats docked there. David noticed nothing new about the place except for bags of white gravel stacked in the carport next to Toshi's pickup truck.

As he walked unsteadily through the parking lot, David McAdam's head moved back and forth across the luminous cross hairs of a telephoto lens. He could not have heard the muttered curses of the photographer struggling to keep David's face in focus from the tan government-issue sedan twenty feet away.

David put his hand on the door to the bar and pushed it open. Before he entered, he looked back at the car. The sun was blinding and reflected off the windshield. David could not make out if someone was inside.

At that moment a finger pushed down on the camera's release, capturing his image on a surface of film.

Entering Toshi's, David recalled what he liked most about the place: hardly anyone bothered to look up as you walked in the door. He had to wait a moment to let his eyes adjust to the darkness before he went any farther into the bar. At first he could see what most people saw when they entered Toshi's—the fishing net and floats hanging from the ceiling and the life preservers and laminated mounted fish on the walls. What you'd see in most bars up and down the Keys.

But David also noticed other things most people overlooked, like the hand-carved Indonesian masks and the statuettes of Balinese spirits behind the bar. A radio was on, but it was tuned to one of those Miami stations that catered to old folks, playing things like Tommy Dorsey live from Roseland in between Dentu-Cream commercials.

David recognized one or two of the three or four customers. One of them, a young Asian woman at a table, watched him take a seat at the bar. David had never seen her before. On the table in front of her was a big stack of hardbound books, and she was with someone David knew, the fisherman with a testosterone problem.

The fisherman was of some undetermined Mediterranean extraction and covered with thick masses of hair—his face, arms, and probably every other part of his anatomy. David imagined that his pants and shirt were actually made out of his hair, only processed and cut to look like clothes. He was extremely aggressive, always looking for a fight. And oversexed. David could hear him making clumsy, obvious moves on the woman.

In his Zorba the Greek accent he undoubtedly played up, he was describing a fishing accident. "It didn't hurt as much as you might think," he purred. "The hook, it came out very clean with the knife. I stayed on the water and got me half a dozen snook before I came back. But I got this scar here. . . ." He hummed softly, pointing to a dark area near his crotch. The woman did not look down, but held her gaze on his face without changing expression. Who was she? David wondered.

"Sign of a good man," someone said to him. He turned and saw Toshi behind the bar with his arms folded, smiling at him. "Good man comes when his name is spoken."

Every time Toshi saw David McAdam, he thought he looked like he had just come in from months in an extreme environment, like a jungle or desert, he wasn't sure which. It was not only the wild hair and beard, or the filthy, sloppy clothes, but it was more the dazed and distant look in David's eyes, a certain disconnectedness that suggested he had cut himself off from the concerns suffered by most of humanity and was now absorbed completely in some private, primitive quest.

Today he looked even worse, as if he had been attacked by a wild animal. The hair and beard were the same, a bit wilder, maybe, than usual. Both his pants and sweatshirt were on inside out, soaking wet and spotted with burrs from the walk through the woods. As usual, David's clothes were tattered and dirty, especially the sweatshirt, which was stained with dried blood from the shoulder to the wrist.

Toshi wasn't so sure how David's shirt got turned inside out. Knowing David as he did, Toshi assumed he couldn't find another one to wear and had to settle on this one. All he did was turn it inside out to hide the stain. Just to be certain his hypothesis was correct, he kept an eye out for scars on David's wrist.

Toshi didn't know why, but he had a special feeling for David. Sure, David was a nice enough guy—generous, funny, and very smart, maybe the smartest person Toshi had ever met. And he was one of the few people Toshi could talk physics with, even though David was one of those applied-science types who had little time for theory.

Toshi thought maybe he was just feeling sorry for David, a helpless, aimless lost soul. But Toshi saw a lot of lost souls in the Keys. In fact, they were in the majority here and he spent a good portion of his time trying to keep them out of the bar.

Maybe it was because he saw David as a victim of nature's relentless tendency to devolve into disorder. Maybe it was because he saw him as someone in the throes of a paradigm shift, tumbling down the slippery slope of chaos like a little wooden airplane falling to the earth after its rubber band had unwound. Hell, maybe it was just because David gave good tips. But Toshi wondered how many times a person could bottom out.

Toshi Murata was the only person David had exchanged more than five words with since moving to the Keys. Toshi had come to the United States in the early sixties from Bali, where he had lived ever since he had deserted the Japanese army in World War II. David learned that Toshi had been an officer with the Japanese Corps of Engineers, assigned to building deep-water ports in Indonesia for the Japanese navy.

But, while hopping from one rain-soaked, malaria-infested island to another, the tramp steamer transporting Toshi's unit had been blown up by a mine. Toshi described for David how he had sat on the prow of the ship as it was sinking and admired the mechanics of a floating mine, its longevity and independence from human manipulation once it had been set.

There it lay, Toshi said, barely discernible as it bobbed in the waves, camouflaged as a coconut or loose debris, dumbly pushed and pulled by the currents as it awaited a victim. But most of all Toshi appreciated the ruthless philosophy behind the mine, that *you had to come to it* for it to do you in. There was no plan or design for this kind of *seppuku*—you simply walked blindfolded into the sword pointed at your guts.

Toshi had been rescued by a fishing boat from nearby Bali just as the steamer began to submerge. He was taken to a village called Kuta, where he lived for twenty-three years. He took a Balinese wife and became a lapsed Shintoist and learned the warm, easy ways of the Balinese.

Until 1964, that is, when the tourists invaded Kuta—

Australians, Germans, you name it. They built big ugly hotels, an airport, and roads where the Balinese could no longer walk barefoot. It was in that year that Toshi moved to the United States, ending up in the Keys, the place that most reminded him of pre-1964 Kuta, where he bought a bar.

"Oh, hey, Toshi," David said. "How about a drink?" Toshi gave him one of his inscrutable looks and then, out of nowhere, he produced a shot of Wild Turkey. David knocked it down effortlessly. Toshi poured another and again David finished it right off.

"Why do you encourage my worst habits, Toshi?" David said, loosening up a little and feeling the shakes go away. He had found that when he had been out of circulation for some time, it took him a while to get back to his ability to speak.

"This is bar, not halfway house," Toshi replied.

David grinned. "And that music, why don't you put on something good, like rock or something?"

Toshi wiped the bar. "You don't want to hear that kind of music. Ruin your ear. This is good music. Big band. So, what you working on these day?"

"Not much. Say, Toshi, do you have any sunglasses I could buy?"

Toshi shrugged and rummaged underneath the bar. He pulled out a cigar box marked "LOST–NOT FOUND" and opened it. Inside were pieces of jewelry, some expensive-looking wallets, condom packages, and other miscellaneous items. And two pairs of sunglasses.

"You welcome to borrow these," Toshi said, " 'til owner come looking for them, of course."

David studied the glasses, one with rhinestones and pointy ends on the frames—clearly unacceptable. The other pair was lime green and had "IT'S A SMALL WORLD AFTER ALL" inscribed in yellow across the top.

"Nothing in a cat's eye, huh?"

"Cat eye?" Toshi said.

"Never mind," David said and looked down at his drink. It looked so warm and glowing in the dim bar. As he drank it down, something stirred in his head. "Say, what did you mean just then when you said I came when my name was spoken?"

Toshi poured again. "Oh, nothing. Two men here this morning asking about you. One of them I seen before few time, policeman in Key West. Other one had badge too."

"Policemen?" David felt his face flush. "You didn't tell them anything, did you?"

"Me?" Toshi said, acting surprised that his friend thought he could betray his privacy. "No, sir."

David felt shaky and in need of a drink. Who was looking for him? And why? He tossed down a Wild Turkey. There, that was better.

"Cosmo there, now he tell them," Toshi said.

David spun around on the stool toward the fisherman—yes, Cosmo, that was his name. He never had liked David for reasons he couldn't fathom other than that David couldn't stand *him*. The bearded maniac was standing up, getting ready to leave. He looked angry.

The Asian woman was gone and David, momentarily confused, wanted to confront Cosmo but was also wondering, thinking, Who was that woman and where had she gone? Cosmo looked at David sitting there, stupid with his mouth open, and walked out.

Toshi had disappeared. David returned to his drink, his mind racing. What could he do now? There were other places he could escape to, another island he owned, this one off the southern coast of Turkey. Then there were also the hacienda in Mexico and the sheep farm in New Zealand.

As David plotted his next move, the news came on the radio.

". . . and today in Washington, the leadership of both the House and the Senate proposed sweeping legislation to respond to the product-tampering epidemic. The bill with the most bipartisan support at the moment would no longer require police to obtain search warrants when obtaining evidence and would substantially limit freedom of speech and the press.

"After the death of a Rochester woman last week, the number of tampering deaths has risen to forty-eight since the outbreak of these homicides three months ago. Police and the FBI are reportedly pursuing leads, but no suspects are in custody.

"In local news . . ."

David tried to tune it out but then, finally, a story came on that interested him, about a panther that had been sighted in the Keys. The report said the panther was last seen on Big Pine Key, just up from Kettle Key, looking disoriented as it ran through the parking lot of a Tastee Freeze Mini-Diner.

The police were alerting motorists and campers to stay in their vehicles, and parents and teachers to monitor the whereabouts of small children. No one was sure how a Florida panther could have strayed down this far into the Keys. Only twenty to fifty of the breed were known to still exist, and they rarely left their home in the groves of Brazilian pepper trees in the Everglades.

While the police hauled out their riot gear to track down the lost panther, David downed his fifth, sixth, or seventh Wild Turkey and said to himself: "They know you're here."

"What?" someone asked. It was Toshi.

"Do you have any meat?" David asked him. His tongue felt heavy, numb. "In your refrigerator, I mean."

"Some lamb. You want to come to dinner tonight? Somebody here you might like to meet."

David got up from the bar. "Uh, no . . . thanks. I just want to buy it from you." Toshi shrugged, disappeared, and came back with a plastic bag swollen with six pounds of lamb chops. He dropped it on the bar.

David dug around in his pockets, not an easy thing to do with his pants on inside out, and came up with a crumpled hundred-dollar bill. "That's all I have," he said, handing it over.

Toshi studied the picture of Benjamin Franklin on the bill, reminding him of one of his favorite American figures from the class he had taken thirty years ago for becoming a citizen. Franklin was a scientist, did some work in electrical conductivity. He was also a pretty funny guy. When Toshi returned with change for the drinks, David was gone.

Outside, on the edge of U.S. 1, David began to leave pieces of lamb, Hansel and Gretel style, on the path through the pine woods leading back from the highway to California Key. He spread some of the meat in the rushes at the rim of Kettle Key and dropped chunks of it in the marl separating the two islands.

He continued the process on his own island, leaving lamb on the path to his house, on the steps of the porch, and into his bedroom. David lay down on the bed and placed the last piece of lamb—the largest piece—on his throat and went to sleep.

Chapter 10

"Well, Mr. McAdam, it certainly wasn't easy finding you," Hugh Lawson said as he wiped mud from his black Florsheim wing-tips. He was perched on top of his briefcase, set vertically on the floor of David McAdam's living room. Hugh had had to slog through the muck to get to this little island at the ass-end of the United States.

Across the room from him, hunkered down in a dark corner, McAdam sat silently, radiating anger. He didn't offer Hugh a seat. Even if he *had* offered one, Hugh probably wouldn't have taken it.

McAdam's house looked like a landfill. Scores of empty liquor bottles were scattered among mounds of candy wrappers, frozen dinner trays, and other assorted garbage. A quick count of the bottles indicated McAdam favored vodka, with Wild Turkey running a close second. And Fudgesicle sticks—hundreds of them all over the place. What in hell were *they* for?

Hugh couldn't imagine how a human could live in such squalor, especially one as rich as McAdam. But one look at the computer genius told the story.

The photographs Hugh had taken of McAdam from the parking lot at Toshi's Bar and Marina bore no resemblance to the FBI file picture of a razor-sharp young computer scientist. The man must not have owned a mirror, or if he did, he avoided it like a vampire. Bits of food hung from the great gnarly beard that hid much of his face. Hugh expected something to come flying out of McAdam's dreadlocks: long, thick, and matted.

McAdam was a boozer, borderline if not hard-core alcoholic. Hugh's cop instincts told him McAdam wasn't into drugs, but it would be tough getting through to this man anyway. Judging from his failure to get two words out of him so far, Hugh guessed it would probably be tough anytime, even without the booze.

If Hugh hadn't worked so hard to find McAdam, he probably would have turned around and gone back to Washington. But he had pulled out all the stops to find McAdam, bringing in a team of about fifty FBI and INTERPOL agents working around the clock. Hugh even brought in the State Department, the Securities and Exchange Commission, the Federal Marshal's Service, and a couple of foreign embassies to help.

McAdam was supposedly a computer wizard, perhaps the only person who could do the job for the FBI. Hugh still couldn't figure Ed Brady's vehement reaction to the idea of bringing him into the investigation. When Hugh suggested it, Brady flew into a fit, roaring about security and propriety and anything else that came to him.

But Hugh wouldn't back down. He threatened to pull Agriculture off the case and turn over data collection to the FBI. Brady finally gave his OK, providing McAdam was fed only selected information about the case and he agreed to help without any threats or intimidation.

Fat chance. It was obvious McAdam had gone to great pains to hide himself from public attention. He had changed names several times, had himself declared legally dead, and for years covered almost all his tracks as he moved from place to place.

Operant word here was *almost*. As Hugh discovered, California Key was one of maybe one hundred pieces of real estate McAdam had acquired in the early eighties, apparently when the drum beats in his company, Pan-Tech, were getting louder. Using dummy corporations and third-party transactions, McAdam had bought farms, islands, and estates in remote parts of the world and then dissolved the corporations and erased the trails connecting him to the acquisitions. It had all been done on computers, which he had just about invented. Hugh never had found out where McAdam kept his money, reportedly in the nine figures.

Now that he had McAdam, Hugh was going nowhere in a hurry getting him to help out on the investigation.

"Listen, Mr. McAdam, I don't particularly like having to come down here, disturb your privacy. But I'm running an investigation of the highest national priority. To date, product tamperings are responsible for forty-eight deaths in nineteen states all over the country. And those are only the ones we know about. We think there're probably more.

"This doesn't begin to describe the panic the tamperings are causing. They've given nearly every lunatic in the country a license to do whatever damage they can pull off. We're seeing an epidemic of hit-and-run crimes—arson, bomb scares. Last week in New York City alone there were . . ."

A long, weary hiss floated out of McAdam's corner. Then a voice, labored, like a prisoner in solitary confinement.

"What's it got to do with me?"

Hugh's head shot up like a bloodhound catching a scent. Maybe McAdam was coming around. He spoke carefully.

"These tamperings are doing far more damage than murdering people, if that isn't bad enough. This is a new kind of crime, it gets into your home, into your mouth, making you question everything you buy. They're acts of random violence, with no apparent connection between killer and victim. And anybody can tamper if he really wants to: your wife, the kid next door, that guy you're competing against for a raise.

"And now the investigation is floundering because almost all the information on the case was destroyed by a computer virus. I need you to recover that information and create a viable system. Your country needs you."

"I repeat the question: what's it got to do with me?"

Hugh felt the tropical moisture beading off his brow. "The economy," he said, grabbing at last straws, "the stock market is taking a beating. Imagine, people not being able to trust the products they've been brought up with. Where would all that leave you, your millions melting away. Don't you care about that?"

Hugh thought he saw a smile on McAdam's face. "What I care about is my privacy, which you continue to violate with your presence here. Why don't you leave now, Lawson? The tide will be coming in soon. You wouldn't want to have to swim away from here in your Brooks Brothers suit."

"Listen, McAdam, time is killing us. The tamperings are getting worse, more frequent. This project shouldn't take more than a few days of your time.

"You'd continue to have your privacy and independence. We'd provide all the equipment you need, expense account, as well as a modest honorarium."

McAdam laughed, a nerd's snigger. "Honorarium? Oh boy, where do I sign? No, Special Agent Lawson, you'll just have to find yourself another errand boy."

Hugh glared at him and McAdam glared back. Hugh had to remind himself that it was *his* idea to get McAdam into this.

"Very well," Hugh said solemnly. "Two final things. First, you probably know there are subpoenas outstanding for you to appear before a grand jury. Seems you left your former employer, PanTech, with some funds and designs they think belong to the company."

Hugh touched a nerve. "PanTech wasn't my employer," McAdam exploded. "I *owned* the company, controlling interest. I built it and they used me, my work, and them dumped me when I wouldn't play the corporate executive for them.

"And those were *my* designs I took with me. The money too. I sold my shares, even though their damn lawyers tried to stop me. But I had a right to. They want to dispute that, fine. As much as I can't stand lawyers, I still have access to some very mean ones who'll shut down PanTech with a word from me."

Hugh held up his hands, the innocent bringer of bad news.

"One other thing. I spent a lot of the Bureau's time tracking you down. When I get back I'll have to file a report on this trip. The report just might, though I'm not saying it will, but it could get out to the wrong people. Like the press, I mean."

David McAdam was quiet for a moment. He knew Lawson was blowing smoke at him.

"I'll move," he said.

"We'll follow. I can post twenty-four-hour surveillance on this island. We could bring a boat or two into this vicinity, even get a helicopter to buzz by every fifteen minutes or so."

McAdam stood up. He was taller than Hugh thought.

"You guys are something. You're sworn to uphold the Constitution and what do you do? Invade my privacy, threaten me—"

"Nobody's threatening you, McAdam," Hugh said, an edge to his voice. He started to get up. "I'll leave my card. Meanwhile, I'll get in touch with Mr. Benjamin Slade. My people tell me he's the best in the business anyway."

"*Sandy* Slade?" McAdam said sarcastically. That was a name he hadn't heard in a long time. Hearing it didn't bother him as it might have a few years ago. Still, he had to admire Lawson's last-ditch effort to salvage this trip to Florida.

"So now you really want to screw up the USDA's database."

Hugh shrugged and stood up to leave. He brushed off his pants and picked up his briefcase. Just then the lock on the briefcase gave out from all the pressure of Lawson's weight. FBI documents, maps of Florida, and packages of Ex-Lax tumbled out onto the floor.

The last thing to fall out was the copy of the collected poems of William Butler Yeats he had picked up in Rochester to be ready for Ed Brady's next quiz.

David had started to laugh at Lawson fumbling with his bag and then, spying the book, he stopped in his tracks. David had read some Yeats, but like most computer scientists, never had given much time to poetry.

David picked up the book. He fought back a sudden wave of nostalgia for all the good things he had left behind to live in isolation here. Important things, like new rock music, computer-parts outlets, and books. Good books.

He turned the book over in his hands. It had been recently purchased, with a coffee stirrer poking out of it. What was this FBI stooge doing with it?

He thought for a moment. Maybe he had underestimated Lawson and his kind. Maybe Lawson knew something about poetry, could bring him books if he asked him.

"OK," David said, "this is the deal. First, I help you and no one but you knows my whereabouts. Absolutely no one. That has to be in writing."

"Done," Lawson said, triumphant.

"That's not all of it," he said. "Second, I use my own equipment. It's in storage, but I'll tell you where it is and how to transport it here.

"Third, anytime you want to see me, you have to call first. I don't have a telephone, but I'll give you the specifications for the telecommunications system I'll need. Deliver that and the USDA software when you bring me my system.

"Fourth, the USDA answers to *me* through you. As far as data collection for this investigation, what I say goes."

"Now, hold on. . . ." Hugh objected feebly.

"Fifth, you leave this book here when you go."

Hugh ran his hand through his hair. "Anything else?" he said.

"Yeah, I have a list of books you can deliver with the equipment."

David tried hard to remember exactly how he had gotten a table at Toshi's with a cup of coffee and four aspirin in front of him. He closed his eyes and rubbed his knuckles over them. Burning his throat with the coffee, he got all four aspirin down in a single gulp.

What he could recall was the FBI helicopter hovering over his house, churning up a cloud of dust and scaring the hell out of the birds on California Key. It lowered six crates containing all the things David had told Lawson to send him.

David also managed to remember unpacking the crates and struggling with the components into the house. Man, was he out of shape.

From then on the memories got fuzzier. With effort he could recall staying up about thirty-six straight hours as he set up the new computer system and tinkered with the generator to boost his power supply.

Then he took his first swipes at the USDA's database. What a mess it was, data all but completely hemorrhaged out of it. But that FBI agent—what was his name?—was right: it didn't take David long at all to begin to whip the database back in shape.

Already he had written a program and recovered all of the data lost to the virus. And then he had gone about the job of redesigning the database into a fast, smart system with a lot more capabilities than the USDA had given it. Who knows, he might even be able to turn it into a halfway respectable database.

Now, slurping coffee at Toshi's, one more memory of last night came back to haunt him—it was that of finishing off his second quart of Wild Turkey over the thirty-six-hour stretch. He was paying for it now. His head was pounding, his teeth ached, and he had to go to the bathroom but didn't want to risk losing everything in his stomach by getting up.

Then a pleasant voice came to him through the murky swamp of his brain. It was soft, sympathetic, and vaguely foreign.

"Feeling better?" the voice said.

David looked up. Standing next to him was a tiny woman with an excruciatingly beautiful face and short black hair that rose up in a forest of tiny spikes. She looked oddly comical in a big white apron. Then David recognized her as the woman he had seen with the hairy fisherman.

"Uh, a little," he said. "Do you know how I got here?"

"You walked through the door," she said, deadpan. "Not too well, you bumped into a few things. But you were all right once you sat down."

"How long have I been here?"

"Let's see, it's three forty-seven. You came in at one fifty-four. About one hour and fifty-three minutes ago."

"About?"

"Yes. You talked quite a bit. From what you said and what my father told me about you, I feel I know you already."

"Your father? Who's that?"

"Oh, of course, excuse me," she said, bowing. "My father is Toshiko. I am Nara Murata."

Chapter 11

Four days had passed since Hugh Lawson and the FBI invaded David's life and roped him into helping with their computer chores. If that wasn't bad enough, Lawson was now calling him twice a day, checking up on the status of the database. David, who had retrieved all Agriculture's data lost to the virus and then reconstructed the entire database into an infinitely better one in a couple of drunken hours, told Lawson he was still working on it.

The reality was that David was becoming interested in the tampering investigation. Purely as a computer exercise, of course. He realized Lawson and the FBI were concerned about the mayhem and the fifty or so human lives lost from the tamperings. But that didn't really concern David. He couldn't be bothered by a few dozen units of down wetware.

But he also knew that if he turned over the database to Lawson, the special agent would just thank him, laying on the flag and country crap, and that would be the end of it. No more investigation. David could go back to his computer games and vodkas and mango juice.

After four days of studying this case, David was getting hooked. It was the first real thing he had done in a long time. He didn't want to let go just yet.

He had read through every word and data point twice

in the massive USDA file. He knew that the FBI's top priority at the moment was finding the man Carla Moon had met in the bar the night of her death, the one with the ponytail. The database contained transcripts of interviews with more than thirty of Moon's family and acquaintances. Strange, not one of them knew of any boyfriend or close male friend.

From the database, David called up a picture and physical description of Carla Moon—twenty-four years old, five feet nine, red hair, beautiful. She was a graduate student in film and an accomplished photographer. It seemed odd that she had no one in her life.

No one in her life. That was a good one, coming from David McAdam, hermit extraordinaire. He of all people should have understood, *appreciated*, Carla Moon's desire to be left alone, to assert that primal urge to withdraw from one's species. Besides, was it so strange to want to dissolve one's ties to a hostile world?

He had to watch himself. He would look pretty odd himself if someone put him under a microscope as he was doing to Carla Moon.

Between David's skill and the modem networked through the satellite dish he had installed on the roof, no computer in the world was safe from him. It was a relatively easy thing to use Moon's Social Security number to learn everything that was stored about her on computer.

The FBI had ruled out drugs as a motive. David first looked at Moon's bank records for the past year to see if she had been moving money around. She had only $205.00 in her checking account and a CD fund valued at $18,350.00 under her and her father's name—Gerald W. Moon. The largest monthly balance of her checking account for the entire year had been in June—$784.36.

How had she paid the rent with so little liquid cash in the bank?

With a little digging, David found the name of the company that managed Carla Moon's apartment building. The company had accounts at three Rochester banks. In one of them Moon's rent checks were cashed.

He keyed in a command for the computer to override the bank's computer security and gather information on Carla Moon, or whoever it was who paid her rent. David was sure it wasn't her.

The computer was now searching for the name on the checks.

"Come on," David pleaded to the slate gray computer screen. "Give me the man in the bar."

The name flashed on the screen: Gerald W. Moon. Carla's father paid the bills.

"Shit," David muttered.

He got up and went scavenging for a drink. He flinched as he entered the kitchen, the smell was so bad. Cups and plates covered with layers of mold filled the sink, green from an unhealthy-looking fungus. A sea gull, roosting on the windowsill, boldly stared him down.

"You're the cleanest thing in here," he said to it. Maybe the bird was a sign of impending revelation. He needed a little inspiration. A drink would do.

Gingerly, David extracted a glass from the pile. He looked around for soap, but there was none to be found, so he simply ran water over the glass and fixed a vodka and mango juice. It still seemed like morning.

Back at the computer, David checked Carla Moon's credit history, one of the easiest things for hackers to do. Most of them just went into the TRW computer files and ripped out everything they could get. But TRW mostly gave you bad credit histories—late payments, bounced checks. David was looking for more: hotel charges, air or train travel, car rentals, gifts, anything that might point to a lover somewhere.

He quickly wrote a program for his computer to break into the mainframe of the major credit card companies and decipher their passwords. It took a bit longer to get through their security than that of the Rochester bank. But in a few minutes David was looking at Carla's charges for the past year on her American Express and Diner's Club cards.

He was disappointed again. Moon's only major charge was for a camera bag she had bought through a mail-order company.

Next he tried the Rochester police records and came up with nothing more than a record of the warning she had gotten from a cop the night she was killed, and one for a speeding ticket she probably got when she was late for class. Still no sign of the man in the bar.

David stopped for a moment. He was going about this all wrong, simply throwing darts by probing whatever computer file came into his head. He had to back up a minute, approach this systematically as he would in debugging a computer. He needed to get to know Carla Moon, get a feel for her.

This time he wrote a longer program, giving the computer much broader orders to break into any file showing Moon's Social Security number. These contained the documents of her life—job applications, school records, tax returns.

He started with her parents. Her father worked for Eastman Kodak, no big surprise in Rochester, where he managed a classified research contract for the Defense Department on optics for high-flying aircraft. For a moment David thought of going into Defense files—there was probably a security clearance for Gerald Moon—but held off on it.

Moon's mother, Gloria, was a part-time teacher of deaf children, and did a lot of volunteer work with the deaf in Rochester. The only other child was Carol, eighteen years old, who worked in a Rochester boutique. From her tax return of last year, David noted extra income she had earned from playing drums in a group called Bullet-Proof Vest. David thought he might like Carol and wondered what kind of music she was into. Metal, judging from the name of her group.

Her sister, Carla, was an average-to-good student—B's and C's in high school, with a couple of A's here and there, mostly in art and photography. She had done better at the state university in Binghamton, where she had gotten her bachelor's two years ago in, no surprise, art and photography.

From old credit card charges and traveler's check records, David learned she had taken a year off, traveled around Canada and the United States, a summer in Europe, and then back to "buckle down" in grad school. Find a life.

David paused. He had found nothing in Carla Moon's life to suggest suicide. She had a successful life, did what she wanted, had no psychiatric history.

But maybe, just maybe, she had met a guy in college or during her travels. At first he charms her with his looks, maybe, his energy, eccentricities appealing to an art student. As she gets to know him better, he gets weird on her, demanding in strange ways, kinky maybe. Then violent, episodes of beating, followed by insanely profuse apologies—"It'll never happen again, I swear"—flowers, presents. The whole damn syndrome.

But Carla isn't the type to stick around for more abuse. She dumps him.

But he doesn't go away. He writes her long, passionate letters, calls. She never answers the letters, won't take his calls.

One day he decides to look her up. He tracks her down on campus, follows her home, breaks into her apartment, and poisons her.

Poisons her? "Oh, come on, McAdam," he said out loud. Would a guy like *that* poison somebody, a woman he's mad for?

Strangle or shoot maybe, beat or stab, but *poison*? Get real.

This was going nowhere. What was he trying to prove anyway, playing detective? He would probably be better off just sticking to his computer games.

To wrap things up, David looked up Moon's graduate school transcript. First semester—a film production course, film theory, about what you'd expect. Straight B's.

Second semester, more of the same. She had audited an art history course, and the grades were—

Huh. David stopped to look at the grades. In high school and college, Moon had been a B student—better than average, even good—but not outstanding. Now, sticking out like a traffic light among all the B's was the grade for one of her second-semester courses: Kurosawa and Feudal Japan.

She got an A+.

It was the only A+ Carla Moon had ever gotten in her high school, college, and grad school career. Curious, David asked the computer for more information on the course, who taught it. A name came up—Mitchell Bryer, Ph.D.

Who he? David asked. Bryer's academic history, a list of his publications, lecture fees he reported to the IRS, came tumbling out.

And then the really interesting news—tucked into Bryer's confidential file were three complaints of sexual harassment. From students.

Using Bryer's Social Security number, David ran a check on him. Bryer was married, his departmental resumé at the university said so. No police record, but a record did surface of a paternity suit filed against him three years ago by one Marsha Cordts. Case settled out of court.

I'll bet it was, David thought.

He pieced it together, saw the situation. Professor Lothario, always on the lookout for fresh prey, spots a lovely young co-ed in one of his classes. Lovely young co-ed is overwhelmed that the hip professor could be interested in her, and responds to his offer of a beer after class with a "Gee, sure, OK."

Beer leads to dinner leads to bed.

Before she knows it, co-ed is seeing a lot of Professor Lothario. In fact, he's the *only* man she sees. She can't tell anyone, not friends, certainly not her family, because the professor has sworn her to secrecy. To ice the deal for himself, he gives her an A+ for the class, grade inflation being what it is.

But Carla Moon gets tired of the sneaking around, knows she's stuck in someone's fantasy. She tries to get out.

Why not just dump the schmuck? Why meet at a bar?

Maybe Carla thinks it's the right thing to do, tell him face-to-face. Or maybe there's something else, maybe he's threatened her with something, won't let her graduate. Can he do that? She doesn't know.

Or maybe he still has a set of keys to her apartment. She wants them back.

David thought of something and shot back into the police records on the case. Yes, there it was, the detectives on the scene had made a note that the door to Moon's apartment had been barricaded with a bookcase the night she was killed. Two locksmiths had been called in to get it open and the fire department did the rest.

She wanted to keep Professor Lothario out.

But where was the good professor? He had a set of keys, could have gone to the apartment after the bar and spiked Moon's milk while she was taking pictures back at the hotel. He wasn't even a suspect.

David wondered: Why hadn't the FBI noticed the A+, come to same conclusions as he? He checked the USDA database. No wonder Lawson was sick of the thing, it was programmed to search her grades for only the current semester. David sensed he was on to something. The lead wasn't much, but it was more than the FBI had. It would be fun to rub it into the special agent's nose.

This called for a celebration. Earlier that day David had spliced together several songs onto a tape he called "Medley of Madness." It included "Brain Damage" by Pink Floyd, "Psycho Killer" by the Talking Heads, "Lunatic Fringe" by Red Rider, the Beatles' "Helter Skelter," and others. This seemed like an appropriate time to play it, so he turned on the stereo full volume, bass to the max.

David braved the kitchen again, this time fixing a Wild Turkey over ice. He looked for the sea gull but it was gone. As he struggled with the ice tray, he realized that something was happening to him. He was used to dealing with abstractions, not people. From the scattered pieces of data, he could see Carla Moon emerging as a human being, a young, ambitious woman just starting out in life. Although he didn't want it to happen, the abstraction was becoming real to him. He felt anger and outrage toward the killer who had taken away her life.

David wasn't sure about this Special Agent Lawson. What would he do with the information David collected, his theories? Maybe he would just brush it all aside or claim David's discoveries as his own. At that moment David knew what he had to do: go to Rochester and confront this Professor Bryer. But how would he arrange it?

On his way back from the kitchen, David, to his horror, realized he had forgotten to replace a microprocessor in one of his computer's backup units. If the main system crashed, he would have zero backup, no fail-safe storage. Where was the damn replacement part?

Hadn't he just the other day run a Fudgesicle stick through that processor? On his hands and knees, he followed a trail of sticks to a corner behind a stack of back issues of *Computer World* Toshi had given him. Maybe that board was back there. . . .

"Anybody home?" a female voice called.

The stack of magazines went tumbling as David suddenly stood up. In the doorway to the living room was Toshi's daughter. What was her name?

She wore shorts and an oversized black T-shirt with R.E.M. emblazoned in red across the front. David noticed the variety of earrings she wore, as well as the tiny gold bead tucked behind one of her nostrils. Her hair was cut short and styled into punk spikes. In her hands were a bucket, broom, mop, and a canvas bag. She looked him straight in the eye.

Nara, that was her name.

"Hi," David said. "I was just looking here somewhere

for a microprocessor for my PT fail-safe unit. You want something to drink?"

"No, thank you," she said. "I hope you don't mind my coming in on my own. I knocked but no one answered. Where can I put these things?"

David eyed the cleaning equipment suspiciously.

"When I met you four days ago, you said that you needed some help getting organized,' she said, sizing up the house. Her face did not change expression as she surveyed the boxes and packing materials in the trashed living room. There was the slightest hint of disgust when she saw through the screen door the great heaps of cans, bottles, and assorted waste drifting on the back porch.

"Garbage in, garbage out," David said with a straight face. He waited. No reaction.

"I would have come sooner," she said, "but I promised my editor I would write enough columns for the next month while she's on vacation."

Now he remembered. She had just graduated from Bryn Mawr College and now wrote some kind of advice column for a Key West daily. "You wrote, uh, thirty columns in four days?" David said, trying to stall her so he could process the larger implications of what was going on here.

"No, only twenty-six. We don't publish on Sundays. So, where do we get started?"

"We? Hey, I don't remember asking for any help. I'm fine here. So, if you don't mind . . ."

"O.K. by me if you want to live like this," she said. "But I brought some things for lunch and I'm hungry. Where's the kitchen?"

"Through there," he said, pointing, relieved to get rid of her.

Nara gathered up her stuff and went off. Except for

his talks with Toshi and Lawson, David hadn't had a conversation with anyone in the past year as long as the one he had just had with her. And only one of those people had been in his house.

She came back into the living room.

"Could this be what you're looking for?" she said, holding in her hand something David couldn't quite see from the corner where he was kneeling.

"Hold on, let me take a look." He tripped over the magazines and came stumbling out to the middle of the room. Son of a gun, she had found the microprocessor.

"Thanks," David said and took it from her. "Where was it?"

"In your microwave oven. Good thing it wasn't on."

David wondered what had inspired him to ask for help getting organized. His life was in excellent order. Had Toshi put her up to this?

He went about installing the prodigal microprocessor and got back to the screen. From the kitchen came strange sounds and smells. Standing at the stove, Nara was humming something from the Balinese top forty as she stir-fried. David noticed she was standing on one leg.

"What's going on here?" he said, perturbed.

Nara did not look up and kept on stirring. "Nothing, just making lunch. Are you always this friendly to your guests?"

"Only the uninvited ones. There seem to be a lot of them lately. What's R.E.M. stand for?"

She looked at him. "Are you kidding? I thought you were supposed to know something about music. God, I suppose if you still listen to the Beatles you probably *don't* know R.E.M. Do you have anything recent? Some Depeche Mode perhaps?"

"Sounds like an ice cream flavor." He squinted at her. "What did you mean, I was *supposed* to know something about music? How did you know that?"

Nara smiled, an inward, inscrutable smile. "Uh, my father may have mentioned it. And I looked you up at the newspaper."

David felt moisture between his fingers. "Looked me up? What are you, another snooping reporter?"

"Don't worry," she said, waving a wooden spoon at him. David felt drops of broth shower his face. Unaware of spraying him, Nara went back to her stirring.

"I checked the microfilm files. A story about you mentioned your interest in music. But that was a long time ago, when people still listened to the Beatles."

"So what do *you* know about music?" David said, taking a step closer.

"I know what I like."

"Oh really? And what's that you're making?" It smelled good.

"Oh, nothing with a name. I'm just using up some things going bad in your refrigerator. Some rice, chicken, dates, and peanuts. When I'm through, I'll help you work out a schedule."

David tried to think. Those things didn't sound like anything he kept in *his* refrigerator.

Dates? Dates!

He hurried back to the living room. Just before this interruption he had picked up on something that flashed by on the computer screen. Something about dates—the timing of Carla Moon's death and how it related to other tamperings.

But he was too late. The information was gone. It was something he could check out again later.

Then he thought of something else and ran back into

the kitchen, where Nara was scrubbing the inside of the refrigerator while the Balinese stew bubbled on the stove.

"What schedule?" he asked nervously.

"Grab a mop and we'll talk about it," she said.

Chapter 12

"If Lawson calls while I'm gone, tell him I was working so hard, night and day, on the USDA database that a part blew on my computer and I had to go into Key West to pick up a new one."

David was giving Nara house-sitting instructions as she drove him to Miami International Airport in Toshi's 1966 Ford pickup. He had a ticket for the first flight to LaGuardia, where he would pick up his connection to Rochester.

"What if he calls more than once?" Nara asked, keeping her eyes straight ahead. Even with two pillows behind her on the seat, she had difficulty seeing the road. She kept both hands on the big steering wheel.

"Improvise, then. Elaborate on that basic theme. For instance, you could say that I got the wrong part the first time and had to go back. Or the part was defective. Or that I had to go up to Miami for some software or computer paper. Or that I was up on the roof, fixing the antenna. . . ."

Nara said nothing, letting David work off steam. All morning long he had been on edge, worked up over the least little thing. She tried to understand what he was going through. Here he was, going out into the world for the first time in a year. She noticed he even had trouble speaking, putting thoughts together, it had been so long since he had been with other people. He was like a patient waking up from a long coma.

Not only that, but he was feeling the first stages of alcohol withdrawal. Nara had given him a tough regimen: he was allowed one drink every half hour for the first week, one drink an hour for the second week, one drink every three hours for the third, and so on.

David didn't like it, but he went along. At least he said he would.

Nara had done everything she could to make this trip as easy for him as possible. She pre-reserved his seats for all flights and insisted on driving him to the airport. By studying a road map, she estimated the trip from Kettle Key to the airport at about 171 miles, or three and a half hours with a couple of stops.

When David had failed to show up at the bar that morning as planned, Nara had gone to the house. She searched all the rooms—there must have been thirty of them—but he was nowhere to be found. Through a window she saw him down by the small beach, watching the ocean.

Ever since she had come to work for her father three months ago, Nara had been bored. She could never admit that to Toshi. But she met no one she could talk with. At the bar, the talk was all sports and fishing. In Key West it was drugs and sex, not necessarily in that order.

The first time she saw David she knew he was different. To Nara, whose job it was to dispense practical advise and moral guidance to the decadent people of the Keys, David represented a project. He was a fallen genius, a brilliant original gone to seed who needed someone to lead him back from the edge of self-destruction.

Nara didn't kid herself. She knew David wouldn't get better unless he wanted to. If she could get him to trust her, to allow her to direct the drive and discipline she knew he had at his own problems, then he might have a chance.

David *was* a challenge. It was hard keeping up with him. Nara had majored in philosophy and physics at Bryn Mawr, so she was no slouch in the brains department. But David's mind worked like a bubble gum machine—ideas, refinements of ideas, and conclusions popping out, followed by long periods of silence.

He was in one of his silent periods as the truck, with its old muffler, rumbled into Miami. David yawned, making a show of covering his mouth in Nara's presence.

"Tell me again why we had to hit the road at five o'clock to make a ten thirty flight."

Nara didn't answer him. The truth was, she hadn't known how long it would take him to get ready. But he had been surprisingly docile, letting her trim his hair and beard and putting up no argument when she drew a bath for him. They had to wait a while as rust-colored water passed through the faucets. Obviously the tub hadn't been used in a long time.

She looked over at David as he gazed out the window at signs flashing by for places with names like Leisure City and Hialeah. After a year of living in seclusion, everything he saw looked alien and threatening. Concrete and asphalt, for as far as the eye could see, made his eyes ache. Cars and trucks choked the road and blew throat-burning emissions into the air.

Nara downshifted as she exited U.S. 1 for the airport. She looked at David again. Cleaned up and dressed, he didn't look bad at all. She wondered where all of this would lead with him.

"Do you know what happened to the panther?" David said.

"What?" Nara said over the roar of the engine.

"The panther, the one that was loose in the Keys. I was wondering what happened to it."

"Oh yes, we sent out a reporter to cover that story. They caught him, sent him back to the Everglades."

"Shit," he muttered.

"Why do you ask?"

"Whoa!" David shouted, the windshield rushing up at his head as Nara slammed on the brakes. They stopped just before hitting the station wagon in front of them. David blinked his eyes several times, getting rid of the stars circling in front of them, and felt his head for blood. "What's going on?"

"Roadblock," Nara said. "The police are checking cars heading for the airport. Sorry about the stop."

"Roadblock?" he said, feeling muscles tighten around his heart. Up ahead he could see the airport terminal. Stretched out before it was a snarl of cars and buses grilling under the morning sun. Police and heavily armed soldiers waded through the traffic, checking cars and luggage and frisking people. "Is there a problem at the airport?"

"A problem?" She turned to look at him, astonished. "You really don't know, do you?"

"I must have been living on an island for the past year or something," David said. "Know what?"

"What's been happening." Her hands tightened on the wheel, as if to steady herself. "I don't know where to begin. The country's under siege, David. It started three or four months ago with the first tamperings and just . . . grew.

"At first they seemed to just go after milk—the tamperers, I mean, poisoning it indiscriminately. And then it was fruit—grapes and peaches. I was still at Bryn Mawr at the time. Everybody there was freaked; you couldn't be sure of anything you put in your mouth. They even put security guards in the cafeterias, mostly for the parents.

"Now it's totally out of control. This week they're putting glass in cat food. Last week it was rat poison in supermarket salad bars. Every day you hear about bomb scares, prison riots, and the crime rate reaches a new record each week. Airports and grocery stores are hit the worst, so that's the reason for the roadblock here.

"The newspaper I work for gets at least one telephone threat of some kind every day. It's become a joke in the office. We think something's wrong if we *don't* get one, that's how bad it is."

David's tongue dug into his cheek. Maybe it wasn't such a good idea getting out like this so quickly, going up to Rochester. He wasn't sure he was ready to deal with people on quite this scale.

"The worst part," she said, her voice getting shaky, "is that nobody trusts anything or anyone anymore. You can't even trust milk. Especially milk."

David drew in a deep breath as the sound of boots came closer along the side of the truck. He looked over as the face of an explosive-sniffing German shepherd filled the window. The dog's head was snapped back with a pull of the leash by a policeman. Another cop, a young woman with a hard face, stared at him for long seconds and waved them on.

They were approaching the entrance to the terminal. David saw clumps of people around the front, piling out of cars and buses. He swallowed hard. Nara pulled the truck over to the curb. David couldn't move.

"Are you OK?" she said.

David sat still, watching the people entering the terminal. He could see their anxious sunburned faces as police patted them down and inspected their luggage.

Nara saw what was happening. "David, listen to me," she said softly, firmly. "You are going to pick up your bags and get out of the truck. Then you will go inside the terminal to the Delta counter and ask them the gate number for your flight.

"Then you will go to the gate and wait for your flight to be called. You will then get on the plane and everything will be fine. Call me at the house when you get to New York and then Rochester. I'll help you every step of the way. Do you understand?"

"Yes," he said, and gathered up his gear. As he opened the door, Nara took his hand and put something in it. David looked down. She had given him a pair of sunglasses, the French cat's-eye kind he wanted.

"Be careful," she whispered.

Chapter 13

"Are you *sure* we never met before?" the woman said to David as she eyed him up and down for the fourth time.

David looked over at her. Her hair was orange red, henna they called it. She wore a tie-dyed T-shirt over a spreading torso and bracelets up and down her arms. Posters of the Grateful Dead and Jefferson Airplane were taped to the cement block walls around her desk.

She was Mitchell Bryer's secretary. David tried to hide from her behind his new sunglasses and a copy of *Moby Dick* Lawson had sent to California Key. He felt way too exposed, sitting in the hallway of a sub-basement of a campus building as students shuffled by, all of them looking at him. He had been there nearly an hour waiting to see Bryer.

David was doing his best to keep to Nara's schedule. The problem, though, was that he didn't own a watch and couldn't be sure when his half hours passed. So he took guesses, downing from time to time the little bottles of Wild Turkey he bought off a stewardess on the plane.

On the floor in front of him was his old nylon duffel bag and a PanTech lap-top with a portable modem he could operate out of a pay phone if he had to.

It had occurred to David on the plane that he might need some identification to see Bryer, to get him talking.

On his arrival in Rochester, he had to scout around the airport to find a telephone where he could use the laptop to call up his computer on California Key and program it to get him into the FBI's files. But most of the public phones were the stand-up kind.

A fifty-dollar tip to a lounge waitress got him a phone at his table. David had to be careful now. The FBI would not appreciate his breaking into their classified files. Slowly, deftly, he used the computer to study the FBI's system, try out different pass codes, and finally slip through into of one of the most world's heavily guarded mainframes.

One of his favorite kinds of programs for breaking into secure files was a Trojan horse. The principle was simple: design a program that resembles the one you want to break into so that it slips past the security. Only give it additional instructions to decode all the passwords to the main file. David customized the program with Boolean logic combined with a Monte Carlo random sequencing.

His lap-top was nothing special, just a standard one he had Lawson send him. It gave him access to his souped-up supercomputer back in Florida. Through it David could get through just about any electronic security code in less time than an ace safe cracker breaking into a high school locker.

It was easy to do if you knew the basics. David had always thought of computer electronics as a lot like music, where eight notes in the scale could be arranged into Brahms' First Symphony or "Third Stone from the Sun" by Hendrix.

Same with computers, but much simpler. Computers ran on only two notes—*something* or *nothing*, pulse or non-pulse—the essence of the binary system. Only when you arranged those into a sequence like *something, nothing, something,* or 12 *somethings,* 456 *nothings,* and 110 million *somethings* did it mean anything.

The key to cracking a code was playing the possible combinations in a logical way. It also helped to know something about the people who did the programming at the other end. They were the kind of people David knew well—computer jocks who followed a few basic rules with minor variations. The more sophisticated they were, the better he knew them, and the more easily he could slip through their mazes.

Once in, it was easy to root around and dig up files. David called up an image of Special Agent Lawson's FBI identification badge on the lap-top, reproduced it in scale, inserted his own picture in Lawson's place, and had it laminated in a machine.

"Now I remember," the secretary squealed. "It was onstage at the Woodstock II concert. That was, like, six years ago."

She was standing up now. "My God, that *was* you, wasn't it? I can't believe it. You put on the concert. You had the beard back then, but not the dreadlocks. What was your name, anyway?"

David tried to act nonchalant as his legs began to shake. "That's very flattering," he said in as level a voice as he could muster. "But it wasn't me."

Actually, the woman was right, it had been David whom she had seen at the concert. Woodstock II had been his last, and most ambitious, concert project way back when. He had managed to get the same site as the original Woodstock for a three-day concert, but that was where the similarity ended. David's Woodstock was a flop, a dismal failure. Fewer than five thousand people and only four acts showed up for it. He lost two million.

Worse, *Rolling Stone* sent up a reporter to cover the concert, and she panned it so badly that the story made the cover and David's reputation as a loser was sealed. And during this time Sandy Slade and his salivating lawyers were trying to freeze David's assets and get him brought up on embezzlement charges, among other things.

To cap it all off, his marriage was disintegrating. It was no big surprise to him that Caroline, his wife at the time, wanted out. He even suspected that she was fooling around on him, leading a double life. Not that it really mattered anymore.

They hardly saw each other, as Caroline was busy setting herself up as a New Age guru named Telipinus, a channel for a Hittite mystic-king who had lived in the fifteenth century B.C. Without David's knowledge, she used some of his savings to buy property in Arizona, a dude ranch with cottages and meeting hall. She traveled around, making speeches and gathering a flock of disciples who joined the sect, the only requirement being they had to pledge a lifetime of devotion to Telipinus and turn over all their money to her.

Caroline's timing was impeccable as always. She sued for divorce immediately after David left PanTech and cashed in his principal share of the company's stock.

It was a good time to split, which was exactly what he did.

The door to Bryer's office opened and out stepped the professor himself. With a young woman. This one was very thin, arty-looking in black turtleneck, jeans, and massive earrings that looked like hubcaps to a Karmann Ghia.

"Doreen," Bryer said to his secretary, not noticing

David, "I'll be at the library until my three o'clock with the dean."

Doreen's eyes, wide open and shifting from Bryer to David, caused him to look down. He studied David, his eyes locking onto the beard, dreadlocks, and dirty jeans. David took the cue to flash his new FBI badge.

"I have a few questions for you," he said in his best Joe Friday voice, "about Carla Moon."

He watched Bryer closely as the color drained from his face and seemed to bleed into the red bandana he wore around his neck. Silently he led David into the office and carefully closed the door. Bryer dropped into his seat behind the desk and waved David into a chair next to it. David noticed Bryer's hair, a nice trim baby-banker cut.

"OK, Mr. Bryer," he said, getting right into it, "I'm investigating the poisoning death of Carla Moon. How well did you know her?"

Bryer sat still for a moment and folded his hands in front of his mouth. His eyes, narrow slits, looked carefully at David, evaluating. "You don't look like an FBI agent," he said.

"I'm under cover. Would you like to check my credentials again?"

"That won't be necessary. It's Agent Lawson, isn't it?"

David swallowed. "Yes. Now, about Carla Moon."

"Well, what can I say?" he said, spreading his hands and leaning back, relaxed. Saying with his body: See, I have nothing to hide.

"I read about it in the newspaper. Terrible thing. And she *was* a student in this department, was she not?"

Lying bastard, he was blowing wind in David's face. "Did you *know* her?" he said sharply, losing his cool.

"I'd have to check my records. She may have been in one of the classes I teach. But I really don't recall."

David thought for a moment. He really wasn't handling this very well. It was hard enough for him to carry on a conversation with something other than a computer, much less get a net over this weasel. Time to play hardball.

"Mr. Bryer—"

"It's *Dr.* Bryer."

". . . are you able to remember giving Carla Moon an A+ in your class?"

The eyes flickered momentarily. "What? No. I have graduate assistants who handle that sort of thing."

David kept up the heat. "In your nine years here at the university, you have given out exactly five A+'s, all to female students. One of those students was Marsha Cordts, who settled a paternity case against you out of court. Another was Carla Moon. Does *that* help you remember?" Bryer's eyes lost their languid self-confidence. "Mr. Bryer, were you with Carla Moon at the Rochester Hilton bar the night she died?"

Bryer did his best to appear outraged. Maybe he was. "Now, just a moment. What is going on here, Agent Lawson? Are you implicating me in her death?"

There it was. David had two ways to go, to ease off or to let him have both barrels at once.

"Yes," he said flatly, pulling the trigger. "We have reason to believe you were with Ms. Moon at the bar that night. Also, we found entries in Ms. Moon's diary, references to the affair you were having." David made up the bit about the diary. Not bad for a beginner, he thought.

"Preposterous," Bryer snapped, "Carla never kept a—"

"A diary? How do you know that?"

"All right, all right," Bryer said wearily. "I recall. She

was a student in my Japanese cinema class, one of those annoying kind who don't leave you alone. They bug you after class, they're standing there waiting at your office door as you arrive in the morning. I might have run into her that night. I don't know."

David looked at him contemptuously. "What did you talk about that night?"

Bryer reared up, like one of those harmless lizards that spread their wings when something attacks, trying their damnedest to look dangerous. "Did you hear anything I just told you?" he said, indignant. "I said I didn't even recall if I saw her that night."

"Bryer," David said calmly, "why don't you just face it? You have a history of hitting on your students, it's all in your file. And you and I know that Carla Moon was one of them. So make it easy on yourself. Tell me all about it."

Bryer flicked his wrist, as if swatting away a fly. "I have an appointment, Agent Lawson, and you have no evidence. If you want to talk further, I suppose you'll have to proffer charges." He got up to leave.

"One last thing," David said, pulling out the picture of Mitchell Bryer with a ponytail he had copied at the library from the school's yearbook. "When did you get your ponytail cut?"

Bryer's eyes were wide open now. He slid back into his seat.

"I want to see my lawyer," he said weakly.

Chapter 14

From the window of the Lear jet, David watched as the Rochester suburbs shrank to the size of a circuit board, the streets like circuits, the shopping malls and buildings like transducers. He had always enjoyed flying, especially the feeling of being detached from the world, leaving the ants far below.

In Rochester he had got tired of sitting in a john, the only place where he wouldn't be seen by anyone. So he found an idle private plane at the commuter terminal and stuffed some loose change in the pilot's pocket. The pilot eyed David's dreadlocks, wondering what kind of drugs or terrorist weapons were in the duffel bag. When David produced his FBI badge, the pilot relaxed and told him he could take him only as far as Baltimore, but there he could get a flight straight out to Miami. That was good enough.

The plane reminded him of the PanTech company jet, outfitted with fax machine, wide-screen TV with video and laser disk hook-up, Jacuzzi—the works—encased in plush wall-to-wall carpeting. David used to take that jet up whenever he felt like it, sometimes sitting up front with the pilot and watching the clouds rush at him. That was before.

And this was now. David poked around the cabin and

checked out the sound system. It looked pretty good, although not up to his personal standards. But the music—what crap! David could barely bring himself to touch the Julio Iglesias, Zamfir, and New Age CD's. Behind a CD called "Rainfall in the Big Sur," he found Laurie Anderson's "Big Science." Someone, whoever owned this plane, probably bought the CD thinking it was a collection of whale noises. He dropped it into the player and spun the volume dial around to the max.

Behind a well-stocked bar he found a telephone that could get him into his computer back in Florida. He hoped he might get some answers, or maybe some questions, by searching the computers of the Beverly Farms Company.

He was running out of ideas. After leaving Mitchell Bryer sobbing on the floor of his office, he was reasonably sure that the professor had not killed Carla Moon. No doubt he had carried on an affair with her, maybe even blackmailed her into continuing it. But the little shit wasn't a murderer.

David would call Lawson later with the news he had found the man in the bar. Lawson would no doubt be grateful. He hoped the special agent never found out that he had borrowed his name and badge for a while, all for a good cause. David was also tempted to call Nara and tell her how he had nailed Bryer, whom the FBI had been frantically seeking for weeks.

But he just didn't feel like gloating. Finding Bryer was not bringing David the sense of victory and satisfaction he had expected. It was mildly enjoyable watching Bryer squirm, but David now felt only irritation, like a prickly rash on the back of his neck, that Carla Moon's killer was still at large.

There were at least three possible scenarios, he figured. One, Carla just had the bad luck to pick up a milk carton someone had spiked on the supermarket shelf. Two, somebody besides Bryer wanted her dead. Or three, something else happened, the poison got into the milk some other way he hadn't figured out yet. Which was why he was looking into the Beverly Farms Company, the dairy which produced the poisoned milk Carla Moon had drunk.

David brought the phone and a Wild Turkey from behind the bar and dialed an access number. On his first pass at the Beverly Farms files, he came up empty. The screen on the lap-top scornfully flashed the "NOT ACCESSED" message. Amazing. His modified Trojan horse usually could get him into just about any system. And then he realized, the telephone signal from the plane must have fluctuated, causing a break in the transmission.

He tried again, this time running a check on a computer system he knew well—PanTech's. Within seconds the lap-top was overflowing with data from PanTech's mainframe.

No problem with the signal transmission. Something else, some kind of electronic chastity belt he had never seen before, was preventing him from getting into Beverly Farms's secrets.

So he did something different this time. He wrote a much more general program to assess the problem and suggest options for getting around it.

David entered the program and sipped his Wild Turkey as he waited. In her machine-like voice, Laurie Anderson sang about twentieth-century madness in "O Superman." The light in the cabin grew dim as the plane flew into a cloud. Up came the answer on the lap-top's screen: the Beverly Farms Company no longer existed.

Just three days ago it had been taken over by another company, and its name was already gone from the access files he searched.

He pressed a key to retrieve all historical records on what was once the Beverly Farms Company. Words and numbers pulsed over the screen, every scrap of information on the company up to the day it was absorbed and erased. Then he studied the records of Beverly Farms's new owner—American Milk, Inc.

David took it all in, absorbing and collating it in his head. Suddenly he felt a change in cabin pressure as the plane wheeled around, preparing for descent into Baltimore. He went forward to the door of the cockpit and entered.

The pilot, jotting down his landing instructions, looked up.

David threw three hundred dollar bills into the pilot's lap. "Take me to Washington," he said.

Chapter 15

The Dairy Division of the USDA's Marketing and Inspection Services is in the South Agriculture Building in Washington. One of the largest federal office buildings, South Agriculture is six stories high and sprawls over three city blocks. It is connected to the older, ornate building on the Mall by two arches, known as the Bridges of Sighs, which hang over Independence Avenue.

The South Agriculture Building is about three thousand feet across the Mall from the FBI building.

Mile after mile of corridors, stairways, and offices form a maze of bureaucratic monotony. In less than three minutes of walking the hallways of South Agriculture, David had already lost his bearings. He was following Dr. Stefan Kramer, Director of the Dairy Division, who had come down to the lobby from the second floor to pick him up.

It had been years since David had been exposed to this much concrete and fluorescent lighting. They passed frosted glass doors stenciled with names like "LIVESTOCK SLAUGHTER," and "SCREWWORM SPECIALIST," and "POULTRY PROCESSING." David, already self-conscious, had to wear a big, conspicuous visitor badge attached to his coat. But that was probably the least uncomfortable thing he was wearing.

At National Airport, David had been glad he had that FBI badge, the security was so tight. But the badge didn't stop him from getting grabbed and body-searched five times before he got out of the terminal. With his hair and clothes as they were, David felt like a deer on the first day of hunting season. He escaped in a taxi straight for Washington.

"Since when did the cops start searching people without a warrant?" he asked the taxi driver.

The driver clicked his tongue in shame. "Police do what police want," he said in a West Indian lilt. " 'Specially in airports now. Ever since them tamperings started, mon, things not right."

David noticed the big Rastafarian dreadlocks under the driver's wool cap. He asked if he knew of a barber who would cut his hair.

The driver laughed and said, "Sure, I take you there myself."

They drove to a building in the Adams-Morgan section of Washington, the music of Yellowman throbbing from an open window. The driver led him up to an apartment where David submitted himself to a crew cut and a shave in the kitchen by the driver's girlfriend, who asked him over and over, "Why you want to cut these beautiful locks?"

When she was done, his hair covering the kitchen floor, David tried to give her fifty dollars, but she would take only twenty.

Their next stop was a men's store on Connecticut Avenue. There, David quickly picked out a conservative suit, shirt, tie, and shoes. He left his old clothes in the changing room.

When the driver dropped him off in front of the South

Agriculture Building, he leaned over to David, shook his hand, and said, "I hope you get the job."

Now his new clothes, especially the big, heavy shoes, were driving him crazy as he marched down the USDA hallways as Special Agent Hugh Lawson of the FBI. But David had to look impassive, as though he did this every day. He noticed no one was looking at him now that his hair and clothes blended perfectly into his surroundings. That was what he had intended, but he hated the uniform.

Kramer walked with a noticeably hunched back, his eyes straight ahead. He seemed vaguely hostile and didn't speak a word until they reached the second floor.

"Everywhere you go now, you are forced into a confrontation with a cop," he said. "This is the Department of Agriculture, for crying out loud. How are you supposed to run an office with this kind of harassment?

"It's a damn nuisance," Kramer said, working himself up. "It takes nearly a half hour to get through the door in the morning with all this important security. You go to lunch, and police are watching the food lines in the cafeteria to make sure no one poisons anything. The Constitution is just going to hell."

David was relieved when they reached their destination, the Dairy Division. Kramer led him into his office, spare and chilly, devoid of decoration. Under a plate of glass on a small conference table was a poster showing equipment used in milk processing. A tall, thin woman in a black dress sat at the table and looked up at them.

"OK," Kramer said, "Special Agent Lawson, this is Dr. Iris Butler, one of our facility review specialists. I believe you wanted to speak with her."

Butler kept her seat as Kramer made his introductions. She nodded. David tried to see her face behind the steel-rim glasses and wiry hair that hung like a screen around it. She had a light port-wine stain on her neck and jaw-line.

"I have to be on a plane to our field office in Illinois in two hours," Kramer said, an edge to his voice. "Can we get on with this?"

"Fine," David said. "As I told you on the phone, I'm just back from Rochester, where I—that is, the Bureau—is running down leads on the tampering crime there. I have a few routine questions for you."

While he talked, he was aware of Iris Butler watching him with a steady gaze. More than a little paranoid, he wondered if she recognized him. No, she was just listening.

"Up in Rochester, I went through the records of Beverly Farms Dairy, the company whose milk was poisoned in the tampering. They showed the milk was inspected by the USDA a couple of days before the tampering death of Carla Moon. I have a couple of questions about—"

"*Mr.* Lawson," Kramer broke in, taking pleasure in doing so, "let me clarify something. Dr. Butler was not inspecting the milk per se, but rather the processing facilities at Beverly Farms. There *is* a difference.

"Her role, and that of this office, is not to grade milk. *That* is the provenance of the Food and Drug Administration. Ours is to carry out the dictates of the Agricultural Marketing Act of 1946 and to ensure that USDA-approved plants comply with 3-A standards."

"Fine," David said, letting Kramer's officiousness slide off him. "But you were there. I was hoping you could fill in the blanks, tell me what you inspected—how you did it, what you found."

Kramer's eyebrows jumped. "That's a tall order. We

look for many things during a survey. Butler, why don't you brief him, in layman's terms, of course."

Butler frowned at her boss's rudeness. "Basically, the Beverly Farms survey followed our standard operating procedures," she began. "I looked at the general conditions of the physical plant—the receiving cans, the milk trucks, the storage facilities for cheese, butter, and dry products.

"Then I reviewed the plant records on quality control, frequency of milk pickup, how tests are conducted. It's quite routine."

"Tests? For what?"

"Oh, various things. Purity of the raw milk. Presence of tuberculosis and brucellosis. Many of the plants now do a Charm II assay, a test for the presence of pesticides, herbicides, and antibiotics, like tetracycline and sulfamethazine."

"What would all that stuff be doing in milk?"

"Well, the antibiotics are administered to sick cows. Some farmers don't wait until they're well to milk them, and the antibiotic gets passed in the milk."

David felt an unpleasant bubble rise in his stomach. "Go on," he said.

"And, of course, there's mastitis. Beverly Farms has had a couple of cases of it this year, so I spent a lot of time checking the records on their tests."

David was interested. "What exactly is mastitis, Dr. Butler?"

"An inflammation of the mammary gland characterized by an increase in somatic cells in the milk and pathological changes in mammary tissue," she recited. "Even nursing mothers can get it."

"Oh," he said. "What sort of evidence do you have that a cow has it?"

"Oh, red, inflamed udders. Or general sickness in the cow. Usually it will turn up in the samples."

"Mastitis, how do you check for it?"

Kramer groaned. "Perhaps you should walk him through the CMT. He seems to have all day."

Butler ignored him. "The quality-control representative at the plant runs a CMT—California Mastitis Test—at the site. It measures the concentration of somatic cells in a milk sample. Any milk with more than trace amounts should get pulled."

David stood up and began pacing. "The Beverly Farms Dairy. Did anything turn up in that inspection?"

"Such as what?" Kramer said.

David ignored him too. "Do your recall, Dr. Butler?"

"I'd have to check the DA-151. But I don't think there were any problems, other than the usual residue I find in valves, that sort of thing. As I said, it was a routine survey."

O.K., David thought. Here goes nothing. "What is BST?" he said, watching Kramer's face.

The division director, aware of David, put on a puzzled look. "Do you mean RBST, the growth hormone?"

"I don't know. It was mentioned in the Beverly Farms files."

"It stands for recombinant bovine somatotropin," Butler said. "It's a growth hormone that stimulates cows to produce more milk."

"Did you know that Beverly Farms was conducting tests on BST?" David said.

"Now, just a minute," Kramer said, "BST is a drug. Ergo, responsibility for monitoring it falls under the purview of the Food and Drug Administration. Why don't you go waste *their* time?"

David fought back a smile. "Did you also know that

Beverly Farms was into all kinds of other things besides milk and yogurt? For example, they're doing genetic engineering, developing new strains of efficient cows, immune to certain diseases and able to produce more milk using less feed."

"I hardly think—"

"Not only that, they had a contract with a medical research company doing experiments on artificial blood. They were actually trying to manufacture blood in cows that can be transfused into humans."

David leaned his back against the wall. "What I want to know is, Who would want to stop this kind of research? The small dairy farmers, the family businesses, who feel threatened by super-cow? The environmentalists, who are worried about the new chemicals?

"Who would go so far as to put poison in Beverly Farms milk, killing someone to force the company out of business?"

Kramer and Butler were quiet for many seconds.

Butler blinked. "But Beverly Farms isn't out of business," she said. "I just saw it in the National Dairy Association newsletter this morning. It's been bought out by American Milk, just like so many others."

"So many others?" David said, and he sat down again to hear more.

Chapter 16

There's something I like about hospitals.

I can't quite put my finger on the reason, but they are somehow reassuring, even comforting. Even if they are hectic, hospitals have an underlying order one can cling to. Hospitals have purpose, decisions are made for you—calmly, scientifically.

I was following a red stripe on the floor which I had found as soon as I entered the building. The stripe led to the intensive-care ward.

A light smell of industrial cleanser hung in the air. I could make out the odor of its ammonia base, a raspy, not altogether unpleasant smell. The hospital must have used one of those germicidal cleaners that attack the lipophilic viruses like herpes simplex 1 and rhino-38.

The walls, floors, and even the ceilings, it appeared, had been recently scrubbed. The antiseptic purity absorbed all sound and sensation, like a newly fallen snow.

Despite their seeming cleanliness, I wore thick gloves. The cancer was thick here. One could almost see it hanging in the air.

Two young residents in blue scrubs wheeled around the corner, nearly running into me. One of them produced a weak smile and excused himself while the other went on with the story he had been telling: ". . . when I told her she had to curtail her activities during her recovery, she asked me if that included sex. I said no and she said, 'Good, my husband's going out of town for a week.' "

The white walls smothered their laughter as they disappeared down the hall.

The red stripe led me to an elevator, where I folded my arms tightly and waited. I looked around, hoping no one would show up at the elevator banks and ride up with me. I disliked elevators and sometimes needed to hold the walls when I rode in them.

Stairways had already been ruled out as a possible means of getting to the ward on the fifth floor. Hospital stairway exits often are locked; I pictured myself trapped in a stairwell, running from floor to floor like a mouse in a maze, hoping to catch someone opening a door.

Around the corner came a woman, approaching the elevators. Go away, I said to her in my mind. Find another way to go upstairs. Use the stairway. Just stay out of my elevator.

She pushed the Down button and smiled at me. At that moment the Up light flashed and the door slid open. I jumped inside and quickly pushed Five.

Elevators present a paradox. They can provide a zone of safety, comforting relief from the unrelenting openness of the outside. But they also demand a surrender of even more of the control one relinquishes in bits throughout one's day, throughout one's life.

Elevators are greedy: from anyone riding in them they require a major commitment of control, of confidence in the strength of unseen cables and machinery, faith in the competence of faceless technicians.

I steadied myself in a corner of the elevator, my hands flat against the walls.

On one of the walls was the inspector's certificate, old and yellowed, a relic. I read the tiny print that vainly tried to assure me the elevator was safe for up to eighteen people. But it didn't say it was safe for one person.

This was a traction overhead elevator with a speed of 350 feet per minute and a capacity of 3,000 pounds. That meant that it could hold 18 people averaging no more than 167 pounds. I hadn't weighed myself that morning.

I counted thirty-one words in the certificate: six *the*'s, four *and*'s, and three *in*'s. There were also two *emergency*'s.

Control, control.

The doors opened onto the fifth floor. I looked around for the red stripe and a familiar face turned toward mine. Dr. Peck, my mother's physician, came toward me and shook my hand.

"Can we go somewhere and talk?" he said, trying hard to keep his smile from cracking.

He led me into a waiting room with battered furniture and rows of fast-food machines. A man was stretched out on a sofa, a newspaper covering his head.

Dr. Peck was nervous, reluctant to talk, so I just blurted out, "Well, how is she?"

"She's comfortable now," he said in the most soothing bedside manner he could muster. "The home she's in has its own ambulance and paramedic, so she received prompt treatment as soon as she was found."

"When did they find her?"

"Uh, about ten thirty this morning. She didn't come down for breakfast, so the staff assumed she was sleeping in. She does that sometimes, they said."

Nonsense, I thought. She never slept in. She was always up before everyone else, bright and early. The staff was dangerously lazy.

"What's the prognosis?" I asked.

Dr. Peck shifted his weight, much more of it since I had last seen him. "We'll have to see. It's the glioma again. Apparently it's not responding to the chemotherapy. We're seeing more advancement behind her left ear, near the base of her neck. It was the reason your mother lost consciousness.

"The unit in this hospital is very good with these things. They'll do some tests—X rays, scans—and see what we're looking at."

I was getting impatient. "So it's still the cancer," I said. "If it's behind her left ear, then it's probably at the stem of her brain. Depending on what stage it's in, it could be inoperable. You could try radiation, but that's dicey at best."

Peck was, at first, speechless and then his face flushed. His look was one most physicians had when confronted with a layman who knew something about medicine.

"Now, hold on here," he said indignantly. "We don't have any results on which to base that opinion. Granted, that's all a possibility, but it's the worst-case scenario. For your mother's sake, I think we should—"

"What about her fall? Was she injured?"

Peck stood up. "A bad bump on the forehead. It broke the skin. It will cause her some pain but no more than the pressure caused by the growth."

"And the medication?"

"She was given eight milligrams of morphine sulfate solution for the pain and Decadron to relieve some of the swelling. I think it best that you speak with the specialist in charge, Dr. Heymann. We can just go down the hall and I'll introduce you—"

"That won't be necessary. You were on your way out."

"As you like. I'll drop in on her tomorrow. Call me if there's anything you need."

A new physician for Mother. "Thank you, doctor."

A ward nurse told me where she was, in a long room with a series of beds partitioned by curtains. As I walked through the ward, the voice of a woman coming out of sedation rose above the murmuring. "My son, where is he, the bastard? That son of a bitch, he put me in here. Where is he?"

Then the nurses got to her.

In the space next to Mother's bed a family of Koreans or Chinese—there must have been at least thirty of them—were crowding in to see a patient. I could not see whoever it was in the bed.

Then I stood before Mother's space and pulled back the curtains.

When I was much younger, maybe eight or nine years old, Mother fractured her hip while packing for a family vacation. She was standing on the top of a suitcase, trying to mash it down so that my father could lock it.

But she slipped off and fell toward the bed and cracked her hip against the baseboard. Our trip to the Grand Canyon was canceled as Mother had pins inserted into her hip.

Papa gathered my sisters and me, and we visited her in the hospital. I had never been in a hospital before. Papa led us down long, dim hallways whose polished floors receded into floor-to-ceiling windows and then dropped off the edge of the earth.

I recalled the faces in white smocks passing like ghosts. Their smiles were precise and reserved and belied a weariness toward us and a desire to be someplace else, far away.

We came to Mother's room. I remembered being fearful, expecting to see her strapped in bed, writhing in pain. But she was completely relaxed, happy, and had done her hair and put on makeup before we arrived.

It was then I began respecting hospitals; you could trust them, I concluded.

Then when I was thirteen, I was diagnosed as having cancer and had to spend a year in the hospital. I had such privacy as I had never known, no one but Mother visiting me there. It was the most wonderful year of my life.

And now, with the curtains parted, I saw her again. I was prepared for the tubes and the machines but not for the sight of her physical condition.

A hideous bruise, purple and red and oozing lymph, covered most of her face. Off her jaw hung a blood-soaked bandage that flapped loose like a dead man's tongue.

They had taken off her wig, and I could see the thin clumps of hair dotting her scalp. Dried blood ringed what was once her hairline, and speckles of it were lodged in her pitiful hair.

The skin on her face and bare arms was more shriveled and liver-spotted than I remembered. Her eyes throbbed behind closed lids. The sheets had not been pulled back over her, and one of her breasts was exposed through the nightshirt.

Explosions went off in my ears. The shock waves blew me over onto a tray. My head slammed against it as I went down. I curled up on the floor, covering my head.

Another memory of my childhood: on hot summer nights I would sneak in the dark onto the porch of a neighbor's house, ring the doorbell, and then run and hide in the bushes and watch with giddy delight as the porch light came on, the door would open, and a figure in a robe would appear, look around (not seeing me, hidden in the dark), and close the door and turn out the light.

I reached up and jammed my finger on the call button next to my mother's bed, held it there for many seconds, and ran out.

Chapter 17

Nowhere in the universe is the terror of openness more real than in the prairies of the Southwest. Here, one can find no relief from the vast stretches that explode in all directions and sink into the mouth of the voracious horizon. The wind, unchecked by trees or rises in the landscape, gathers force and rages over the plains, screaming into one with the force of a tidal wave.

Alone in the prairie grassland one is shrunken and dissolved, stripped of boundaries and orientation. The bloated sky and unyielding earth are like the two hands of God coming together to crush those foolish enough to stand between them.

Diaries of the Oklahoma pioneers—the Sooners and the Boomers—are filled with stories of men and women driven mad by weeks and months on the plains. They described the Alice-in-Wonderland sensation of moving without going anywhere, driving their mule teams into what seemed like infinity, the boundless, unchanging landscape.

Some pioneers, disoriented and unhinged from the effect, were known to have attacked their traveling companions and murdered their wives and children before turning their rifles on themselves. There were even accounts on record of grisly torture and cannibalism.

But the horror buried beneath the reddish-brown prairie soil stayed mostly silent, rarely evoked, except when squeezed out by the terrible weight of the wide open spaces.

Other than Papa, I had few friends when I was growing up. My mother used to joke that if it weren't for him, I might never have learned to speak. I knew that wasn't true; I received very good marks for recitation at school.

We moved a lot but only within Oklahoma. With some effort I could connect the name of a town—Enid, Anadarko, Duncan, or Altus—with a house or a pet. But over the years those places became a single blurred composite of a hot, dusty town somehow anchored to the earth, mile after desolate mile from anyplace else.

Papa was a geologist specializing in prospecting and exploration. He was considered the best in the state, and all the big companies back then tried their best to hire him. They offered him handsome salaries, houses, cars, and shares in the company's stock. One company even promised to put his children—all four of us—through college if he joined up with them.

He listened to them all but gave each one the same answer. Papa believed he did fine on his own but had one thing money couldn't buy—freedom. He could choose whom he worked for and when. The only drawback came when he finished prospecting a site and had to pull up stakes to move on to the next one, sometimes in less than a year.

My sisters—all older than I—complained about the moving. But I didn't mind. People didn't matter much to me, one was as good as another. They whisked past like the scenery from a moving car and vanished without a trace. I could be content anywhere as long as Papa was around.

I couldn't imagine a wiser man than him. He seemed to know something about everything. Whenever I came up with a new hobby—stamp collecting, astronomy, or bird watching—I could count on him to answer any question I had about the subject.

And I was his best friend too. He would lift me up onto his knee and whisper in my ear: "Tonto, you're the Lone Ranger's most trusted companion."

Together we would watch the Lone Ranger on television whenever we lived close enough to a transmitting station.

Papa's last job was in Cimarron County up in the Panhandle, deep in the High Plains country. The closest school to us was in Texas, but we weren't allowed to attend it. Instead we got up at four thirty every morning to make the eight o'clock bell at a school more than one hundred miles away.

Cimarron County wasn't known for much of anything back then. There were some oil fields, but many more after Papa left. In the mid seventies Cimarron became famous when a low-level employee of the Kerr-McGhee Corporation there was contaminated with plutonium, complained about it, and was shortly thereafter killed in a car accident. The employee was Karen Silkwood. I never knew her.

We moved again when Papa got another offer in southern Oklahoma. This time we found a house in Lawton, a good-sized town in one of the most oil-rich parts of the state. Papa said we could stay here a while. That made my sisters happy, but I didn't much care.

Sometimes on weekends Papa would take me with him on trips to the oil fields. We would drive for what seemed like days through the prairie, and Papa and I would have our best talks.

"Do you know where the word Oklahoma comes from?" he asked me. It was like a test.

I thought long and hard and ventured a guess. "I'd say . . . 'home of the oaks.'"

"Hmmm, not a bad guess. But there aren't many oak trees here. The state tree is the redbud. And the state flower is the mistletoe. Would you believe it? A parasite is the state flower!"

Papa was doing what he usually did, stretching it out, playing the game of will-you-ask-me-or-will-I-give-in-and-tell-you? As usual, it was I who caved in.

"All right, Papa, tell me. Where does Oklahoma come from?"

He smiled, getting what he wanted. "It's a Choctaw word that means 'red people.' Okla means 'people' and humma means 'red.'"

"Really?"

"Of course. There's a lot of Indian blood in the state, about seventy or so tribes. Most of them were forced to come here from the East. Remember the Five Civilized Tribes on the state flag?"

It was another challenge. I remembered them—five C's and one S.

"The Seminole, the Cherokee, the Choctaw. . . ."

"I helped you with that one."

" . . . the Creek, and the . . . " I was stuck.

He gave me a moment. "The Chickasaw," he said.

I always forgot the Chickasaw. Then I thought of a question.

"Papa, since we live in Oklahoma, does it mean that we're red people too?"

"Yes, I suppose it does," he said, rubbing my head.

I had been to oil fields before but had never dreamed one could be as big as the one Papa brought me to. In the middle of it stood a massive refinery—a castle of steel surrounded by forests of huge oil derricks that shot up to the sky from the flat prairie. Orange flame crackled ferociously from the top of gas towers burning off the residue of the crude.

My ears hurt from the deafening clang of hundreds of drill bits smashing into rock beneath the ground. Pistons on the mud pumps attached to the rigs churned and snorted. Papa watched for the big oil trucks that roared past in every direction, raising red dirt into the air.

He led me toward a group of rigs—Apache Estate #2—that he had prospected twelve years earlier, just before I was born. He told me it was one of the most productive fields in the country, each rig averaging around three thousand barrels a day.

To get to the field we took a shortcut through the refinery. I stayed close to him as the sun disappeared behind a canyon of pipes as big as school buses. Steam hissed from valves inches from my legs. Before we escaped from the maze of the refinery, Papa gently put his handkerchief over my nose and mouth.

We came out next to Apache Estate #2. Even with the handkerchief covering my nose, the awful smell of sulfur caused my head to spin. I blinked hard and kept my eyes on the ground, following Papa's steps and holding back vomit.

A man in overalls and a hard hat came up to greet us. Papa introduced me as Tonto, and I shook his hand. He was the rig supervisor. I looked at his face. Every wrinkle and fold was etched in black, as if he had been made up to look much older. When he smiled he showed white teeth coming out of black gums.

"I hear you signed on to prospect the Stehle Field," he said to Papa. He had to shout above the noise.

"Yeah, right along the Red. Think we'll strike?"

The man laughed. "You ain't missed a gusher in what . . . one hundred straight shots?"

"Ninety-four," Papa said, and they both laughed.

The rig supervisor and Papa strolled together and talked. I stayed behind and gawked at the derricks like a farmer on his first visit to the big city. I wondered if this place would sink down to China from the weight of the rigs and the machinery on ground punctured with so many holes.

I hoped Papa wouldn't be here when it happened.

Suddenly three men carrying monkey wrenches as big as tennis rackets hurried past me. They scrambled up a ladder to a monstrous oil rig that belched smoke at its base.

The men disappeared within a tangle of scaffolding and pipes around the pump. Papa had told me the pump forced drilling mud into the bore hole. The mud actually was a heavy fluid that kept an even pressure in the hole and carried crushed rock out to the surface. As long as mud was pumped into the hole, everything was fine. If the pumping stopped, you were in the Dutch, Papa said.

A blast of steam issued forth from the mud pump and the pump shut down.

Men were running everywhere, hiding underneath trucks and below scaffolding planks. Out of nowhere Papa appeared, snatched me up, and carried me running back into the refinery. Papa's friend, the rig supervisor, followed us into the refinery, and we all dived beneath the same pipe.

Papa put his arm over my head. Dirt caked my lips and face.

"What happened?" I heard Papa say.

"That was Big Bertha," the roustabout said, "owned by British Petroleum. Its mud pump's been acting up last couple days. Looks pretty bad right now—"

He was cut off by a loud rumbling noise and a gushing sound from the sky. Rocks flew everywhere and clattered over the refinery tubing above us. From the ground where we lay, I saw jets of mud streaming down, followed by a shower of greasy black oil that washed over us, covering us from head to toe like death itself.

Chapter 18

I was entering the sixth grade the year we moved to Lawton. Many of the children in my class were new, having been stationed with their parents at the Fort Sill army base in town. The army kids lived in a village out near the base, coming to school in a separate bus, always sticking together.

The Lawton kids called them the Sillies.

The military children were used to this kind of treatment from the locals. Many of those in my class already had gone to as many as six or seven schools. They openly showed the contempt for civilians their parents felt privately.

They called the local kids Okies.

The military children considered me a despicable Okie even though I never joined the local kids as they taunted them with chants of

> Sillies, Sillies,
> Such hillbillies.
> Pull down your pants
> And water the lilies.

And the local kids treated me with the same small-town suspicion reserved for outsiders. After years of practice, I had become adept at melting into the background, never raising my hand in class even if I knew the answer to a question, going home immediately when school let out.

In Lawton I tried as usual to stay in the shadows and especially out of the rivalry between the Fort Sill and Lawton kids. But my status as an outsider to both groups endowed me with an unwanted prominence. I had no gang to back me up, so everyone picked on me, chasing me after school, beating me up, fouling my school locker.

At recess I stayed off to myself away from the others, usually with a rock or handful of gravel to throw at my enemies if they came for me. I took to standing at the fence on the edge of the school grounds, watching convoys of green trucks roll past on their way to the military base.

One day a voice came from behind me as I stood there. "Know what's in those trucks?"

I pulled back my hand with the rock inside and turned.

"No, wait a minute," he screamed, hands stretched out and eyes fearful. I recognized him, a boy in my class named Richard Farnsworth. I had noticed him before as a misfit among the Sillies. He would have been a misfit anywhere. "How do *you* know what's in them?" I said, letting down my arm.

"My dad's an ordnance officer at Sill. It's his *job* to know."

"What's ordnance?" I said but wished he would leave.

"Bombs. Artillery mostly. But my dad's doing top-secret stuff. They're building atomic bombs to drop on the Russians."

"Who're the Russians?"

"Shoot, don't you know anything? They're the Reds."

So I wondered why the army would want to blow up people in Oklahoma, the red people. Maybe they didn't like the way their kids were treated at school. If they ever dropped bombs, they would have to pick a time when their kids weren't in school. They would never get away with it.

I refused to believe him until we began air-raid drills in class. The teacher explained that if the alarm sounded, we were to squat under our desks and cover our faces and chests with our bookbags. Two or three times a day the alarm went off, sending us scurrying and giggling under our desks.

I remembered one time crouching under the desk, counting the wads of ancient chewing gum underneath it, and waiting for the alarm to stop. But it didn't. Across the aisle from me a girl sobbed into her bookbag, a puddle of urine expanding on the floor around her.

The alarm was stuck and the teacher had stepped out of the room. We stayed under our desks for what seemed like hours before our teacher came back to get us.

At night I sat next to my father as he watched the news. Whenever I tried to ask him a question about the Reds, he would shush me and keep watching. Sometimes he would mumble something under his breath like he was swearing at the TV.

I caught fragments of the broadcast, words and names dropped dispassionately like bombs from the sky— blockade, President Kennedy, missiles, and Cuba.

"What's going to happen, Papa?" I asked when the news was over.

"I don't know, Tonto," he said.

I was stunned. It was the first time Papa couldn't answer a question. Whatever it was that was going to happen would be terrible. Not knowing was worse than knowing.

"It'll be just like we did to the Japs," Richard Farnsworth explained. "One minute you're drinking your Yoo-Hoo, and the next minute you're a pile of ashes."

Every night for the next several months I would wake up in the darkness, drenched in sweat, and then lie shivering under my bed until morning, waiting to be turned into ashes.

After the explosion at Apache Estate #2, I had to talk Papa into taking me with him again to watch him work. I could usually wear him down with my begging. I had just turned twelve.

We did not have to drive very far this time to get to the site. The Stehle Field was an empty stretch of grassy prairie along the Red River that divided Oklahoma from Texas. You could see the river from Stehle.

I wore a St. Louis Cardinals baseball cap Papa had gotten me for my birthday. But there was no sun that day, clouds were out. It was unusual to see clouds in this part of Oklahoma except in the flood season. Papa said it was good it was cloudy, his men worked better out from under the sun.

As we parked near Stehle Field I noticed children playing around a cluster of tents off to the side of the range. I asked Papa who they were.

"Indians," he said. "They set up camp here and they'll be looking for work when the rigs go up."

The Indian children looked poor—deathly skinny and dressed in rags.

"Should I give them something to eat?" I said. "Maybe some milk from the cooler?" We had brought a picnic lunch with us.

"Indians don't drink milk," Papa said. "It makes them sick."

"Really?"

"Yes. Their stomachs can't take it."

I followed Papa out to the range, where a few men sat talking in pickup trucks. They were Papa's crew. Two of the men had been passing a bottle wrapped in a paper bag. One of them was smoking a cigarette. I saw them put the bottle and cigarette down when we got nearer.

All the men climbed out of their trucks.

"Too cloudy to work today, Burt," one of them said to Papa. The men laughed.

They began unloading equipment and Papa spread out some maps on the back of a pickup. He talked a while with one of the men, the surveyor, who took one of the maps and left in a truck with another man.

They were going out to dig holes in another part of the range.

Every so often I would look over to see what the Indian kids were doing. They had gone inside the tents.

I noticed that everywhere Papa went, he carried a black metal box. In the car he had explained that the box contained charges and explosives he used to explore an oil field.

Papa said he would first study the surface of a field, looking for any sign of oil, like seepage of crude oil or a certain kind of rock formation. But the Oklahoma fields were secretive, he said. They rarely revealed from the surface just where the oil was hiding. So he had to do something else to map the field, to discover its secrets.

Papa and the surveyor would make several visits to the field, examining soil samples and slopes in the ground. Then they picked out certain spots all over the field where they would drill shallow holes. In the holes they put the explosives and charges.

Papa then hooked up microphones to instruments set up around the field to record how fast the echoes from the explosions reached the microphones. The speed of the echoes, Papa said, told him what the rock in the field was like so that he could make a map of the underground. The map showed the oil men where to drill their holes.

Today Papa was going to map a part of the field near where the trucks were parked. When I scrunched up my eyes I could see the holes already dug out in the field around us.

Papa told the men to follow him with the equipment. Then he came over and said to me, "Tonto, the Lone Ranger has to go do his duty. You stay here and watch the horses."

I smiled when he rubbed my head. I watched him walk away with the black metal box.

And I watched him as he went out into the range with the men behind him struggling with the instruments. They placed pieces of equipment around the field where Papa told them to. One of the men dropped what he was carrying. I couldn't hear what Papa said to him.

The prairie was quiet. A light wind chilled my bare arms. I took a seat up on the hood of our car and turned my Cardinals cap around, catcher-style.

Even with the clouds in the sky, the group of men standing around a hole in the field shimmered in a mirage. I could see men running here and there on Papa's instructions, and I could just barely make out Papa kneeling down before one of the holes, a man standing beside him. The man made a motion to his hip and then to his mouth.

I could not remember what hit me first, the flash of light and blast of red dirt, the thunderous sound of the explosion, or the ground rushing up to my face as I was lifted off the car and thrown down. Through the smoke and dirt I could gather fractured images of choked screams, a man appearing and disappearing, and then a glimpse of the distant prairie.

I felt myself to see if I was all still there. My ears rung from the explosion and I felt a dense ball in the pit of my stomach. I managed to sit up.

And then it began to rain. It fell on my head and arms and washed over the terrifying openness of the prairie.

It rained red.

I rode home in the cab of the surveyor's pickup. In the back was Papa, covered by a piece of tarpaulin. I had seen him when they carried him in from the field, both of his legs and one of his arms blown off, his face imbedded with shards of rock. I also looked into his eyes, black-red holes, that now knew the answer to any question I could imagine asking.

"Don't cry, Papa," I said.

"Get that kid out of here," one of the crew screamed.

The surveyor, coming in from the range after he heard the explosion, took me away. The surveyor, Papa, and I went home together. None of us said anything.

Soon after the funeral I got sick, and Mother kept me home from school for a long time. When I went back, the children treated me differently, left me alone, the way I wanted it to be.

Papa died leaving us in debt, never having saved anything and speculating on property in the eastern part of the state. His friends said he had planned to prospect the land. Mother sold it immediately.

Within a year after Papa died, Mother married a man who drove a cement mixer for the Halliburton Company.

She used to say she didn't have much choice in the matter. With four mouths to feed, she took the first man who came along.

I remember the day she brought him to the house to meet us. My sisters and I had to put on our nicest clothes and our best behavior. Mother instructed us not to call him Papa, but rather Mr. Gough.

He arrived late for supper, looking tired and glassy-eyed. He was a big man, with massive shoulders and no neck. His eyes were small like black marbles that looked hard at my sisters and me. After he left we all agreed we would try to talk Mother out of marrying him.

"He gives me the willies," Daisy said.

But Mother wouldn't hear anything from us about Mr. Gough.

"You will all make do," she said, "and you will learn to love him as I have."

Mr. Gough moved in a week later. At first things were calm, everyone making an effort to get along. But he began to stay out late, come home drunk expecting dinner, then go to bed.

And he was mean, frighteningly so. Once I found him in the bedroom with Daisy, who was struggling to break free of his big, truck-driving hands that held her wrists. When I screamed, he let her go and slapped her. He warned us never to tell Mother or he would hurt us bad.

Rose and she, the oldest two, left home five months after he moved in. They went to Arkansas to stay with cousins. We never heard from them again.

My next older sister, Lilly, finished her junior year of high school and then dropped out to get married. When she left, she didn't say where she was going. I had nowhere to go, so I remained at home with Mother.

Just weeks after Lilly left, a wolf began to prowl our

house, looking for me. It was a big house, but try as I might, I could never stay hidden from the wolf for very long. Even in my best hiding places it tracked me down and took me in its jaws. I held onto banisters, furniture, myself, but the wolf would just take me and take me.

Shortly after the wolf's first attack, the red days started. They surprised me with their virulence, slamming into me like a hurricane. I would be so unclean and sick throughout the red days, sometimes barely able to move. They got worse and worse, and I missed a lot of school.

The scent of the red days hung in the air. If it weren't for the scent, the wolf might have forgotten about me. But it lodged in the wolf's nostrils, driving the animal into fits of hunger. I was its prey.

Where were you, Papa?

Then the cancer struck and I ended up in the hospital for surgery. A neoplasm the size of a baseball was removed from my bowels.

My recovery was slow. I was weakened by the toxins the doctors pumped into me to kill the cancer cells. I graduated from high school a year later than scheduled.

Afterward, I went away and stayed many years—college, graduate school. As always I kept my distance from people. They were carriers of cancer and didn't know it.

Meanwhile I watched and waited to burst forth in the ripeness of time. I stayed quietly in the shadows. I knew how to do that.

Chapter 19

After weeks of living out of a suitcase and shuttling back and forth from Rochester to Florida to Washington, Hugh Lawson was glad to be home. Not that things were so terrific here. Pat had taken the kids with her to her mother's place in Richmond, to get away from the house for a while, she said.

Hugh knew she was uncomfortable staying at home alone while he was on assignment. Now that he was back in Washington, he was sure everything would be fine.

But Pat decided to stay a while longer in Richmond "to help Mom with some projects," she said. Not that there weren't any projects to be done at *their* place. Hugh said nothing, wanting just to keep the family peace. He thought it was a bit too much on the kids, having to travel one hundred or so miles each day to school in Arlington, then back to Richmond. Pat insisted she didn't mind the drive, and the kids would be out of school soon anyway.

He resigned himself to seeing the family only on his rare free weekends. He came down to Richmond on a late Friday night, pushing his old Pontiac and cutting a half hour off the usual two-hour trip.

Pat's mother, Gladys, lived on Dresden Terrace in a

gritty working-class neighborhood passed over in Richmond's recent upscale development. Hugh, who had grown up in one of the better suburbs of Fayetteville, North Carolina, had never been comfortable at his wife's house. His father was a major general stationed at Fort Bragg for most of his career. Hugh attended private schools, worked summers at a tennis club, and was president of his fraternity at Chapel Hill. He never could connect with Pat's family, their loud conversations and indifference to his work and interests.

Pat was chilly toward him when he arrived, but he was careful not to push her. He ended up on the living room couch while she shared her mother's bed. As the hours passed slowly, Hugh felt the weight of the night heavy on his chest. He fought back thoughts of Pat beneath him, her eyes sealed tight and cheek pressed against the pillow, and finally fell asleep around five just before Lynn woke up screaming.

That morning Pat enlisted him in a series of chores that gave them little chance to talk. While they emptied the basement of what seemed like fifty years of old newspapers, Hugh asked her what he thought was an obvious question:

"Can't your mother sleep on the couch tonight?" he said. He was dragging a load of plastic bags out of the dingy basement. They were filled with newspapers, old clothes, and junk accumulated over years of purposeless collection. Soot and mildew clung to their bodies and clothes.

Pat glanced over her shoulder and blew a strand of hair from her face. "Hugh, you know about Momma's back. Her arthritis has been acting up lately, giving her fits. Her chiropractor retired, you know."

Hugh wasn't going to back down that easily. "I slept

on the couch last night, it felt fine. At least *ask* her, will you?"

They dropped the bags at the end of the driveway. Pat rubbed her hands on a rag. She squinted from the bright sun and looked down the street.

"This block's hardly changed from the way I remember it," she said. "Bobby McGuire used to live in that green house there, three doors down on the other side of the street. That house was the same color green when he and I used to date. You remember Bobby from my twenty-year reunion, owns a chain of car dealerships in southern Virginia?"

Hugh said nothing. Gladys called them to lunch from the front door.

The kids were already at the table when Pat and Hugh came in. His face was streaked from newsprint, provoking teasing from Roger and Lynn. The parents made a show of washing up before sitting down.

"Hugh," Pat's mother said, dishing out spaghetti and meatballs, "was that couch comfortable for you last night?"

"Uh, sure, fine," he said absently. He had been thinking about the tampering investigation.

"'Cause it's fine by me if you want to go upstairs tonight. I'll be all right on the couch."

"Momma, Hugh and I already discussed it," Pat said, tearing apart a piece of garlic bread. "He's fine on the couch."

Hugh started to object when Lynn began begging him to feed her lunch. Ever since moving to Richmond, Lynn, four years old, had regressed, and now had to be fed like a one-year-old.

"Please, Daddy, please. Please."

"Lynn, you can feed yourself," Pat said.

Hugh relented and began stirring pasty tomato sauce into Lynn's chopped spaghetti. He then scooped a portion into the spoon and moved it slowly toward his daughter's mouth. She sat still, watching him.

So far so good. Out of nowhere Lynn's hand swept around and grabbed the spoon, spaghetti flying and tomato sauce spattering her face.

"OK," Hugh signed, "let's try again."

"*Drink*, Daddy" she commanded.

"You want something to drink?" he asked. Lynn nodded resolutely.

He got up and went to the refrigerator. He stood before the big white box. It was an old Kelvinator Gladys couldn't give up. The thing rattled when the freon cooled and had to be defrosted every couple of months.

The refrigerator always had been a friendly presence to Hugh, something more than just another appliance. It was there for you, offering up a midnight snack or an ice cold beer just when you needed one. He thought of the many times he had gone to the refrigerator for something to keep up his strength when the kids were infants, screaming in the middle of the night.

But now, with the tamperings, the refrigerator was dangerous, forbidding. Taking something from it was like playing Russian roulette, or walking through a mine field. Death lurked on the clean, brightly lit shelves and bins. Anything was possible.

Hugh reached for a new carton of milk. Before he opened it, he carefully inspected the protective seals and tamper-resistant packaging. As best as he could tell, the carton was secure. He opened it and poured some into a baby cup. A vague sense of foreboding passed through him as he handed the cup to Lynn.

He thought of the tampering case and how it was getting away from him. He could see it unraveling as he struggled to come up with anything substantial to go on, a few decent leads, a suspect. Tamperings were proliferating all over the country, and nearly every Bureau field office was being pulled into the case.

And the leaks were getting worse, more brazen and frequent. Last week Hugh had laid a trap to flush out whoever was singing to the press. He wrote Eyes Only memoranda to the three people he suspected: the principal USDA agent assigned to the case, the Bureau's public affairs liaison, and Dean Stiles.

In each of the memos, Hugh described his plans for continuing the investigation. Each one contained information different from the others. He distributed them on the same day and waited to see what information from which memo would turn up in the papers.

To his horror, the next day's editions of the *New York Times, Atlanta Constitution,* and *Boston Globe* carried pieces of *all three memos.* Hugh would have to bring this up in his briefing on Monday with Brady. The deputy associate director would probably go through the roof.

Hugh was surprised how often he heard from Brady, usually eight or nine times a day. Whenever Brady wanted a meeting, Hugh would get a call from someone at the Bureau, someone different each time. The message would direct Hugh to some highly irregular meeting place—a hotel lobby, a coffee shop. Last week they had met in the Bonnard room at the Phillips art gallery.

Hugh went along with Brady's idiosyncracies. What else could he do? He felt the tamperings reaching into his private and professional life, poisoning him in small doses.

"Dad!"

He spun around and saw Roger, eyes wide, mouth open, pointing over Hugh's shoulder at Lynn. Hugh turned to see her in the high chair, the entire cup of milk running down her head, over her face, and dribbling to the floor.

Hugh went for a paper towel, but Pat got to it first. "Here, let me do it," she said, pushing him back into his chair.

Chapter 20

Hugh Lawson squinted through the fogged-up glass doors of the sauna. "You're sure that's him?" he said, his voice sounding flat and foreign as it echoed off the white marble and tile of the fitness room.

The attendant nodded, a glaze of perspiration shiny on his black face. "Yessir," he said. "Mr. Brady always takes his sauna at three, right after his rub-down."

Hugh gazed in at the mass of white flesh that seemed to drift in and out through the steam. He was in the basement of the Infinity Club, one of Washington's more exclusive private men's clubs. A call had come this morning, another anonymous voice, with orders for Hugh to meet Brady at the club at three.

Hugh had spent the better part of an hour scouring the club's cavernous lounges and reading rooms, peering over newspapers at ancient men in red leather chairs. Finally a doorman suggested he try the fitness room.

Now, standing before the sauna, Hugh paused. He had good and bad news for Brady and wondered if this was the best time for it.

"You want to, I can get you a towel and you can join him," the attendant said. "Or you can wait 'til he comes out. Either way, don't matter to me."

Shit, Hugh was wearing his firearm, a Beretta semiautomatic. He couldn't very well leave it in a locker. But he had on a light three-season suit. The attendant said, "Huh?" as Hugh opened the glass door and went in. Brady didn't seemed surprised to see him. As best as Hugh could tell through the fog, no one else was in the room. He took a seat on the bench next to a pitcher of water.

"Sir, I have some news I thought you would want to hear. About the investigation."

"Go ahead, Lawson," Brady said. "We're alone in here."

"Sir, that consultant I brought into the investigation, the computer specialist. It seems he has found the man in the bar, the lead suspect in the Rochester tampering."

"'Seems'?" Brady growled. "What do you mean, 'seems'?"

Damn, it must have been one hundred twenty degrees. Hugh loosened his tie. "That is to say, sir, the suspect is now in custody. He's admitted to being with the victim the night of her death."

"And your . . . consultant found him, eh?"

"That's right, sir," Hugh said, his mouth dry.

"Posing as you, isn't that correct?"

Hugh looked up quickly at Brady, tendrils of steam rising off his forehead and pink shoulders. "Sir?"

"How did you find out all this?"

"McAdam called me himself, just over an hour ago. I confirmed with Rochester police. The suspect is—"

"Mitchell Bryer, professor of film at the University of Rochester," Brady said. "Claims he had an affair with the victim, one of his students, but denies any role in her death. Rochester P.D. thinks he's telling the truth."

Hugh sat, speechless. How did Brady know all this? And what did he mean by McAdam posing as him?

"Your consultant seems to be overstepping his boundaries, Lawson. It *seems* he had a replica of your Bureau identification when he met with Bryer, who gave your name as his interrogator.

"McAdam is clever, perhaps too much so for his own good. He came very close to doing serious harm to this investigation.

"Think about it, Lawson. If Bryer were the killer, he would have easily escaped conviction, even arrest, due to McAdam's charade."

"It won't happen again, sir," was all Hugh could manage. So much for the good news.

Brady mopped his brow with a towel. "I'm certain of that," he said. "So where is the investigation now?"

Hugh took a breath. Sweat was pouring down his head. "As you've advised, we're taking each tampering as it comes. No one is even looking for a connection among these incidents. And you should know, there's been a . . . setback in the investigation."

"What now?"

"It involves the milk carton from the Rochester tampering. It disappeared."

"Disappeared?"

"I can't understand it. It was in Chemical Analysis on its way to Fluoroscopy and seems, appears, to have been lost. I've had them turn the place upside down. There's no trace of it anywhere."

Brady shook his head. "A major piece of evidence disappears in the middle of the FBI," he said, his voice trailing off. He slapped the towel over his thigh. "Fluoroscopes, computers," he muttered with contempt. "No wonder we're having so many problems. Where do they get us?

"When Hoover and I ran the Brinks investigation, we

had nothing of the kind. We cracked the case, just good men doing good police work.

"We're addicted to this technology, Lawson. No sooner do we get a fancy piece of machinery than we forget how we ever made do without it. I honestly believe people today think they're smarter than their forebears because they have a computer in their office."

"Sir, I've been meaning to discuss something with you. I believe someone, or some group, is trying to obstruct this investigation."

Brady turned and looked at him. "This is very serious, Lawson. On what do you base your suspicions?"

Hugh nonchalantly tried to adjust his briefs, which felt like they were glued to his crotch. "Well, sir, I've mentioned the press leaks to you. Some of the most classified information on the case is in the papers even before my agents see it. And there's no end in sight.

"And now there's this, the stolen evidence. I'm convinced that a key player in the investigation, someone on the inside, is actually attempting to undermine the tampering investigation. That, or the press or an unfriendly nation has infiltrated a mole of some kind."

"I see your point, Lawson. Whom do you suspect?"

Hugh sat for a moment, breathing in hot air. "Two possibilities. One is the USDA liaison to the investigation, John Durkin. I'm keeping tabs on him."

Hugh was reluctant to go on. Like most people in law enforcement, he secretly despised informants. What he was about to do was no less than squealing on a colleague.

"The other is . . . Dean Stiles," he said slowly. "But I have nothing concrete, no evidence pointing to him. You have to understand that."

Brady nodded. "Of course," he said, reassuring him. "Stiles. Interesting theory."

"Sir—"

"Don't worry, Lawson. Let me handle it. You have enough on your plate. Now, what else?"

"One other thing. McAdam mentioned something about a new lead in the investigation. Had to do with a big New York milk company. He asked me if we could spare some men. . . . "

"Out of the question," Brady snapped. "That man is a loose cannon, Lawson. Get down there immediately and talk to him. Remind him he has one job to do and hasn't delivered on it. Tell him he is as close to the investigation as he will ever get. If he tries anything else, he'll be up on federal charges."

For a moment Brady disappeared in the fog. Hugh felt a wave of dizziness passing over him. It took all of his energy to stand up and stagger out of the sauna.

Edmund Brady, flush from his rub-down and the moist sauna heat, daubed his smooth chest. He reached under the bench, where his finger found a button. He pushed it twice.

Brady lifted the pitcher from the bench and poured the remaining water over the hot stones. Steam rose around him, hissing in his ears. The strong heat felt good.

He relaxed and let his thoughts drift. Brady had heavy thoughts that needed to fall from his mind from time to time of their own weight. Since he knew no one who could appreciate these thoughts, they were best left inside.

For years he had watched, high from his place at the Bureau, as human events unfolded. There were secrets he knew, knowledge so sensitive it defied classification. Many were the times he had known what the headlines would be weeks in advance. A word from him had put major events into motion. He had been part of some of the greatest historical moments of his day. Members of Congress sought his favor. Presidents feared him.

Ed Brady had developed a keen sense of history and appreciated its elegant clarity. Like a distant object, a satellite, observing the turning of the tides, Brady watched as the rhythms of history played themselves out. How easily one could predict the outcome of an election or the fall of a nation. So much the easier if one manipulated those events.

He knew that progress was now coming to a standstill. Humanity had reached the proverbial glass ceiling, had gone as far as it could go.

Now the regression was beginning. Public faith in institutions—government, churches, industry—was failing. It was only a matter of time before they would collapse.

The door to the sauna opened. In walked the attendant, carrying a fresh towel, a pitcher of ice water, and a portable telephone on a silver tray. He carefully placed the tray on the bench next to Brady and took away the empty pitcher.

"Thank you, Ulysses," Brady said. "I'll be out momentarily."

Ulysses bowed and left. Brady used the towel to wipe his eyes and hands. He punched in seven numbers on the telephone.

After one ring, a voice came on.

Brady said, "This is the Fulcrum. Get me Command."

Another voice came on. It never took long.

"Lindt?" Brady said. "Yeah, never better.

"Listen, a favor. Recall that situation we discussed last

week? Correct. I want you to move on it now. Yes, full surveillance."

Brady looked at the pitcher of water as Lindt went off the line, checking a schedule. Beads of sweat rolled down the pitcher. The water was pure and clear, much like history itself, Brady mused.

Lindt came back on.

"Two agents?" Brady growled. "Is that the best you can do? No, that's not enough. Put a full team on it.

"All points must be covered thoroughly. Yes, the usual arrangement. I want updates every three hours."

Brady rang off and placed the telephone on the silver tray. Ice clinked against the crystal pitcher as he poured water into a plastic cup.

He held the cup, admiring the water, and drained it with loud slurping noises.

Chapter 21

The entrance to the parking lot of the Carefree Food Store was clotted with traffic as wary police searched incoming cars. At the front of the line was a white van with red lettering on the side that read: "THE SAFETY ZONE COMPANY." And below that: "*We Specialize in Residential Security.*" A policeman, a member of the new anti-terrorist force, was searching the back of the van.

Inside, one of the two men in the front seat took off his Nike baseball cap, mopped his brow with a neon red wristband, and said, "Man, tell me again why you keep the windows open and the air conditioning off on a bitch of a day like this."

The man, the younger of the two by about fifteen years, was LaCharles Jameson. Like anybody with two good eyes in his head, he could see that all the other cars in the parking lot had their windows up and the air on full blast. This was a good day to be at home, drinking something cool and grooving on MTV.

"Ever watch animals in a zoo?" the other man said. His name was Tom Harmon and he owned the Safety Zone Company.

"Notice how lazy and paranoid they look? Being in captivity spoils them and they know it. Everything is

done for them, their food, shelter, even sex is *given* to
them.

"Now take air conditioning. It's just another example
of how our environment is controlled for us. We can't
handle extremes of any kind. Chilly? Turn up the ther-
mostat. A slight headache? Take a pill. We've lost our
primitive edge, tampering with Mother Nature."

LaCharles rolled his eyes. The man was on *that* shit
again. "Hey, just answer me one question," he said. "Did
Mother Nature give us the brains to be able to *make* air
conditioning, or what? She prob'ly laughing at us right
now, sweating here like pigs."

Tom was about to tell him that pigs don't sweat, but
before he could, he heard a tapping sound from behind
the van.

"Uh-oh, the cop found your stash," LaCharles said
with a straight face.

Tom got out to see what the trouble was. LaCharles
stayed in the van and watched in the side mirror as Tom
talked with the sweaty cop, who was holding up something he had found in the back. LaCharles recognized it
as a battery pack for a motion detector. The detector was
one of their most popular items.

The cop probably thought the pack was a bomb or
something. What LaCharles had a problem with was,
What terrorist in his right mind would try to smuggle
bombs or guns or *anything* through this kind of security?
Dude'd have to be out of his fucking mind.

Now Tom was giving the cop a pen and paper, and the
cop was writing something down. LaCharles had seen
this before: the cop read the sign on the van for residential security and was looking for a moonlighting situation. Happened all the time at grocery store checkpoints.

Tom just took the cop's number, cool as you please, and closed up the van.

For all his bullshit about Mother Nature and the rest of it, Tom was a decent dude. LaCharles knew that Tom had risked some business by taking him on as an assistant. It was obvious to LaCharles, who was black, that Tom's clients, who were mostly white, got nervous when a black person who wasn't their maid was in their house. And now that Tom was selling the business, he made sure in the contract that LaCharles could stay on as a technician with the new owners if he wanted to.

Tom climbed back in the van. "You a popular guy, Tom," LaCharles said. "Might want to open you an employment agency."

"I just told him LaCharles Jameson would be calling him in a couple days. If you don't, he'll come looking for you."

"Yeah, right," LaCharles said. "So how does it feel? Tomorrow you'll be out in the country with your trees and bugs and all that other shit. No more of these road-blocks. Where you say you going?"

"Union Center, West Virginia."

"Union Center," LaCharles said, turning it over in his mind, seeing the place. "Yeah, I heard of it. That's where all them dudes in sleeveless down jackets and CAT hats go and drink Budweiser and shoot little animals. They *love* nature there."

Tom smiled. He felt good and was enjoying his last day on the job. Today even the cops and the roadblocks rolled off his back.

As he parked the van, he thought: Just imagine, in three days he and his family would do something he had dreamed about for years. They were breaking free of so-called civilization to go to a saner, more secure world. A place where they could have more control—over the food they ate, the air they breathed, their *lives*.

For years Tom and his wife, Chloe, had been unhappy, feeling out of place wherever they lived. They yearned for another kind of life, healthier and more fulfilling. Especially Tom, dissatisfied with desk jobs, bouncing from one meaningless position to another. It was the topic of conversation whenever they were alone together—out to dinner, in bed after sex. They never seemed to stop thinking about it.

He knew there was more to life than a mortgage and a retirement plan. And both of them were appalled with the deterioration of the environment and the quality of life. You never knew what you were eating anymore, what with the hundreds of chemical agents used in food products.

And now the final straw: the tamperings. Tom couldn't understand why everyone had been so shocked when it started. It was almost inevitable. We threw the boomerang—over-population of the planet, excess consumption, and the corporate depersonalization of life. It was bound to come back and strike us.

Those who could see where all this was leading were not sitting still, waiting for it to happen. A new movement had been spawned as thousands of people left their artificial lives behind to find something better. Tom and Chloe had met some of them in Breakaway, the support group they had joined for people trying to get back to nature.

They met others here and there, in the Outward Bound program Tom did, or at the shooting range, and through survival courses. Everyone said the same thing: you can't trust anything or anyone anymore. The system was falling apart. No one trusted private industry or the government, especially the government.

Where were *they* when the shit hit the fan?

The Harmons had sold the Safety Zone lock, stock, and barrel. At midnight tonight they finally would be rid of it. They had sold their house, liquidated their bank accounts, tore up their insurance policies and cut up their credit cards, and were pulling their kids out of school. Tom and Chloe had no doubt they could do a better job teaching them themselves.

Tom and Chloe had talked about what moving would mean to the kids. They even talked it over with them, that is, with Melanie and Jeremy. Their third child, Shane, was still an infant.

Jeremy, nine years old, was enthusiastic about dropping out of school and living in the country. But Melanie, their oldest, was Tom's main worry. She was a rebellious fifteen and refused to discuss the move. Whenever Tom or Chloe tried to bring it up with her, they got nothing but stone cold silence.

Sometimes fear punctured their exhilaration over leaving. They were pioneers, giving up their old life and putting everything on the line. There would be no more complaining or blaming their problems on "the system." Freedom, real freedom, was a scary proposition.

But the decision had been made. They were doing it, heading for a life-enhancing environment in West Virginia. Very soon they would be free of all. . . this.

The oil smell of hot asphalt rose in Tom's nostrils as LaCharles and he crossed the parking lot toward the store. Somewhere brakes screamed and a horn blared. Ordinarily, Tom would have gotten his lunch at a supermarket, but LaCharles liked the steak sandwiches at the Carefree deli counter. Tom was buying.

"Man, I don't get it," LaCharles said above the traffic noise. "Why you want to go and put yourself and your family through all that shit for? I mean look at it, here you have running hot water, MTV, and nice fresh food at the local grocery. Out there you be raising your own food, working yourself to death miles from nowhere."

"Fresh food," Tom repeated, disdain in his voice. They were entering the supermarket, where the processed food buried in layers of marketing and deceptively pristine displays seemed unwholesome to him. Now more than ever.

He smelled the stale tobacco on the breath of the cop who body-searched him before he could go through the turnstiles and into the store. Armed guards paced each aisle, carefully watching the shoppers. The products were stored in cases and dispensed individually to prevent anyone from removing a product from the store, spiking it with poison or a foreign object, and returning it to the shelves.

As they started out for the deli counter, Tom said, "This is progress, huh? Let me give you a tour of this place."

"Tour?" LaCharles said, frowning at what he anticipated was coming. "Shit, you need to get you one of them little buses to be giving a tour."

Tom led him into the produce section. Everything there was in heavy tamper-resistant packaging. Baskets full of plastic fruits and vegetables hung on the walls and were arranged to give the section a "country" look.

"Well, let's see. All this looks pretty healthy, huh?"

"Yeah, the kind of shit you always eating."

Tom pointed to the tomatoes. "Take those, for instance. Nice juicy red tomatoes. Can you tell if any have been treated with methamidophos?"

"Metha-what?"

"Methamidophos. It's a pesticide that can do major damage to your nervous system. And look at that glistening pile of broccoli over there. Now, that's a great source of parathion residues, great for cancer. And those nice plump strawberries just might have been sprayed with carabyl or endosulfan, very bad for the liver and kidneys."

"Man, what's the point?"

"And now," Tom said, "we enter the seafood section. Look, a special on coho salmon. You never know, the one you get might contain sewage or industrial residues, or an insecticide like aldrin or toxaphene. Do you have any idea what they can do to your gastro-intestinal system?

"You could get a good case of paralysis from the mytilotoxin in those fresh Pacific mussels or the venerupin in the oysters. The boss and his wife would love some of that."

LaCharles was feeling a little queasy. "Yeah, I'd like to be feeding him some right about now. Lots of it."

Tom kept going. "Did you notice the smell of fresh-baked bread coming from the bakery section? It's fake, a fragrance they pump into the air. You may also be breathing in ions that are pumped in to make you feel better, stay longer and spend more money."

They passed a heavy guard with a razor-burned neck, who eyed them suspiciously. "Now the dairy section," Tom said, happily oblivious. "Here we have products as different as brie cheese and ice cream bars that can contain the same bacteria, capable of killing pregnant women, little children, and old folks. Oh, but you don't fit any of those categories, do you, LaCharles? So you don't have to worry."

LaCharles had a weak stomach and it was bubbling now. "Shee-it," he said.

"And milk, see how well protected it is? If it's in paperboard, it can easily become contaminated with dioxin, one of the most potent cancer-causing agents known to man. Who needs a tamperer, huh?"

"You sick, anybody ever tell you that?"

Up ahead was the deli counter. As they walked through the meats, Tom took LaCharles by the arm. "Now, this is what your steak sandwich is made of. I'll bet you seventy-five percent of this nice pink marbled meat has residues of growth hormones or antibiotics in it. Don't forget the preservatives and the dye.

"And speaking of progress, ever actually *see* a slaughter house, how unsanitary it is?"

"Man, don't."

"I worked in one for about four months when I volunteered to collect information for the Humane Farming Association. Sometimes the high-speed eviscerating machines they use to rip out the intestines on poultry chew up chicken shit and stomach residues into the meat. A stomping grounds for salmonella poisoning, botulism, and more allergies than Nike has sneakers.

"Hey, here's the deli counter. What'll you have?"

"Alka-Seltzer," LaCharles said, weak. "Make it a double."

"O.K., what've we got this afternoon?" Tom said as he pulled into traffic. Neither of them had had any lunch.

LaCharles scanned the clipboard on his lap. He was feeling a little better. "Let's see. We booked solid. Next up is regular maintenance on one of them passive infrared intrusion-detection systems. Mmm, somebody likes his security."

"That's a service contract, right?"

"Right," LaCharles said. "Then we have, uh-oh, Miz Tribble's motion detector again. That'd be the second time this month she put in a service call.

"I swear she wants my body. What you think she be wearing today? Last time it was some lacy black thing. Low-cut, as I recall."

"What's after that?" Tom said.

"After that, something about an access control system. Thing says here that's it's been locking up, not responding."

"What kind is it, the new generation of AT&T?"

"No, some other kind. You ever hear of Defender?"

"Yeah," Tom said. "It's a new system by PanTech. They're trying to break into the card-key market. You'll probably be getting a lot of calls on that one."

LaCharles looked at him. "Man, I can't believe you want to sell this business. Home security is got to be one of the hottest things going right now. You could expand this company—shit, take a computer out to the woods with you and run everything from there."

"Maybe I should have sold the company to you. Sounds like you've been giving it a lot of thought."

"Who knows? Maybe these new owners don't work out, I'll just start my own company."

"You'd be good at it."

"Yeah, lots of black folks want home security too. I could expand into small businesses. Open a shop, hire me a couple of techs, and spend the day out at the track with Miz Tribble."

"Here we are," Tom said, parking the van on the street. "The passive infrared system. Top of the line."

He went into the back of the van and removed the black tool case. LaCharles looked around for spare parts for the infrared system, in case they needed replacing in the house. Save him a trip to the van.

"I could get me my own business card printed up," he said to himself as he rummaged through a repair kit.

Tom went on ahead, up to the front door of the single-unit apartment building. He looked up in the corner of awning over the porch. The red eye of the detector stared down at him.

He rang the doorbell.

Chapter 22

Back from the hospital, trying to keep busy. Day off from work, at least relief from that tedium. Raining, so I can't work in my garden.

I have resigned myself to the fact that Mother will die soon. She looked especially pitiful and helpless in the hospital today. The nurses no longer look me in the eye when they come into Mother's room. They know.

Although I wear gloves when I visit her and sit a safe distance away from the bed, the cancer cells swarm in the air around me like mad bees. The nurses don't care, they're immune by now. I was painfully aware that each breath I took in Mother's room added millions, billions, of new cancer cells into my body. The risk is great for me now. Another visit and I might very well contract it.

The best way I knew to keep my mind off it was to go through my scrapbook.

I kept a record of my achievements in a locked drawer of my desk. It was a secret delight to unlock and open the drawer and carefully remove the scrapbook, hidden beneath sheaths of paper.

Newspaper articles, magazine stories, editorials, everything I could find went into the scrapbook. I subscribed to magazines and papers from all over the country.

Of course, the local papers in the towns I visited gave the incidents considerable attention. Usually I would begin a subscription to a city's papers just before I vaccinated that place, just to be sure I wouldn't miss anything.

When I could not subscribe, I would go to newsstands, bookstores, and libraries for copies. For foreign publications I would make a weekly trip to the library and copy almost anything that looked appropriate.

On television there were special reports, news programs, and interviews about my work. I wanted to tape them, so I was finally motivated to learn how to record with my videocassette machine.

I was certainly causing a stir. All the major weeklies featured my achievements as cover stories. I especially enjoyed collecting headlines from the prestigious papers. Imagine: front-page coverage in the *New York Times* for six consecutive days in May!

But there were papers that deliberately played down my accomplishments. The *Chicago Tribune,* the *Christian Science Monitor,* and the others—I knew who they were. Even on days of unusual achievement one could see the efforts of these papers to push the incidents to the background. Did they believe their coyness would discourage me?

It occurred to me that I might want the foreign articles translated, to learn what an observer from another country might say about my achievements. I even called the language departments at a local university about their translation fees. But I realized someone might ask unwelcome questions about my interest in these stories. I finally had the good sense to stop myself.

Instead I looked up certain key words and kept an eye out for them as I went through the foreign papers. In

German publications they used the word *Vergiftung*, meaning "poisoning." In Spanish I was known as *El Envenenador*.

It seemed that every day I'd find some reference to my work. The album was filling up quickly. I enjoyed holding it in my hands, feeling its heft and substance and smelling its soft gray leather cover. It was the largest album I could find—three hundred pages. Soon I would have to start a second one.

I looked down on them all—the reporters, editors, press men, delivery boys—scurrying to get out the word about me. And all the millions of people reading about me, people I would never meet but whose lives I touched. The thought filled me with an almost unbearably gorgeous feeling. My skin pulsed with the intense thrill.

It was control. A push of the button, a pull of the string, and the world bent its knee before me.

I sorted through the publications, separating the national press from the local, and then re-sorting by city, state, and region. While I worked I kept the papers in an airtight bag, protecting them from corrosives.

With small, extremely sharp scissors I cut out the stories, taking care to include the date and name of the paper or magazine. I wore gloves to protect the ink and paper from any soil or acid on my skin. Then I slid the clipping into a transparent, non-static plastic pocket which fit securely in the tabs of the album.

Here was a big one in the *Los Angeles Times,* front page. And, how nice, they followed up in the back with an analysis of how my achievements have exposed the fragility of our economy and society. Nice try, *Times,* but *Atlantic Monthly* and *Newsweek* beat you to it.

One article I did not save appeared in the *New York*

Post. It was a maudlin exploitative front-page appeal to the "The Tamperer," calling on him to end his "reign of terror."

Below the headline were forty-eight grainy photographs in three rows with the caption: "YOUR VICTIMS."

That made me see red.

Victims?

Frauds, pompous fools. As consistently tawdry and low-brow as that paper was, the story represented new depths. How dare they refer to these people as *my* victims!

I sat down immediately and poured out my thoughts in a letter to the editor. I pointed out to him, if he cared to know, that by merely inhabiting a body, we were victims.

These people, these "victims," were chosen for this role by a greater concatenation of events, a divine judgment, if you will. They took the poison themselves. No one forced them to, certainly not I.

I, I was merely an instrument of fate, a messenger. Nothing more than a doctor on his rounds, immunizing faceless patients against a disease.

And I informed him that, most obvious, not all of these people were subjected to *my* immunizations, that there were many charlatans who copied my methods.

But I never sent the letter. They can trace those things.

Instead I studied the pictures of the faces printed on the front page, the vacant expressions and colorless skin. And then a new thought blossomed in my mind, a realization that I had never actually *witnessed* the effects of my work, never seen the people take the poison and fall.

It was as if my work had never been fully consummated. The distance between my subjects and me was comfortable, but left a hollow feeling. A sense of separation.

I thought: Why not get closer? Why not be there as they took the poison? Why not observe their faces as they struggled for breath? Why not?

From nowhere a buzzing noise slapped me on the head. What—was it the cancer already?

I laughed, actually laughed out loud. It was the doorbell.

The world on the other side of the peephole in my door is like the view through a fish-eye lens. Or the reflection in a drop of water.

As I looked out into this world, I saw a man in work clothes holding a black box. He was young and tall and seemed to stand on top of the world, to anchor it with his feet.

Why was my chest suddenly constricted, as if seized by a heart attack?

Papa?

I quickly opened the door.

"Yes?"

The man's face came closer. "Hi there. Tom Harmon, the Safety Zone. Here to take a look at your infrared system."

The sun was cold and bright, washing over the day behind him. In the foyer of my apartment, dust particles, massing like cancer cells, floated in and out of the uneven shadows. Out in the street, another man, a black one in a hat, came rushing up.

"But there's no reason," I said, struggling to order my thoughts. "That is, the system is working perfectly."

The man smiled. Light wrinkles at the corners of his eyes and mouth. His mouth.

"Well, that's good to hear. This is just your regular maintenance check. Part of your contract. You get no-cost testing and servicing every four months."

If I turned him away, he might get suspicious. A security company, he might speak to the police.

"Very well. Do you need to come in?"

"For a minute. We'll inspect the circuits and wiring inside the door and around back. Mr. Jameson here will take care of the front. I'll do the back entrance."

I let them in. The particles in the air churned and scattered as they rustled around the foyer. I watched the particles, not breathing them.

"Would you mind showing me the back door?" he said.

"No, come."

I led him through the hallway, keeping him away from the rooms. A fear shrieked in my ears: Did I leave the door to the study open? Would he see my scrapbook, notice the headlines?

"I don't recall your being here before," I said, trying to distract his attention as we passed the study. From the corner of my eye, I saw the clippings spread out on the floor. But he was looking at papers on a clipboard and didn't see them.

"Well, says here that last time you were due for a service check, no one answered the door. And we always call at least twice if we miss somebody."

"I travel a great deal," I said. "For my work."

We reached the rear entrance. "So, this'll be the only time I'll be coming here. The company is coming under new management, effective tomorrow."

"Oh?"

"Yeah," he said, looking through the high window in

the back door. "Say, that's a nice garden you have out there. Are those amaryllis, the red ones?"

He began unscrewing the cover to the security device. "I'm a bit of a gardener myself. Vegetables, miniature ones. Just an experiment, really, but they're doing well. Gives me hope. Everything looks pretty good so far in here."

Normally I do not encourage conversations, especially vapid ones. But I wanted to learn more from him, about him. I said, "Hope, you said. For what?"

"Oh, I'll be growing them—organically, of course—for distribution to restaurants. I've sold the Safety Zone and we're moving out to the country."

An idea, like a seed, germinated in my mind. I looked back down the hallway, but did not see the black man. "You have a family?"

"Yeah, and that's the main reason we're leaving, to give them a better life. Hmm, this wire here is showing signs of corrosion. It's part of the backup alarm, so it wouldn't affect the integrity of your system."

"A better life?"

He looked at me strangely, as if I should have understood him. "This can't be it, can it?"

"It?"

"I mean, having to run a magnet over your kid's cereal to check for needles and razor blades. Or to have to inspect everything you buy for signs of tampering. I just want to get out where it's clean and peaceful, a place where I can call the shots."

"I see."

While he wasn't looking, I studied him, evaluating his height and weight. How much cyanide would I need for him? How much for an entire family?

I did not want to arouse his suspicion, but I had to ask one more question. "Where are you going?"

"There," he said, tinkering with a wire. "This shouldn't give you any problems.

"Oh, you just asked me a question. I bought a place, a hundred acres. It's really not too far from here—"

"Yo, Tom." It was the black one. "You got the electrical tape?"

"Right here," he said, and disappeared down the hall.

Damn, I almost said aloud. I needed to know where he was going. No matter, I could look him up in the telephone directory, his name was right there on the work order.

He looked like a promising subject for an experiment. It would be simple enough to track him down when the time was right.

Chapter 23

Hugh Lawson, hair dripping wet, hovered over David McAdam as he fiddled with the controls to his oven.

"I forget," David said, "do you have to put it on the Preheat setting before the Bake?"

"Just put it on Bake," Hugh grumbled. He slung his water-logged pants and jacket over the makeshift clothesline in front of the oven.

Crossing over to McAdam's island from Kettle Key, Hugh had slipped in the lousy muck and had actually gone under. He managed to keep his briefcase out of the water, but everything in his pockets—wallet, maps, pipe tobacco—were soaked. Last time he was here all he had to do was take off his shoes, roll up his pants, and wade across. Who would have expected the goddamn tide to come in up to his crotch?

David McAdam owned no coat hangers nor a working clothes dryer. So, while waiting for his clothes to dry, Hugh was forced to wear a pair of filthy, moth-eaten sweatshirts and equally ratty pants. They were the least repulsive things in McAdam's Salvation Army wardrobe.

At least the house looked better. Even the trash on the porch was bundled up and bagged. And, miracle of miracles, McAdam had gotten rid of the beard and the Neanderthal hair. He looked semi-respectable.

Hugh moved to one of the overstuffed chairs in the living room as McAdam, in his usual manic style, tried to sell his theory on the tamperings.

Humor him, Hugh told himself. You need his cooperation. Brady gave strict orders to get McAdam moving on the database and off the investigation.

Hugh tried to listen to McAdam over the music—angry, destructive punk stuff with serrated notes and a chip-on-the-shoulder attitude. The noise had been blasting at Hugh since he arrived. He knew McAdam had put it on to grate on him, but he was beginning to lose his tolerance.

"What *is* this music?" he finally said, hoping McAdam would get the hint.

"Oh, it's 'New Nails' by Mission of Burma. Of all the American postpunk bands, they had the sharpest edge. Awesome guitar, huh?"

"Can't you turn it down?"

McAdam frowned. "That would attenuate its artistic integrity."

Hugh gave up and let his mind drift. His eyes wandered around the shabby living room. Water marks hid in the shadows of corners and along the molding of the ceiling. He noticed the walls and the windows sweated a glaze of water. A rich, heavy odor of mildew clung to the overstuffed furniture, infusing the air.

McAdam marched around the room, waving his hands and gesticulating wildly. "The—the FBI's basic problem with this investigation," he said, "is that you have agents running down every piece of glass that turns up in a box of granola. Know what I think?"

"No," Hugh said, giving him rope.

"Ever hear of chaos theory? The study of patterns that exist beneath apparently disorderly events, like weather?

Anyway, I've been playing with this theory and looking at the tamperings, doing some runs on a program I designed.

"For instance," he said, typing a command into the computer set up on boxes on the floor, "if you study the tamperings over the past four months, their frequency appears random." A graph appeared on the screen, with little black and white skull-and-crossbones symbols scattered all over.

"There, you see a rise and fall in their incidence around the time of the dairy tamperings, which are highlighted in white. But if you look at their *relative* frequency, you notice patterns."

McAdam did another calculation and the black skull and crossbones were redistributed in a wavy pattern. "See? Immediately after the word gets out on a dairy-product tampering, you see a sharp increase in tamperings around the country, especially in the area where the product was spiked. Then it quickly goes down until the next one.

"I call it the Pied Piper effect. There's the Rochester killing," he said, pointing to one of the skull and crossbones. "You see a little bolus in the curve right after it . . . there . . . representing tampering activity in the last week.

"Oh, and by the way, four of the five dairy tamperings involved some form of cyanide, and potassium cyanide was used twice."

"Listen, McAdam," Hugh said wearily, "the Bureau has been through this already. Professionals, experts who've been studying these kinds of things for years, have gone through this backwards and forwards. And they come to the same conclusion each time: these tamperings are random and they will be investigated as such."

David got up from the floor in front of the computer and began pacing excitedly. "Just—just assume for a moment that the dairy tamperings *are* the lead incidents. If you nail the person or persons responsible for *these* poisonings, then all the others will die down."

Hugh started to say something but stopped himself.

"What possible motive could you come up with for poisoning milk?" David asked. "Criminal insanity? Maybe. But a tamperer doesn't even get the perverse pleasure of watching his victims die."

"Suppose, just suppose the motive is simpler, the oldest one in the book?"

He paused, looking out the window as a fishing boat—a two-decker outboard—moved slowly past, sunlight glinting off something in the bow. Where had *that* come from?

"Unbridled greed," David whispered.

"What? What was that you said?" Hugh shook his head as McAdam, like a man possessed, began riffling through a pile of printouts stacked in a corner. He seemed to find what he was looking for, and tore a string of sheets from the stack.

"Remember what I told you about on the phone?" McAdam said, excited.

"You mean the milk company in New York?"

"I didn't go into it in detail. Sometimes walls have ears."

He handed the printouts to Lawson. "These are copies of the last two quarterly reports of the American Milk Company. Look at the earning statements at the bottom of that page."

Hugh studied the numbers, still humoring McAdam

but getting tired of it. He noticed that the company's revenues in the second quarter were nearly fifty percent more than in the first. "Mmmm, not bad," he hummed.

"Not bad?" said an incredulous McAdam. "Just hold a moment." Containing his excitement, he fished through another pile of papers.

"This," he proclaimed, displaying a graph before Hugh's face, "shows the comparative performance of the top ten dairy companies this year and last. Look at those figures."

On the first graph Hugh recognized the names of several of the more familiar companies—Kraft, Borden, Sealtest, and others. Kraft clearly had the lead among them, but Hugh knew that earnings for a single year did not necessarily indicate the overall long-term strength of a company. But in the second quarter this year, the American Milk Company was suddenly a strong sixth among the giants.

"And that's only part of the story," David said, pacing around the room. "If you look at the top one hundred dairy companies over the past ten years, you'd find that American Milk managed to make the list only twice, and then just barely."

"In the space of a few months—from March to July—the company's S&P rating went from A to triple A. It's now one of the hottest issues on the American Stock Exchange and is considered blue chip by most brokers."

"I've never heard of it," Hugh grunted.

"Right," David said, "that's another thing. Most companies play this kind of growth to the hilt—cover stories in *Forbes* and *Business Week,* specials in the *Wall Street Journal.* Believe me, I know: the more publicity, the more investors."

"But *this* company," he said, more quietly now, "appears to do everything in its power to stay out of the limelight. It just doesn't figure."

"So they like a low profile," Hugh said, getting impatient. "OK, McAdam, I'll bite. Bottom-line it for me."

"*Bottom-line it*? Oh, brother."

"C'mon, McAdam. What did you find?"

David stopped pacing and squatted down next to Lawson. "Do you remember the names of the dairy companies whose products have been tampered with?"

"No, but I have a feeling you're going to tell me."

David handed him another printout. "This is a list of 'em, five in all. Next to that list are data on the corporate acquisitions of American Milk in the past three quarters, taken from the company's confidential computer files."

Hugh studied the printout. Four of the five companies directly affected by the tamperings were on the list, as well as a few others. Each company had been taken over by American Milk within a week or so after the news of the company's misfortune had gotten out.

"Notice the buy-out prices," McAdam said, getting closer to Hugh. "In some cases they're over half the value of the company before the tamperings."

"No doubt about it," he said quietly, "American Milk is dirty."

"Wha—" was all Hugh could get out before McAdam cut him off.

"Listen for a minute, Lawson. Now comes the good part. This phenomenal rise of American Milk's fortunes has coincided with the rise of one company executive. His name is Falco, Rutland Falco, a v.p. at American Milk. A real bastard, one of the nastiest and I've seen the worst. He's the one who initiated the takeovers of those companies.

"Falco has been buying up what are called put options

on stocks of companies whose products are about to be tampered with. He profits when the value of the stock falls after word gets out on the tamperings.

"He protects himself by doing it through his company. American Milk is now owner of some of these companies, since they bought up controlling interest.

"The problem is that none of this is illegal. You could put him away now for insider trading, mail fraud, and a few other things, but I don't have anything linking him directly to the tamperings. But there are a couple of dubious-looking transfers of funds he's made that I haven't checked out.

"Falco is a one-man pestilence," David said with anger in his voice. "I've seen more than my share of his kind: *corporate* types who hide behind the interests of the *shareholders* to get what they want. He'll let nothing stand in his way. I call him Dr. Doom."

"Now, hold on a minute," Lawson snapped. "I can see where you're going with this, and I don't mind saying it's horseshit. Plain horseshit.

"For one thing, not all of the companies taken over by American Milk were victimized by tamperings. Your list says so. All this is corporate hardball—aggressive takeovers, survival of the strongest. Good, honest capitalism."

David groaned.

"This . . . theory of yours," Lawson went on, "it's pure fantasy, you know that? You discover a company that's turning a healthy profit, chewing up the dead wood, and you scream like Chicken Little.

"Do you honestly believe a major corporation would go out and do in its competitors by poisoning their products? And you want me to commit agents to this craziness? If you ask me, you're still carrying a grudge from getting the boot from PanTech."

David quickly turned to the window to hide his face, which was turning bright scarlet. Special Agent Lawson never knew how badly he had burned him with his remark about PanTech. Seething, David noticed the fishing boat was still in sight, drifting on the gulf with no one on deck.

"Let me ask you something," Lawson said. "How do you account for the fact that three different kinds of cyanide were used in the dairy tamperings?"

David turned from the window, not answering at once. "Elegant variation," he said, almost to himself.

"What?"

"Elegant variation. It's an editorial term, when writers strain to add variety to the words they use. The variety becomes forced, obvious."

"I don't get it."

"I didn't think you would."

Hugh tried to control his irritation over McAdam's presumptuousness. Thousands of hours and millions of dollars had gone into the investigation in the past four months. Some of the best law enforcement minds in the world had studied the tamperings, picked them apart. And along comes this snot-nosed geek who thinks he knows it all and tries to run the show.

McAdam was the genuine article, a bona fide resident of the fringes. He was bright enough, perhaps even brilliant, but Hugh had serious reservations about how far he could be trusted.

"By the way, McAdam, how did you get all this information on American Milk?"

"Oh, I had to go into some of the corporate computer files and lift a few things. It's really no big deal. With this system I can get into just about any database or file I want. I even got some pictures of Falco. Want to see them?"

Hugh was incensed. "Do you know that unauthorized entry into a computer file is a violation of the 1986 Computer Fraud and Abuse Act?"

David shook his head. "So book me, Dan-o. *You* dragged *me* into this, remember?"

"And another thing," Lawson said, "how is it you have so much time to jerk around, playing with numbers, when you're *supposed* to be working on the USDA database? While we're on the subject, just where do you get off *impersonating* me in Rochester? That's *another* offense you've committed.

"You've got exactly seventy-two hours to deliver the USDA database in perfect condition or be brought up on charges. Am I clear?"

There it was, David thought, the real Hugh Lawson. A rigid, red-eyed, programmed, dangerously simple cog in the bureaucratic machinery. David looked at him sitting there in grubby sweats, wet hair, and wondered who in his right mind would have put *him* in charge of this investigation.

"Do they still call you guys 'untouchables'?" David asked.

Lawson straightened up in the chair, immediately defensive. "Why do you ask?"

"No reason," David said innocently.

"You hear it once in a while, mostly from glib, overly urbane media people," Lawson said. "It's supposed to be a compliment, that federal agents are incorruptible."

Ironic, David thought, how one word could have such different meanings. Talking with Nara on the way to the airport, he had been reminded of a consulting trip he had made to India in the mid seventies when PanTech was just getting off the ground. His project was to help the Indians build a mission control for their space program.

David learned, after overhearing a few conversations and asking a few questions, that the aerospace engineers and computer scientists he was working with all were Brahmins, the most exalted of the Hindu castes. The dark, faceless people who dug ditches and hauled away the dirt from the launch-pad construction site were Harijans—the Untouchables.

To David, the caste system was fascinating and repulsive. It seemed to operate from some mindless, cosmic software program called dharma that determined at birth one's station in life.

He raised the issue with Ajay, a young electrical engineer he had befriended. Ajay tried to explain that the Untouchables were considered part of a big schematic that wasn't so much concerned with this one transitory lifetime but a much more complex, long-term system. David wasn't persuaded.

He looked at Hugh Lawson, the Untouchable, and imagined him hauling dirt for a living. The way Lawson looked, it wasn't hard to do. Besides, it would probably be better for the investigation if Lawson took up ditch digging.

Then David thought of something else.

"Oh, by the way, Lawson, I traced that virus that ate the USDA's data."

"Huh?"

"It came from a source somewhere inside the FBI Building in Washington. That's the best I could come up with."

"What?"

Chapter 24

David finally managed to get rid of Lawson by letting him have a computer diskette with no more than the first ten percent or so of the USDA database on it. Lawson still didn't know he had finished restoring the whole thing. And now David was less inclined than ever to co-operate.

Before Lawson would leave, he demanded that David turn over the evidence on the computer virus. David said, "Sure, why not?"—not that it would do him much good. Whoever planted that virus knew what he was doing, having made a copy that could have come from any terminal in the FBI building.

Something was indeed going on at the FBI, and Lawson wasn't talking about it. David slipped into the FBI's classified files and checked Lawson's record as a special agent. Not only was his record undistinguished, Lawson was a rookie, never having run a major investigation.

What brilliant mind at the FBI would put him in charge of such an important case?

Well, not much he could do about it. David had other fish to fry. Make that sharks. As he nursed his drink at Toshi's, he mulled over his next steps.

They all led to Rutland Falco.

It was during his stop in Washington, at the Department of Agriculture, that David had connected American Milk and the tamperings. There was more digging to do before he could move on Falco, some dubious-looking bank transfers he had been about to run down when Lawson showed up at his doorstep.

But computer analysis would not be enough to bring down Falco. David knew this guy, knew he was smart and ruthless. It would not be as simple as walking into his office and scaring him with an FBI badge.

David glanced hopefully at the big round alarm clock ticking loudly and conspicuously on the bar. Nara had given it to him as part of David's new regimen, to get him back on schedule, she said.

According to her, David's main problem was that he was out of sync with something she called the "Big Wheel." The best he could make of her assessment was that he had fallen out of some larger order in her complicated Hindu–Buddhist–Balinese worldview.

So now he had to keep track of himself. That meant reflecting on his actions and keeping a daily journal. He also had to know, within a half hour, what time it was. The worst part was that he had to limit himself to one drink an hour. For starters.

David figured he had started this drink about forty minutes ago. If he had another one now, he would have to wait an hour and twenty minutes before he could have the next one. What the hell, he thought, the whole country is in debt anyway. He made a motion toward Toshi, who was at the other end of the bar doing his books.

"You pretty quiet today," Toshi said, the slightest hint of a smile in his eyes as he poured Wild Turkey. "Nara making you give up talking too?"

"Cute. Say, where is she anyway?"

"In Key West, at newspaper. Usually get home about five."

George, Toshi's handyman, came into the bar from the back, wiping grease from his hands with a rag and muttering about an engine he had just repaired. "Shit, I don't think they had the goddamn thing gapped the entire time they owned it. Took me damn near two hours to tune that sucker up."

He disappeared through the front door. David felt a light tugging on his foot and looked down. A puppy, no more than a couple months old, was nibbling his shoelaces.

"What's this?" he said, leaning over and clumsily patting its head. David saw traces of at least four breeds in it.

"Supposed to be dog," Toshi said, frowning. "Nara found it on highway. Another one around here somewhere. She collect stray."

"Toshi," David said, "can I borrow your truck again tomorrow? I've got to get to the airport again."

"Sure, no problem. Where to this time?"

"New York."

"Hmm, Rochester again?"

"No, New York City. I think I've got him this time."

"Who?"

"Dr. Doom, the prime tamperer, the grandaddy of them all. We get him and the tamperings stop, I know it. He's there, probably planning his next little surprise as we speak. But I'm going to squeeze him, get him out from under his rock."

George came back in, this time carrying the bags of white gravel David had noticed out front the last time he was here. Puffing and complaining, he took them into the back, through the door.

"Tell me, why you got to chase this guy?" Toshi said. "Let FBI handle."

"Lawson." David worked the name out of his throat like early morning phlegm. "He wouldn't know the tamperer if he walked in and announced himself. The guy's unbelievable.

"Every time I call up the computers at the major newspapers and magazines looking for information on the tamperings, there's something on Lawson. He's really milking this thing, spending all his time giving interviews, appearing on talk shows."

"You talkin' about the FBI?" George said. David hadn't realized he had come back in. "They're still hangin' around."

"What?" David said. "Where?"

"Out front. I seen 'em there all day, two guys sittin' on the side of the road. Must be bored shitless."

David jumped up from his seat and went to the window, his head swiveling back and forth. "Where? I don't see anything."

George came over. David could smell the Thunderbird on his breath. He wondered: Is that what I smell like?

"Y'see over there? Set back in that little road what cuts into Kettle? There, about twenty yards north. See?"

David squinted his eyes. Across U.S. 1 he could make out the shape of a sedan hidden in a grove of pine saplings. A flash of light came off something metal, a bumper or mirror. Then David remembered the boat near the house this morning.

"That son of a bitch," he hissed.

George snapped his head around to look at David. "What did you . . . ?"

David rushed back to the bar. "Toshi, got a pen and paper?"

"Help yourself," he said, pointing toward the end of the bar.

David tried to clear his head and think for a moment before scribbling out a note. "Give this to Nara for me, O.K.?"

"Sure, no problem. What's going on?"

"Celebrating Halloween a little early this year," he said, and walked out the door.

Later that day, Agent Ron Westheimer, in the front seat of the FBI-issue sedan parked along U.S. 1, nudged his surveillance partner, Phillip "Buddy" LaCroix. Just minutes earlier they had relieved the day-shift team.

"That's the girl, isn't it?" Westheimer said. "One written up in the day report?"

A young woman in a loose-fitting caftan and big straw hat had just come out of the bar and was crossing the gravel parking lot. She came to the edge of the highway.

Buddy LaCroix peered through his binoculars. "Can't say for sure. The hat's in the way of her face. But I would bet on it. Report says she's Oriental, Indonesian background."

Westheimer checked his watch: 5:12. He jotted down a note in the watch journal. "O.K., she's entered and accounted for."

"So what kind of eats did you pack?" LaCroix said.

"Christ, Buddy, you just ate less than an hour ago."

"Surveillance gives me an appetite. The guys on the boat have a microwave. We get cold sandwiches."

About three hours later, Westheimer spotted the girl coming out of the woods and onto the shoulder of the road. He looked over at LaCroix, who was dozing soundly now. Westheimer didn't want to wake his partner, so he carefully lifted the binoculars off LaCroix's lap.

Visibility was poor. It was twilight and a light fog was settling, but Westheimer saw the same big caftan, the same floppy hat they had seen earlier. He made another entry in the watch journal: "Female Oriental, acquaintance of surveillance subject, observed returning to bar."

In the other seat, Buddy LaCroix snored and rolled over.

Chapter 25

Rutland Falco felt two fingers lightly squeeze the muscle in his back stretching from the collarbone to the base of his neck. He had been watching night fall from high above Manhattan in the World Trade Center. Miniature lights illuminated the streets as toy cars gridlocked the intersections and herds of tiny people filled the sidewalks.

The view reminded him of *The Third Man,* that old mystery with Orson Welles and Joseph Cotten. In particular he was thinking of the scene where Welles and Cotten are alone in the big Ferris wheel in Vienna, arguing over Welles's trafficking in diluted penicillin in the postwar city.

Falco remembered Welles's argument as the Ferris wheel reaches the top of the ride, maybe five stories over Vienna. Orson shows Cotten the little Viennese strolling beneath them, no bigger than dots, he says. Even governments think no more than that of their people. So why is his old friend Cotten so worked up over a few faceless, nameless dots being erased by a watered-down antibiotic?

What a scene. Falco turned, half expecting to see Joseph Cotten standing there. Instead it was Chester Garrett, president of American Milk.

Garrett, usually a healthy, domineering presence, looked old and tired. Rumor had it he was trying to make a golden parachute for himself and retire. That would leave a big hole in the company Rutland hoped to fill.

"How's my star quarterback?" he said affectionately.

Rutland smiled. "Pretty good, Chet. You pulling off?"

"Yeah, I can't keep up with you young studs anymore. Any news on Dixie Dairy?"

"They're running scared. Our people in Atlanta tell us their management is desperate to scrape up some cash, even petitioning the federal government as a small business. Would you believe it? Sounds like they don't want us as their new bosses."

Chet laughed too loudly, as always. "How's our cash situation?"

"Great," Falco said. "I've got investors lining up, not even knowing what they're buying into. I figure we'll have enough commitments by the end of the week to buy out Dixie Dairy's shareholders."

Chet slapped him on the back. "Terrific, just terrific. After all this is behind us, I want to have a retreat with the vice presidents. Maybe at Tahoe this year. I'll want to talk with all of you about restructuring, getting some new blood where it's needed, if you get me."

No, Rutland *didn't* get him, but knew better than to ask. Garrett left Falco alone with his thoughts in the palatial office.

He rubbed his face and remembered he had a date with Claudia in a half hour. He went into his private bathroom and turned on the light that gleamed from the imported Italian tile and gold-plated fixtures.

He loosened his tie and turned on his razor. Rutland had a system for everything he did: getting dressed in the morning, eating, and making money. Routine provided stability. And it was important for him to know as much about his surroundings as he possibly could. He hated surprises.

He began shaving, starting at the left sideburn and working his way methodically around his face and neck. There were a few flecks of gray in his beard, and the skin around his eyes was loosening. He had given some thought to getting a skin tuck, but he liked being the only senior executive in the company who had not had cosmetic surgery.

Rutland also liked the idea of being the whiz kid, the enfant terrible. The pressure was intense and he kept killer hours, but he didn't mind the spotlight. It only made him dance faster.

As he worked the razor around his jaw, he thought about the Dixie Dairy deal, he thought about Claudia, his mistress, and he thought about himself.

He did his best thinking while he shaved. Falco was on the verge of accomplishing one of his biggest goals—single-handedly doubling the holdings of American Milk since taking over Mergers and Acquisitions a little over a year ago. The Dixie Dairy deal would put him over the top.

His face clean, Falco started on his neck. He attributed his remarkable success early in life to his ability to get inside the minds of the people around him. When he started out in business, he knew he lacked the pedigree and contacts of the Ivy League pussies around him. Everywhere he looked he saw guys with fewer brains and guts than he moving up because of whom they knew and married. They dressed well and spoke smoothly. He knew he needed an edge.

He learned how to be competent but not threatening,

to appreciate that flattery might work well with one person but not with another. He kept notes about people. He remembered spouses' and children's names, and he recorded miscellaneous personal information about those he wanted to get close to. He watched and waited.

At American Milk, he worked his way into the Mergers and Acquisitions division. Working one-on-one on real estate deals, he found that his ability to get into the minds of his adversaries worked well. But before long he had too many adversaries—teams of lawyers and accountants scheming across the table from him.

How could he read into those inscrutable faces? How much power did they really have? What were they like on the tennis court?

He was losing his edge. Information was everything, and his hunger for it was insatiable. He needed more.

Falco took people to lunch. He began to cultivate contacts inside and outside the business. New York, he found, was a network of gears, tight little groups of people who shared information with each other but expected something in return. Falco sought out people whose teeth touched many gears, who were plugged into all kinds of information—key loan officers at banks, lawyers, and political types.

It wasn't long before he could touch important pressure points and make things happen. Sometimes he paid for the privilege. And it was risky. He could tell no one he was using insider information, especially the people he worked with.

Falco's deals became more and more important to American Milk. Promotions came, bigger money, perks. Of course he wouldn't let anyone in the company stand in his way. The joke going around was that Falco had his own hit squad to get rid of the flotsam in front of him. The "disappeared" of American Milk, they were called.

Then his big break came—the tamperings. A string of dairy companies was going under because some nut was poisoning their products, and the public lost all confidence in them. Falco offered the drowning companies a hand, and they grabbed it gratefully. He didn't even need insider information to acquire them.

The mandarins of American Milk balked when he proposed the idea of taking over Pure and Simple Milk Inc. in Maryland, the first of the ill-starred companies. Change the company's name, he told them, and make it a subsidiary of A.M. Get it back on its feet. Then watch the profits roll in. He laid the old Cash McCall story on them, that A.M. was performing a service, saving jobs. They went for it.

Falco was fearful that American Milk's competitors like Borden and Sealtest would catch on to his system. So he began to buy put options in various companies, including those that might get nailed by a tampering. This allowed him to have a foot in the door of a company even before its reputation was damaged, but it also stretched American Milk's resources, scaring some of the company sheep.

Soon his gambling was paying off big. His deals brought in huge amounts of cash when he sold off pieces of a company or when the company held a big fund for employees' pensions. And Falco wasted no time stripping flabby management whenever he found it.

The tamperings continued, and Rutland Falco was always there, first in line to bail the poor companies out. Some of them were only marginally profitable. Falco needed a big one, a grand slam, to really make his reputation.

He had been following a company in Minneapolis—the Sweet Creams Company. It was run by a bright group of young people who were tearing up national markets with an array of upscale dairy products, like Brisken Glatt gourmet ice cream and Sweet Creams Lite children's milk. The stock on the company was privately held by the management and employees, preventing Falco from starting a hostile takeover.

It was a confident, well-financed operation—that is, until traces of cyanide turned up in the corpses of nine Sweet Creams customers. Then the bottom dropped out of the company. Stores would not even carry its products.

Soon Rutland Falco showed up with an offer to pump capital and life back into Sweet Creams. With his offer came the full weight and integrity of the American Milk organization to restore Sweet Creams to its rightful place in the industry. All he wanted was controlling interest in the company.

The Sweet Creams management jumped at his offer. Falco stood back and let the Young Turks of Sweet Creams redesign the subsidiary's image and create a new line of products even better than before. The news of an earthquake in China helped everyone forget the Sweet Creams tampering incident, and the new subsidiary was in the black within months.

Everyone forgot, except Rutland Falco, who had to sell off his best Robert Rauschenberg to pay his associate, Garl Julian, for adding the cyanide sprinkles to eleven cartons of Brisken Glatt.

Finished with his neck, Falco splashed on some aftershave and straightened his Hermes tie. He put on his vest—they were in that year—and the suit jacket, all tailor-made on Saville Row.

As he prepared to leave, Falco noticed a soft green glow on one of the four desk-tops he kept on the other side of the office. There was a message on the screen of the computer in which he kept his most confidential files.

That was strange—only he knew the password and it was protected by a quarter of a million dollars worth of software security. Who could have turned it on? He came over from his chair and peered at the screen that asked the question :

HOW MANY COWS DOES IT TAKE
TO SCREW IN A LIGHT BULB?

What in the hell . . . ? Falco pushed the Return key. The message changed:

IT'S A MOO POINT

Chapter 26

New York was at its darkest and grimiest when David arrived later that night. The taxi from LaGuardia slid through the dank streets obscured by steam billowing from vents. Streetlights flickered, and whole blocks were dark from a brown-out. A bomb had gone off earlier that day in a main power station.

This was Dr. Doom's territory. David knew he was at a disadvantage here. He had never followed anyone before and wasn't even sure what he wanted to accomplish by trailing Rutland Falco.

He did know he wanted to flush him out, cause him to make a mistake. Already David had begun to tamper with Falco's computer files, moving things around and leaving messages on his computer screen. Even better, he had discovered a big deal Falco was working on, a hostile take-over of a dairy company in Atlanta. If David could swing it, the deal would never happen.

Hit Falco where it hurt—in the money belt.

The taxi left David in front of the midtown Hilton. He wanted the biggest, most anonymous hotel in the city. Disguised in hat and sunglasses, he checked in under a fake name and refused a bellhop's offer to help him to his room.

Once there, he immediately went to work. Through a

portable computer connected to the mainframe on California Key, David could do a raft of mischief. For starters, he programmed a tap on Rutland Falco's home and office phones, as well as continued surveillance of his computers.

With the taps in place, he could check the progress of Falco's deals. David was most interested in the financing—how Falco was raising the money to buy out the company. This was David's pressure point. The place where he could squeeze Falco.

From American Milk's computers David had a list of all the investors Falco was lining up for his takeover. Mostly they were managers of aggressive mutual funds. David knew those managers would jump like rats from this deal if they suspected anything questionable about it, if it appeared anything could go wrong.

So David composed a little story and disguised it as an article from one of the many financial wire services everyone in the investment world subscribed to. The story was about "poison pills"—measures taken by companies to prevent others from taking them over.

David's story was about such creative poison pills as the one at the Dixie Dairy Company of Atlanta. There, the company had put a clause in its charter that guaranteed enormous sums of money for its senior executives in the event of a takeover. These sums were big enough to put the company deep in debt and therefore unattractive to take over. If you bought the company, you bought the clause.

Tomorrow, every one of Falco's investors would see that story and wouldn't be answering his calls for a long while.

David lay back on the hard Hilton bed. He closed his eyes and listened for waves breaking on the beach of

California Key, but all he heard were horns and sirens on Sixth Avenue nineteen stories below.

He wanted to call Nara, but the phone in his house probably was bugged. She had done a great job of helping him pull off their charade for the FBI, even wearing high heels under her caftan when she left the bar to make herself look taller.

And the look on Toshi's face when David had walked in the bar wearing the caftan and big hat and carrying the shopping bag—if only he had a camera!

David realized he could communicate with Nara by computer. He had showed her the basics of operating the mainframe. Before he checked in with her, he wanted to do one more thing.

Yesterday, back in Florida, when he had been studying Falco's personal financial accounts for any link to the tamperings, David noticed something that brought him up short. He had been checking transactions that had taken place around the time of each dairy tampering. Most involved big amounts, nothing less than six figures.

But exactly one week after the March tamperings had been reported, Falco moved $25,000 from his account to the East End Art, Incorporated, whatever that was. These tamperings had killed eleven people in the Minneapolis area who had eaten ice cream laced with potassium cyanide. The incident had drawn particular attention because the wife of a state senator was one of the victims.

The company that manufactured the ice cream—Sweet Creams Dairy—was now owned by American Milk, courtesy of Rutland Falco. Just when David had been about to dig further, Special Agent Lawson had showed up at his front door.

The lap-top was now set up on the generic desk in the generic hotel room. David typed in a question:

WHAT IS EAST END ART, INCORPORATED?

In seconds, the computer brought up the answer from the files of the New York City courts, where the company had been incorporated. East End Art was owned by one Garl Julian at an address on Avenue C on the Lower East Side.

Then another file came up, this one from Mercantile Bank of New York, where East End Art had an account. It showed records of two payments to the company, each from different numbered accounts and each in the amount of $25,000. The second payment was the one David had found in Falco's file. The first one had been made almost one week before the Minneapolis tamperings. Other than the fund transfers from Falco, the company had no other financial activity in its history.

East End Art was set up to allow Falco to make the transfers.

David was trembling. This was it, his direct link between Falco and the tamperings.

Questions, questions were flying through his brain. What were the transfers for? And how did East End Art fit in?

A quick check of phone company records showed no listing for East End Art. David figured as much. It was a dummy corporation.

Lucky for him, the court record of incorporation included Garl Julian's Social Security number. David ran a check on it. Within seconds Julian's miserable life story crawled out of the computer like an infestation of poisonous insects.

Garl Julian had been born Garl Giuliani on March 9,

1951, in Fresno. Expelled from high school. Juvenile record of car theft, drug dealing, and assault.

Enlisted in the army in 1968 and served in the Special Forces in Vietnam. Dishonorably discharged for desertion in 1970. Convicted for possession of cocaine with intent to distribute, 1971, suspended sentence. Arrested for assault and battery on a social worker, 1972, no conviction. Convicted for attempted armed robbery and another assault and battery, 1981, jumped bail and was later recaptured. Did five years in Folsom Prison and was released on parole. Present address: unknown

He sounded like a real sweet guy.

He also sounded like the kind who would put poison in ice cream, if the price was right. Fifty thousand dollars, that's what Falco paid him to kill nine people and destroy the Sweet Creams Dairy. And while the company lies in ruin, Rutland Falco extends a helpful hand and turns a hefty profit for American Milk.

Why had Falco paid off Julian with a fund transfer? Why hadn't he just used cash?

Maybe he had no cash. Maybe he thought no one would ever think to look into his personal finances. David wasn't sure.

And where were the records on the other tamperings, like the Beverly Farms Dairy in Rochester? He would have to look into that.

Then multiple alarms went off in his head. Was Falco planning another tampering? Were any other deals underway with Julian?

David quickly confirmed that no other transfers had been made from Falco's to Julian's accounts, even within the last hour. Nothing.

As the exhilaration of his discovery wore off, fatigue set in. David opened his duffel bag and removed the few things he had brought along from Florida, some extra clothes, a toothbrush, and the journal Nara wanted him to keep. David also had brought along her big clock, which showed that it was already a little after two. The morning would come quickly if David was going to follow Falco from his apartment.

Before he went to bed he typed a message that he would transmit to Nara. She would find it when she woke up.

HI. SETTLED IN—ROOM 1967 AT THE HILTON. THE YEAR "LIGHT MY FIRE" WENT NO. 1. FOUND A STRONG CONNECTION BETWEEN FALCO AND ONE TAMPERING (SO FAR). HE USES A HIT MAN NAMED GARL JULIAN. NEED YOU TO WATCH COMPUTER TO SEE IF ANY TRANSFERS ARE MADE OUT OF FALCO'S ACCOUNTS AND INTO JULIAN'S. THAT WILL INDICATE A POISONING IS ABOUT TO OCCUR. IF YOU SEE ONE, CALL ME IMMEDIATELY.

WILL SEND MORE INFO AS I GET IT. MISS YOU. D.

David thought a while about sending the last part— "miss you"—and decided to delete it. Then he changed his mind and typed it back in. Just before he transmitted the message, he erased it again.

He jotted down a few notes in the journal before he fell back on the bed and slept fitfully.

Midtown Manhattan at noon was an anonymous blessing and an overwhelming curse. Hordes of aggressive New Yorkers stampeded past David in every direction on Fifth Avenue. It was all he could do to keep sight of Falco ten feet ahead of him.

As best as David could tell, Falco was unaware of

being followed, first from his apartment, then to three buildings in the space of four hours. He hadn't bothered to check in at his office downtown in the World Trade Center.

David guessed Falco was paying calls on his investors, trying vainly to keep them interested in the deal. As Falco pleaded and begged in someone's office, David waited in the lobby below, hiding behind a newspaper. Each time he saw Falco coming out of an elevator, the rising young executive looked a little more stressed out.

Falco turned a corner off Fifth and crossed on a green light. David was close enough to bump him into the way of an oncoming taxi. The impact would at least fracture his hip. It was tempting, very tempting, but he held off. Falco crossed the street cleanly.

David wasn't sure, but he thought he saw Falco look over his shoulder as he entered a trendy-looking restaurant. Just in case, David melted into the doorway of a Club Med booking office. He pretended to study posters of plastic-looking people working hard at being Bohemian, lying inside some sort of tropical hut and stuffing themselves on fruit. Inside the office, a tan young woman studied him up and down and threw him a look of cold contempt.

So far David had had pretty good luck finding places to hang out while waiting for Falco. Earlier that morning, he had found a bar open at six across the street from Falco's apartment building. The bar had a window with a clear view of the building. And now, two doors down from the restaurant, he noticed a deli with stools at the windows.

He might as well get something to eat. Falco might have a long day visiting investors.

Chapter 27

Rutland Falco sucked on the breasts of his mistress. It was his favorite part of their lovemaking. He curled like a hook on the edge of the bed with her chin on the top of his head and his lips firmly attached to a nipple. She locked her fingers at the middle of his bare back.

His lips worked fast and machine-like. He sucked on one breast and then another, sometimes both together. He was greedy and aggressive, especially today. He sucked hard, bit, and sometimes drew blood.

Claudia winced and groaned from the pain but didn't push him away. He seemed to know just how much pain he could inflict before she would object. Since meeting Rutland, Claudia had taken to carrying antiseptic in her purse. For her part, she dug her fingernails into the soft meat of Rutland's upper thighs. As he groaned with pain and pleasure, she made red grooves up his buttocks.

The rest of their lovemaking was for him just an acting out of expectations. He never enjoyed intercourse as much as he enjoyed her breasts. But he pretended for her sake that the rest of it was satisfying for him.

He went through the motions and made the requisite sounds. Occasionally he would seem to lose control in passion. He knew this excited her. But that, too, was staged for her benefit.

Early on, Falco had been careful to delineate the boundaries of their relationship. He wanted it understood from the beginning what he wanted from Claudia and what she could expect from him.

Their experience of each other was confined to nine rooms twenty-six floors above Manhattan. Rutland insisted they meet only at the company's suite at the Waldorf, never at his or her apartment. He would be the first to arrive at the suite, precisely at a specified time. Claudia would arrive five to fifteen minutes later, alternating between the Park and Lexington Avenue entrances to the hotel.

They met at different times during the day and night, depending, usually, on Falco's schedule. There were occasions when Claudia would arrive at the suite and Rutland would not be there. He had not given her a key, so she had to leave and wait for his next call. He had forbidden any calls to his home or office. Sometimes she made a point of not showing up even after agreeing to meet. Claudia believed Rutland secretly liked being stood up, that her independence piqued his excitement.

The last time they were to have met, Rutland had not appeared. Claudia had waited two weeks for the next call. When it came she was in the middle of a meeting in her office with an important Swiss book dealer who was deciding to which of the major New York auction houses he would consign a collection of rare first editions.

Claudia had known him for years, before she had become general manager of Christie's. He liked her and she enjoyed doing business with him. The collection he offered was an important one and would fetch a healthy commission.

She was careful not to press him or to appear too eager even though she would have killed for that consignment. So they chatted easily, gossiping about other dealers. Claudia was surprised that he knew about her divorce, which had been settled quietly less than three months ago. She steered the conversation to business.

"Americans are my best customers," he said in flawless English. "Because you have so little past, you adore old things."

They were interrupted by a soft knock on the door. Her secretary passed her a message. The meeting went on, with the dealer agreeing to look at a proposal from her. She waited three hours before she got back to Rutland, who wanted to see her immediately. She told him she first had a few calls to make, which was partially true.

Later, as she left the building and stalked a taxi, Claudia thought about breaking things off with Falco. She wondered if seeing him like this really brought her any happiness. She had never believed their affair would turn into anything more. And Falco's intensity and drive, at first attractive to Claudia, now seemed obsessive and increasingly repugnant.

Part of the reason she was attracted to him was because he was so different from her ex-husband, Gayle. With him, Claudia was always in control. She could predict his response to any situation. And everything she did was fine with him. Their relationship had devolved into little more than a business partnership in the last five years of their marriage.

But Falco never relaxed or confided in her. She was constantly on guard about him, never sure if she was saying or doing the right thing. She even doubted her ability to please him sexually.

Sometimes she believed he had picked her out for a hostile takeover, like one of the failed companies he bought out. When she looked into his eyes she tried to deny to herself the madness she saw in them. To her, Rutland was capable of almost anything. He only revealed himself to her through his obsessions.

He did everything in his power to control the space around him. One time at the Waldorf, when he had thought she was in the shower, she had seen him pacing off the dimensions of the bedroom. She laughed and asked him if he sold real estate on the side.

But he did not laugh. In fact, he was deeply angered that she had caught him in such a private, personal act, as if she had spied on him while he was on the toilet. She felt a fissure forming in the ground of their affair and never brought it up again.

When she arrived at the suite, she found him agitated and restless. The first thing he did was to ask her which entrance to the hotel she had used. She tried to soothe him by holding him and stroking his head. They sat on the bed and she massaged his neck.

Then he began to babble. Claudia had never seen him this way before. In spasms of words and phrases he told her that someone had invaded his private computer files containing information on his business deals. Whoever was doing it was not content to tamper with the files. Rutland also was receiving threats and taunting messages on his office computer screen. The messages were terrible puns with references to cows and dairy products.

"This morning the message was: 'How was the moo shoo pork last night, udderly delicious?'—exactly what I had ordered out for," he said, panic-stricken.

"That means my telephone lines are being tapped. Maybe yours too. I took a chance by calling you, even on a public phone."

"But, Rutland, who would be doing this?"

She felt a chill when he looked at her with an expression that said "so you don't believe me either." But he simply said he wasn't sure. It could be almost anyone in the industry, possibly a jock in the Securities and Exchange Commission. Falco had questioned everyone who worked for him, but turned up nothing.

He told her this was all happening at a time when he was attempting a takeover of a company called Dixie Dairy. It would be a coup if he pulled it off, he said, but now the whole deal was in jeopardy. Investors were dropping like flies. He could not understand how he could have been so wrong in underestimating the company's business savvy. Now he was under surveillance, perhaps by Dixie Dairy itself.

"Another thing," he said, "I think I'm being followed."

"What?" Claudia almost laughed but didn't dare. "By whom?"

"I don't know. Someone. I noticed him this afternoon on my way to lunch at Pauline's."

"What did he look like?"

Falco lit up a cigarette. Claudia had never seen him smoke before. "Scruffy-looking. Unshaven, sloppy clothes."

Claudia tried to be rational. "Rutland, this kind of thing really doesn't go on, does it? I mean, surveillance and threats. You've been under a lot of pressure lately. . . ."

But Falco already was tuning her out as his mind raced over his problems. He wondered if they intersected in whomever was harassing him. He wondered if getting rid of this person would end his problems.

Claudia, trying to comfort him, unbuttoned his shirt

and rubbed his chest. She licked his ear. Falco grunted, rolled over, and fell upon her breasts.

In the lobby of the hotel, Claudia checked her makeup in a mirror and smoothed her skirt. She left through the Lexington Avenue exit even though the cabs were more plentiful on Park. She turned up Lexington and disappeared into the shadows of the skyscraper canyon. The traffic moved, sluggish and tense.

As she walked she glanced over her shoulder in search of a cab with its light on, almost impossible to find during lunch hour. It probably would be best to head over to First Avenue or Sutton Place to find one going uptown.

Crossing 54th toward the Citicorp Building, Claudia's scalp began to tingle and her shoulders tried to shake off invisible hands she felt were encircling them. Once she made it to the other side of Lexington, she stood on the curb and watched the pedestrians behind her clear the intersection.

But she saw no one looking at her. She continued on 54th, but the feeling of being followed persisted, even grew. Was someone trailing her, or was Rutland's paranoia taking hold?

She ducked into the Citicorp Building and was comforted by the swirl of lunchtime crowds. The building's ground-floor lobby was New York at its anonymous best, with restaurants, shops, and a big Conran's cloyed with humanity. In the center of the huge lobby, students of a dance school were giving a performance with piano accompaniment.

Claudia pretended to study the menu outside a Danish smorgasbord restaurant. She looked over her shoulder and saw three people standing in a row looking directly at her. Through the drops of perspiration beading in her eyelashes they looked like the silhouette figures one saw painted on the sides of buildings in lower Manhattan.

One was a waiter in a tuxedo smoking a pipe, another was a thin woman with many shopping bags, and the third was a man in soiled, baggy clothes tapping a newspaper against his leg.

Claudia looked inside the restaurant and saw a very blond woman in white overalls spooning herring into a cup. She kept her eyes to the wall in front of her and walked sideways to her right. She found stairs that led down to an exit.

At that moment the sound of an alarm, like the wail of foghorn, filled the lobby. Claudia felt her body quake from the impact of the noise that ratcheted up and down the lobby, off columns and stairwells.

She turned and saw scenes from Bosch. People everywhere were hunched over covering their ears. The face of the woman with the shopping bags was contorted in a scream, but her screams were drowned out by the alarm and by other alarms going off by the elevator banks.

A small girl, a dancer in a red tutu, ran past Claudia and up a flight of steps. Bouncing down past her, rhythmically and *Potemkin*-like, was a child's stroller. Claudia moved instinctively toward the stroller but was pushed back by the crowd churning toward her.

The mob was like a single monster with many heads, each face open in a silent scream. As people crushed against her, Claudia tried to cling to the wall.

But the crowd, fearful of an explosion from a hidden bomb, kept churning. It caught her like a chameleon snatching a fly and pulled her down the stairs to the street.

The hot city air blew into her face as she burst through the door. The street was in chaos. Hysterical people broke through store windows with their hands to escape the crowds. Some collapsed on the street.

Fire hydrants sprayed plumes of water up and down the block. Overturned cars, some with people still inside them, were being set on fire by rampaging gangs.

Trapped in the crowd as she was, coming up alongside her, was the man in the soiled, baggy clothes she had seen inside. He looked at her, his eyes open wide with fear, and was swept past. They went on for about half a block when the crowd began to break up and Claudia could pull herself free.

Fire engines, rescue trucks, and police cars were stuck in the lunchtime traffic and could not get close to the riot scene. Shopkeepers frantically pushed customers out of their stores so they could close security gates before the stampeding crowds arrived.

Claudia stood and caught her breath. Behind her, a second wave of people streamed out of the Citicorp Building, adding to the tumult.

Remembering that she was being followed, she looked around for the scruffy-looking man in the oversize clothes. He was nowhere to be seen. She turned and walked twenty-two blocks to her office and did not look back once.

Chapter 28

Rutland Falco, up at dawn and wearing sunglasses on a cloudy Sunday morning, caught a number six subway heading downtown. It had been more than two years since he had ridden the New York subways, and he remembered why. If the heat and stink didn't get to you, the mangy, shiftless people hassling handouts or the lost out-of-towners with their stupid questions would. Fortunately, Falco's subway car was empty all the way down to Astor Place, where he got out.

The streets were almost empty. Not even the homeless were up yet. Falco walked east past the hulking Cooper Union building onto St. Mark's Place, and continued down bombed-out blocks and through parks with only brown fuzz where grass once grew.

Heading down Avenue C, Falco looked up quickly when the steel-plated door to an old brownstone squealed open. A sickly-looking young person in black clothes oozed out, sniffed the air, and went back inside.

As Falco crossed the street, a car passed, full of kids with expensive clothes and haircuts heading home after a night of standing in line to the trendiest clubs in town. They shouted something, but he ducked his head and kept on walking.

Falco was reasonably sure he wasn't being followed.

Just to be sure, from time to time he eased into a doorway or stopped to read a poster, casually looking around to see if he saw anyone. He had taken the extra precaution of using the stairwell in his apartment building that morning and going out the back delivery entrance.

Whoever was tailing him seemed to want him to know it. Even Claudia had noticed the guy a couple times. Neither of them had gotten a good look at him other than they both agreed that he was in his late thirties or early forties, average build, with a week-old beard and baggy clothes. He would appear and disappear on the street, at restaurants, and in the lobbies of their office buildings.

Falco was certain he was connected somehow to whoever was tapping his telephone and computer files. The computer tampering and tail both had begun at the same time.

Was blackmail his game? Had Dixie Dairy found out about Falco's takeover plan and sent this man up to squeeze him out?

Rutland was waiting for the shakedown that never came. The tension was getting unbearable. He decided he would get the guy before he got him.

He followed the addresses on Avenue C, whenever the buildings had addresses, until he found the familiar Latvian meat market with the sign in front *Se Habla Español*. On the wall next door, he found a row of buttons and rang apartment E. He rang fourteen times before a voice crackled through the intercom. It was Garl.

"Who the fuck *is* that?" He sounded out of sorts.

"It's your friend from uptown. Are you alone?"

"Wha—? Shit. Do you have any idea what time it is?"

"This won't take long. C'mon, buzz me up."

"Wait." A few minutes later the door buzzed open. Falco scanned up and down the block and went in.

Garl Julian, dressed in a stained, ripped T-shirt and brand-new shiny red Everlast boxer's trunks, let him in. The place looked as if everything strewn around the loft had been left exactly as it had been four months ago when Falco was last there.

Off to one side of the loft was Garl's weight bench surrounded by assorted dumbbells and weights stacked on the floor. Falco noticed the dust on them. On the other side stood three easels, each with a different sample of Garl's awful paintings.

As a marketing ploy Garl called them his Vietnam collection, depicting, as he would explain to anyone willing to listen, abstract images of his experiences in the Special Forces along the DMZ. One was bright, lurid bursts of red and yellow over clumps of dark green.

Garl came up next to him. Rutland could smell his wretched breath. "You like that one? I call it 'The Smell of Napalm in the Morning.' Remember, from *Apocalypse Now*?"

"How much?" Falco asked, feigning interest.

Garl rubbed his belly. "For you . . . forty-five thousand. Interested?"

"Maybe. Sounds like you're big-time now."

Garl Julian knew Falco was brown-nosing, angling for a favor. But he didn't mind a little deference to his art. He got it so rarely. He sat down on a floor pillow and motioned Falco to take a seat on the weight bench.

"I get by, Falco, mostly on the payment from my last job for you. But you didn't come all the way down here to Alphabet City to admire my paintings."

Falco looked at Julian, finding it hard to imagine him as the go-anywhere-anytime commando he had been in 'Nam before he was busted. He was thin and bony with a long neck and prominent Adam's apple. He had a high, whiny voice and he scratched himself a lot. Garl looked like a geek, not a professional assassin.

"I wanted to discuss with you a resumption of your last job for me," Rutland said.

Garl laughed and coughed. He had a bad case of dry-mouth. "What, you want me to put a land mine in a pizza?"

Falco scowled at him. "I'm being followed. I don't know by whom, but he's been tailing me for about two days. It's the same guy each time, so I'm quite sure he's working alone."

"You're 'quite sure,' huh? Well, Falco, since *you* could make him, he's either a chump or he's setting you up for a shakedown."

"Don't you think I know that? Only he hasn't come forward with any terms."

Garl scratched his head. "So why do you want me to off him? What's he got on you?"

"Some potentially damaging information. Very damaging."

Garl suddenly looked serious. "Hey, he don't know about that little job I did for you, right?"

This gave Falco an idea. If Garl thought the black-mailer had something on him, he would play along like a good scout. "I believe he may. He's somehow gotten into my private computer files. You name might have appeared somewhere."

"Shit, you told me you had all this cleaned up and under control."

"I said I *believe* he may have something on you. Any-way, this is too important to close our eyes and hope everything is all right."

"Yeah, sure, that's easy for you to say if it's my ass

that's hanging out. He's probably carrying some insurance under his jacket."

"I thought you'd find a more discreet way to handle it."

"Right, why don't I just take him to lunch at the '21' Club and ask him to leave us alone. That's how you guys do it."

Falco stood up. "OK, Garl, if that's the way you want it."

Julian stood up on the pillow and held up his hands for Falco to wait. "Now chill out, dude," he said. "I got a personal stake in seeing this is done right once and for all. I can clean up my own messes, even if I don't see what it is I messed up here."

Falco allowed a small smile. "What did you say you wanted for that painting?"

"Well, like I said, fifty-five thousand."

Falco nodded his head and said gravely, "Yeah, how do you place a value on great art?"

"Right," Garl said. "Our usual arrangement?"

"Half before, half after. Only this time we do cash. No transfers like last time."

"Fine with me. When do we start?"

"You'll hear from me," Falco said, getting up to leave. He dipped into a pocket and pulled out a roll of bills.

"Here's five hundred. Clean up. Get a haircut and a suit. Now I owe you fifty-four five."

Julian took the five bills and threw them toward a table. "I mean it," Falco said, "you have to go where I go, and as you look now, you'll be picked up for vagrancy."

He was halfway out the door when Garl called, "Yo, Falco, you forgot your painting."

Chapter 29

Garl Julian moved the barrel of his M-21 rifle a tad and looked into the high-powered Weatherhill Sniperscope on top. Perfect. The cross hairs marked a *T* just behind the left ear of the guy following Falco. Garl made a sound in his throat, like a gun going off.

The M-21 had been the rifle of choice of Special Forces snipers in 'Nam. It was an old, heavy model with bolt action and flash suppressor. But it packed a wallop.

Garl had ripped it off when he did supply officer duty in 'Nam. He kept it oiled and combat-ready; he had even had the barrel extended and a couple more twists added inside to improve its accuracy.

If he pulled the trigger now, the bullet would go straight through the man's cerebellum and splatter the rest of his brains all over the place. Lights out in a hurry, just the way Garl learned in the Special Forces. The barrel was resting on the ledge of the passenger-side window of Garl's rental Toyota. Maybe that's why they call it the "shotgun" side, he thought. He had brought the rifle along more for fun than anything else. It was pointed at the window of a Greek restaurant across the street from Falco's apartment building.

It was already dark, so no one could see Garl playing with the rifle. He didn't intend to use it—yet. Falco had told him to waste the guy quietly, make it look like an accident if possible. More important, Garl wanted to see the color of Falco's money before he moved on the guy.

He would get his first installment tomorrow.

Garl stowed the rifle in the backseat and put his stocking feet up on the seat and rubbed them slowly. Man, did they ache.

Since six-thirty in the fucking a.m. he had been on them constantly, starting at Falco's place. Garl had to dog the man every step of the day until he picked up the tail shortly after lunch. Once Garl made the tail he had to follow *him* following Falco, a goddamn parade up and down Park Avenue.

The tail was some grubby-looking guy, looked like a private badge down on his luck, with no backup Garl could see. But he was just another hustler, number seven million and one in New York. If he was a private detective, it would have been just too funny—a dick chasing an asshole.

Falco said he wasn't going to change his schedule, even with two guys following him. Otherwise, the tail might be tipped off.

Later in the evening, after Falco went home, Garl followed his mark to the restaurant. The guy took a place at the window and put something down on the counter next to his drink. Garl couldn't make out what it was.

Whoever the guy was, he knew how to nurse a drink. He had been in the bar about three hours and was still on his first one.

So Garl had to wait.

Waiting was something he was used to doing. When he had been seventeen he had enlisted and waited for what seemed like forever to get into the army. Once he got in and was sent to 'Nam, he couldn't wait to get out of the country. He was sure his number would come up at the fire base along the DMZ where he was stationed.

When that didn't happen, he tried to stow away on an aircraft carrier headed stateside. But they nailed him and he did a year and a half in a Saigon stockade.

Back in the U.S. he got nailed again, once for possession with intent and then for armed robbery. He waited through more than five years of hard time before he made parole. The jerk he pistol-whipped at the K-Mart he tried to knock over *did* have to be the police chief's brother-in-law. And now Garl was waiting for a break as the assholes from the galleries stuck up their noses at his paintings while he hung his guts out on canvas.

Wait, wait, wait, wait, wait. Fuck it.

Garl remembered a poster he had seen somewhere, maybe on a cell wall in Folsom, of two vultures on a fence and one of them says to the other: "Patience my ass, I'm gonna kill me something." That's exactly how Garl felt.

He began to feel circulation return to his feet as he massaged them. He checked his watch: 11:09. How much longer would the guy be staying? Garl wanted to go in there and tell him he could go on home, that Falco was staying put for the night.

That was when the idea came to Garl how to waste the tail. He saw the shape of the whole operation. It was perfect, maybe one of his best ideas ever.

He still had a lot to do to get ready. Leaving the headlights off, he started the car, pulled it out onto the street, and headed downtown.

Garl thought: this time tomorrow the guy will be history.

Inside the Thasos Restaurant on his bar stool at the window, David tried to fight back frustration and fa-

tigue. He had been there for nearly four hours. What had
he accomplished?

Rutland Falco obviously wasn't going out tonight.
Not only that, he hadn't made a single false move all
day, nothing that David could tell, anyway. David had to
admit it was good seeing Dr. Doom's deal go sour on
him. But Falco wasn't showing signs of cracking, and
David had only forty-eight hours until Lawson would be
back at his doorstep, demanding the USDA database.

David made a decision then and there: he would give
it one more day trailing Falco, then confront him with
the evidence. He wasn't sure how or where he'd do it—
probably in a public place like his office or a restaurant.
There was nothing David wanted more than to see this
slimeball go down.

He was sure that if Falco was stopped, all the other
tamperings would stop. Covering Falco would be like
cornering a rat. David knew he'd have to be careful.

It probably would be a good idea for him to get the
telephone number of this restaurant and send it down to
Nara when he got back to the hotel. David collected his
clock, which he had placed in front of him on the
counter. He drained the last of his Wild Turkey—the
only one he had had all night—and went looking for
the phone.

He realized he was hungry. Maybe this restaurant
served food to go.

At the pay phone near the restrooms, David jotted the
number on the only piece of paper in his pocket, a hundred dollar bill. Circulation was returning to his legs. He
hadn't moved in three and a half hours.

He turned to look for a waiter and heard a scream followed by shouting in the back of the restaurant. He followed the bartender into the restaurant, where a crowd

had gathered around a table. The bartender pushed through and David followed him.

The scene was awful, sickening.

On the floor, a man was giving mouth-to-mouth to a woman. Another man sat on her legs as she bucked and twitched. The woman's legs were losing tension as the mouth-to-mouth grew more desperate.

"Call an ambulance," someone shouted from the crowd.

"It's too late anyway," David heard someone behind him whisper.

"Can't you take her somewhere?"

"Get back, everybody," barked a waiter, pushing hard at the people toward the front. "Give us some air."

The crowd pulled back reluctantly, but David realized it didn't matter. The woman's legs had gone slack. The man administering the emergency breathing looked up helplessly.

David, not wanting to be recognized, moved to the back of the crowd. A man in a running suit grabbed his arm.

"What happened?" he demanded. "Did she choke on something?"

David shrugged and kept moving.

"She was poisoned," someone said, "I saw her. She was drinking coffee when she fell over. It must have been in the sugar."

"Oh, my God," another person screamed. "I just had sugar too."

David was at the door. He couldn't stand any more and had to get out. He looked back quickly at the crowd moving away in horror from the latest victim of Dr. Doom's greed.

Chapter 30

The next day Nara did things that kept her near the computer screen in David's house. She couldn't go outside, the FBI was still watching. So she cooked, getting ready for her big Galungan feast next week. She didn't really enjoy cooking, but a good deal of the preparations were already done. Earlier that day, her father had brought over a suckling pig that was now in the oven.

After much thought Nara had decided to invite David to the Galungan feast. It was a big decision because she had never celebrated Galungan with anyone other than her family. Even in college she had always had a private celebration, sometimes requiring that she rent a motel room just for one night when she shared a dorm room.

Until she met David, she had never met anyone with whom she wanted to celebrate Galungan, the most important holiday for Balinese. Toshi cautioned her. He reminded her that David had never been to Bali and might find it hard to understand their customs, especially the things he'd see at a Galungan feast.

But Nara somehow knew David was different. She trusted him and was certain he'd understand.

As the pig roasted in the oven, Nara checked the kitchen cupboards for seasonings. She had managed to prod David into cleaning up most of his house, but these cupboards had a long way to go. David had merely hidden away his filthy dishes inside them.

Beneath the counter was a long row of cabinets. From deep in her larynx came a sound of disappointment and surprise as she swung the cabinet doors open. Row after row of Wild Turkey, vodka, and mango juice bottles were tucked away behind pots and pans encrusted with what looked like dried spaghetti sauce.

Nara felt her cheeks burning. The bastard, he had agreed to get rid of every drop of liquor in the house. She went through all the closets and cabinets, finding hundreds of bottles. Nara called George at the bar and asked him to hire someone to take the bottles away. Suspicious of George's eager interest in the project, she called her father to take care of it for her. She left the mango juice.

As she supervised the removal of David's liquor, she kept one eye on the computer screen set up on a box on the living room floor. So far she had received two messages from David. Both of them had scared her.

In the first one David said he had discovered a connection between his suspect, Rutland Falco, and a professional assassin. He gave Nara instructions to call him immediately if funds were transferred from Falco's accounts to the assassin's.

In the second message David tried to assure her that everything was fine. That made her even more nervous. He gave her the telephone number at his hotel and another one for a restaurant across the street from Falco's home. Just in case.

In case of what? she wondered. What was going on?

She tried to keep her mind off David by working on letters to her advice column, called "Just Ask Jock," in the *Key West Daily.* "Jock" was the name of the man

who had written the column for years, sort of a self-
styled Hemingway type who had fallen over his typewriter from a heart attack while advising a reader what
pound test to use when fishing for snook.

The publisher wanted the name of the column to stay
the same, but Nara tried to expand the readership. Sometimes she wondered if it had expanded too far.

Her first letter was from yet another endist, one of the
growing number of people who believed in endism, that
the end of the world was at hand. Endists pored over the
Bible, the zodiac, Nostradamus, or whatever they could
get their hands on, searching for signs and portents of
the world's imminent collapse. Nara was seeing more
and more letters from endists since the tamperings had
started.

And now the letters were getting alarmingly specific
about when the end was due, like this one:

> Dear Jock,
> I find that not all of my friends are fully aware
> the world will end on August 19. Yesterday one of
> my oldest and dearest friends asked me to be a
> bridesmaid at her wedding. Jock, I think it's great
> that Dolores (not her real name) has found some-
> one and wants to share her life with him. And the
> last thing I want to do is hurt her in any way.
> The problem is that her wedding date is set for
> October 25. As you can plainly see, time as we
> know it will cease nearly two months before Do-
> lores's scheduled big day. How do I tell a dear
> friend that I cannot, in good conscience, accept her
> invitation? This problem is keeping me up nights,
> so I ask for a speedy reply. Sign me,
>
>   Knows too much on Islamorada

Nara paused for a moment, mulling over possible responses. The easiest thing to do would be to take the Ann Landers route and refer the woman to a shrink. She had never answered an endist, concerned that she might encourage more of this kind of thinking. But now she would take a stab at a reply.

She rolled a sheet of paper into her typewriter and pecked out:

Dear Knows,
    The philosopher Kierkegaard once wrote: "Dread is the possibility of freedom."

Staring into space, Nara caught a slight jump on the computer screen.

"Hmmm," she said as she looked closer. The screen showed that a withdrawal of funds from one of Rutland Falco's many accounts had just been posted by the bank. The withdrawal was for $27,500.

She checked on the other side of the split screen on East End Art's accounts. No change there, so Falco's withdrawal hadn't been transferred to Julian's accounts.

Nara went back to her letter. She sat for long minutes, but no thoughts would yield themselves. Something was tugging at her. Something urgent.

She looked up again at the computer and stared at it for a long time. The withdrawal had been the only activity all day in Falco's personal accounts. David said Falco usually made hundreds of withdrawals and deposits each day. But today no other withdrawals or deposits had been posted. Why?

What if he used cash to pay Julian this time?

And then she knew in an instant: the $27,500 was hit money and David was the next target.

Garl Julian brought a glass of scotch to his lips and sucked through the ice. He watched as the man who had been following Falco for the past two days settled onto the next stool at the counter, with a view of Falco's apartment.

The man, a little filthier than he looked yesterday, fished around in a pocket of his coat and brought out a big alarm clock and placed it on the counter. What the fuck was *that* for? When the waitress came over, he ordered a Wild Turkey.

Garl had been at the bar for forty-five minutes already. Everything was going according to plan. He had spent another day tracking these two idiots around Manhattan and was sick and tired of it. Tonight, right here in this bar, Garl was going to whack him.

Garl had tailed him to the Hilton, the big one over on Sixth, and bribed a bellhop into getting him his name—Herman Melville. The name was probably fake, but it didn't matter. In a little while his name would be John Doe down at the city morgue.

It was while spying on Melville last night that Garl had remembered his joke to Falco, a pretty good one, he thought, about putting a land mine in a pizza. Back when he had poisoned the ice cream in Minneapolis for Falco, Garl had found the hardest part of the job was finding cyanide, the poison that was being used in the other tamperings. The idea was to make the police think the job was another of the tamperings that had everyone tearing their hair out.

Falco told him not to tell anybody about the job or

even mention he was looking for cyanide. There was too much heat.

Garl got a guy he had done time with to get him a job in a pharmaceutical plant in Jersey. Garl tolerated it until he found the cyanide stores used in drug processing— the kind he was looking for—and boosted some of the stuff. He didn't quit for a while after the inventory clerks discovered the missing cyanide, so no one would connect him with the few missing grams of poison.

Garl needed only half of the cyanide he had boosted to do the job on the ice cream, so he kept the rest of it for a rainy day. He had even thought about using it on a few smart-assed gallery owners and art collectors.

But here was his rainy day—Herman Melville, the world's worst private detective—Garl's duck in a barrel. Garl made sure to get to the bar before Melville so as not to get him suspicious by coming in and sitting next to him. He had already picked up the cash Falco owed him, the first half, from a commercial safe deposit box.

Garl decided after this job he would take Falco's money and blow out. New York was getting dangerous, with all these bombings and other scares. And he had always wanted to see the Southwest, to check out the art scene in Santa Fe. Maybe he'd buy a Toyota. He really liked that car.

As he sipped his drink, he fingered the glass vial in the side pocket of his jacket. It was filled with cyanide and the top could be opened inside the pocket with a flick of his thumb.

He peered through the window and thought about his Toyota parked three blocks away. Too many times on *America's Most Wanted* somebody got nailed for a perfectly good hit by leaving his wheels too close to the scene.

Garl touched the vial again. Santa Fe was calling. He was itching to get on the road.

Fighting back panic, Nara placed a call to David's room at the Hilton. No answer. The operator came back on and Nara asked to be connected to the concierge, where she left an urgent message for David to call her as soon as he got in.

He shouldn't even go to his room, she added to the message.

For all she knew, Garl Julian was there, waiting.

She found the number for Thasos Restaurant, from which David watched Falco. Was he there now? she wondered. She prayed he was as she dialed.

Busy.

She tried again. Busy again.

Suddenly she had an idea and ran out of the house toward the beach on California Key. She waved her arms, hoping the FBI boat would see her in the dark.

It was nowhere in sight.

Nara tried to shut out the fear and focus her thoughts. She could call the New York City Police Department. No, she told herself, with all the stories you heard about recorded messages answering 911 calls in New York, that might waste valuable time.

Back inside, she searched David's bedroom for Hugh Lawson's phone number in Washington. Then she remembered: David had put Lawson's business card and other important papers in the top drawer of his clothes chest.

And there it was, just as he had left it.

Before she called Lawson, she tried the restaurant one more time. Still busy. She punched in Lawson's number on the telephone and waited.

A secretary answered. Not letting her fear get in the way of the task at hand, Nara explained the problem—Falco, Julian—as quickly as she could. The secretary told her to hold, she would have to beep Lawson, who was about to be interviewed for *Nightline*.

About three minutes later, Hugh Lawson was on the line.

"You mean McAdam has been following a possible multiple homicide suspect without my permission?" was the first thing Lawson said after Nara had gone through the situation all over again.

"He *tried* to tell you, Mr. Lawson," Nara said, trying to restrain her anger, "but that's not important now. His life is probably in danger."

Lawson was unmoved. "And whose fault is that? You want me to arrest a prominent corporate executive just like that? On what grounds?"

Nara was beginning to understand what David had said about Lawson. What had he called him, a dead battery? "Mr. Lawson," Nara said, "I'm not suggesting you arrest him. Just please, send someone over to the Thasos Restaurant. I don't know what street it's on, but I'm sure you could find out. David may be there, as well as the hit man, Julian."

"*Hit man?* Are you jerking me around?"

That did it. "Is this getting through?" Nara said through clenched teeth. "Someone's life is in danger here, maybe others if you don't get off your ass and do something.

"Now, I can transmit to you some evidence, computerized financial files, that show Falco has been transferring money to Julian. The transfers occurred around the time of one of the tamperings.

"David thinks Julian did the poisoning and was paid

before and after by Falco. Exactly $25,000 was paid a week before and after the tampering. This should be enough probable cause to warrant *something*."

Lawson didn't say anything for awhile. Nara heard some commotion in the background as he was being called for his interview. "All right," he said. "Send the information up now. Use the same number you just called. But I'm not promising anything."

Nara hung up and read through David's instruction for transmitting on the modem. She typed in the proper commands and the data were on their way to Lawson.

Now all she could do was wait. She said a prayer to Vishnu, the Great Preserver.

"You're telling me that Lynyrd Skynyrd, the *group*, was named after a *gym teacher* in Jacksonville, Florida?" Garl Julian said to Melville, the guy tailing Falco. "I don't believe it."

He sat back on his bar stool, feigning great surprise. But Melville was low-key and didn't make a big deal out of Garl's disbelief.

"Yeah," Melville said. "The teacher was named Leonard Skinner, taught at the high school where the group came from. He used to give them a hard time about how they looked—their hair and clothes—so they named the band after him."

"No shit?" Garl said. He laughed into his drink, a big wet laugh. "I just love that group. Remember 'Give Me Back My Bullets'? Too bad that dude got wasted in the plane crash."

"Ronnie Van Zant," the guy said. "I never much cared for southern rock."

Garl looked hard at him but let it go. Normally he

would have jumped on any barfly who gave him lip, but he wanted to do this quiet.

He had struck up a conversation with Melville, or whoever he was, about a half hour ago. He was angling for a shot at the guy, just one shot. Garl kept the conversation light, no personal questions to get the guy suspicious. He didn't even ask him his name.

He wanted the dude to trust him.

"So what kind of music *do* you like?" Garl said.

The guy took his time answering, as if it were an important question. "I suppose my tastes run in different directions," he said. "I like a lot of the old stuff—British invasion, Hendrix, the San Francisco groups, although I think the Dead are overrated. I thought the art rock stream was interesting—Roxy Music, David Bowie, and that crowd—leading to punk and the New Wave. I liked the Clash. Ever hear their 'Sandinista' album?"

Garl wondered: who was this guy? A private detective who looked like a garbage collector, sounded like a *Rolling Stone* music critic, and knew enough about computers to break into Falco's hush-hush files?

He seemed like an interesting guy. It would almost be a shame to ice him if he ever got the chance.

"Hey, I gotta use the head," Melville said. "Watch my drink for me?"

"Sure, you bet," Garl said lightly, pressing his fingernails into his palms to contain his enthusiasm.

When he was sure the guy was gone, Garl dipped into his pocket and popped open the vial of cyanide. His eyes moved over the room and his arm reached out over Melville's drink. He dumped the powder into the drink and swirled it around with a swizzle stick.

Garl looked at the drink. Good, you couldn't see a trace of the cyanide.

He used the opportunity to wipe his prints from the swizzle stick, the countertop, and the bar stool. Less than a minute later the guy came back. Garl kept his eyes fixed on the counter.

"You notice if anybody left that building across the street?" Melville said.

"You mean the brownstone? Naw, nobody left."

"Reason I asked is that I'm waiting on somebody. He lives there."

"Oh yeah?" Garl said. He picked up a bowl of beer nuts, being careful to keep his fingers only on the napkin that sopped up the grease inside the bowl, and held it out to the guy. "Want one?"

"No, thanks," he said. He put his thumb and first two fingers around the rim of his glass.

Garl held his breath and clenched his teeth. He was ready. He knew where the kitchen was, having noticed it earlier. When the guy keeled over from the cyanide, Garl would slip out through the back delivery entrance.

"I was hoping to make a phone call," the guy said casually. "But somebody's been on it for a while."

Garl's eyes crossed from the tension. *Drink the fucking drink,* he screamed in his mind.

"Hey, let me buy you a drink," the guy said to Garl. "You've finished yours."

Garl's eyes flashed. "Sure," he said, "but only if you drink *yours* first."

The guy laughed. "That's OK. I'm in no hurry. See that clock? I'm trying to keep to one drink every three hours."

Garl heard his own teeth grinding. "See, man, I got this . . . thing about drinking with somebody. Like, I got to stay even with him. Know what I mean?"

"No, not exactly." The guy waved at the waitress. He

kept his other hand on the glass of Wild Turkey and slid it over the counter toward himself.

Then several things happened and Garl watched them as if they were in slow motion. First, the telephone rang and Melville turned his head toward it.

Then two guys in dark suits who looked like narcs or federal agents came through the front door. They looked around and one of them made for Garl immediately.

The bartender was moving toward the phone and Melville was stuck between watching him and getting up to answer it. The narc at the door, the one who had seen Garl, came toward him, his hand moving inside his suit jacket.

Garl jumped up from the stool, bounced off Melville swiveling on *his* stool, and broke for the kitchen. Someone shouted something at him, but he only heard the sound, not the words.

He pushed through the swinging doors and knocked a tray from a waiter's hands. Garl kept moving toward the delivery entrance as the tray exploded on the floor.

From the corner of his eye, Garl saw a figure in white moving toward him. Then, from out of nowhere, a black guy in a suit and real short hair swung around in front of Garl and leveled a revolver in his face.

"Freeze," the guy screamed.

Garl stopped in his tracks and heard the other agents coming up behind him. They did the usual—pushing his face against the greasy kitchen wall, shaking him down, and rooting through the vial and money they found in his pockets.

They put handcuffs on him as they read him his rights. It seemed like a long time since he had last worn handcuffs.

Chapter 31

Ladies' night at Toshi's Bar and Marina attracted the usual set of drifters, bikers, and other losers, as well as an occasional blue-haired dowager from Key West chasing half-priced Kamikazes with chardonnay. David McAdam sat patiently at a corner table as Nara, working alone, scurried from table to table taking orders and serving drinks. He hadn't seen Toshi all night and wondered where he was.

The television above the bar was turned on to a game show. David watched as a young marine in his dress blues tried to answer a question the same way as his wife. When he got it wrong, the wife, a petite blonde about half his size, beat him over the head with a cardboard sign. The studio audience laughed hysterically.

Just as she was about to let fly with another shot, the network cut in with a special report. Garl Julian, in handcuffs, was being led through a crowd outside a New York federal courtroom building. An FBI agent put his hand on top of Julian's head as he was hustled into the back of a car. Moments later Rutland Falco followed him.

David strained to hear the reporter above the barroom noise. Mostly he was concerned about being named as part of the investigation. But he needn't have worried.

Lawson and the FBI were soaking up all the credit. The reporter promised an exclusive interview with the special agent later that night.

At the table next to David, a woman maybe twenty years older than he was throwing hard looks in his direction. The rim of her brandy snifter was smeared with bright red lipstick. David looked over his shoulder to see who the lucky fellow was, but there was nothing there but a wall. He was relieved when Nara finally joined him, sipping a glass of water.

David led off with: "Hey, Nara, where's Toshi tonight?"

Nara had learned to overlook David's disregard for courtesy. He meant well but had the misfortune of lacking basic social graces. She was trying her best to do something about it.

"He's in Key Largo," she told him.

"What's he doing there?"

Nara was surprised. "He never told you about his friend, Gisela? I thought you knew."

"Toshi has a *girl*friend?"

"Mmmm. They've known each other for years. By the way, you look very nice this evening."

David ducked his head, embarrassed. "Took a shower and washed my hair before I came over. Even washed my clothes."

"Well, I'm honored! What happened at your house with the FBI?"

Nara did not see Cosmo, the hairy fisherman, at the bar raising his empty glass and obnoxiously waving it in the air. He glared at David, who ignored him.

"They left a couple hours ago. Boy, you'd think they'd at least show a little gratitude to me for finding Falco for them. Lawson, sheesh, he just about chewed my ear off over the phone, telling me the only reason

I'm not in the slammer is because it would be too embarrassing for the *Bureau*.

"But they picked up Falco after Julian spilled his guts. He's being charged with nine counts of homicide, among other things, for the Minneapolis tampering deaths. They'll be eligible for parole in about three hundred years.

"Now *I've* been ordered to stay put on California and Kettle Keys. The FBI confiscated the USDA database and threatened to take my whole system away if I don't come up to Washington and explain the enhancements I made in the database."

David looked at his scrubbed fingernails. "But I made a copy of the database without their knowing it. In fact, before I came over here I was looking at the dates of the tamperings. If you remove the Minneapolis incident from the string of daily tamperings, you start seeing an interesting pattern. I'm not sure what it means yet, but it's interesting."

"When?" Nara said.

"When what?"

"When do you have to go to Washington?"

"Oh, next week sometime. For my command performance they're rounding up all the feds involved in the investigation. Lawson'll call me when they're ready. As if I had nothing else to do.

"The FBI even wants to take me to the airport. I get the feeling they don't trust me."

"Well," Nara said, "I'm sure everyone will rest easier knowing at least one of the tamperings was solved."

"Until the next tampering," he sighed, feeling more cynical than usual. "Maybe Lawson was right, that I went after Falco out of revenge."

Nara was puzzled. "But you didn't know him, did you?"

"It wasn't revenge against Falco personally, but against his *kind*. The greedy stop-at-nothing sons of bitches like Sandy Slade at PanTech who rob you of your ideas, ruin your reputation. . . ."

David fell silent, suddenly aware that he was making a spectacle of himself. Nara knew he was frustrated, having built up so much hope that Falco was his Dr. Doom.

David looked over at the next table. The woman was gone. He hadn't seen her leave. His gaze settled on the bowl of rice crackers in the middle of the table.

"These tamperings," he said softly, "they're strange crimes, if you think about it. I mean, what does the tamperer gain from them? Except for Rutland Falco, there's no profit motive involved.

"If they are random acts, the killer doesn't even get the satisfaction of seeing his victims die. It's like dropping bombs from a B-52 two miles in the sky: killing by remote control. I think, I fantasize, that if I could just figure out what motivates this guy, then I would be closer to finding him."

Nara thought about the file in her office where she kept bizarre, chilling letters from deranged minds. How many had she received? A hundred? Two hundred?

She wondered who these people were, how they looked, and what they did for a living. Any one of them could be Dr. Doom. There were thousands of them out there, walking the streets, waiting to snap.

"I guess everybody has a theory about the motive," she said. "Mine is that the act of tampering makes whoever's doing it feel more real. In some bizarre way, the tamperer asserts himself by causing the police and media to scramble as they do.

"He thinks: *attingo ergo sum.* I tamper, therefore I am. But somehow I don't think his motivations are penetrable. They must be like a teenager's sexual fantasy—private dreams remotely connected to reality."

"That's probably it," David muttered. "Dr. Doom is just some kid."

He nervously tapped a finger on the table. "Nara, there's something going on with these tamperings, something I've been missing. I just can't quite get it."

"Listen," she said, "I ought to get back. Will I see you later?"

David didn't want her to leave. "So tell me," he said, pointing at a partition at the entrance to the bar, "what is that wall doing there? It wasn't here last time I was in the bar."

Nara turned to look at it. "It's something I asked my father to put up to keep out *leyaks*—evil spirits. The wall prevents them from entering this place. You should have one in your house."

She stood and took David by the hand. "Let me show you something else. Then I really have to get back to work."

Nara led him through the fire exit in the back and into a small outdoor courtyard that sparkled with white gravel raked into wavy patterns. So this was what the bags of gravel had been for! Set on top of the gravel, next to the door, was a wooden bowl filled with dry rice.

"We are living in bad times," Nara said solemnly. "The world is confused, out of balance. This can only mean one thing."

"Yes?"

She shrugged, as if resigned to the role of bearer of

bitter news. "We are in a terrible phase of Siva. He cre-
ates the rhythms by which all life flows, but he is also
the Great Destroyer. He is now in a phase where he is
siding with the demons just as Vishnu, the Preserver and
Siva's counterbalance, is in a weak incarnation.

"Siva is very unpredictable. I am fearful, David, that
he is now taking on the aspect of the hunter who delights
in killing his prey and dancing around, awash in blood.

"This is a temple I have built to appease him. The rice
is a sacrifice. So far my prayers have protected us—you,
my father, and me."

"Speaking of sacrifices," David said, "I noticed my
stock of booze has disappeared. I hope you put it to good
use."

"That's poison and you know it," Nara said sharply.
"You promised me you'd get rid of it. I don't particularly
like playing Molly Hatchet for you."

"Who?"

As David and Nara argued in the fading sunlight, a
pair of headlights on a truck flashed across the parking
lot, illuminating the outlines of two figures sitting in a
sedan. The FBI was still at it.

The lights went out and Toshi climbed out of his truck
and went inside.

"I have to get back," Nara said. "You can stay here
and pray if you like."

"Uh, I'll join you." To David, Nara was a walking co-
nundrum: a Bryn Mawr summa in philosophy and
physics who practiced arcane Balinese traditions. He
caught a heady whiff of perfume as he followed her back
into the bar.

Inside, they found an ugly scene developing as
Cosmo, in a drunken rage, was stalking Toshi, screaming
at him for neglecting his customers, meaning himself.

Toshi, flustered, hurried behind the bar, fumbling with his apron strings. Cosmo snatched a beer bottle and smashed it on the bar, spraying glass in all directions.

"Hey!" David shouted from deep in his diaphragm. "There was a deposit on that bottle."

Cosmo spun around to face David. He began to slowly wave the jagged bottle like a street fighter with a knife.

"You hide behind a woman," the fisherman spat with contempt. He slurred his words like Zorba. "Maybe I cut her too."

Cosmo came toward them, weaving like a punch-drunk boxer. His thick hair beetled over his eyes and his face. David bent down at the waist, as if bowing, and started in a dead run across the bar room.

The faces of the barflies flashed by as he picked up speed and then slammed into Cosmo, driving his head into his ribs. David heard a cracking sound and they tumbled together through Nara's new partition.

Before he blacked out, David thought: that wall really didn't keep out the bad spirits.

He awoke in a strange room. Candlelight flickered across threatening faces leering from the walls. Tiny figures with many arms seemed to dance around his head.

His head . . . it throbbed with the intensity of the worst hangover he could ever imagine, with a sinus headache thrown in for good measure.

David felt a hand lightly touching his shoulder. He looked up at Nara encased in the dark, a twist of candlelight revealing alternately one of her eyes or her wan smile.

This was her room, he realized. The faces on the wall

were from her collection of Balinese masks and shadow puppets, the figurines representing Hindu gods.

He turned toward Nara on the bed. "Did the bull manage to win that last bullfight?" he asked. He vaguely remembered hearing a siren and watching Cosmo being carried out on a stretcher.

"Don't talk," Nara whispered. Slowly, quietly, she came toward him. David did not move as she nuzzled her face against the area between his neck and shoulder. She leisurely moved her face toward face and began rubbing her right cheek against his left one.

Nara reversed cheeks, caressing her left one over his right. She alternated strokes, right against left, left against right. Each of her movements was carefully deliberate, beautifully, painfully slow.

As Nara's head turned side to side, her lips brushed over his, leaving traces of exotic tastes that filtered to his tongue. David lost count of the number of times she stroked him this way, aware only of the roar of blood in his ears and below his belt.

David's hands found her robe and he tried to slide it off. "No," she said, holding his wrists, "you shouldn't touch my clothes."

He shrugged, yielding to the strange customs, the ritual that governed her actions in even this, the most private of moments. Nara shrugged off the robe, her golden-brown skin glowing in the candlelight.

In the excitement of the moment, David's knowledge of the operation of his belt somehow lapsed. He fumbled helplessly as Nara giggled in the shadows. Finally, losing buttons and his hard-on, he was naked.

David tried out Nara's cheek stroke on her. Giggling, she pulled away.

"Your beard," she laughed, "it tickles. Let me do it."

She started up again and moaned a soft sigh or sighed a soft moan, he wasn't sure which. He felt heat flush his skin, spreading from his chest and down to his lap. They wrapped themselves around each other, forming a single charged integrated circuit.

With what sounded like a hurricane in his ears, David heard something else, but could not make out what it was. He listened: it was Nara's laughter.

They lay silently for several minutes. David looked around the room.

"Nara?"

"Yes, David?"

"Why do you have a poster of Muhammed Ali on your wall?"

She smiled. "If it was on the floor it might get dirty."

David snorted.

"A few years ago," she began, "I saw an interview of Ali on television. Barbara Walters, I think. Anyway, Ali was asked to explain his philosophy on boxing.

"He said that whenever he was in the boxing ring, he divided the ring up into zones. In his mind, I mean. Some zones he called his safety zones, where he knew he could return if he got into trouble.

"Then there were the danger zones where his style of boxing was less effective. His lateral movement, shuffling, even rope-a-dope suffered in these areas. These he made a point to stay out of unless he had to go into them for some specific reason.

"He said he was in the danger zones more often than not during his fight with Joe Frazier. I assume he meant his first fight with Frazier, the one he lost.

"So, Ali formed the boxing ring into what Huizinga calls the 'consecrated spot.' This is an area like a stage or a church altar where special rules apply. The area tolerates only its own kind of absolute order. It is this order—ephemeral and beautiful in an imperfect and unstructured world—that I so admire.

"And that's why I keep that poster on my wall."

"Oh."

Neither of them spoke for several minutes until David said, "Nara?"

"Yes," she said sleepily.

"Was it my imagination or were you using only your left hand a few minutes ago?"

"When we were making love, you mean?"

"Yeah."

She rolled over on her side, facing him. "It's a Balinese custom," she explained. "We use our right hands for eating, and only the left can be used when making love."

"Oh." He lay quietly for a moment. "When was the last time you did it?"

"Did what?" She wanted him to say it and he knew it.

"Make love," he finally said.

"My sophomore year at Bryn Mawr, with a Swarthmore boy, a senior. It was my first time."

"How was it?"

"OK. But not as good as with you. When was your last time?"

He laughed. "You know, I honestly can't remember. It must have been with Caroline, but I haven't seen her in, gosh, five or six years."

"Is she your wife?"

"Was. Last time I heard from her, she had given up being a goddess to her cult and was selling real estate in Southern California. I feel like I've been an Untouchable."

Nara smiled, nearly asleep. "You were simply in a state of nonaction. I was untouchable until yesterday."

"Huh? What do you mean?"

Her voice was fading. "I finished my period yesterday. According to Hindu law, mourners and menstruating women are considered impure, untouchable.

"But don't worry," she added. "I'm on the pill. I've been planning this since I saw you in the bar the first time."

And then her breathing grew heavy and steady. She was asleep.

David watched as the shadow of one of Nara's Siva statues was projected five times its size on the wall. In the restless candlelight the eight arms of the Great Destroyer turned like spokes on a gear.

As David watched them spin hypnotically, he felt a charge of electricity in some primitive part of his brain.

"Yes, of course," he whispered. A moment of enlightenment, like the way Einstein must have felt, riding the streetcars of Berne, fitting together the puzzle of space and time.

David dressed quietly and went outside. Along the shallows of Kettle Key the sounds of birds, insects, and frogs were incredibly loud, almost overwhelming. They reminded him of heavy machinery in PanTech factories. The intensity and repetition of the noise of motors and assembly lines, with the overlay of echoes and p.a. pages, neutralized sensation, drowned out thought. He felt momentarily disoriented, unsure of where he was.

He began to walk the short beach beyond the marina, trying to collect his thoughts. All along, he had felt something was missing in his analysis of the tamperings, that some connection had been overlooked. There was so much information on the case, so many variables, that he hadn't really looked carefully at the *timing* of the tamperings.

That is, until this evening when the FBI had gone and David could look over the computer files again. With Falco and Julian out of the picture, he could now eliminate the Minneapolis ice cream tamperings from the investigation.

He called up information in the database on all the tamperings and then isolated those involving dairy products. He wrote a quick program that produced this summary:

Date	Location	Number of Victims Discovered	Cause of Death
March 5	Dundalk, MD	1	hydrogen cyanide
March 6	Dundalk, MD	1	hydrogen cyanide
March 6	Dundalk, MD	2	hydrogen cyanide
March 8	Dundalk, MD	1	hydrogen cyanide
April 2	Newark, NJ	2	sodium cyanide
April 3	Elizabeth, NJ	1	sodium cyanide
April 3	Rahway, NJ	4	sodium cyanide
April 4	Newark, NJ	3	sodium cyanide
April 4	Linden, NJ	1	sodium cyanide
April 4	Jersey City, NJ	2	sodium cyanide
April 18	Minneapolis, MN	3	potassium cyanide
April 18	Minneapolis, MN	5	potassium cyanide
April 19	Minneapolis, MN	3	potassium cyanide
May 1	Rochester, NY	1	potassium cyanide

David stared at the summary for two hours before he deleted the data on the Minneapolis tampering. That left three dairy tamperings, each in a different state and each involving a different kind of cyanide.

Elegant variation.

What the summary didn't show was that milk had been poisoned in each one.

But the *dates*, that was the interesting part. With the

Minneapolis dates out of the way, David could see a pattern emerging.

He was assuming things Lawson would have laughed at. First, that one person—Dr. Doom, the real one this time—was responsible for all the milk tamperings. Two, that the actual poisonings themselves happened only once in each location rather than several times. And three, that most of the victims bought the milk and brought it home, but didn't drink it for a while, which would account for the variations in the times of death.

David checked a calendar: the dates did not correspond to the phases of the moon or to any astronomical phenomenon he could discern.

Something else was at work, some other force was driving Dr. Doom. But David could not perceive what it could be.

Until now. Nara's remark about her menstrual period was the key that had unlocked a drawer in the Chinese cabinet. A piece of the puzzle was now in his hands.

He looked back at his own footprints on the beach behind him as a wave seeped forward and erased them. He bent down and took a handful of wet sand and squeezed it in his fist, water dribbling out.

He spoke to Dr. Doom:

We are probably not very different from each other. We are both governed by the same physical laws, our bodies are affected by the same chemical and electrical processes. You eat, sleep, grasp, feel heat and cold as I do.

You had parents, perhaps brothers and sisters. You grew up, experiencing pain and triumph. You have sat in rooms and walked on streets.

We may even like the same kind of music, share a dis-

like for crowds, appreciate a good joke. We have our
fears, memories, and hopes. How different can we be?

He closed his eyes. The picture of Carla Moon's
young face floated through his mind, and the chokes and
shrieks of the creatures in the darkness became the cries
of the now nineteen victims of Dr. Doom.

They told him to open his eyes. He opened them.

The mask covering Dr. Doom's face had fallen away.
The face was much smoother, softer than he had imagined. It was that of a woman.

Chapter 32

The tampering epidemic was causing a huge increase in the work load of many of the regulatory agencies of the federal government. Congress was inundated with letters and calls from a fearful public demanding action. In its usual fashion, Congress steered the complaints toward the agencies.

Besides the FBI, offices of the Food and Drug Administration, the Bureau of Alcohol, Tobacco, and Firearms of the Department of Treasury, and the Environmental Protection Agency were ordered to beef up their inspections.

The most beleaguered was the Department of Agriculture. Within the USDA, the Agricultural Marketing Service had responsibility for programs to insure the quality and safety of the nation's milk supply.

One such program granted USDA approval to certain dairy plants around the country. Approval was given only after a plant passed at least two unannounced inspections a year. The inspections covered all aspects of dairy production and processing.

Participation in the program was voluntary. In fact, dairy plants sought USDA approval so that grocery stores, wholesalers, and others would buy their products. The buyers counted on the USDA inspections as a marketing device, a way of reassuring their customers that the products they bought were independently tested and upholding the image of milk as pure and wholesome.

The USDA inspected many kinds of dairy products, including butter, cheese, and ice cream. It also examined so-called specialty items like yogurt and dip.

The USDA also examines the raw product from which these products are made. That raw product is milk.

The USDA inspections program was run out of Washington and through a national field office in Glen Ellyn, Illinois. Most inspections were done at the local level and by the Glen Ellyn office. When inspection loads got heavy, the Washington staff helped out by taking on some of the visits to the dairy plants.

In the past three to four months, one of the Washington staff members pulled into the inspection program was Iris Butler, Ph.D.

Butler's office was in the complex of Dairy Division offices on the second floor of the South Agriculture Building. She had a number of things to read and initial before she could leave for the day. Having come in early that morning, she wanted to go through some of the paperwork piling up in her in-box. She was anxious to leave before lunch—she had a good deal of driving ahead of her.

The most important document for her attention was the one on top of the pile. It was marked "URGENT: SIGNATURE REQUIRED." Butler knew what it was before looking at it. She had been working on it for months. It was the newly revised listing of dairy plants subscribing to the USDA Salmonella Surveillance Program.

A salmonella alert had been issued for a number of southern states. Salmonella bacilli festered in inadequately pasteurized milk and could cause typhoid in humans.

The names of the dairy plants in the salmonella program were as familiar to her as the names of customers to a good salesman. Butler had visited several of the plants and run white gloves over their equipment.

She checked the list one more time before signing off on it.

The list would go on to Dr. Stefan Kramer, her supervisor and director of the Dairy Division. When she finished reviewing the list, Butler drew a pen from the cup on the desktop and signed on the top of the title page.

She returned the pen to the cup. Always the inspector, she apprised her desk. Counterclockwise were the cup of pens, ballpoint and felt-tipped, a cup of sharpened pencils (number 2.5), in-box, digital clock, out-box, pad, and "current" file. Each object on the desk was in its proper place, as if it filled a space only it could occupy.

Iris Butler did not like nameplates and did not have one on her desk, even though it was common practice in the division to do so.

She placed the signed list in her out-box. The next item for her attention was the latest postings of inspection assignments for June. The postings were never released until two weeks before the first inspection of each month. The field inspectors grumbled that they never had enough time to prepare for the travel expected of them.

But there was nothing to be done about that. The list came down to her, through Kramer, from the Secretary's office. It was a new policy, intended to sharpen the inspection process, as the departmental literature boasted. Butler knew better: the policy was to mollify Congress.

The postings arrived in a sealed envelope marked

"CONFIDENTIAL." Butler felt the contents, thicker than last month's.

She opened the top drawer of the desk and removed her letter opener. Her eyes rested on its serrated edge. A flick of the wrist and the envelope would be cut.

"Dr. Butler?"

She looked up quickly. Standing over her was Stefan Kramer, his hands fumbling in his pockets. He pulled out a handkerchief and blew his nose.

"Are you busy?" he said.

She frowned and tilted her head, resigned to the interruption. Kramer sat down in one of two matching chairs in front of the desk.

"I've just come from Tonnesen's office," he said. Rolf Tonnesen was administrator for the Agricultural Marketing Service and the highest authority Kramer ever came in contact with at the department.

"You may have heard about the shake-up going on over at the FDA. They're under the gun like the rest of us, but didn't do well in the budget wrangling this year."

Kramer fingered his horn-rimmed glasses and adjusted his fly-blown wool tie over a stain on his shirt. Butler could see his eyes on her capillary hemangioma, a port-wine mark on her neck and jaw she had had since birth.

"The upshot is, they need warm bodies. They're behind in their inspections and have put out a general request to the regulatory agencies for voluntary assistance. It fell in Tonnesen's lap here."

Butler fidgeted in her seat, wary of what was coming.

Kramer went on. "Tonnesen brought in all the division directors for a brainstorming session. Helen Sykes had to come back from a vacation at Bethany Beach to attend.

"Anyway, we want to help the FDA out, even if it

might crimp us a bit. So, we've been ordered to donate, if you will, personnel to the FDA, just to get them over the hump. They especially need people like you— Ph.D.'s in food engineering—to head up some of their teams."

He paused to look at Butler. She wasn't about to help him out.

"So, I'm offering them two people from Dairy: Glenn Dewitt and you."

The letter opener made a sharp clattering sound on the desk when it fell from Butler's hands. Heads turned in the office.

This is it, she thought bitterly, the government version of a pink slip. Farmed out on loan.

"Keep in mind that this is only temporary," he said, his voice syrupy. "There will be no reductions in salary, and we'll hold your slot here until you're finished at the FDA.

"You'll be assigned to the Product Surveillance Division. It's a good group, I know the director. You can start on Monday."

Butler's face remained rigid. "Why me, Dr. Kramer?"

He let out a long breath, the poor world-weary bureaucrat.

"It's that old thing," he said, trying to be as offhand as his coldness would allow. "Somebody's got to do it. And it might be good for you, a tonic if you will."

"A tonic?"

He pulled on his tie. "Well, Butler . . ."

Butler?

". . . in the past three of four months your performance has been, well, lackluster. Not up to your usual standards at all. I'm still waiting on that salmonella assessment. And your absenteeism has been well above the divisional average."

As I sat there behind my desk, I watched as words drained from Kramer's mouth like sanious pus from a running sore.

The air around him was thick with cancer cells. Mushroom clouds of them drifted toward me. I braced myself for the contact.

I felt my entire system shudder as they hit me, leaching through my skin toward the veins. Even as I backed away, the cancer cells kept up their attack.

And later, I was ravaged and weak. Kramer had left but his cancer lingered behind.

The wolf of the red day, prowling the high meadows, pauses to turn his nose downward to gather in the scent carried on the wind. From the scent he evaluates his prey, its strengths and weaknesses. The wolf knows his prey before seeing it.

He sets off toward the prey in an easy lope. He sees no reason to hurry. His prey is limping.

It is stricken with cancer.

Chapter 33

Iris Butler's mother lode was stored in the most innocuous of places—the refrigerator. It was well hidden there but, more important, well preserved by the cold at the lowest setting. She kept it in three reinforced aluminum bags inside a cookie tin at the back of the bottom shelf.

The tin box was cold to the touch, having been there for weeks. Inside were layers of foil to be peeled away to get to the treasure. Butler removed it carefully over a large piece of seamless plastic.

The fine white crystals glistened in the bright kitchen light. This was the instrument, she mused, the medium for the arrival of a new age. A vaccine for the most ravaging disease—cancer. Four kilograms of pure potassium cyanide.

Butler put on surgical gloves, withdrew three syringes from her overnight bag, and pulled back the plungers. She set the syringes down and went about preparing the solution. With a sterilized eyedropper, she squeezed distilled water into a stainless steel bowl.

Then carefully, carefully, she eased a measuring spoon into the package and withdrew enough for her standard 300 milligrams. The crystals were sightly settled from packing and stayed firmly in the spoon.

She tapped the spoon once over the bowl, and the

crystals cascaded like an avalanche of fine snow over a clear mountain lake. They quickly absorbed the water and began to melt into solution. A few crystals floated on the surface. Butler stirred them in with a sterilized glass rod.

The syringes lay quietly on the linen cloth spread out on the kitchen counter. Their needles extended beyond the room, stretching with a consciousness of their own around corners, through windows, and into the pulpy core of the human machine.

Butler then fed the cyanide solution to the hungry syringes. The plungers filled up quickly.

and aching Pleasure nigh, turning to poison while the bee-mouth sips.

She would put the syringes to work soon. The time was drawing near.

The hospital was still when she arrived later that night. She had been to the hospital every night that week, except for the night she had spent in West Virginia. Deep caverns of space engulfed her as she padded down the hallway toward the intensive-care ward. A distant sound of a janitor's wet mop slapping time on the floor punctured the silence.

An old woman with a mustache and a black dress was on duty at intensive-care reception. Butler had to get past her to get to Mother's room. She hung back in a doorway until the receptionist stepped away from her station. Then she bustled past, keeping her head down and eyes to the floor.

Mother's room was dark, the only light coming from the life-support equipment hovering like mourners around her head. On a table in a corner was a bouquet of red chrysanthemums Iris had sent. Someone had put them in a specimen bottle. Whoever had done it no doubt had assumed Mother would never wake up to see them there.

A red light twinkled on one of the life-support machines, registering each fluctuation in Mother's blood gases. The green electrocardiogram signal was a thin strand holding onto Mother, keeping her from being sucked into the Beyond. An oxygen tube was taped to her nose, and an IV line fed into her arm.

The cancer had attacked her brain and taken root in her spinal cord. It then had invaded everything, eating her alive.

Another one, a victim of her own existence. The cells of her body were a firing squad of billions of cocked guns ready to go off at any time. And now those cells that had protected her, sustained her life, had turned on her, become venomous. She was no more than a sack of chemicals ready to explode.

Look at you there, lying helpless in the dark. It is lonely, isn't it? You'll get used to it. You may even come to like the loneliness, as I did.

Now you can feel how I felt when you threw me to the wolf. Mr. Gough, the wolf of the red day. Your husband. My stepfather.

He was a monster and you, you never kept him away from me. You just let him have me. You stayed back and pretended nothing was wrong, everything was fine.

You were terrified of being left alone, like Papa did to you. So you let him have me whenever he wanted. You just disappeared into the parlor, closed the door, and turned up the volume on the television. That way you didn't have to hear my cries or, worse, his grunts of plea-sure.

You never had to know his wolf smell and the awful look in his eyes as he had his way. His hands, huge and rough, seemed to come from all directions at once.

And after, when he was done, the awful eyes avoided mine as he prepared to lumber away, back to his wolf's hole, whispering a vague threat in my ear before he left.

I was helpless as you are now. I had no place left to hide. He came at me and held me in his jaws, forcing me to look into his horrible mouth. I was just a sick little girl, thirteen years old.

It was because of the wolf that the red days came. They came like cancer, exploding from inside. Every month they exploded, hitting me with the fury of a wild animal. They haven't stopped since.

So now it's your turn to be helpless, to be at someone else's mercy. But, you see, there is no mercy, only the sheer dumb implacability of nature.

Where was the "free will"?

Who to hate? What to sue for? How to get even?

Butler watched the weak electrocardiogram signal, fluttering like a suffocating moth under a bell jar. Only drugs and machines kept Mother alive now. It was all rather predictable—tedious, really. Iris's main concern was staying clear of Mother, keeping herself from being infected more than she already was by being in the room with her.

She studied the life-support equipment around Mother, giving special attention to the IV system. It was a standard system, with a bag of electrolyte solution hanging at the top feeding nutrition through a tube directly into one of the main veins in her forearm. The tube was attached to the vein through a cannula insertion.

Butler fingered the clear tubing from the electrolyte bag. She was looking for access to the tube. Her heart was beating so hard it felt like it might jump out of her chest.

She followed the tubing until she came to a rubber stopcock. Connected to the stopcock was another tube leading to an instrument to measure pressure in her veins. No access there.

Butler searched farther down the tube. The closer she got to Mother, the more vulnerable she was to the rabid metastasis of her cancer. She came to another connection, this one a piggyback junction leading to another IV bag that permitted the nurses to administer other fluids.

Where was the way into the main line?

Butler's heart skipped a beat as she came to a third stopcock. This one had no connecting line. It had an insert for a hypodermic needle. This was it, her access to the main IV.

She turned off the stopcock to the electrolyte bag, cutting off the flow of liquid. Then she drew out one of the loaded syringes from her bag and inserted a plunger into the back of the vial. Working swiftly and surely, she pushed the needle into the third stopcock.

With her thumb she pressed on the plunger and, mesmerized, her eyes followed the cyanide solution as it streamed out of the needle and dripped down the tube.

Iris's legs felt rubbery, her head light. She steadied herself and let her eyes close. Alarms were sounding on the life-support machines, but she remained calm, languid. Her body felt heavy, her mind incredibly lucid. She saw each object in the room as sharply defined, as occupying a distinct space only it could occupy.

She tried to make herself leave, but had difficulty doing so. She had never been so close to a subject before and felt an odd attachment to it, as a child does to its feces. But she also felt empty, as if the wolf of the red day had not been fully appeased.

Iris moved slowly, like rising after a deep sleep. She reluctantly left the room, pushed through a door to a stairwell, and forced her heavy legs to carry her down the stairs.

She knew, as she had never known anything before in her life, that she could never go back to the shadows as before. Being this close to a subject was intoxicating, and she knew she could never again be satisfied with a distance between her subjects and her. She was willing to take risks now, to emerge from the darkness.

"I think this will be a rather simple matter," said the young lawyer with the spotty mustache sitting across from Iris. "No more painful than it has to be."

He adjusted his tie, a green and orange monstrosity fortunately covered by his vest, and opened the folder on his desk. Thick, ragged sheafs of paper were stacked high on the desk and the credenza behind it.

The walls of the office were covered with a shiny wallpaper of a tacky zigzag pattern. Long strips of it were peeling from the wall around an air duct. Cigarette burns pocked the yellow carpeting.

The view from the window of a mini-mall parking lot was slightly obscured by a wilted potted ficus whose curled brown leaves littered the floor around it.

Iris had just come from the funeral home where a man reeking of gin unceremoniously had handed over the brass urn containing Mother's ashes. She had brought the urn to her meeting with the lawyer, hoping it might encourage him to hurry things along.

Iris wondered: why don't people's possessions go

with them when they die, just disappear, and spare others the tedium of cleaning up their messes?

"Your mother left no will and you were the only relative we were able to locate," he said. "Do you have any idea where the other children are at the present time?"

"No."

"Hmm," he intoned and returned to the folder. "I see the estate consists primarily of a house in Oklahoma. Strange she didn't sell it when she came east."

"Hmmm," she said in reply.

He is probing me, looking for an opening to attack me as a neglectful child. He will have to do much better than that to get me to reveal anything.

Mother never sold the house because she expected to return to it someday. She said she wanted a place where all her children could visit if the world got too heavy for them.

In the dense fog of her medicated mind she completely forgot that her precious daughters had never once called or visited her since the day they moved out more than thirty years ago. I'm the one who stayed behind in Lawton all those years. I'm the one who took care of her, brought her east to be closer to me. I'm the one who paid her bills, visited her every week, took her on walks in her wheelchair while she raved madly about the wonderful food in the nursing home.

As her senility grew worse, Mother would ask me during my visits where Rose, Daisy, and Lilly were. After a while I grew tired of manufacturing excuses and just told her they were too busy to visit. But it didn't matter.

"Such sweet girls," Mother would say each time. I chewed on the insides of my mouth to keep from screaming.

I received no help whatsoever, not even so much as a

word of gratitude from my sisters or Mother for the burden they had placed on me all my life.

Now I'm the one who has to bury her.

"The court will rule on your mother's estate, but I frankly don't see any problems here. In the absence of the other heirs, you are the obvious beneficiary.

"I'll draw up the papers and set a hearing. With a little luck we can dispose of this in a month or so."

"Fine," Butler said.

"I, uh, see you have the ashes there in the urn. Do you plan to have a service?"

"Why do you ask?"

He tugged on his tie. "Well, I just thought . . . There might be some family or friends, maybe some residents of the nursing home who might wish to pay their last respects."

"I don't think so."

He shrugged, stood up, and extended his hand. "Very well, I'll give you a call when a hearing date is set."

Iris held up the urn, keeping both hands on it. She did not take his hand.

You can keep your cancer to yourself.

The receptionist, who was plucking her eyebrows with tweezers and a small mirror, never looked up as Iris left.

She crossed the street to her car in the mini-mall parking lot. Next to a video rental outlet, at one end of the row of shops, was a black dumpster.

She went straight to it, her eyes avoiding the yawning space of the parking lot and the highway beyond it. She looked around quickly, seeing no one.

With only a little bit of effort she threw the urn up into the dumpster and walked away, brushing away a layer of fine grit from her hands. She would scrub them when she got home.

* * *

After leaving the lawyer's office, Iris went home to her apartment on Capitol Hill. She rented the ground floor of a brownstone and had exclusive use of the garden out back. In the bedroom, she packed a change of clothes, toiletries, and a pair of binoculars.

Wrapped in a towel at the bottom of the bag was a small leather case. It looked like the kind used by physicians, diabetics, and well-heeled drug abusers. The case contained syringes.

It also contained vials of mercuric cyanide, a form of cyanide she had never used before.

She drove west through Washington into Georgetown and continued out MacArthur Boulevard. Just before reaching the Maryland line, Iris slowed alongside the Dalecarlia Reservoir, one of the principal sources of water for Washington and the neighboring suburbs.

The driver of the car behind her honked as she rolled by the reservoir. She parked her car, a gray Volvo, in a shady, unobtrusive spot and took in the reservoir. She sat and watched for an hour. The smooth surface of the water reflected only the blue cloudless sky.

As best as she could tell, a single chain-link fence was the only barrier around the reservoir grounds. She had already visited the McMillan, Reno, and Georgetown reservoirs around the city and kept notes on each one.

Dalecarlia looked the easiest of the four.

It would be a simple matter to cut the fence, especially there at the bottom of that slope, unseen from the road. There, no one would see her slipping through and dumping several kilograms of cyanide into the water.

She would have to do all four of them in the same day. Otherwise, the security that was sure to be added after the first reservoir was done would make subsequent work much harder.

What a multiplier effect! She could successfully inoculate thousands of subjects in a single stroke. This water was consumed by some of the most powerful people in the world. Perhaps the president himself would drink it, or even Stefan Kramer.

Iris had created a makeshift laboratory in her basement to manufacture cyanide. But she would have to make more cyanide, much more, to realize her dreams. She might have to acquire additional equipment for the laboratory, storage facilities.

Perhaps she could take out a loan at the bank.

But it would have to wait. All things happened in time.

She started the car and continued out MacArthur Boulevard toward the Beltway. From there she would head to Takoma Park, where her subjects—Tom Harmon and his family—were now preparing to move to their new home in West Virginia.

Iris glanced at her bag on the passenger seat. Now was the Harmons' time.

Chapter 34

"Jeremy, I'm afraid you're just going to have to find another home for Boris," Tom Harmon said.

"But, Dad . . ." Jeremy whined, not looking his father in the eye.

Tom set down the case of beef jerky he was loading into the truck. He had a tendency to stand stoop-shouldered, so he made an effort to stand up straight.

"Now, son, we've talked about this, remember? There's no room for pets in our new house in West Virginia. Besides, Boris would have a hard time making the trip we have in front of us."

Jeremy held up the box turtle, wisely closed up in its shell. "So what should I do with him?"

Tom scowled. "Haven't you learned anything I taught you about independent thinking? Where we're going, I'll be counting on you for resourcefulness, maturity. Can't one of your friends take him, somebody with a big yard?"

Suddenly Jeremy's face lit up. "I know. I can let him go in the woods next to the old pigeon-racing club. There's plenty of places to hide there."

"There you go."

Jeremy took off toward the woods behind their house. Tom was proud of his boy, coming up with a natural solution to the problem by returning the pet to the wild. He hadn't been too pleased when Jeremy had brought the turtle home one day last week. Keeping a pet was just another version of the master-slave relationship humans imposed on nature.

Tom and Chloe had tried to instill in their children some reverence for nature by eating only organic food and giving up air conditioning. They let their yard grow out naturally, without cutting or fertilizing it, even though it had cost them a lawsuit with the neighborhood association.

Sure, there were times when they'd catch Jeremy underneath his bed eating a Twinkie or Melanie drinking out of a polystyrene product, but they could forgive that. They had realized long ago that as long as they remained in what was mistakenly called civilization, they would never be quite safe from inorganic toxins.

Tom went back inside to get the last of their things. Chloe was seated on the floor nursing Shane.

"Tom, where's Melanie?" Chloe asked him. "She hasn't cleaned out her closet yet."

"Dunno," Tom said. He hadn't seen their eldest since breakfast. "I'll look around."

He strained under the weight of the four remaining boxes, three of canned milk and one of ammunition. As he loaded them onto the truck, a motorcycle rumbled to a stop in front of the house. Tom watched as Melanie hopped off the back. The cycle, driven by Bob or Ed or whoever it was this week, roared off, leaving a trail of carbon monoxide in its wake.

"Melanie, just a minute," Tom said, putting his hand on her shoulder. "Your mother's been looking for you. She asked you a week ago to pack up your things, and you haven't even started on your closet."

She shrugged off his hand and walked silently into the house. Tom held back, saying nothing, and thinking: this will all change soon. No more punk music and black clothes and blatant hostility. Getting back to nature would purify them all, wash away the sins of civilization.

While Chloe and the kids got ready, Tom spread out a map over the hood of the truck and studied it. He had made the trip twice before but never with the kids along. It was about an hour's drive from Takoma Park to the West Virginia border, and then another three or four to Union Center, including pit stops.

Tom would take Jeremy in the truck and Chloe would follow in the Bronco with Melanie and Shane. He was anxious to get on the road.

As Tom concentrated on the map, he did not notice the gray Volvo parked at the other end of the block. From time to time, gloved hands would raise a pair of binoculars to the driver's eyes.

Tom went inside to round up everyone. Nobody was around; the house was quiet, bare, stripped to its essentials. And then it hit him: *this was it.* They were really going to do it, burn their bridges. Tom felt conflicting sensations of giddiness in his head and a dull nausea in his stomach. Under his shirt he felt the money belt that contained all of their savings. A sound of someone crying came from upstairs.

Melanie slammed her door when he looked in on her.

Control, he commanded himself, *center the emotions and contain them.*

He felt a sharp pain in his gut, followed by a slow burning sensation. His ulcer was acting up again.

He patted his shirt pockets and found the package of enteric-coated peppermint oil capsules and another of deglycyrrhizinated licorice tablets prescribed by his homeopath.

Tom chewed a couple of tablets and swallowed the capsules without water.

The crying was coming from the bathroom. Inside, Chloe was pulling a mud-soaked shirt over Jeremy's head, the boy sobbing and out of breath. It was then that Tom noticed the tracks in the hallway.

"He fell in the pond letting his turtle go," Chloe said. She had the water running in the bathtub that they had scrubbed clean for the walk-through this afternoon by the new owners of the house.

"Boris died, Dad," Jeremy wailed, his face and hair coated with muck. "I tried to save him, but he drowned in the pond."

Shit, Tom thought, and then Shane started crying in the next room.

Heading west on Route 1 in central West Virginia, Tom navigated the truck around another hairpin turn. He eased up on the accelerator but did not brake. It was raining cats and dogs.

"Can't you hurry up?" Melanie pleaded, crossing her legs. At their last rest stop, a diner, she had insisted on having coffee—three cups—over Tom and Chloe's objections. Now she was struggling to hold her bladder. The rain didn't help matters much.

Melanie had stayed off to herself at the diner, sitting sullenly at a separate table, listening to some heavy metal garbage on her Walkman. Tom wanted to go over to her and try to talk her out of her funk, but Chloe said it would only make matters worse. Melanie was just going through something, Chloe explained, nothing more than passive aggression about their move.

Melanie and Jeremy switched cars for the last leg of the trip. He was getting car sick and needed to lie down on the backseat of the Bronco. That put Melanie in the truck with Tom. The two of them exchanged maybe a dozen words during their three-hour ride together.

"It can't be far," Tom said, peering into the twilight through the rain running over the windshield. Melanie couldn't hear him for the Walkman. The road straightened out and Tom checked the rearview mirror on the side of the truck. Chloe was still with him. Good girl.

He could see the Bronco, with its vanity plate that read "SECURE," a vestige of the business he had just sold. Next to it on the fender, a sticker read: "ESCAPE TO WILD AND WONDERFUL WEST VIRGINIA." There was also one on the bumper.

Something told Tom that he was near the house, Box Number 7 on Route 1, Union Center. Maybe it was the bridge over the swelling creek they just passed over or the split rail fence that followed the road on the right. He had been there only twice before in February when he purchased the house. This had to be it.

Up ahead he saw a mailbox next to what looked like a slight break in the brush: a road. Tom slowed down and hit his bright lights.

"Lucky seven, lucky seven," he chanted, hopeful, nearly desperate. Melanie recrossed her legs. He pulled up next to the box.

"This is it," he said triumphantly, and flicked his brights on and off. Chloe did the same.

Saplings and thick weeds grown up on the road gave way as the truck lurched forward. Melanie held her breath as the taut suspension on the truck bumped and squeaked over the potholed road. The rain was letting up and shredded clouds opened to let the evening sun come through.

The house was not yet in view, and Tom thought it a good idea to try to talk to Melanie, get her to open up with him a little. All of them would be in pretty close quarters in their new place, and it would probably be a good idea to call a truce and mend fences here and now. He had to catch her when she turned off the Walkman to turn over the cassette.

"Melanie," he said. "I want you to leave the Walkman off a second."

"What? Why?"

"I want to talk."

She let out a long hissing sound and folded her arms tight. But she left the damn machine off.

"A move is never easy," he said, trying to choose his words carefully. "I remember moving from Pittsburgh to Washington when I was a kid, having to get used to a new neighborhood, to make new friends. I didn't like it at all at first. But you know what happened?"

Melanie sat stone silent. Her long, straight hair covered her face from him.

"It worked out," Tom said. "I made new friends, even made the baseball team at school. It's going to be hard on you and all of us at first, but I promise things will get better.

"I want you, all of us, to be safe. Coming out here, giving up our old lives, means that we're free of things we only thought were important. I want you to think of our new place as a castle, protecting us against the world."

The truck jerked heavily and a low branch scraped across the roof. "All the time, it's only what you and Mom want," Melanie said suddenly. "You never think about *us. You* wanted to come here, not me. I didn't want to do this.

"I liked where we were. I had friends and even school was OK. But you didn't like it, so we have to move. You had to drag us way out here, where nobody is. My friends will never come and visit, they think this is stupid anyway. And no concerts will ever come here."

Tom gripped the wheel, trying to keep the truck on the road. "That's exactly my point. You might miss your friends and concerts at first, but we'll find new things to do out here. How about giving it a chance?"

Melanie wasn't listening to him. Instead she was craning her neck toward something out her window. "What's that over there?" she said.

Several yards down the slope next to the road was a family of seven, eight hulking natural gas rigs, bobbing like feeding chickens. Each was about ten feet high and made out of heavy steel. The pumps were actually down in the ground operated by a motor and beam above that moved up and down. The earth and trees around them had been torn up by bulldozers.

"What *are* they?"

"Pumps," Tom grumbled angrily. "Natural gas pumps. A lot more of them than when I was here three months ago."

"But what are they doing here?"

Tom let out a long breath. "We own about a hundred acres of property here. I got a good price on it because in West Virginia you can own land but not what's under it. It's called mineral rights."

"You mean these pumps belong to someone else?"

"That's right."

"And they can put as many here as they want?"

Tom shifted into a lower gear as the truck descended a

ridge toward the house. "Not exactly. They're supposed to consult us before they do."

"Oh."

The truck got stuck in a puddle, and Tom found some rocks along the service road and worked them under the tires. When they made it to the house, Melanie snatched the keys and dashed inside. Chloe pulled up in the Bronco, spattered with mud.

The house, a five-bedroom contemporary with solar panels built into the roof, looked smaller than Tom remembered, and the yard around it where he planned to plant vegetables was grown over with weeds. Chloe got out and stretched.

"Home sweet home," Tom said.

"Dad! Mom!" Melanie shouted from the house.

Tom and Chloe rushed inside. Chloe squealed as a huge cobweb snagged her ear and wrapped around her face. As he ran toward Melanie's voice, Tom first noticed the green and yellow paint splashed over the house and then the windows broken clean of their panes. Every one of them.

"In here," Melanie called from the bathroom.

On entering the bathroom, Tom felt like he had been sprayed with a pesticide, the smell was so bad. The floors of the bathroom were smeared with excrement, the toilet stuffed with it. Someone had taken some and written a message on the wall. It was barely legible.

"Rust never sleeps," Chloe read.

On a ridge above the road leading to the house, Iris found a safe perch that gave her a splendid view of her subjects. With the binoculars she could see right through a big picture window into what appeared to be their living room.

Butler pretended not to see the flock of natural gas pumps mindlessly banging at the earth below her, a slight that would have disturbed her if she had thought about it.

Using the binoculars, she could observe the Harmons' frenzied reaction to the condition of their new home, registered in their faces. The place looked almost unlivable. But none of that mattered to her.

It is very nearly perfect. I did not see a single house or car as I followed them down that last road.

The subjects could not have seen me with their boxes piled to the ceilings of their trucks. Besides, I stayed well behind, always out of sight.

And now they are completely isolated. They are alone with me. For the first time I will be able to observe an inoculation. It is a worthy experiment.

The who, what, and where of the experiment have been solved. The only questions remaining are when and how.

Jeremy tugged on his father's arm for the third time.

"Wake up, Dad," he whispered fiercely. Tom didn't move. Jeremy turned to Melanie standing behind him and said somberly, "Maybe he's dead."

Melanie rolled her eyes in the darkness. "You dweeb, he's just tired from cleaning the house all day. Here, let me try."

She pinched her father's nose with her fingers, hard, and watched his face. Deprived of oxygen, Tom jerked violently, but Melanie hung on. He was awake in seconds.

"What's the . . . what? Melanie? What're you—?"

"Dad, shush. Listen, we heard something outside. Jeremy and I did."

Jeremy rushed forward. "Dad, somebody's been screaming outside. It's been going on for hours."

"It just started a few minutes ago," Melanie said. "It's weird, Dad."

Chloe began to stir as Tom rolled out of bed. "Stay with the baby," he said to her and went straight for his boots, parka, and shotgun. The floorboards were cold; in West Virginia everything was colder, hotter, dryer, or wetter. His muscles ached from the lifting and cleaning he had done all day.

He threw on his clothes, loaded two casings of shot into the gun, and slammed it shut.

Downstairs, he disarmed the security system he had installed, opened the back door, and trained his ears to the blackness. At first he heard nothing and then the sound floated to his ears.

It was more like many sounds: loud, purposeful, agitated. Tom thought of a crowd at a baseball game jeering the umpire. He pointed the shotgun up in the air and advanced, crouching, toward the woods.

Shadows moved against the trees along the service road. He released the safety and lowered the gun. The sound was getting louder.

"Who's there?" he challenged.

"It's us, Dad." Melanie and Jeremy.

Tom came toward them. "What are you . . . ?"

"Listen," Melanie said, and they all looked toward the sky.

Tom squinted and could make out a dark, jagged form in relief against a cloud. He smiled.

"Geese," he said. "Canadian geese flying home for the summer."

"They sure make a lot of noise," Jeremy said.

"Yeah, there must be at least a hundred in that flock," Tom replied. "They're late getting here."

He tried to imagine what it would be like to be in the flock as it flew north, to see the relentless churning of the wings and single-minded determination of the geese responding to nature's will.

"It's freezing out here," said Melanie. "I'm going inside."

Tom replaced the safety on the shotgun and drew close to Jeremy. "Melanie's not much of a nature lover," Jeremy laughed.

"She's catching on," Tom said. "We all are."

"Dad, is this home now?" Jeremy asked, needing reassurance.

"Yes it is, son," he said and slung his free arm around the boy's narrow shoulders.

Iris returned the next day and stood watch for three hours in the morning and came back in the afternoon. Her subjects worked hard cleaning and fixing their vandalized house. Through her binoculars, she studied them carefully, even taking notes on their heights and weights.

Later in the afternoon, a truck came up the roadway to the house, rattling over the potholes. Butler watched it stop in front of the house, and an old woman with white hair got out, carrying a tin box. Butler could not make out what was in it. The woman knocked on the door.

Harmon's wife came out of the house and onto the porch, her child in her arms. She and the old woman talked for a moment, and then the woman lifted the lid off the box. Mrs. Harmon made a great show of looking into the box and fawning over whatever was in it. She waved at the truck and a man got out, shuffled to the porch, and entered the house with both women.

Butler slowly drew the binoculars away from her face. She thought for several minutes. Insects pecked at her skin, but she didn't feel them.

She rolled up the neck cord of the binoculars and started on her way back to the car, hidden off the road.

She walked quickly. She had found her "how." She only needed to answer the "when."

Chapter 35

The next day Iris Butler started her assignment at the Food and Drug Administration. She took notice of the similarity between her new office and the one she had just left at the USDA. The building, the office, even the people looked the same.

Her new director was surprised to see her three days early, but was obviously happy to have her there. At least that was different. He introduced her to the staff and showed her to her desk. She spent most of her first morning filling out personnel forms. The director had them processed immediately. He was in desperate need of help and did not want to lose her.

The office cleared at lunchtime. Butler went to the assignment officer's desk and searched it for his "watch" list of food-processing plants to be inspected. She found it in a drawer and read it.

The list was foreign to her, the product and plant codes completely different from the ones she was used to seeing. But at the back of the list she found the definitions for the codes.

Her eyes widened as she read through the codes. The FDA had responsibility for inspecting many more products than the USDA. She went to the state index and found West Virginia.

There seemed to be hundreds of product listings, each presenting different opportunities and challenges for her. She read them all, assessing and discarding scenarios for the Harmons.

One inspection was for a frozen dinner plant in Charleston. She wondered how well mercuric cyanide would assimilate in a frozen host.

Somehow she could not picture the Harmons eating frozen dinners.

She had another idea, one she had gotten while watching the old woman stopping by her subjects—the Harmons. Iris had figured out what the woman had in the tin box. It was something she had made for the Harmons, a cake or some cookies. There must be hundreds of mountain women in and around Union Center who brought welcoming presents like those to newcomers. It was a fine old tradition.

Skimming through the long list, Butler found what she was looking for, a bakery in Clarksburg, not more than twenty-five miles from Union Center and her subjects. Its principal product: Golden Summer Apple Pies.

She knew precisely what to do. She would put in immediately for the Golden Summer inspection. Her supervisor had already assured her that she could do any inspection on the "watch" list.

Milk and pie. What a lovely combination.

Chapter 36

Chloe Harmon could not remember a time when she had actually looked forward to going shopping. But now, after days of digging out of the mess they now called home and dealing with her children's constant complaining, she was anxious to get out. Chloe, normally uncomfortable around people other than her family, was surprised to find herself craving contact with others.

The house had turned out to be not as bad as it had first looked. The worst thing was the smell, which they were almost rid of, thanks to hours of scrubbing. A good paint job would take care of the exterior and the windows would cost something to be fixed. The whole incident had drained Chloe of enthusiasm for coming here. But she had to keep up a brave face for the kids.

She drove into town with Melanie, their first stop the Union Center general store, run by Dorris Loftus, the sweet old woman who had brought them the German chocolate cake. Tom said Dorrie was probably just coming around looking for customers. Chloe scolded him for his cynicism.

Tom wasn't used to good neighbors and hospitality, having grown up in the city. Chloe was from a small town in Pennsylvania, and had known women like Dorrie all her life. They were the pillars of the community, arranging welcome wagons and baby showers, bringing their "best dishes" to wedding parties and funeral lunches. German chocolate cake was probably Dorrie's best dish.

Union Center wasn't much: a post office, Dorrie's store, two or three clothing shops, and a Tastee Freeze. Muddy pickup trucks roared up and down Main Street. Chloe noticed a few kids and pointed them out to a diffident Melanie. She hoped Melanie would make some friends here.

They parked the Bronco and climbed the steps to the porch.

"Oh look, honey," Chloe said, pointing to an old swing hanging from the porch roof.

Melanie screwed up her lips and said nothing.

Inside the dark store, Chloe found things she hadn't seen since she was a girl: Mary Janes and Red Hots in jars on the counter, nickel Popsicles, and original Barbie dolls, probably worth a fortune to a collector. She scooped a handful of Mary Janes out of the jar and left a dollar on top of the cash register. She smiled at a sign on the wall behind the counter that read: I'm not slow, just half fast.

She found Dorrie in the back, taking inventory of her sewing supplies. She was visibly upset about something. Chloe gently tried to get her to talk. Soon Dorrie was telling her about her set-to with the Rameesh cult.

"There was two of them in the store this morning," she said, still trembling a bit. "A boy and a girl. I've seen them before. Very nice-looking.

"They floated around a bit, looking at my gardening tools. I knew they was up to something, but I never push customers.

"Then, when nobody else was in the store, they came

up to me. Said they was interested in gardening supplies but wanted to make a deal. I'd *give* them the supplies they needed and in return they would bring in flowers every week for me to sell."

Dorris snapped a rubber band around a stack of doilies. "I told them, first, that I don't trade merchandise. Looks bad on the books.

"Second, they should try to sell to the florist and get cash. Now, I happen to know that the florist gets his flowers from a nursery in Morgantown. He's been doing business with them for years, and those Rameesh people wouldn't have a prayer trying to sell to him.

"Imagine!" Dorrie said, really into it now. "Me competing with the florist. Why, he's married to my favorite cousin."

Dorrie laughed and Chloe felt a little better. "Well, let me tell you, they didn't like that one bit. One of them, a girl, started into a fit, stomping around, calling me names and saying nasty things. Said they would boycott my store.

"I said fine, I don't need customers like you. Boy, did that set them off. I was all set to call the sheriff when they left.

"I'm sorry for going on like that. Was there something you needed help with, dear?"

"Yes, there is, actually. Whoever vandalized our house tore up the garden. I can't bring myself to understand why they would do that on top of everything else. But we're going to need more fertilizer than what we brought with us. We use the organic kind. Do you carry anything like that?"

Dorrie thought a moment. "Can't say as I do. Folks around here go for the chemicals. But I could order some for you. It'd be here in two weeks or so."

"Fine," Chloe said.

Dorrie rose slowly from the stool and led Chloe to the front of the store. Chloe looked around. Where was Melanie? she wondered.

"Terrible thing about your house," Dorrie said, searching behind the counter. "I cannot fathom what possesses people to act like animals.

"You know, I've heard that those Rameesh people are having some hard times," getting back to the subject on her mind. "Seems their leader spends money like there's no tomorrow and is pressuring the kids to sell more flowers.

"But every once in a while I'll see a new one amongst them. You can spot them right away, they ain't been programmed yet like the others. You can see in their eyes how miserable they are, but they don't dare say a word. I really feel sorry for them."

She brought out a farm catalogue and thumbed through, mumbling names of fertilizer. "Here's one called Nature's Own. Sixteen-fifty a bag and made in Morgantown. Listen, I can have my cousin bring a few bags in his truck. You'd have it in a couple days that way."

"Thanks," Chloe said. She folded her arms and rubbed them as she looked around the store. "Dorrie, have you seen my daughter, Melanie? She was here a minute ago."

"No, dear," she said, "maybe she's outside taking a stroll."

Chloe felt the hair on her nape bristle. She picked up her bag and raced toward the front door, pushing it open. Outside on the porch swing sat Melanie between two smiling clean-cut teenagers. A boy and a girl. Rameesh people.

"Melanie," Chloe said quietly, firmly. "Let's go."

"But, Mom, we're just talking."

"I'm not arguing, young lady."

Chloe took her daughter's arm and pulled her to her feet. One of the teenagers—the girl—grabbed her other arm and pulled. Melanie screamed and fell back on the swing.

The boy came up behind Chloe and took hold of her arms. She spun around, surprising him, and kicked him hard in the shin with her clog. He crumpled to the ground.

Chloe picked up her sobbing daughter, led her to the Bronco, and got her inside. She locked the doors and fumbled for the keys.

Just then the Rameesh girl appeared next to her at the window. She mashed her face against the window, her face contorted in a grotesque mask. She made animal noises, flicked her tongue in and out like a snake. Melanie screamed.

Chloe finally found the key and jammed it into the ignition. The Bronco started up and Chloe floored the accelerator, grinding back gravel.

"We'll come visit you, Melanie," the girl cried as the Bronco pulled away. "Soon."

Chloe held Melanie all the way home.

Chapter 37

A car was driving me out onto the dangerous open road. It was taking me to a place beyond these mountains where I could do my work.

The lines on the highway were faded. The shoulders were soft. There were no clear boundaries to contain the awful potential of this vast openness.

Up here, high in the mountains, the road was a thin strand suspended in the air. As I went higher, the drop on both sides got steeper, more menacing. Around each sharp curve I braced myself for the wolf of the red day, mouth open and thirsty for blood, to be waiting there in the middle of the road.

The best I could do was hold onto the wheel and keep my mind from the thought of the explosions going off inside the engine and of the violence of the wind hitting the car.

Again I was at the mercy of a mindless machine and unseen faces. It was an occupational hazard, throwing myself into constant deadly risk.

Through the windshield I could see the front fender eating the highway and then, through the rearview mirror, I watched as it was spat out behind. Cars, driven by shadows, shot past from the opposite direction. The steering wheel, nothing more than a worthless prop in front of me, became wet and slippery.

What if a tree fell on the car?

What if a tire blew out?

What if a runaway truck came screaming down on me from the other direction?

What if the brakes failed?

What if the road up ahead was washed out or ruptured with holes?

What if the driver of a passing car suddenly had an epileptic seizure, was drunk, or was a maniac hanging in the balance looking for a companion to the grave?

What if lightning struck?

What if a bird smashed against the windshield, blinding me?

What if, by driving the slightest bit too fast or too slow, I reach a gas station just as a robbery is taking place and I become trapped in a deadly cross fire?

What if one of the explosions propelling the car was too strong and took me and the car up in a fiery blast?

The terror of being alive, of being exposed constantly to the disease of life.

Walls of green flashed by on either side and, just beyond, behind them, the statistics were lining up for their tickets. They streamed through the turnstiles, placed their bets, and took their seats to watch the race.

They clapped their hands in unison and chanted:

AUTOMOBILE ACCIDENTS ANNUALLY RESULT IN

50,000 DEATHS

2,000,000 DISABLING INJURIES

1,400,000 YEARS OF HUMAN LIFE LOST

760,000 HEADS TRAUMATIZED

275,000 BROKEN LEGS

509,000 BROKEN ARMS
317,000 PERMANENT DISFIGUREMENTS
WHICH ONE WILL *YOU* GET?

A sign appeared in a green wall: Clarksburg—12 miles. And in an instant I saw the unbearable truth.

I was a cancer, hiding in a cell, traveling through an artery toward an organ.

A stout, sweaty man in a polyester shirt and trousers led Iris from the only office of the Golden Summer Apple Pie plant to the processing section. They passed steel vats, each the size of a small house, that mixed the sugar, flour, water, and butter for the pie crusts.

Butler kept her eyes straight ahead as they walked.

Many tons of air hover over me. The deep hum of engines rattles in my chest. The cancer is spreading in my body.

The red days are constant now. They cannot be ignored. The wolf is pinning me down, suffocating me. It will have to be silenced.

"I want to see your distribution facility," Butler said.

"Distribution? You bet."

The man, the manager of the plant, spoke as they walked. "I'll bet they're keeping you inspectors busy up there in Washington, what with all these tamperings."

Butler looked at him with contempt, the poor nervous insect. On his cheek was a piece of tissue to which the blood from a shaving cut was coagulating. He wore cheap cologne that made her eyes water.

"We're always busy," she said.

"Uh, you bet. You know, we passed the last inspection with flying colors. FDA guy—what was his name?—

said we ran a tight ship here. His very words, a tight ship."

"We'll see," Butler replied. She looked around the large room and saw no one. "Is this the central distribution facility?"

"Yes, ma'am. Everything made in this plant goes out from here directly into the trucks. No human hands touch the pies. It's all done automatically, the latest in hygiene technology."

"Show me where the pies are boxed."

"Right this way," he said, taking her to a section of the conveyor belt covered by a plastic hood. "Under here the pies are boxed automatically. From here they get stacked in big cardboard boxes and are loaded into the trucks."

"Where will these pies be sent?"

"You mean these ones going through now? Hard to say exactly. We're getting shipments ready for some local runs—over to Parkersburg and up to the Wheeling area. I think we have an order to fill in Salem."

"I'm going to have to ask you to stop the conveyor belt and lift the hood."

"Ma'am?"

"I need to do some routine tests on one of the products before they're boxed. Can you let me see some of them?"

"Oh sure. You won't disturb any of the pies, will you?"

"Disturb?"

"Make them unfit for sale's what I mean."

"No. I'll just extract a small amount of filling to check for preservative levels, ingredients, that sort of thing. The product won't be disturbed."

He took a walkie-talkie from his belt and spoke into it.

"Judy, will you shut down conveyor belt number two in the packing area? Yeah, a few minutes. Stand by."

I felt my strength returning, surging into my fingers. The wolf of the red day has been held at bay for the moment. I have control.

The manager drew back the plastic hood, exposing the plump yellow pies. They looked like hens on their way to slaughter. Iris would sacrifice one here and take another.

The walkie-talkie beeped and a voice came on, asking the manager to come to the control room.

Perfect, he will be gone for the inoculation.

He appeared somewhat nervous about leaving. Iris gave him a big reassuring smile—all was well, nothing to fear.

He walked off.

She set down her bag and smoothly removed from it two of the ten syringes she had loaded before setting out from Washington. The needle passed cleanly through the crust. She trembled, her eyes partially closed in pleasure as a gram and a half of mercuric cyanide in solution emptied out into the pie.

She carefully replaced the empty syringe and drew back the plunger on the other one. Butler repeated the procedure on another pie, and lifted it from the conveyor belt. It fit nicely in the bottom of her bag.

Then she realized that she would need a sample of the pie filling to take back to the FDA. Fortunately, she had brought along an empty syringe, one that would show no cyanide residues in tests. She drew out her sample.

Butler gently closed the lid of the conveyor belt and set out looking for the manager. She was a dutiful inspector. She would take a sample of the pie crust dough before stalking the Harmons.

* * *

Her subjects did not seem to be home when Iris arrived from the Golden Summer bakery. She climbed to her spot above the road, careful not to disturb the pie in her bag. Iris was a fit woman with wiry muscles in her arms and legs. With little effort she reached the top of the ridge.

She watched the house for several minutes. There was no sign of life. She decided she should get to work quickly. The Harmons could return any time now.

She scrambled down the ridge to the road and approached the house. The Harmons already had cleaned up much of the mess that had been waiting for them when they arrived two days ago. The front porch was spotless.

Butler drew out the pie from her bag. In Clarksburg she had purchased a pie tin, one with a big floral print, and put the pie inside. The tin would give her gift a homey look. The tin was still warm, and Butler left it on the welcome mat. But she immediately realized that if it stayed there, an animal might get to it. She placed it on a windowsill next to the door.

The pie needed something more, something . . . personal. Butler dug in her bag and found a pen and pad of paper. She scribbled a note:

Welcome
Bon Appetit!

and tucked it under the pie.

As she began to leave, she changed her mind. "Bon Appetit" was too sophisticated. She wrote another one:

Welcome
Enjoy!

*   *   *

Night was beginning to fall. She climbed up the ridge, back to her spot where she would wait for the experiment to begin.

Chapter 38

Earlier that day Tom and Chloe had agreed that the family needed a trip away from the house, something to nurse their wounds. She had wanted to see the Dolly Sods cranberry glades, a part of the Monongahela National Forest in the eastern part of West Virginia. Jeremy looked at a map and lobbied for a visit to the Smoke Hole Caverns nearby. They got an early start and tried for both.

After about an hour's drive through the Appalachians, they found the Monongahela Park and Dolly Sods. None of them had known that it actually was a tundra area, one of the few south of the Arctic Circle, as the park ranger explained.

"Strange," Chloe said as she followed the nature trail on a catwalk. The experience with the Rameesh kids had upset Melanie terribly, and she had stayed close to Chloe, gone everywhere she went. The tundra area was bleak and rocky, moon-like. Branches grew out of only one side of the wind-battered trees. The sun was bright, but the air was eerily cold for June.

As Shane slept in his Snugli and Melanie followed her every step, Chloe imagined this was what the earth would look like after the ozone layers had been depleted.

Or after an atomic holocaust. A cloud passed over the sun, making her shiver.

Chloe could never tell Tom that she was now having second thoughts about moving to the country. So far nothing was working out for them: their house had been senselessly vandalized, and Chloe and Melanie had been accosted by fanatic teenagers, all in the space of a few days. She was afraid to look ahead, to even think what else could go wrong.

At the Dolly Sods ranger station, Jeremy picked up a leaflet about the Caverns and read it aloud as they ate lunch.

"Look, Dad, they have a four-foot turtle that grew out of the rocks," he said, excited.

They drove north in search of the Caverns. When they found them, a Closed for Repair sign was posted in front. Jeremy obviously was disappointed but tried to be brave by not showing it. Why hadn't that park ranger said something to them when they asked him about the Caverns? Tom wondered.

As they headed home, Chloe pulled a handful of Mary Janes from her bag and handed them out. Tom passed on them, but Chloe was surprised that Melanie took one. It was a small gesture of peace, a good sign.

Chloe, humming as she drove, started singing "Barbara Anne" by the Beach Boys. Before long they were all singing, even Melanie. Tom broke them up by trying to imitate Brian Wilson's falsetto, failing miserably.

They went through every Beach Boys, Beatles, and Motown song they knew. Melanie introduced them to songs by Metallica, a heavy metal group, until Shane started crying. Melanie hushed up, giggling.

The entire crew, including Tom, was asleep when Chloe pulled into their service road early in the evening.

As they bumped their way toward the house, everyone woke up. Melanie was the last one to stir.

"Oh good, we're home," she said, yawning. Tom looked over at Chloe and touched her hand. He hoped that some good was coming out of their misfortune, that maybe Melanie was finally coming around. Chloe read his thoughts and smiled back at him.

"I'm hungry," Jeremy announced.

"You're always hungry," Melanie said.

"How about a picnic?" Chloe suggested.

"A picnic?" Jeremy said. "But, Mom, it's getting dark."

Chloe mussed his hair playfully. "Don't you think I can see that? I meant a picnic on the living room floor. Indian style."

"Neat," Jeremy said.

They all stretched as they got out of the Bronco. Tom handed Jeremy and Melanie things to carry in, and Chloe picked up Shane, still in the Snugli.

"Hey, Dad, look," Jeremy said, excited, "Somebody's been here today." He held up the pie tin resting on the front windowsill, the note fluttering to the ground. Tom picked it up and read it. Jeremy opened the tin and announced, "Wow, apple pie. Can we have some, Mom? Please?"

"We'll see. Maybe after dinner."

"Good Lord," he said, "these people must subsist on starches and sugar. We're gonna get fat living here."

Chloe peered over Tom's shoulder and read the note. "Hmmm, nobody signed it," she said. "I wonder who left it. Probably a friend of Dorrie's. These people really are sweet out here."

"I'll bet it's from one of Dorrie's competitors trying to

muscle in on her territory," Tom said with a straight face. Chloe gave him a shove as he entered the house.

The sun was burning out behind the Appalachian foothills. The Harmons' house was an island of light in the gathering darkness. In the kitchen, Chloe set about making dinner. She needed pliers to turn on the oven, stripped of its knobs, to heat up the pizzas they had picked up on the way home.

The apple pie sat on the counter where Jeremy had left it. Chloe looked at it, thinking she could put it in the cooling oven after the pizzas came out. Then she could dollop some vanilla ice cream over it.

After all this junk food, they would have to get their diet back on track, she thought to herself. But for now they would do it the easy way.

Just then Melanie entered the kitchen, carrying a kerosene lamp and looking like the frightened child that she was. "Can I help, Mom?" she said.

Chloe felt her eyes mist. She came toward Melanie and tenderly put her arms around her, holding her close. Melanie hugged back.

"Let's get dinner, sweetie," Chloe said.

Chapter 39

On the stage of the FBI auditorium, Hugh Lawson tapped the microphone hooked up to the podium, causing a squeal of feedback that made heads jerk in the audience. He tried to size up the audience from their clothes, a tricky maneuver in Washington. He saw a lot of striped suits, tweed, and silk scarves, all mid- to high-level types, and some FBI brass, including Ed Brady.

In the back of the auditorium, among the contingent from the FDA, sat Iris Butler. She had not wanted to come to this meeting, preferring instead to bask in the glow of her latest achievement. Given the choice, she would have been at home, scouring newspapers and magazines for clippings and savoring the memory of her subjects, the Harmons, obligingly taking their vaccine.

There was so much to take in, but so little time. The reaction was incredibly swift.

The children went first, since their systems were the smallest. The adult subjects were much more interesting. They thrashed around for over a minute and flailed their arms as they experienced a sensation of being suffocated with nothing covering their mouths.

The man beat his hands on the floor, trying to get to the children. Note: he lost function in the legs. Then his jaw muscles spasmed and locked, leaving his mouth gaping open. He died that way.

The woman was quite strong. She managed to stand and get to her baby. But the $Hg(CN_2)$ did the job and she collapsed as she reached the child.

The entire scene was fascinating, like films of the effects of Zyklon-B gas in the showers at Treblinka. I would have liked to have recorded the experiment, to study in detail the subjects' reaction times and responses. Another compelling experiment would be to gauge reactions to various kinds of cyanide.

I realized only one thing could be more satisfying than being that close to a subject, and that would be to move from the passive to the active, to directly inoculate the subject myself.

Up in front of the auditorium, Hugh Lawson was ready to introduce David McAdam, but the featured guest was nowhere to be found. He beckoned over one of his agents, the one assigned to escort McAdam up from Florida. The agent made his way over, stepping carefully through the cables on the stage floor.

Hugh put his hand over the microphone. "Where the hell is he?" he demanded.

The agent held out his hands. "Sir, it was Mr. Brady. I was in front of the men's room when he came by and asked me what I was doing there. When I explained I was waiting on McAdam, he ordered me to the auditorium."

"Fuck," Hugh said, and then realized his hand was off the microphone. The reaction from the audience was a mixture of shock and hysterical laughter. Hugh was perspiring again.

He unfolded his notes and the agent drifted off. "Ladies and gentlemen," he began, "I apologize for our small technical problems. I first want to express the appreciation of the Bureau for your coming here today, especially those of you who were just notified about the presentation this morning.

"By way of introduction, my name is Special Agent Hugh Lawson, in charge of the tampering investigation. Today we have brought together the key agencies of the federal government involved in this investigation, as well as representatives of offices engaged in product regulation, inspection, and related activities, to demonstrate an important new tool in our ongoing efforts to bring the tampering epidemic under control.

"Some of you are aware that the FBI, working in conjunction with other agencies, has been developing a computerized information system that will provide faster, more reliable data analysis than before possible. We have engaged a consultant, David McAdam, formerly of the PanTech Corporation, to assist in this project. But before I introduce him, let me give you a bit of the history of the case.

"Approximately four months ago—"

All heads in the audience turned as David McAdam burst through the door and ran down the center aisle to the front. He jumped up over the front of the stage and joined Hugh at the podium.

Hugh, flustered, took his seat in the audience next to Ed Brady.

"Thanks, Lawson," McAdam said. He pulled something from his back pocket, a black box.

"What I have here is a high-density Bernoulli box"— he inserted it into the computer on stage—"that contains about one-fifth of the database I designed for the investigation. Its capacity is approximately fifteen times that of an ordinary floppy disk."

He typed in a command on the keyboard, and a table of numbers appeared. It was the same summary of the dairy-product tamperings as the one he had created in Florida.

"This screen shows all the dairy tamperings to date, as well as their locations, dates, and types of cyanide used. Milk tamperings have occurred in three cycles so far—in March, April, and May. No other product tampered with shows such a pattern. And—this is crucial—those other tamperings occurred *around* the milk tamperings.

"Each milk tampering took place in a different state and involved a different kind of cyanide. The Minneapolis incident involving ice cream has been removed because the killer has been found."

Unexpectedly, the audience applauded. David hung his head and shuffled his feet, embarrassed. Hugh Lawson fidgeted nervously, wondering what was next. He had warned McAdam to stick to the technical aspects of the database and not to mention any facts of the case.

McAdam touched a key and a graph appeared, with brilliant yellow, orange, and green lines. "Here you have a graphic illustration of the dates of the tamperings. What I've done—and the program can do automatically—is to work backward from the actual date that each tampering death occurred.

"The database is programmed to compute the average period of time between when milk was brought home from the store and then consumed. It also factors in the average time it takes dairy companies to distribute their milk. For you data people out there, my source for the averages is the National Dairy Association."

He pointed to places on the graph. "You can see the different dates for the tampering deaths, clustering around each cycle. What accounts for these differences?

Well, not everyone drinks their milk immediately when they bring it home. What else? Milk, even the same milk from the same plant, is not always distributed at the same time. Also, milk moves faster in larger grocery stores than in smaller markets."

McAdam typed in another command. In the front row of the audience, Brady leaned over to Lawson and whispered fiercely, "What is he up to? Didn't you talk to him like I told you to?"

Hugh tried to think quickly. "I told him in no uncertain terms that if he—"

"There," McAdam said, pointing. "This is the most interesting graph. You folks in the back will have to take my word on this.

"I won't bore you with the statistical details. They're here if you want to see them. I have estimated the exact day each tampering took place. As you can see from the spacings of these points on these curves, the data show a regular interval of twenty-eight days between each tampering incident.

"Twenty-eight days," he said. "What, besides these tamperings, takes place in twenty-eight day intervals? Anybody?"

He paused for several moments, giving his students time to think. They grew restless.

He feigned great surprise. "No takers? I'm surprised, such a sophisticated group as this."

He put his hands in his pockets and began pacing. "Over the past few days I've been reading through the medical literature on premenstrual syndrome."

Hisses from the audience. "Sexist," someone hooted. McAdam, more than a little nervous, held up his hand, asking the audience's indulgence. He was relieved when the noise stopped.

"Let me explain, then you can boo me off the stage. In a normal menstrual cycle there are two phases: the follicular, the first half of the cycle, and the luteal, the second. During the luteal phase some women, only some, suffer from a condition known as LLPDD, sort of a subgroup of PMS.

"There's still no consensus in the literature as to what causes LLPDD. It's not even clear where PMS comes from. According to an article in the *New England Journal of Medicine,* the symptoms can be nothing more than irritability or fatigue, but it has been linked to more severe things like depression, panic attacks, and violent outbursts."

McAdam stopped his pacing and stood next to the computer. "LLPDD begins about a week before menstruation. For most women who suffer from it, LLPDD stops when menstruation begins.

"But for *this* woman," he said, pointing to the screen, "LLPDD may go through into menstruation itself. It sets off *something,* a well of rage or evil, call it what you will.

"One thing appears certain: the killings will continue if she isn't stopped."

Brady grabbed Lawson's arm. "Get him out of here," he ordered.

Lawson rushed up the steps, waving McAdam off the stage. He was intent on inflicting some degree of pain on McAdam when he reached him. Instead he tripped over one of the cables, sending sparks flying from the back of the computer. The sparks ignited a pile of packing material, and a small fire began to spread over the stage.

Someone pulled an alarm and four agents took up fire extinguishers, spraying them over Lawson and the stage.

In the confusion David McAdam quietly left the auditorium.

Brady shook his head. Around him, the front rows were emptying of people. Brady was in no hurry. He had a few words for his special agent who was up on the stage, flat on his butt, spitting white foam and massaging a rapidly swelling ankle.

The auditorium was almost deserted. All the way to the back, in a far corner, Iris Butler sat still in her seat. Her knuckles were white from gripping the armrest. Her unblinking eyes were riveted straight ahead. She breathed in short spasms, as if the air had been knocked out of her lungs.

It is important to know one's enemies. For a long time my only enemies were the wolf of the red days and his friend, cancer.

But now I realize I have two more enemies: Hugh Lawson and David McAdam. One is a bumbling fool, greedy for publicity that should have been reserved for my accomplishments.

And McAdam. He is getting too close. I am safe momentarily because no one believes him. But that could change.

I will have to visit each of them soon. I must be steady and draw in my power.

Chapter 40

Before Hugh could escape from the FBI auditorium, he was cornered by Ed Brady, who ordered Hugh to meet him at J. Edgar Hoover's grave at four that afternoon. Hugh, nursing a painfully sprained ankle at the time, managed to have the presence of mind to ask Brady where the grave was.

"Down past the cenotaphs," Brady grumbled, "don't be late."

Hugh looked up *cenotaph* in the dictionary: "a tomb or monument erected in honor of someone buried somewhere else." That was no help. He had to call around to find out the name of Hoover's cemetery.

The grave was in the Congressional Cemetery, thirty-five acres of rolling meadows sloping down to the Anacostia River in Southeast Washington. Hugh learned it was the official burial place of U.S. senators, although most of them preferred interment in their home states.

The cemetery was home to the remains of an odd assortment of characters, including John Philip Sousa, the march king; Matthew Brady, the Civil War photographer; and Taza, the son of Cochise. In 1864, twenty-one women had been killed in an explosion at the Washington Arsenal while preparing rifles for Union troops. Fourteen of them had been buried in the cemetery.

None of that mattered to Hugh, who was frantically searching the cemetery grounds for Hoover's grave. The day was hot and sticky as another notorious Washington summer arrived early. He had wrapped his ankle in an Ace bandage, but that controlled only the swelling. The pain throbbed mercilessly.

It was now 3:56. Hugh had four minutes. Brady did not tolerate tardiness.

He managed to flag down a service truck loaded with lawn mowers. The driver, a groundskeeper, vaguely nodded his head toward a line of centophs when Hugh asked directions to Hoover's grave.

Hugh hobbled through the rows of ugly tombs, dedicated to congressmen buried elsewhere. Up ahead he saw a figure leaning against a stone cross: Ed Brady.

The special agent was sweating and out of breath when he reached the grave precisely at four. His ankle pounded with pain. He mopped his face and neck with a handkerchief.

Brady had taken off his jacket and hung it on the cross. Hugh noticed he wore suspenders and a belt. Except for the two of them, the cemetery was empty of the living.

For several minutes Brady did not acknowledge Hugh's presence. Instead he kept his eyes down as if in meditation. Cicadas buzzed in the distance.

"This is one of the more peaceful places in Washington," Brady said at last. "Even at the Bureau, the floors have ears."

"Sir?" Hugh said.

"You know, Lawson, death isn't so bad. Look around you. See how quiet and orderly? Everything, everyone, in their place. We pity the dead, beat our chests over them, but we are only pitying ourselves.

"Mr. Hoover would have appreciated this order. He also would appreciate what you and I are doing."

"Doing, sir?"

Brady looked at him for the first time. "Restoring order, Lawson. Bringing normalcy to replace this madness we call society. We're close, very close, to achieving our objectives. I am of the opinion that when Mr. Hoover was director, that was his objective as well. Restoring order."

Hugh followed Brady's eyes to Hoover's gravestone. Above his name were those of his parents and sister. Clover and crab grass sprouted over the plot.

"I try to get here every day," Brady said quietly. "Can't always manage it, though."

"Did he have a big state funeral?" Hugh asked, hoping to stir pleasant memories in Brady. "Twenty-one-gun salute and all that?"

"Absolutely not," Brady snapped. "It was a simple family service. I was there."

Hugh let it drop. He looked up at the massive blocks of the D.C. Jail that rose along the Anacostia and overshadowed the cemetery. The windows were narrow slits of reinforced glass.

Good, Hugh thought, give the convicts a view of the cemetery. Let them see where they're going when they get out.

"Any news from West Virginia?" Brady asked.

"Yes, sir," Hugh said, digging around in his pockets for notes. Where were they? Brady crossed his arms, impatient.

"Here we go. I sent a team of forensics specialists from Washington yesterday. With luck, there'll be some fresh evidence, even after the locals have slopped over the scene. Agents and local police are questioning suspects, including members of a local religious cult who were involved in an altercation with the victims. I'm expecting an update when I get back to the office."

Hugh paused a moment. "The county sheriff stopped by the Harmons' house to investigate an harassment complaint filed against a couple of the cult members. He was quoted as saying that the scene he found on the living room floor reminded him of pictures he had seen of Jonestown years ago. He also said that he had a difficult time prying a screaming infant from his dead mother's arms."

Brady was watching Hugh closely. "Mmmm, some good leads. And you're checking out the possibility that one of the family members may have poisoned the pie."

"Yes, sir."

"What about the other pies?"

Hugh nodded. "The West Virginia state police are coordinating a recall of all Golden Summer apple pies. The state public health service is running tests on them.

"So far, one has been discovered with enough cyanide to wipe out a battalion. It's been sent to the FDA laboratory in Cincinnati for evaluation. They have a library of cyanide samples there, including the ones from the original Tylenol tampering case."

Hugh put away his notes. "Another thing, sir. West Virginia detectives found a note in the Harmons' garbage. It said: "Welcome. Enjoy.' No signature. They also found a couple of tins, including one with traces of apple pie filling. We're checking into the possibility that the pie was left as a gift, so to speak."

Hugh paused again, collecting his thoughts, wondering how he could best break this next item to Brady.

"Go on, Lawson," Brady said, "you wanted to say something?"

"Mr. Brady," he blurted out, "the contents of that note appeared in this morning's *Cleveland Plain Dealer.* I have no idea how it could have happened. The West Virginia authorities claim only three of their people saw the note and are beyond reproach. The editors at the paper aren't talking, of course. I have absolutely no idea how this could have happened."

Brady pulled his jacket off the cross and began strolling. Hugh followed until Brady stopped in front of a pink marble gravestone, this one inscribed with the name Clyde Tolson.

Hugh recognized the name immediately. He looked at Brady. "Sir, weren't there some rumors about Clyde Tolson and Mr. Hoover, that for many years they were—"

"My *point,* Lawson, in showing you this marker is to illustrate what the press does with information. Newspapers are rumor mills. Oh, very sophisticated ones, I'll grant you that. But from simple observations they draw complex conclusions. From innocent statements come vicious lies.

"I knew Mr. Tolson. He was a good friend of Mr. Hoover's, a confidant. Nothing more, I assure you. But the papers and book publishers can at least appreciate the profits that can be made from a whiff of scandal."

Brady drew closer to Hugh, who smelled something familiar on Brady's breath. He recognized it as caramels.

"The press are part of the problem, Lawson, but, make no mistake about it, they will be part of the solution."

They drifted off down a brick path grown over with weeds, past a row of mausoleums. Some of the doors to the crypts, the ones whose families had died off, were sealed.

His eyes on the ground, Brady said, "Today Congress is meeting in an extraordinary session to decide whether to move forward on suspending certain First Amendment rights, at least for the duration of this crisis. Freedom of the press is high on the list.

"It's hard to predict what will happen. But, of course, the Bureau will stand ready to enforce the law of the land. We can only be patient."

Hugh puzzled over Brady's remarks. Did he *want* Congress to restrict basic rights? Then something occurred to him, something he had been meaning to ask Brady.

"Sir, in going through some old files, I discovered you were involved in the investigation of the Tylenol tamperings."

"You're referring to the Chicago incident of 1982, I presume. Yes, I personally oversaw a good deal of that operation. Now, *that* was a missed opportunity."

"Sir?"

"An opportunity," Brady said quickly, "to catch a tamperer."

"Reason I ask, I was wondering if you've seen any connection between the current tampering incidents and the Tylenol."

"No, no," Brady said, swatting at flies buzzing in his face. "No apparent connection other than cyanide has been used in each.

"There have been many other tamperings since then, Lawson, both here and abroad. Recall the attacks on Israeli produce in France, West Germany, and Italy. In 1984 the Man With 21 Faces terrorist organization threatened candy manufacturers in Japan with cyanide tampering.

"And, of course, the Chilean grapes incident of 1989. Imagine, Lawson, just two grapes with an infinitesimal amount of cyanide in them brought an entire country's agricultural output to a standstill and set off a storm of panic here at home. And look at what we have today. Nothing less than national hysteria."

They had reached the tree-lined road leading to the cemetery entrance. A saccharine smell of cut flowers rotting on a grave wafted into Hugh's nostrils.

"One other thing, Mr. Brady," Hugh said. "Just before coming here I got a call from a Jack Lavelle in the director's office at the Food and Drug Administration. Lavelle was calling for the director, who reminded us that a month has now gone by with no reports of a dairy-product tampering.

"You will recall our arrangement with the USDA and the FDA. If thirty days go by with no report of a dairy tampering, the entire data collection for the investigation is transferred to the FDA."

"Yes," Brady said, "I recall that arrangement. It's a pity. Agriculture has been doing an excellent job."

Hugh bit his tongue. "Tomorrow the FDA will take over the budget and responsibilities for all data collection and database management. Lavelle says they plan to use their own system, not the one David McAdam demonstrated this morning."

"Well, the silver lining in the cloud," Brady gloated. He slapped his cheek at a fly that had already flown away. "I don't think Mr. McAdam will be causing us any more mischief anyway. I've already seen to that."

Hugh turned toward him. "What do you mean?"

"Ah, here's my car," Brady said, pointing to the black limousine soundlessly pulling up at the gate. The driver, a young agent-in-training, hopped out and opened the back door.

"Sir, what did you mean by that? What have you done about McAdam?"

Brady snatched a fly in midair and squeezed it in his fist. He climbed into the limousine. "I have a luncheon meeting with the director of the Bureau and the president tomorrow, Lawson. Have a full update on the investigation on my desk first thing in the morning."

The driver slammed the door and skipped around to the front. The limo pulled off, leaving a cloud of dust in Hugh's face.

Chapter 41

The red days were relentless this time, the worst they have ever been. Wave after wave raged into me in measured contractions, each more terrible than the last.

I tried to breathe my way through them—short, short, long; short, long, short; short, short, short. I focused on a picture of Papa on the table next to the bed, clinging to the warm image as the waves kept coming, crashing over me, until, entirely drained, I passed out.

When I awoke, the waves had stopped and I was calmer. Oh, it was still there, the red day, lurking like a wolf, eyes glowing. Saliva oozed over its fangs as it toyed with its prey. It was resting now, gathering strength.

Yet I knew the wolf had tasted the blood. It would want more.

I saw light through my bedroom window. I could move my legs the forty-eight steps to the back door and into the garden.

Coin-sized clover poked through a bed of lush long-stemmed amaryllis. I rolled up my sleeves and went to work on them, gouging out fistfuls of soil under the clover, catching every root.

The face of Special Agent Hugh Lawson came to me— short hair, closely shaved, speaking to reporters on the *evening news, appearing on the covers of major publications. The world looks to him for answers. It scours his words for hope.*

I have seen much too much of Mr. Lawson in the past several weeks. My accomplishments are being subsumed by his unvarnished ambition, his grandstanding for publicity.

Don't forget, Mr. Lawson, I made you. I gave birth to you through my creativity and suckled you with my work.

And now, Mr. Lawson, you have grown too big and too fast and have thrust yourself into the awful openness with me. Your clean face has grown too large and has multiplied orders of magnitude beyond the acceptable limits.

There is room for only one of us, Mr. Lawson. You will have to be erased from the picture.

And after you I will see to David McAdam.

I looked at my hands and then down at the ground, where yellow and red amaryllis lay torn and useless like aborted fetuses.

Of course, I thought, how perfect. How utterly perfect.

I finished the job, tearing out the remainder of the garden, flower by flower. Like everything else, they would all have to die anyway.

Before Iris left her house, she checked herself in the mirror. What has happened to my hair? she wondered. Is the Washington humidity the cause of this shapeless frizz? And her eyes . . . they needed work. She couldn't visit Special Agent Hugh Lawson of the FBI looking like this.

Mr. Lawson had a new house, a little love nest over the river in Arlington. Traffic was light, for most of the good children of Washington were safely at home, eating their dinner and drinking their milk. Iris drove within the speed limit, calling no unnecessary attention to herself.

She had prepared weeks ago for a possible visit to Mr. Lawson in case he got too close to her. He no doubt rested comfortably, secure in the knowledge that his unlisted telephone number kept his wife and him safe.

Even though Iris did not include them in her scrapbook, she had clipped and saved every story she found about Mr. Lawson. Amazing how all the stories appeared to be written by one reporter.

All except for a story appearing in one of those sleazy supermarket tabloids that dug a bit deeper than the usual pap. From it she learned where Mr. Lawson had gone to college (University of North Carolina at Chapel Hill) and that his wife was a nurse.

A call to the alumni affairs office at North Carolina yielded an address for Lawson in Herndon, Virginia. Promising lead, she thought, but she wasn't quite satisfied. Her training told her that reserach data were only credible when they were collected with the proper controls. Research was an important part of the hunt. She still had one more source of data to tap.

She then called around the Northern Virginia hospitals and found a Patricia Lawson, R.N., on the staff of Fairfax Hospital.

Pretending to be a cousin of hers stranded at Dulles Airport, Butler got an all-too-willing candy striper to give her Nurse Lawson's home address and telephone number.

It was a new listing on Franklin Street in Arlington, no more than twenty minutes from her own place.

In a toilet bag on the car seat next to me were two syringes fully loaded with vaccine for Mr. and Mrs. Lawson. Perhaps they had children. Even better.

As I drove west I headed into the sun setting behind the flimsy high-rises in Rosslyn. Great power surged through me, high-tension pulsations emanating from my fingertips. The power took over the car, turning the steering wheel, pressing the accelerator, switching on the headlights.

With this power I could will the sun down from the sky. A beam of sheer energy from the middle of my fore-head seized the sun and forced it to set more quickly.

Darkness cloaked her as she entered Arlington and turned onto Franklin Street.

Lights glowed through the windows of the neat little houses on the tree-lined street. Cape Cods, most of them, some with bird baths and lawn lamps. Comfortable homes. Comfortably safe.

Butler found the Lawsons' and parked across the street, headlights off. Odd, she thought, there was only one light on upstairs. All the other homes were lit on the ground floor, people eating dinner or watching television.

She waited and watched. The light went out, but no other light in the house subsequently came on. Did the special agent and nurse turn in early?

Butler checked her watch, enough light to see from a street lamp two doors down. It was 8:19.

A short time later the same light came on again. 8:29. And then, at 8:59, it went out again.

Then she realized: it was a lamp timer. No one was home.

She turned off the interior car light before she opened the door. From the toilet bag she took a pair of surgical gloves and put them on. She got out, softly closing the door, and went toward the house.

The porch was dark. She touched the bell and then

crouched in the shadow of a large juniper tree in the adjoining yard.

Nothing happened.

There was no fence around the yard, so it was easy enough to go around back and find the kitchen door. Through the window Butler could make out boxes on the floor but little else. She tried the door, but it was locked.

Inside me the power was building. My skin barely contained the energy growing to the magnitude of a nuclear reactor. What was a mere door in the face of such power?

I touched the door. It melted away and I entered the house.

It became easier to see in the darkness. Stepping around boxes and sheets, she found a pool of mail on the floor of the foyer. Most of it was addressed to Shep and Jody Lovejoy.

Was this the wrong house?

No, Shep and Jody were the previous owners, and their mail was not being forwarded. Iris found two letters addressed to Hugh and Patricia.

This was the right place.

She could not remember the last time she had been in someone else's house. Strange, the air conditioning was on. Perhaps Hugh and Patricia would come home soon. She went about her business.

Back in the kitchen Iris made a space on the cluttered table and put down the toilet bag. Inside it were two syringes each loaded with 300 milligrams of potassium cyanide in solution, about twenty times the lethal dosage. She removed the syringes one at a time, faint moonlight glinting off the needles.

She checked all the cupboards. Cans, nothing but cans! That wouldn't do.

She opened the refrigerator. A milk carton—opened—that was promising. She could simply squirt the solution inside.

Opening it, Iris had to step back from the offensive odor of the sour milk. Closer inspection of the refrigerator revealed mold colonies on nearly everything—floating in orange juice, growing up the sides of a casserole.

She didn't need to vaccinate this house. There were enough bacteria here to immunize the planet. Besides, no one in his right mind would touch this food. No sense wasting excellent cyanide. It would keep.

I didn't care about the family anyway. All I wanted was the star special agent.

I was growing bored of this tedious sneaking about. Yet I was still infinitely powerful, invulnerable.

I would meet this unsanitary policeman, Hugh Lawson. I would meet him face to face. It would be simple.

I would just make an appointment.

Chapter 42

Hugh Lawson was tired. He was tired of restless nights in the FBI's basement lounge. He was tired of bad coffee, greasy food, and Alka-Seltzer. He was tired of frustraton and failure, the only real results of his investigation. All his life Hugh had never dreamed when he slept, at least not that he could remember. But now the little sleep he could manage was punctured by nightmares, unsettling violent episodes in which he was chased by faceless pursuers, after which he would wake up sweating and more tired than before. His eyes burned and his joints ached, and he frequently caught himself staring off into space.

Hugh had not been home for nearly a week. Usually he worked long into the night, alone in his office on the basement floor of the FBI. He kept a change of clothes at the office, a black suit and two shirts he had laundered every other day. Loose threads began to sprout from their collars and cuffs.

It seemed the longer the hours Hugh kept at the office, the less productive he was. Up to this point he had been able to juggle his office and home life, even managing to help his career along by appearing on talk shows and in news magazines. But now he was cancelling everything—press conferences, interviews, lectures. He simply lost the stomach for it.

Occasionally someone in the office would notice his lined face and unfocused eyes and sympathetically ask if he needed any help. That usually snapped Hugh out of his funk, and he would scowl at the remark and get back to work.

One person who never asked was Ed Brady. Throughout the investigation the associate director had usually called Hugh eight to ten times a day. Hugh had even taken to carrying a pocket phone. But since his meeting with Brady in the cemetery, Hugh had not heard once from his supervisor. His calls were returned by subordinates. He felt cut off, adrift in the eye of some fierce, relentless storm. For the first time in his life, Hugh felt out of control. He felt like a victim.

He tried to keep the creeping paranoia in check. At the cemetery Brady had said David McAdam wouldn't be causing any more mischief. What did *that* mean? Hugh turned it over in his head many times, even checked the computer to see if any additional agents had been detailed to California Key. Nothing came up.

To escape Washington, Hugh returned to his final refuge—his family. He slipped out of the office early on a slow Thursday afternoon and headed to Richmond. He wanted to surprise Pat and the kids, maybe pick up some small presents on the way.

Traffic on southbound Interstate 95 moved like a winter glacier. Hugh beat often on his horn to no effect. Water oozed from the air-conditioning vents on the dashboard, dripping on his Bass Weejuns. As a fog of exhaust fumes settled over the highway, Hugh stared out over the expanse of idling cars and began to think about his life. He did this infrequently, the idle time imposed by gridlock forcing him to reflect.

On the surface things looked fine. He had a happy,

healthy family, a new home, and a good job despite the temporary setbacks in the office. The future looked bright for Hugh Lawson.

And yet something pecked at his confidence, his sense of security. What it was he couldn't quite say—some vague foreboding, an uneasiness that everything he had worked and sacrificed for could unravel in an instant. His fear, if you could call it that, was completely irrational, he knew that. But it was there, a malignant presence asserting itself in his weak moments.

For no apparent reason, and certainly without his wanting to, Hugh began to think about the Harmons, the most recent tampering victims. He had read through their file from cover to cover and felt a strange connection to them he had never had toward a victim. In reviewing the file he was surprised by the surges of anger and outrage aroused in him. Those feelings boiled over when he got to the statements by family, friends, and coworkers. Reading the statements, Hugh heard the same painful refrain in each of them: the Harmons were basically good people who wanted a simpler life, a chance to start over together in a new place.

Was that too much to ask of life? Had the Harmons violated some law of nature by not only wanting happiness but by seeking it out, trying to make it into reality? And was this their punishment, a random poisoning at the hands of a maniac? Hugh wondered what his punishment would be for wanting happiness and for translating his desire into deed. Did his ambitions exceed his destiny? For a moment he saw himself as Tom Harmon, happily oblivious to the evils lurking around him, unprepared for attack from unseen forces.

A horn blared in Hugh's ear, tearing him from his

thoughts. He looked up and saw a stretch of asphalt in front of him. He was holding things up.

Not knowing if it was from the anticipation of seeing his family or the effects of inhaling so much carbon monoxide, Hugh felt uncharacteristically giddy pulling into Richmond two hours later. He stopped at a Walmart along the way—the only store he saw—and picked up toys for the kids and perfume for Pat. He even got something for Pat's mother—guest towels—knowing it would please his wife.

In his haste to get to the house, Hugh took the corner onto Dresden Terrace a little hard and his tires squealed loudly, provoking a flurry of curtain openings and hard gazes from the small brick houses along the block. The house was at the dead end of the street, perched above a small creek dug to catch runoff from the James River. Ever since the nearby factories had shut down, the smell from the creek wasn't as bad as it used to be. Climbing the steps to the house as fast as his sprained ankle would let him, Hugh noticed the lawn was scorched almost white from the early summer heat. Pat's station wagon was not in the driveway.

Gladys, Pat's mother, came to the door, still in her robe at six in the evening.

"Well, you just missed them," she said in her slow drawl, crossing her arms defensively and looking off down the street. She didn't invite him in.

"Where'd they go, Gladys?" Hugh asked quickly, setting down the presents. "Is anything wrong?" He tried to look past her, to see if anyone was inside.

Gladys took in a long breath and let it out slowly. Her eyes moved from the street to the top of a dirty magnolia tree in the neighbor's yard. She shook her head.

Hugh felt the pulse quicken in his neck. He had been

trained to know a liar when he saw one, and Gladys was certainly one. What was she hiding? he wondered.

"To that new place downtown," she said, "I can't think of the name. One with all the stores."

Hugh thought a moment. "You mean the Sixth Street Marketplace?"

He had been there once. It was one of those theme malls with espresso bars and shops pushing overpriced cookies. And it had been around for years.

Gladys never answered him. She ducked her head and worked phlegm from deep within her throat. Hugh bit the inside of his cheek. This was getting him nowhere. Giving it back to her, Hugh let out a long strangled sigh of exasperation, gathered up his gifts, and stalked back to his car.

He got cheap satisfaction from putting down four loud feet of rubber and watching the curtains flutter as he roared up the street.

Hugh headed north toward the Richmond business district, where he picked up Broad Street, a main thoroughfare that took him all the way to Sixth. The rush-hour traffic was moving in the opposite direction, so he had no trouble making his way into town.

He parked on Fifth Street, just across from the Richmond Convention Center. The first traces of pale pink twilight marked a line above the city's skyline. Hugh puzzled over why downtown seemed so deserted. The sidewalks were clear of people and even the streets were hushed, with only an occasional car or bike moving past. Had a curfew been ordered?

As he approached the Sixth Street Marketplace from the west, Hugh took in the full measure of the place. The Marketplace was actually a group of connected structures sprawling over three city blocks, with high glass

walls and a promenade bridge that crossed over the
street below. One of the buildings, now a collection of
restaurants, had housed Confederate soldiers during the
Civil War.

Part of the downtown renewal of the eighties, the
Marketplace had been conceived as an urban showcase,
an environmentally controlled shopper's paradise. For
reasons Hugh couldn't fathom, he saw the Marketplace
as a comforting symbol of permanence and middle-
American values. He had always believed people needed
things larger than them—religions, political movements,
companies, and buildings—to feel secure. The Sixth
Street marketplace was just such a thing: solid and unchanging, a testimony to man's triumph over nature. He
entered through an etched glass door with a sign welcoming him.

The last time Hugh had been here, the place had been
jammed with shoppers and junior high school kids in tattered jeans and bicycle pants. Now it was eerily quiet.
As he wandered into the main atrium, he noticed the
ferns, browned, curled, and cracking, in planters along
the floor. A spotted fungus leeched up the trunk of a
sickly palm tree. Copper-colored water sputtered from a
fountain in the center of the atrium.

The sound of Hugh's heels on the hand-laid tile floor
rifled off the walls and stairways of the mall. He wandered up a broad aisle, peeking in clothes stores for Pat
and the kids. Except for bored clerks, he saw no one. A
couple in their seventies, wearing matching baby blue
sweat suits and running shoes, passed him, staring in-
tently ahead and pumping their arms furiously as they
walked.

He passed through Food Court, a restaurant boutique,
it was called. Surrounding him was a half acre of white

enamel tables, all empty except for one, at which sat a man in a pearl gray fedora. Hugh's heart beat faster. Maybe Pat had come by this way. Maybe this guy had seen her.

The man's back faced Hugh and he seemed to be staring up at the frosted glass elevators that glided mindlessly up and down the walls with no one inside them. As Hugh approached the man, he first noticed his hair—clumps of it poking out from beneath the hat. A little closer he saw the bald patches. Then the lesions on his neck. Hugh kept on walking past the man and never looked back.

Hugh turned down a narrow aisle and stopped dead in his tracks. At the end of the aisle stood a deer—an eight-point buck at least five and a half feet from his shoulders to the floor. How had he gotten in here? The buck stared Hugh in the eye for several long seconds. Hugh heard a noise from above and glanced up. The buck looked up too. A Victorian ceiling fan clicked slowly to a stop. When Hugh looked again, the buck was gone. But where? The aisle was a dead end.

Somewhere in the mall a child was crying. Hugh recognized the cry as Lynn's, so he started off in a jog back toward the atrium. He came out in a different plaza, a part of the mall he hadn't seen before, where the developers apparently had run out of money and walked away.

There was no fountain here, no dried, decaying plants. Instead there was a carpet of clear plastic over an unfinished cement floor. Electrical cables spilled out from the ceiling and walls like exposed entrails from game. Buckets and ladders encrusted with paint were stacked against a wall. Hugh stepped carefully over the mess in the direction of a row of shops. "Unhh," he groaned as he ran face-first into a mirror reflecting the image of shops across the plaza. Holding his smarting cheek, he staggered back and stumbled over a bucket. When he reached the other side of the plaza he realized he had come up against another mirror reflecting another reflection of the shops.

Holding back a burst of panic, Hugh followed the mirrors around the plaza until he found the aisle of shops. He made his way up the aisle as it zigzagged back and forth like a mountain switchback. The stores—mostly small eateries and gourmet shops—were dark. Why would they be closed at dinnertime?

Peering through the window of a deli, Hugh was surprised to find the shelves, counter, and refrigerators completely empty. Boxes and packing material were strewn over the floor. Next door, a raw bar was stripped bare of everything edible. Up and down the aisle every store was the same—dark and empty, picked over like a Parsi corpse. Some shops were secured by chain-link screens, recently installed.

Hugh saw light in a shop at the end of a switchback. As he drew closer, he heard loud arguing in a foreign language. He kept his hand on his firearm, holstered on his belt, as he edged around the doorway.

It was a produce store, small and overly lit and empty like the others except for a box of artichokes. At the center of the store a middle-aged Korean couple in matching green aprons with "HOW CAN I HELP YOU?" printed across the bib held the box and, amid great shouting and gesturing, pulled it back and forth between them. The man obviously wanted to display the artichokes on a milk crate. He took the box and pushed it down onto the crate with both hands, seeming to screw it on. The woman, seizing her chance while the man lectured and waved broadly at the bare shelves, snatched the box and slammed it down at her feet. She obviously wanted it on the floor.

Hugh shook his head and cleared his throat. The couple snapped to attention with frozen smiles as he entered the store. Hugh swept his eyes over the store and back to the couple, still smiling. He took a moment to think about it and decided to show his FBI identification. They nodded and shrugged their shoulders, respectful but unimpressed.

"What's going on here?" Hugh said.

The man bowed quickly. "Please?"

Hugh pointed with his head. "This store, the others. They're empty. Nothing on the shelves."

The man mumbled something rapidly in Korean to the woman. "Yes?" he said, still polite.

"What happened?" Hugh said impatiently.

"The people, they take everything. Two days ago. Some buy, some steal. Everything gone now. No more food."

Hugh squinted at the man. "Why? Why two days ago?"

The man shrugged and whispered again to the woman. She answered Hugh in perfect English. "We don't know why. Some say it's hysteria. People are afraid more food will be poisoned, so they hoard whatever they can. It's madness, but what can we do?"

Hugh was speechless, numbed by the madness of it all. And somehow he knew this scene was being repeated all over America at this moment. He had heard of the hoarding and looting. He had even heard of plans to ration food. But it had been far away, part of other people's lives. Now he was aware he was seeing it firsthand, the frustration, anger, and fear.

Hugh turned to leave and nearly fell into his wife and

children entering the store. At the sight of them he felt a wave of relief wash over him, a lightness and wholeness he hadn't known in ages. They were finally, mysteriously together and he knew everything would be fine.

Pat was pushing Lynn in a stroller and dragging Roger behind her. She looked harried and tired, but Hugh didn't care. He moved forward to hug her, but she pulled back and drew the children toward her. Hugh thought: she's probably as overwhelmed as I am from the excitement of being together under such crazy circumstances. He forgave her and kept his distance for the time being. She left the store and he followed.

Marching up the aisle, children in tow, Pat said, "What are you doing here?" without looking at him.

"What do you mean? I was looking for you."

Lynn began to cry and Roger snorted, "Not again."

"I called the hospital," Hugh said, "and they told me you had taken a leave of absence. What's the story?"

Pat kept her eyes forward. "What do *you* mean?"

Hugh felt his left eye twitching and perspiration popping out on his brow. "Leave of absence, that's an important move. Sounds like you're looking for something else."

"Something else," she said so softly Hugh didn't hear it.

"We never talked about it, that's all," he said.

"We never talked about anything."

Hugh let it drop. "So what're you doing now?"

About thirty seconds went by before Pat answered. "I'm at a clinic not far from my mother's. Strictly outpatient. They wanted a full-time R.N., but I told them I could only go part-time. The kids need me right now."

This time it was Hugh who avoided looking at her. Roger was sullenly silent in contrast to Lynn's sobbing.

They were coming upon the plaza with the mirrored walls.

"I agreed to consider a full-time position after working there a month," Pat went on. "Next Friday will be a month."

They stepped into the plaza. For a terrible moment Hugh had a vision of them trapped in it forever. He still didn't know how to get out, other than by going back the way they had come. He couldn't reveal his irrational fear to Pat. He sensed things might be bad enough already without him going paranoid on her.

"So what will you do?" he said, knowing the answer. She would turn down the full-time offer and return to her old job and her life with him.

Pat stood still at the center of the plaza and took a deep breath. She looked at him for the first time, and he winced at the maze of bloodshot that filled her eyes. Her knuckles turned white as her fists tightened around the handle of the stroller.

"I don't know," she choked.

Hugh smiled, trying to reassure her. "I know you'll do the right thing," he said.

She turned her eyes away quickly, grabbed Roger by the hand, and with her other one, pushed the stroller toward what she thought was an aisle.

"Pat, hold it," he screamed.

Pat did not look back. Instead she continued up the aisle and disappeared around a corner.

Hugh stayed behind, wondering how Pat and the kids seemed to pass through the mirror he'd just run into.

Chapter 43

"It's Dr. Butler, Mr. Lawson," the secretary said blandly into the phone, as if she were ordering lunch. "Food and Drug. Yes, sir."

She looked up and put on a smile. "If you have a seat, Mr. Lawson will be with you in a moment."

What if I didn't have a seat, would he still see me? Or perhaps he would take longer than a moment? Foolish imprecision, laziness.

It was difficult coming here. The red day has been crippling, one explosion after another in the horribly wide hallways of this sub-basement where Prince Lawson holds court. I've never been here before and it took all of my power to overcome the obstacles in my path, the blind corners and open doors.

I rest my eyes, exhausted.

"Dr. Butler?"

She jumped, nearly bumping into a familiar face, an enemy suddenly real and close. He looked smaller than pictured in the papers, weaker and vulnerable.

"I'm Hugh Lawson." He held out his hand, but she was loath to touch it, to expose herself to his sepsis. She had no choice but to take it. "Would you follow me, please?"

He handed a folder to the secretary. "Corinne, will

you fax these to West Virginia? Gilbert is waiting on them, so put them to his attention."

He led Iris through a labyrinth of offices and store-rooms bustling with activity. She noticed he was limping slightly. Iris surprised herself by speaking to him.

"Wasn't there something in the paper this morning about a tampering in West Virginia?" she asked innocently.

"Yeah, it happened three days ago. They just found the bodies the day before yesterday. It all goes to show you."

"What's that?"

"Well, this is confidential, but we're sure that none of these tampering cases are related. And this incident, the West Virginia one, only strengthens the argument."

"How so?"

"Were you at that circus the other day with David McAdam? There are still a few people here at the Bureau who actually put stock in his one-tamperer theory. The West Virginia incident did not involve milk, but did involve cyanide. It showed no relation to the other incidents on McAdam's list."

"As I understood Mr. McAdam," Iris said, being careful here, "the *timing* of the tamperings was the important factor."

"Yeah, but no one here has even bothered to ask McAdam if the West Virginia tampering fit his ridiculous pattern. He's history around here." Lawson held open a door for her. "In here, please."

"So the West Virginia incident is what is called a 'copy cat'?"

Copy rats, the parasites.

"They all are," Lawson said emphatically. "How do you know who's copying who? They just happen."

He ushered her into a small office that connected to another room crammed with teletype machines, computer terminals, and various other telecommunications devices. On the wall was a large map of the United States stuck with multicolored pins.

Lawson noticed her staring at it. "Would you like to see the map?" he offered.

"Yes, I would. What are those pins?" She already knew the answer.

"They're color-coded, representing the different kinds of materials used in the tamperings over the past four months."

"Materials?"

"Well, the clear ones are places where glass—shards, mostly—were placed in consumer products. We had one case of ground glass in New Hampshire.

"The blue ones are strychnine, very lethal, the yellow are pesticides, over the counter stuff, and the green ones are pharmaceuticals."

"And the red ones?"

"Cyanide. That was the first material reported. Would you care for some coffee?"

"Oh, yes."

A map. What an excellent idea! I'll have to get one.

They each took their coffee black. Lawson settled down behind his desk. "So what can I do for you?"

Iris smiled. "I came here to see what we can do for you, Mr. Lawson. I'm in the Division of Product Surveillance at the FDA. We have an extensive database on non-dairy tamperings, and we heard about some of the problems—"

"It's *Iris* Butler, isn't that right? Don't I know you? Have we met before?"

She smiled again, wider this time, and made deep

grooves with her thumbnail in the styrofoam coffee cup. "No, I'm sure we haven't. As I was saying, we heard that you might be having some problems managing your data, so the division director sent me over to offer our database to you for your investigation."

Lawson swung around in his chair toward the PC next to his desk. "Well, that's very generous. We're . . . ironing out those problems. In fact, the FDA director's office is managing the data collection now. You might want to speak with someone there."

Butler tried to keep the conversation going. "We thought it must be an enormous project, keeping track of all those terrible murders."

"No question about that. We have about two hundred and thirty agents assigned to the case, not counting police and the intelligence community. And I use special consultants, like McAdam."

"That's an enormous commitment of personnel. And they're all under your supervision?"

"Yes, basically. It's the largest deployment of law enforcement officials in American history."

"Really?"

The buzzer sounded on Lawson's phone. He poked a button.

"It's David McAdam, sir." She recognized the secretary's flat voice over the squawk box. Lawson's face reddened.

"McAdam?" he said, perturbed. "Where is he?"

"Florida, sir. At home. Should I take a message?"

Butler blew on her coffee, gazed at the ceiling, and listened carefully.

"No, I'll take it. Send it to me in the outer office."

Lawson pushed another button, excused himself, and left the room. His face was still red.

It was time for Iris to go to work. She dipped into her bag for the test tube with the rubber stopper and powdered cyanide. Covering her hand over the test tube, she stood and waited, one beat, two.

She pulled off the stopper and leaned over the desk toward Lawson's cup. It was too awkward that way. She couldn't reach the coffee.

She went around the desk, keeping her hand over the test tube in case he walked in. She took a breath and dumped in a good half a gram.

Damn!

Some of the white powder did not quite dissolve and floated to the surface. She mistakenly thought the coffee was hot enough to melt the powder. He surely would see it there.

Iris scanned the desk and her eyes locked onto a picture of three freshly scrubbed faces posing before a photographer's screen—Nurse Lawson and her brood. She tried to pull away, but the picture held her there.

With effort she picked up a pencil off the desk and quickly stirred in the undissolved crystals. Then something else caught her eye—a map of Florida with a yellow circle drawn clumsily at the southern tip of the state.

McAdam! *"Florida, sir. At home."*

She took the map and stuffed it into her bag. She hurried back to her chair and waited long minutes.

Lawson would return, drink the coffee, and lapse immediately into severe ventilation brought on by metabolic acidosis. Nausea would follow, and then convulsions, electrocardiographic change, coma, and death. It would look like another tragic heart attack brought on by extreme stress.

And he was so young . . .

She thought of leaving, but Lawson came back with

another man he introduced as a computer specialist assigned to his command. What a specimen—four pens in his shirt pocket and a calculator attached to his belt at the hip. Lawson sat back down, visibly distracted by the telephone call with McAdam.

The computer specialist began asking questions, pressing Iris for details about the FDA database. There was no such thing, she had made it up entirely as a pretext to see Lawson. But she managed to slide around his questions, casting sidelong glances at Lawson as he picked up his coffee and blew on it lightly.

Iris could feel his eyes on her, trying to place her. His lips touched the edge of the cup. He was centimeters from eternity.

Lawson set the cup down and broke into the conversation. "Don, why don't you give Dr. Butler a tour of the setup you have outside?"

"The mainframe?"

"Yeah, I have to get a memorandum off to Brady. Dr. Butler, I appreciate your stopping by. Do you have a card?"

"Uh, no, I don't. I'll just leave my number with your secretary."

"Fine."

On the way to the mainframe lab, Iris Butler stopped and asked the specialist for directions to the women's room. He apologized, explaining that this was a makeshift office and the one bathroom was shared by men and women. She would find it just before she got to the secretary's station. The secretary could bring her back to the lab, he suggested.

Iris thanked him and walked away quickly, past the secretary, not stopping until she was out of the building and down the escalator of the Archives subway station.

In a corner of the dimly lit subway platform, safer in the confined darkness and the ratcheting noise of the trains, she let her heartbeat slow down.

Damn. I wanted to be there when he drank it to see him go down. Damn fucking damn.

The next day Iris Butler watched the news and scanned the papers for word on Lawson's death. Surely it would make the news, he being such a major celebrity. But there was no mention of it. Perhaps they smothered the story, hushed it up to prevent panic.

That must have been it. But they might come looking for her. The secretary and computer specialist knew who she was, where she worked. She had had to give them that information to get to Lawson.

It was a risk going in there, but it was worth it to vaccinate Lawson. Over and over in her mind Iris watched him gag and retch and struggle for breath before collapsing at her feet.

He was big. It might have taken several hours before his body fully absorbed the KCN. In that case he would have kicked and puked for a long time, perhaps fully conscious with the knowledge of his vaccination.

Special Agent Lawson knew so little, far less than he realized. He had not known who and what she was, even as she stood inches from him, spoke with him, touched him. He had not known that yesterday would be his last day. And he had not known that he had given her the location of David McAdam.

It had been a productive visit.

With Lawson gone, Iris expected the news to return to its proper focus. But stepping out of the shadows, even for a few moments, she had been exposed. All these incredibly beautiful months the darkness had shielded her. She had hidden among the vast numbers of cancer carriers who simply took it on faith that she was one of their own.

Now she was exposed and could even feel the first stages of cancer taking hold. Spending time with Lawson, touching him, had corrupted her with his metastasis. She had revealed herself, and, by visiting Lawson's home and office, breathed dangerous amounts of his air.

Iris's thoughts were pulled constantly to the telephone call Lawson had received in his office, the one from McAdam in Florida.

She still had the map. She spread it open on the floor of her bedroom and used a magnifying glass to study the area contained in Lawson's circle. In the middle of the circle was a tiny island named Kettle Key, approximately three-quarters of the way down the Keys.

That would be her destination.

Iris stopped into her office that afternoon. She was looking for an inspection assignment in Florida, preferably in the Keys, to justify her absence.

She quietly pulled the assignment log from a bookcase in her supervisor's office and went down the list of inspection sites. Boca Raton, Bradenton, Clearwater–St. Petersburg, Daytona Beach, Jacksonville. She found nothing for the Keys.

Ah, here was something interesting: a baby-food factory in Tampa up on the Gulf coast. On the way back from visiting McAdam, we'll just drop in unexpectedly and vaccinate some children. Get them while they're young.

Tampa.

And then after, we'll see about those reservoirs in Washington. But in the meantime, concentrate on McAdam.

I won't need an apple pie this time. I'll plunge the needle in him myself.

Chapter 44

The sun, balancing precariously on the horizon, was just beginning to set over the Gulf of Mexico. David McAdam paced his back porch, hands thrust deep in his pockets, eyes on the tops of his bare feet. He stopped for a moment and looked out over the choppy waters of the Gulf.

The sky was awash in watery crimson, a color with a long wavelength at the end of the spectrum. Down in Key West, the sun worshipers would be gathering on Mallory Pier, a daily ritual, to see and be seen at the very edge of the United States.

Thunder rumbled in the distance. A storm was rolling in off the ocean.

David thought: if only people could behave like light. Light was always true to its context, behaving like energy when it moved through the atmosphere or like matter when it was absorbed in his face. But humans, always oscillating between rationality and insanity, never seemed to keep to their context.

Twenty-four people were now dead by Dr. Doom's hand. Many others had been killed by maniacs following her murderous lead. That most sacred of places—the American home—was under siege from an enemy that was still on the loose.

The thrill of David's earlier discovery began to fade in the cold light of reality. He felt no closer to finding Dr. Doom than he had a month ago when he started this.

So what if the killer was a woman? That remarkable discovery narrowed the field of suspects to approximately half the country's population.

David rubbed his eyes, exhausted from staring at the computer screen all night and all day. He had been reviewing furiously the entire USDA file on the tamperings, all the forensics reports, corporate files, interviews, criminal records—everything—in search of female suspects. His eyes swam pink with broken vessels.

His search had also taken him through computer records of hospitals, HMOs, and insurance companies in the United States and Canada for cases of unusually acute premenstrual syndrome. He was looking in patient files for any reference to violent behavior related to PMS. When he found them, he ran cross-walks on the names with criminal records and with names surfacing in the tampering investigation. From all that work he had come up with two weak leads that led nowhere.

The amount of data on the tamperings was so vast and complex that there were times when even David had his doubts there could be just one principal killer, a Dr. Doom. But he plugged along, convinced that the answer was buried somewhere in the megabytes of information he had stored and catalogued.

Meanwhile, the news of another tampering had been broadcast on television this morning. A few days ago, David had finally broken down and bought a TV, had it delivered from Key West. He kept it tuned to CNN with the sound off.

A family of five in West Virginia were the victims. The report said that they had just moved there from suburban Washington. A seven-month-old baby had survived.

State officials and the FBI issued an alert on the tampered product—apple pies this time—and found another pie laced with cyanide sitting on a store shelf. Everyone was bracing for more tampering deaths from the poisoned apple pies that weren't caught in the West Virginia state police recall.

The news of the tampering increased David's agitation. All day he was irritable, sensitive. He was expecting news of another dairy tampering about this time. It had been about twenty-eight days since the last one. Dr. Doom was due.

You must be stopped. Your brand of terrorism is the deadliest. You puncture the shields around our most private selves. You enter our homes, sit at our tables, and violate the protective membranes in our bodies. You transform the benign into the malignant.

The sun was sinking fast. David went inside and looked at his computer screen. He was expecting a transmission from the USDA on the apple pie murders. It usually took a day for the USDA to prepare the data for transmission. He hoped it would now take less time with the improvements he had made in the system. Nothing had come through yet.

Earlier in the day, David had gone back over the FBI's analysis of the timing of the tamperings that had been done early on. Such lack of imagination, the way they examined data. They were fishing, looking for correlations between the tamperings and the lunar cycle. Somebody even tried to tie the tamperings to the zodiac.

They might as well be studying entrails, David thought. Just to be sure, he checked today's data against the zodiac. Today was May thirtieth, putting them in

Gemini, the sign of the twins. Next they would be entering Cancer, the crab. It meant nothing to him.

As he stood before the computer, David's stomach growled in loud protest. He hadn't eaten in thirty-six hours. And then he remembered: last night he had been invited to Nara's big Balinese feast—what had she called it? He had completely forgotten about it.

"Shit," he said out loud.

He hurried inside, put on some shoes, and ran, slipping through the muck, to Toshi's. Racing through the path on Kettle Key, David hoped Nara would let him off the hook. She had seemed to put great store in his being there when she invited him.

Damn fucking luck. Why hadn't he remembered?

David reached U.S. 1 and crossed it without stopping. A gray foreign car off to the side of Toshi's parking lot caught his eye. A woman appeared to be sitting inside. He wondered: Was the FBI now using foreign cars and women to keep an eye on him?

The front door to the bar was locked and a Closed sign hung in the window. Strange, he had never seen a Closed sign there before, especially at this time of the day. He knocked but no one answered.

David, breathing hard from running, found an open door around back through Nara's garden. His throat parched, he checked the refrigerator behind the bar for some water.

"Wow," he said out loud. The refrigerator was crammed with food, kinds of which he had never seen before. Sliced tropical fruit, bowls of rice and sauces, and . . . was that a suckling pig on the big tray on the bottom shelf?

His curiosity piqued, David checked Toshi's room at the end of the hallway behind the bar. He knocked on the door and waited for the sounds one normally heard after knocking on a door—a chair scraping the floor as someone got up, a rustling around, a hand jiggling a doorknob. None came and David entered the room.

He was shocked at what he found. Toshi's room—usually tidy to austere—was strewn with wine bottles, orange peels, beer nut packages, beer nuts, party favors, and stacks of dirty plates.

All over the walls and furniture was every kind of barroom decoration. Miami Dolphin posters were superimposed with cardboard St. Patrick's Day four-leaf clovers. Christmas tinsel sprouted from the eyes of Halloween masks. Even some of Toshi's Balinese wood carvings had been decorated with tinsel and blinking Christmas lights.

The bed, desk, and other furniture had been pulled back to make room for what looked like a dance floor. In the middle were the damnedest things he had seen yet—long, twisted swords with sharp ends.

On top of the desk was an upended carton of Sweet Creams Brisken Glatt ice cream, drooling thick drops of melted macadamia brittle. Multiple alarms went off in the back of David's head.

He ran out into the bar and through the back door. Then he saw Toshi sitting at the end of the pier, doubled over, staring at the water.

David rushed out to the pier and ran up to Toshi. "Are you all right?" he said breathlessly, pulling up at the edge of the pier.

The moment the words came out of his mouth he wished he had them back. Other than being a little ragged around the edges, Toshi was fine. He was bent over trying to repair a hand-held blow dryer. He squinted up at David with his usual inscrutable half smile.

"You could do me two favor, David. One, not to talk so loud. Two, to sit down here next to me so I don't have to look up to your shadow in the sun."

"Sure." David always felt big and clumsy when he was with Toshi. Come to think of it, he felt that way around Nara as well.

"I was just in your room looking for you. It's a wreck. I was worried you were, uh, sick or something."

Toshi kept on tinkering with the hair dryer. "People on that boat there from Texas heard I was engineer and ask me to fix this machine," he said wearily, pointing to a two-masted seventy-two footer.

"Trouble is, I know more about quantum physics than I do about hair dryer. Think you can take look at it?"

David looked down at the mess of parts Toshi dumped in his lap. "So what's been going on around here?" he asked. "And where's Nara?"

Toshi said, "You know law of entropy?"

"Entropy, entropy," David thought quickly, "second law of thermodynamics. Yeah, the definition depends on the context. It can mean a mathematical factor that measures the unavailable energy of a thermodynamic system. Or it can mean the disorder of a closed thermodynamic system in terms of—"

"Energy devolve into disorder, chaos," Toshi said, rubbing his eyes. "Universe running down, falling apart. You see it all around you.

"Look around you. Look at Keys. I come here in 1964 when it was still beautiful place. Now Highway One is big parking lot on weekend. Everything dirty, decaying. Like this hair dryer here."

David did not even try to make sense of what Toshi was saying. It was typical of him to make a point in an elliptical fashion and then leave it up to David to fill in the blanks and draw his own conclusions. Zen bullshit and nothing more.

He looked up in the sky. Dark clouds were massing.

Toshi went on. "Entropy can happen to closed system, as you say. I wonder, David, if law of physics can apply to people. Like entropy, for instance. Maybe, I wonder: greater the order in person, greater the disorder."

David looked at the disassembled parts Toshi put on his lap. "So this is how you get when you reach your point of entropy?" David said, dripping with accusation. "You go on a binge, get secretive about it, and then feel sorry for yourself and your hangover?"

Toshi looked at David, his face old and deeply lined. "You misunderstand. Not me I'm talking about, but Nara."

"Huh? What about Nara? Look, I wanted to see her, to apologize to her. Is she here?"

"No, still in Key West. Be back in little while.

"Her *wuku* over, so we celebrate Galungan last night. Ve-ry intense, David. Balinese coming out of *wuku* can be like bat out of hell."

"OK, Toshi, what is *wuku*? And this 'Goolagong'?"

Toshi flinched at David's clumsy mispronunciation. "Galungan," he corrected him. Toshi stood up slowly and turned away from the glare of the water's surface. He squatted back down on his heels and spoke quietly without looking at David.

"Balinese people have two calendar—one is called *sakka*, that register the movement of moon around earth, and earth around sun, way you do here. This is Hindu calendar, a convenience.

"But more important to Balinese is *wuku* calendar with about two hundred day divided into three-day week, seven-day week, ten-day week. Very complex business. Still not sure I understand whole thing.

"At end of *wuku* year, Balinese have Galungan—big religious festival when all village cut loose. Lots of food, parade, and people go into trance. Some even stab themself with sword without bleeding."

"You mean like the ones in your room?" David said. He was beginning to feel the heat absorbed in the pier seeping through his shorts.

"After Nara's mother die, Nara follow Balinese tradition almost to a fault. I think she somehow keep her mother alive by observing Balinese custom.

"But you know something. I live in Bali twenty-four year before I come here. I marry Balinese woman, have Balinese children, but I never feel like I understand what go on there.

"You think Japanese people just about same as Balinese people—little Asian who eat funny food? Not same at all.

"One conclusion I make is that for Balinese, just about everything they do is ceremony. Even more than Japanese, Balinese have ritual for all occasion. Strict rule control all they do.

"That why I say people subject to entropy. Nara usually very controlled. But on Galungan, she reveal part of herself, another side. A wild side."

David said nothing. He watched the reflection of the storm clouds on the calm surface of the water.

"Where were you last night, David? It was big deal for Nara to invite you, to show you her wild side. I think you better talk to her. She very disappointed."

David tried desperately to digest it all. "I was—I was, I don't even know what I was doing last night."

He looked at Toshi. "What you're saying is Nara follows a different calendar than the rest of us. What you're saying is that she observes patterns that I'm not even aware of, that her life revolves around a wholly different system of measuring time. . . ."

Toshi patted David on the back and went inside, leaving him to sadly ponder how different Nara was from him and how little he really knew her.

Chapter 45

Back home, the transmission David had been expecting was coming up on his computer. The living room was dark, the lamp on the table next to him the only source of light.

He took his place in front of the screen, rolled his head slowly, and lifted his arms. His joints cracked softly. It would be another long night.

He still hadn't gotten anything to eat.

Lightning flashed, illuminating every corner of the room for a brief second. David closed his eyes.

Today is the thirty-second day since the Rochester tampering. Where is Dr. Doom? What is she waiting for?

He thought of calling Lawson again. It had been two days since they spoke. David had called to fill him in on a fine point of loading the database in the USDA's computers. The special agent was angry and made a point of reminding David that he was now officially off the case.

But David still had his computer and could keep tabs on everything going on in the investigation. And here it was, the latest information on the West Virginia tampering crawling down the screen:

FOLLOW-UP INVESTIGATION OF WEST VIRGINIA MULTI-
PLE HOMICIDE STOP CAUSE OF DEATH MASSIVE

CYANIDE POISONING STOP FBI AND DODDRIDGE
COUNTY WEST VIRGINIA SHERIFF'S OFFICE QUESTION-
ING MEMBERS OF "RAMEESH" RELIGIOUS GROUP STOP
HARASSMENT CHARGE FILED AGAINST GROUP INVOLV-
ING VICTIMS STOP NOTE—"WELCOME ENJOY!"—
FOUND IN VICTIMS' HOUSE STOP FBI EXAMINING NOTE
FOR PRINTS STOP POSSIBLE LINK BETWEEN NOTE AND
PIE STOP TRANSCRIPTS OF FBI INTERVIEWS WITH
RAMEESH MEMBERS TO FOLLOW ....

David held his hands to keep them from trembling in
anger. In the silence of the tropical night, he tried desperately to keep an emotional distance from the Harmon
family. Although he had no idea what they looked like,
pictures of them invaded his imagination.

Welcome. Enjoy!

From the depths of his guilt came a poisonous voice
that beat at him.

*You could have stopped Dr. Doom. You could have
prevented these senseless killings . . . if only . . . if only
you had been smarter, more creative, more persistent.
These people might still be alive if only . . .*

David sat still, eyes closed tightly, gathering the scattered shards of his strength.

Stop it, he demanded. *Concentrate. Concentrate on
your data.*

He focused on the computer screen in front of him. He
was more interested in the form than the content of the
report.

*This was not the database he had designed for the De-
partment of Agriculture.*

Perplexed, David turned off the screen. What was
going on? Where was his database?

Goddamn Lawson. David had put in a good half day

on that database. And that was the least of it. Lawson had violated David's privacy and dumped untold shit on him, goading him to build the database. Now they weren't even using the damned thing.

And to make matters worse, this new database was a tired-looking piece of garbage. Clunky and rigid. Just look at the thing, no punctuation, it still needed the old telegraphic "STOP" to separate messages. It had absolutely no *style*.

David turned on the screen again and went to the beginning of the transmission. He began to read:

UNITED STATES DEPARTMENT OF
HEALTH AND HUMAN SERVICES
FOOD AND DRUG ADMINISTRATION

JOINT FDA—FBI TRANSMISSION
MAY 30, 1991

Food and Drug Administration? And then David remembered something Lawson had told him. The FBI had gotten the Department of Agriculture to agree to give up data collection on the investigation if *one month passed without a dairy tampering*.

So now the USDA was out of the picture completely and with it went David's database.

Son of a bitch. All that trouble . . .

But something else bothered him, the same thing that had been irritating him all day. Imagine your worst skin condition and put it in your head. Burning and itching, spreading like juicy gossip in a small town.

Dr. Doom.

Had she stopped tampering? Maybe something had happened to her, she had a bad cold or walked in front of

a bus. Or maybe she'd moved on to something else, beyond milk.

David looked at the screen. Apple pies, the Harmon
family had been poisoned with cyanide in an apple pie.
The lousy FDA database didn't even mention the kind of
cyanide.

*USDA. FDA. What was the difference? One less letter
of the alphabet to deal with. These goddamn government
agencies are interchangeable, anyway, the lines of authority blurred.*

Where did the USDA leave off and the FDA begin?

*And so it was with the people. How different were
their jobs, from the FDA to USDA, from the GAO to the
GSO? Were the people as interchangeable as their agencies?*

What felt like an electric current crackled up and
down David's spine. A click in his head—he could almost hear it—as his mind seemed to shift from mono-
phonic to Dolby.

"Oh, my God," he whispered.

There it was, in front of him all along. What if? What
if?

What if Dr. Doom worked for the government?

He switched off the FDA transmission and quickly
wrote a program for his computer to search the records
of the FDA and the USDA for any personnel changes in
the past month, especially for women. He thought a moment and focused the search on offices that conducted
product inspections.

David jumped as a sheet of lightning seemed to bend
through the window and into his eyes. Errant wind blew
papers through the room, and David raced to pull down
windows on the gulf side of the house. He ran back to
the screen.

He was exhilarated, frightened, and humbled all at once. Up on the screen was one name, a single, solitary name the computer had found in its relentless searching.

The name was Iris Butler.

David hit "ENTER" and Iris Butler's history appeared on the screen like a revelation: Account Officer in the Division of Product Surveillance, FDA, May 24, 1991 to present. Account Officer in the Division of Quality Control and Inspections, USDA, September 30, 1986 to May 23, 1991.

He punched a key to stop the history and thought for a moment. He typed a command.

LIST IRIS BUTLER'S INSPECTION ASSIGNMENTS FROM MARCH 1991 TO THE PRESENT.

Like a bullwhip, the computer snapped out a response.

PURE AND SIMPLE MILK, INC.
DUNDALK, MARYLAND MARCH 4, 1991
USDA ACCOUNT #31-016-478

FOUR-LEAF CLOVER DAIRIES
BEDMINSTER, NEW JERSEY APRIL 1, 1991
USDA ACCOUNT #44-592-316

BEVERLY FARMS DAIRY INC.
ROCHESTER, NEW YORK APRIL 29, 1991
USDA ACCOUNT #02-770-914

GOLDEN SUMMER BAKERY
CLARKSBURG, WEST VIRGINIA MAY 27, 1991
FDA ACCOUNT #WV-97A-24881

THE MOUTH OF BABES BABY FOOD COMPANY
TAMPA, FLORIDA MAY 31, 1991
FDA ACCOUNT #FL-119-06284

David wasn't sure if the explosions in his ears were from the thunder sideswiping the house or from his heart straining against his rib cage. His hands trembling, he placed a call to Hugh Lawson.

David waited for the call to go through. One ring. Two.

Come on, Lawson, pick up your fucking phone.

Three.

And then the phone went dead.

"Shit," he screamed. He waited for the dial tone to come back, tamped on the receiver.

What was wrong? Had his earth station on the roof blown off in the storm? Was it struck by lightning?

Suddenly the power went out. What was wrong now? He had checked the generator just the other day. There weren't any wires for the storm to knock over.

David jumped up as he heard a rattling noise at the back door. He was wound up too tight. It was probably just the storm. Or Nara. Toshi must have told her he had stopped by.

He felt his way through the dark house to the back door and waited for his eyes to adjust to the blackness. He swung the door open. The porch was empty.

Snaky streaks of lightning appeared and disappeared over the angry Gulf. A quick wind whistled through the lattice work on the south side of the house.

David had to get to a phone. He would go back inside and find his shoes and get moving.

As he turned toward the house, a bolt of lightning lit

up the sky and the face of Iris Butler screaming down on him with a loaded syringe.

David jerked up his arm instinctively, but her weight carried forward and drove him to the ground. Iris shrieked and kicked, trying to get the needle into him any way she could.

She scraped his face with her left hand as she raised the right one holding the syringe.

One thrust would do it.

With great effort, David pinned her arms. They wrestled across the porch, each gasping for breath. Damn, she was strong. Stifling his fear, David tried to stay on top, to keep her arms pinned. But she shifted her weight and they rolled down the steps.

David saw stars when his head slammed into the base of the railing. Iris broke free and dashed into the house.

David got up slowly and felt wetness at the back of his head. He peered into the dark doorway. Iris Butler was in there, waiting for him.

She had attacked him with a syringe, probably loaded with cyanide. How had she found him? That didn't matter now. He had to get off the island, find a telephone. His head began to ache, a dull throb near the base of his neck.

Crouching down, he made his way along the side of the house. Rain began to fall, lightly at first, then gaining in intensity. It beat on the sides of the clapboard house. David tried to listen for Iris Butler through the rain and thunder.

He jumped as something big and wet swooped down on his back and over his head. He clutched at it, careful for sharp points.

He let out a breath of relief. It was a branch with leaves knocked down by the wind.

David's head spun around, his mind racing.

Get it together. Suppress the fear. Dr. Doom is out there with enough poison to kill you five times over.

He had to get around the corner of the house. From there he could duck into the trees and make a break for the edge of the island. It was a blind corner. He needed a weapon, something heavy to stop that syringe. He braced himself as he approached the corner, scooping up a fistful of mud.

As he passed an open window, he looked inside. He froze as his eyes drew level with Iris Butler's fist, clenching a syringe. David screamed and jumped back, barely missing the needle swiping past his nose. Instinctively he slung a handful of mud at her. She screeched and backed away as the mud spattered her eyes.

He dashed into a grove of pine and headed for the straits. In the woods, he stayed off the path. Trees groaned overhead, bent by the growing squalls. Branches slapped his legs and raked his face.

Successive bursts of lightning, like a stroboscope, broke the small woods into something resembling a hallucinatory jungle, a primeval forest. He plodded ahead, unsure he was going in the right direction until he reached the straits.

The tide was in and the water was high and rough. He wiped the rain from his eyes and looked across to Kettle Key.

This is it, he thought, bending his legs and preparing to dive in.

David felt a sharp jolt in the small of his back as Iris Butler lunged at him from behind. He saw a flash of the steel needle an inch from his face. They tumbled into the water, Butler's hands jabbing at him.

Coughing water, David searched frantically for a

place to dig his feet into the mud. He held onto her wrists. She leaned heavily into him, their arms locked, and he felt her cold breath rasping in his face. For the briefest moment, holding back her fury, he saw two syringes in her hands.

She kicked at his groin, but missed and hit his thigh. They both went underwater and came up again.

Iris bucked savagely and kicked at him, her long, shrill scream like a knife in his ear.

Then the kicking stopped, as did the screaming. Iris's body relaxed.

Struggling for breath, David let her go. The limp body bobbed facedown in the rough water. He saw the syringe dangling from her hip where it had stuck when they went under together. The other syringe was gone, silted over with oolite at the bottom of the straits.

David dragged her up on land. He stood over her, shivering and wet. He sucked hard for air to fill his lungs.

Iris's wiry hair was plastered to her head. Her face was calm, drained of the insane rage he had seen moments ago. She looked peaceful, a feeling she had probably craved all her life but could never attain. David felt stirrings of pity.

Suddenly her eyes snapped open and she reached for him, her arms wrapping around his neck.

"Papa," she whispered fiercely in his ear. Her hands tightened around the back of his neck, pulling him toward the water.

With his remaining strength, David tore at her arms and shoved her away from him, into the straits. He watched as Iris Butler's body disappeared under the water almost immediately.

Chapter 46

A light breeze, chilly for August, blew up from the Atlantic and pushed the few high clouds lingering over the Keys out to the Gulf of Mexico. Pelicans took advantage of the calm seas around No Name Key by circling for fish and then diving and caroming off the surface with their catch.

Hugh Lawson, waiting for a backup to clear from the bridge connecting No Name to Big Pine Key, watched the pelicans from behind the wheel of the Ford Taurus he had rented in Miami. The traffic stretched as far up U.S. 1 as he could see. In his four trips to David McAdam's, Hugh had never really appreciated the wild beauty of the Keys. Now, sitting in the middle of the bridge, he could enjoy the sea, the good air.

There was a time not too long ago when Hugh had wished he would never have to make this trip again. But his attitude had changed, softened in the five weeks since McAdam brought down Iris Butler, his Dr. Doom. Hugh even considered bringing his son down here on a sort of man-to-man camping trip through the Keys. He had a lot of vacation time coming and didn't know what else to do with it.

The tamperings were beginning to fade away, just as McAdam had predicted they would. Only one incident had been reported since Butler's death. People were putting away their Lilly cyanide kits, stowing them in the same places as their Desert Storm gas masks.

Hugh had to admit that McAdam had been on the right track all along. That was the first of several pieces of humble pie he had to eat.

He had come down to Florida the day before to sign off on a few items with the state police. In a brief hearing he attended, Iris Butler was declared officially dead. McAdam was supposed to have been there to give an account of Butler's death, but he never showed. His signed deposition was enough for the judge.

For over a week the Coast Guard had dredged the Gulf within a two-mile radius of California Key in search of Butler's body. The search turned up one of her shoes, her glasses, and a syringe, but the body was never found.

Hugh led the team that searched Butler's home in Washington. The place was spotless, immaculate, except for the garden in the back, which looked like animals had gotten to it. The search turned up a laboratory in her basement for manufacturing cyanide, a hell of a setup. The team also found unopened boxes of additional equipment and base compounds used in making the cyanide. Apparently she had had big plans that went unfulfilled.

Hugh had discovered the huge leather scrapbook filled with clippings Butler had collected on the tamperings. He felt the hair stand on the back of his neck when he saw a map on the wall of her bedroom studded with multicolored pins, just like the one he had showed her in his office.

Stuffed in a desk drawer among Butler's papers were hospital bills for a Hermione Butler, Iris's mother, who had died of cancer in D.C. General just days before her daughter's death. Her remains had been cremated, but the FBI team had found no trace of the ashes.

The traffic began to move on No Name Bridge. Hugh stepped on the accelerator of the rented Ford, but, not used to its light touch, he nearly slammed into the car in front of him. Horns blared as he stopped to loosen his tie and roll down the windows, but he took his time about it before he got back on the road.

Hugh normally liked to keep the radio on an easy-listening station when he drove long distances. But not now, not when every news break led off with the latest revelation on Iris Butler. He was tired of hearing the rehash of the psychological autopsy the Bureau's Behavioral Sciences Division had worked up on her. People were groping for answers, rational explanations for the rampant evil. It was easier to do now that the killer had a face and a name.

Hugh had hell to pay for the high profile he kept during the investigation. Reporters and camera crews followed him everywhere. He even checked into a motel after they camped on his front lawn in Arlington. The questions were always the same: What had created Iris Butler? How did she get away with her crimes for so long? How many more of her are out there?

No one really knew. But the press had a field day selling papers and advertising time and trying to come up with answers. Iris Butler's last word was grist for their mills.

"Papa."

That's what she had said. At least that was what David McAdam had told Hugh, who added it to his final report. Iris Butler was calling for her father, who had been killed in an explosion when she was a child. One theory held that the trauma of witnessing her father's death in a prospecting accident in 1963 drove her to murder. Another suggested the role of PMS in setting off her psychotic behavior. Psychiatrists rejected any connection between Butler's PMS and her homicidal behavior. Instead they theorized that Iris Butler may have associated menstruation with her father's death or some other traumatic event. The tamperings were acts of sociopathic rage, they said.

Hugh didn't know what to believe. He had enough problems of his own.

Running the tamperings investigation had turned out to be a wash in terms of career advancement. Whatever he had gained by way of leading the investigation and picking the outsider who had found the killer was negated by the fact that Hugh had been a guest on a New York talk show when everything went down in Florida.

Even worse was the embarrassing revelation, fully exploited by the media, that Iris Butler had visited Hugh's office and met with him before her final rampage. For the rest of his life Hugh would have to live with the memory of Iris Butler, McAdam's Dr. Doom, casually chatting and drinking coffee in the bowels of the FBI. He couldn't understand what she had hoped to gain by the visit other than to taunt him, to flaunt her cleverness. She ran off and he was called up to Brady's office, so they never did have their coffee together.

Hugh did not look forward to returning to Washington that evening. He would have some tough questions to answer on his handling of the investigation. His testimony would also be used as nails in Ed Brady's coffin. Hugh could still not quite accept that the associate deputy director for investigations was now on administrative leave pending an investigation of charges of conspiracy to commit murder, obstruction of justice, among other things.

The FBI equivalent of an internal affairs office had turned up evidence that Brady had gone off the deep end and tried repeatedly to undermine the tampering investigation. As testimony to his arrogance, Brady had kept every detail of the plot in his files at home.

That was where FBI investigators had found him, madly muttering poetry and cursing politicians.

Hugh read through the classified report on the Brady investigation in open-mouthed amazement. Evidence had pointed to his boss as responsible for the computer virus, the damaging press leaks, and other shenanigans that had bedeviled Hugh for months. Most unbelievable to Hugh was the evidence that Brady had been plotting David McAdam's murder.

If you listened to the gossip, it seemed that Brady saw the tamperings as a means for clamping down on civil liberties and fulfilling a long-held dream of establishing some sort of cockamamie totalitarian government, something J. Edgar Hoover and he used to dream about together. The Washington mandarins thought he had been pretty close to pulling it off.

Someone leaked the report to the press, setting up a big public crucifixion. Based on interviews, the media claimed Brady had used former agents and selected specialists within the Bureau to carry out his plans. No single confederate of Brady's had been privy to the entire plot. These people had been used for specific jobs and then cut loose, ordered to melt into the background.

The press held nothing back. They spilled the names of the computer scientist who had planted the virus, the top officer in the surveillance unit who had assigned unauthorized teams to watch McAdam, and the public affairs officer who had fed Brady's leaks to the press. The final straw, the one that would really put Brady away, was the name of a former FBI sharpshooter Brady had brought in to hit McAdam.

Another name showed up prominently in Brady's personal files: Hugh Lawson.

It had been hard for Hugh to get through the section about him in the report. Once he had, he read it over and over. He escaped serious accusation, except that of sheer stupidity. The report was blunt about it: Ed Brady picked him to run the investigation because he believed Hugh would never succeed in solving the case.

Hugh still winced whenever the memory of his eager ignorance at the feet of Ed Brady came into his head. Like a mindless robot, he had played the role of pawn to perfection. But now all he could do was watch and wait, resigned to the worst.

One other thing for Hugh to look forward to on his return was his appointment the following evening with a lawyer. Pat had filed for a divorce, catching him completely by surprise. The last time he had seen her was in the Sixth Street Marketplace in Richmond. She refused all his calls at her mother's. So, numbed by the news and the fall-out at the FBI, Hugh went along with Pat's wishes. He would not contest.

Cruising through Big Pine Key, he was tempted to turn off onto one of the side roads and see where it led. But he had only a couple hours before his flight back to Washington, and if he stopped, he might miss it.

"Fuck it," he said, and cut off the highway onto an old trail at the 28-mile marker. The Taurus crunched over the coral rock, past a grove of gumbo-limbo trees. Then it hit him how pristine this place was; even the dirt was clean, no more than the ossified remains of sea life.

He hoped the road would lead to the water, but it abruptly stopped before a dense thicket of thorny brush. The sound of the car door slamming was harsh and out of place. Hugh felt he didn't belong here and wished he hadn't stopped. But he really wanted to see beyond the thicket, to be alone with the ocean.

After fighting his way through, Hugh came to a thin strip of rocky beach shiny with broken glass and bottle caps. Off to the right, on a point that stretched toward him, Hugh first saw a sign—SEA WORLD MINIATURE GOLF—and then the two old men in visors and matching lime green pants. One of them putted into the mouth of a concrete shark. Chattering teenagers lined up for tickets. Hugh headed back to the car.

He would go ahead and do what he had come down here to do: see David McAdam one last time. Hugh wasn't sure why he was doing this. McAdam had already been invited up to Washington for a special reception with the president but never showed. Hugh checked: McAdam had never cashed the check sent to him as a consultant to the investigation.

Hugh wanted to *do* something, to wrap the case up in his mind. He knew McAdam wouldn't want to see him, but that was OK. Hugh would just say thanks, and leave.

Once on Kettle Key, it wasn't far to McAdam's place. Hugh pulled into the parking lot at Toshi's Bar and Marina. The place was deserted—closed and locked. Hugh checked around back but found no boats or fishermen idling about. Nothing about the bar had changed, but it looked desolate and uninviting. Hugh set off for McAdam's.

He had come prepared this time with waist-high boots he put on even before he set out through Kettle Key. But the tide was in and water slopped over the boots and down his pants as he crossed the little straits to California Key. He didn't really care.

As he crossed the straits, it dawned on him that this was the place where Iris Butler had gone down. He had nearly memorized McAdam's statement. Over near the rock at the other side of the straits, she had gone under for the last time.

When Hugh reached California Key, he noticed something different about the island. One obvious thing was the quiet—no loud rock 'n' roll thundering out of the house. Another change was the color of the house. The obnoxious camouflage had been painted over with whitewash.

Closer up, Hugh spotted boards on the windows and a big piece of heavy-duty canvas, the size of a sail, wrapped around the seaward side of the house.

He was surprised to find the front door open. He went inside. The house was dark and musty with shafts of light peeking through the boarded windows and illuminating particles of dust floating in the air.

Hugh's eyes swept the place, but there was nothing left in the house, no garbage, no computer equipment, no McAdam.

Nothing except for a manila envelope stuck to the back of the front door. Hugh pulled out the thumb tack and studied the envelope. His name was written on it.

He opened it and a note, a computer diskette, and a paperback book fell out onto the floor.

Hugh gathered it all up and stepped outside into the light. He read the note, written in McAdam's childish handwriting:

> Lawson,
> You're welcome.
> Just don't follow me. M.

On the diskette was scrawled:

More on Dr. Doom, as if it mattered.

The book was *Moby Dick* by Herman Melville.

Hugh stuffed them into his coat pocket. He stood for a moment, gazing over the island and the Gulf. He tried to imagine where McAdam would have gone—to his ranch in Montana or his coffee plantation in Brazil or his island off the Turkish coast.

Wherever McAdam was, Hugh was sure that Nara and Toshi were with him. Hugh would not follow him this time.